THE MAN WHO CAST
TWO SHADOWS

Carol O'Connell

THE MAN WHO CAST TWO SHADOWS

WHEELER
PUBLISHING, INC.
ROCKLAND, MA

★ AN AMERICAN COMPANY ★

Published in Large Print by arrangement with
G. P. Putnam's Sons in
the United States and Canada.

Wheeler Large Print Book Series.

Set in 16 pt. Plantin.

Library of Congress Cataloging-in-Publication Data

O'Connell, Carol, 1947–
    The man who cast two shadows / Carol O'Connell.
       p.   cm.—(Wheeler large print book series)
    ISBN 1-56895-258-9
    1. Policewomen—New York (N.Y.)—Fiction. 2. New York
(N.Y.)—Fiction. 3. Large type books. I. Title. II. Series.
[PS3565.C497M35 1995b]
813'.54—dc20
                                                 95-34677
                                                   CIP

This book is dedicated to an old friend, Richard Hughes, who does not sleep at night, but spends these hours counseling terrified children over the anonymous crisis lines—and to Covenant House, which shelters the children who cannot go home again.

Prologue

Rain rat-tatted on the plastic hood of her slicker. She could feel the drops, but not hear them. She had come out this morning without hearing aid or bifocals. Her landscape was dream-quiet and blurred free of the small, marring details of candy wrappers and cigarette butts.

The smell of wet dog fur hurried past her. She was slow to focus on the animal's rump before it had gone off the path and up the steep incline of grass clotted with bushes. Now, the dog was jerked sharply at the neck by an unseen hand, and airborne in a backward somersault.

Squinting for clarity, Cora realized the dog's leash was caught up in the brambles. The animal freed itself with a panic of yanks and pulls, then scrabbled up the slanted earth, disappearing over the rise.

Cora tucked in a wind-whipped strand of white hair and became invisible again, her hunter's-green slicker blending in with all the plant life not yet turned to the gray spectrum of deep December.

She looked at her watch. She should leave the park now, she knew that, but an inviting procession of empty benches stretched out along the path ahead, drops of water waxing on their green paint. She sat down on the first bench, minding the old bones which reprimanded her for taking them out in the rain.

But, she argued with the bones, it was only

the rain that made her feel safe in the park. She reasoned that muggers would not work in foul weather, nor did she believe them to be early risers.

Her body's closing remark was a stab of arthritis as she bent her arm over the back of the bench and rested one hand on the wood. A moment later, she felt a tickling sensation on her wrist. A dark spot was crawling about on her white crepe flesh. She bowed her head until the crawling spot on the back of her hand was within a few inches of her nearsighted blue eyes.

She sucked in her breath over long, yellowed teeth.

It was a carrion beetle, a long-lived insect whose vocation was the desecration and desiccation of corpses. But surely this tiny undertaker had come too soon. There were rules of nature to be observed while an old woman still drew breath. Perhaps the insect had become confused by the unseasonably warm weather. No matter, the beetle would have to return for her another day.

And now, a second creature entered her narrow field of unblurred vision, its eight legs in crawling pursuit of the beetle.

Oh, this could not be happening.

This particular arachnid was bound by law to die in autumn and be eaten by its children. The spider had overstayed its life; it did not belong in December. And now the unnatural lawbreaker was within an inch of its prey, the beetle.

Ah, but this was too much violence so early in the day.

The elderly naturalist flicked her wrist and sent the beetle flying far and wide of the spider's jaws.

2

At her sudden movement, the spider stopped, then turned and crawled away, all eight hands empty.

The serenity of the morning restored, Cora stared out across the widest part of the lake, gray mirror of the sky. Slowly, her gaze drifted inland to the narrow leg of water close to the path. More like a pond it was, still and stagnant, darker here. And beyond this pond, and darker still, were two large shapes near the water's edge, two black umbrellas talking—if she knew the stance of conversation. And she did.

The taller umbrella had long legs of tan, and the shorter umbrella had blue legs. Now the blue-legged umbrella was backing away. The tall umbrella shot out one white hand to fetch Blue Legs back to him again.

Cora smiled. Young lovers they must be. And now she deduced that it was a covert meeting. The tall umbrella shifted and turned, showing a flash of white face as he spun round to see if he was seen. He held fast to Blue Legs, who pulled back, wanting to leave him now. Gold hair shone bright against black as her umbrella tipped back and flew from her hand, upending itself in the pond, its handle sticking up as a sail-bare mast. It turned slowly, then twirled fast and faster in a sudden rush of clean, rain-washed air.

The tall umbrella stooped low. Was he retrieving something from the ground? Yes, and he brought it up to Blue Legs' face, and then obscured Cora's view with his umbrella as he danced Blue Legs in a half-turn.

It must be a gift he was giving her, thought Cora, squinting. Blue Legs must be pleased with it, for she had ceased to resist the tall umbrella.

Stunned she seemed, leaning against him now, not struggling at all. Something bright and red adorned the gold hair, flowering to one side of Blue Legs' face as they completed the half-turn, not dancing any longer, but standing still and close.

A prelude to a kiss?

Cora looked at her watch. Well, they would have their privacy, for she was already minutes late. She rose up on aching legs.

Cora was turning away from the lovers as an umbrella was falling to the ground and two large hands grasped the head of Blue Legs. Cora was seconds down the path when the fingers were entering the bright curls, when the golden head was twisted sharply, unnaturally, setting Blue Legs free of the constraints of minutes and seconds as the living understood time.

Chapter 1

DECEMBER 20

Her fixation with machines had its roots in the telephone company nets which spread around the planet.

The child had only the numbers written on her palm in ink, written there so she could not be lost. All but the last four numbers had disappeared in a wet smudge of blood.

Over time, she had learned to beg small change from prostitutes, the only adults who would not turn her over to the social workers. She would put the coins into the public telephones and dial three untried numbers and then the four she knew. If a woman answered, she would say, "It's Kathy. I'm lost."

When she was seven years old, she could duplicate the tones of the public telephones by whistling with perfect pitch to open the circuits for long-distance calls, and she had learned all the international codes. She could also whistle the telephone out of its change. And so the telephone network fed her small body and her fixation. The constants of a thousand calls were the simple message and the last four digits of a telephone number.

All these years later, there were still women, around the globe and all its time zones, all haunted by the disembodied voice of a child who was lost out there in the cyberspace of the telephone company.

Detective Sergeant Riker of Special Crimes Section knew nothing of Kathy Mallory's origins. No one did. She had arrived in the life of Inspector Louis Markowitz as a full-blown person, aged ten, or maybe eleven. Who could be certain about the age of a street kid? And her history belonged to her alone.

The inspector's wife, Helen Markowitz, had washed the child and discovered something remarkable beneath the patina of dirt. A waterfall of clean, burnished-gold hair was parted to expose the glittering green eyes, the painfully beautiful face of delicately sculpted angles and hollows, and the full, red mouth. Kathy's intelligence had seemed like an excess of gifts.

Fourteen years later, according to the homicide report of Detective Palanski, she was lying dead on an autopsy table just the other side of the door.

Sergeant Riker pushed through the door and into the shock of cold air. A pool of bright light surrounded the metal table, the carts, and instruments which included the incongruous carpentry tools of drill and saw. He looked down at the partially sheeted body.

A young doctor stood by the table, masked below the eyes and wearing green scrubs and rubber gloves. They had met previously over other bodies. The pathologist nodded to Riker, recognizing him as less than a friend but more than an acquaintance. The younger man turned his face back to the microphone suspended above the body as he continued to intone the list of statistics.

"... *well-developed female, approximately twenty-five years old* ..."

As Riker bent over the corpse, the overhead lamp highlighted every silver hair and deepened the lines of his slept-in face and suit.

"... *wound and bruising to lateral forearm* ..."

A defensive wound? So there had been a struggle.

Blond curls framed a porcelain face. He squinted past the dried blood of the head wound and the damage done by a feasting of maggots and beetles.

It was the wrong face.

"... *wound to the side of the skull* ..."

He pulled back the lid of one eye, which had lost its roundness and gone all cloudy. Still, this eye was not and never had been green. His own eyes went to the roots beneath the curls. Not blond roots.

Not Kathy.

"... *body sixty-six inches in length* ..."

This young woman was not as tall by five inches, but she was slender, like Kathy, and the same age.

"... *bones of the cervical vertebrae are broken* ..."

Riker was slow to regain control over all the muscles in the face and throat that could prevent a burn-out, I-seen-everything, rummy cop from crying like a man who still had feelings after thirty-five years on the force. He closed his eyes.

"Detective Palanski is a damn idiot," said a familiar voice behind his back. Riker turned to face the chief medical examiner. Dr. Edward

7

Slope was pulling on a pair of rubber gloves. A green surgical mask hung free beneath his cragged and deadpan face. All the anger was in the man's words. Slope had also known Kathy in her puppy days.

"The resemblance isn't close enough to make them sisters."

"Palanski's a kid," said Riker, who said this of everyone under forty. "And it's not like he worked with her every day."

". . . *the hands are crushed, no blood loss. Injury sustained after death . . .*"

Riker opened his notebook and pulled out his pen. He kept his eyes away from the woman on the table, bereft of her sheet, exposed to the lights, the eyes of men, the cold air. "The body was found in the park, four or five blocks from Mallory's neighborhood on the Upper West Side. The victim was wearing a blazer and blue jeans, just like Mallory. And Mallory's name was on the tailor's label."

Dr. Slope was staring down at the corpse. "Kathy Mallory's eyes are so green they shouldn't be legal. How could Palanski confuse the color of her eyes with these pale blues?"

"He wouldn't have touched her eyes," said Riker. "He was scared of Mallory. Even when he thought she was dead, he was scared of her."

". . . *Rigor mortis is still present in the neck and jaw . . .*"

Dr. Slope moved closer to the table, nodded to the younger pathologist, and picked up a clipboard which dangled by a chain. Now he turned back to Riker. "What have you got so far?"

"Coffey's got a preliminary report from the West Side squad. The ME investigator on the crime scene estimates the time of death at yesterday morning between six and nine. An entomologist is working on the bug larvae. Maybe they can narrow it some. Your man figures the body was moved within an hour of death."

All that was written on the page of his notebook was the word "bugs."

Riker didn't have to look directly at the woman to know what was being done to her. The young man with the mask and the knife was making the first incision crossing from shoulder to breast-bone, and then on to the other shoulder, his blade describing a V. In peripheral vision, Riker saw the next slice, the downward motion of the knife hand cutting the body open from the breast to the mount of Venus. The smell of blood mingled with urine and feces. He could hear her liquids running into the holes at the sides of the table.

"Palanski was the first detective on the scene. He figures the park for a dump site."

"And what do you think, Riker?"

"Could be. I don't know. We've only got grass stains on the clothes. Maybe he did her in the park, and then dragged her deeper into the woods so he could have some privacy while he was working on her hands."

And that sound, just now, was the first of her organs dropping onto the scale—a lung, or maybe it was her heart.

"That fits," said Slope. "No blood loss with those wounds. The hands were smashed up after death. I can't see you pulling prints on this one."

The medical examiner slid an X ray out of a large manila envelope and held it up to the light. "The blow to the head wouldn't have killed her.

Her neck was snapped after he stunned her. Fractures indicate a heavy blunt object."

"Like a rock?"

"Could be. By the direction of the bone fragments, I'd say he hit her from the front with the object in his right hand. No bruising on the throat. He probably used both hands to break her neck by twisting the head. Are you staying around for the report?"

"I don't know," said Riker. "Since it's not one of our officers, this one goes back to the detectives on the West Side. It's nothing Special Crimes would have an interest in."

"... *evidence of a recent abortion* ..."

More of her organs were dropping onto the scale. Three times he counted the cold slap of soft tissue on metal.

Riker kept his eyes nailed to his notebook. "I think Dr. Oberon said there were defensive wounds on the arm."

Slope picked up the arm and bent closer to it. "No. More like a restraint bruise. The bastard had a strong grip on her arm. Large hand, too. Oh, and be sure to tell Palanski I'm going to sick Mallory on him. He's ruined my morning. I don't see why I shouldn't have him destroyed."

Without looking up from his notebook, Riker knew that the organs of her torso were all accounted for. The younger pathologist was moving to the head of the table to make the long incision that would begin at one ear and stretch along the top of her crown to the other ear. Then the man would pull the flap of skin down over the face of the girl who was not Kathy. It was done quickly, with the sure strokes of a butcher. Now Riker listened to the saw slicing into her skull. A minute more and her brains would hit the scale. His pen hovered over the notebook as that minute dragged by. And then it was over.

She was gutted and ruined.

Because the woman might have been Kathy, the killer had touched him in his soft places. Kathy Mallory had crept into those soft places as a child and grown up in them.

Later in the day, he would soak his despair in scotch, but not drown it. It would be waiting for him in the morning with his hangover. Tomorrow, the two of them, despair and headache, would be married to one another and sitting at the foot of his bed when he awoke to a new morning, or maybe it would be afternoon, and then they would get him.

For all the days of her suspension from the force, the beautifully tailored lines of her blazers had been uninterrupted by the bulge of a .357 Smith & Wesson revolver. She might have passed for a civilian, but for the uncivilized green eyes. She was settled deep into the well-padded brocade of an eighteenth-century couch in a warm patch of afternoon sun. One slim blue-jeaned leg curled under her, but the running shoe never touched the material. Helen Markowitz had raised her to respect furniture, whether it be the antiques which filled this office with the colors of Persian rugs and stained-glass lampshades, or the cruder appointments of NYPD.

"Talk to him, Mallory," said Effrim Wilde, who knew better than to presume he might call her Kathy or Kathleen on only a few years' acquaintance, or even ten.

The long slants of her eyes were only half-open

as she turned her face to Effrim. "I hope the kid isn't possessed by the devil," she said. She glanced at Charles. "I really hate that."

Charles Butler smiled broadly. Effrim Wilde smiled not at all.

Effrim was a rounded silhouette in the soft diffusion of light from the wide center window. Dwarfed by the tall triptych of arched glass panes, he might have been taken for an altar boy, and not a man in his middle fifties. The aging cherub face was crowned by wavy hair, more salt than pepper now.

"Charles, it's a fascinating problem."

"Nothing fascinating about it," said Charles. "It's garden-variety fraud."

Charles coveted Effrim's pug nose, for his own was constantly reminding him of its size and length. Charles could look nowhere without looking over it, or trying to see around it, or noting the shadow it cast on every wall. He was not a handsome man; he knew that. And he had long ago come to terms with the realization that strangers took him for an asylum escapee, perhaps because of the large egg-shaped eyes and the undersized blue marbles that rolled around the vast white surfaces, giving him the look of having been taken by surprise.

"Give it up, Effrim. I'm not dealing with that kind of nonsense," he said, rising from a Queen Anne chair and inadvertently looming over the smaller man. At six-four, Charles's looming was unavoidable.

"It isn't nonsense, Charles. I have the data—"

"The Russian or the Chinese? Never mind. I'm not terribly impressed with either. Those experiments have never been duplicated to my

12

satisfaction. I'm not buying it. Why don't you fob the case off on Malakhai?"

"Malakhai, the debunker? I thought he was dead."

"No, he's in retirement now, but I don't think a small boy will cause him any undue exertion. He won't charge you much for fifteen minutes' work." Charles turned to Mallory. "Malakhai is an old friend of the family. He toured Europe with Cousin Max when he was a practicing magician. This was all a bit before your time."

"Charles, I'm not concerned about the expense," said Effrim.

"Good, not that he needs the money. Shall I call him?"

"Absolutely not. Every case he ever worked on became a sideshow. What we want here is discretion. We're talking about a little boy, a very troubled little boy."

"Are we?" Charles rose off the balls of his feet, smiling pleasantly. "I thought you were sucking up to the boy's father because he controls a grant committee. It is that time of year, isn't it? When the think tank passes the hat? I only deal with legitimate gifts, measurable gifts."

"Levitating objects? That's not a gift?" Effrim's eyes rounded in mock incredulity that Charles would not see things his way. But then, Charles saw Effrim's every expression as a mockery of honest sentiment.

"Effrim, you know the boy is a fraud. He's not levitating anything. And it's no good appealing to Mallory. She's not overly sentimental about small children, little old ladies or dogs. Nor does she believe that inanimate objects can fly without

13

a physical activator. And the proper term is 'psychokinesis.'"

"Well, you would know the technical jargon better than I," said Effrim, waving his hand in the expansive gesture of concession. "I stand corrected. Thank you."

"And if the boy levitates food, it's called a food fight."

"Thank you, Charles."

Now Charles watched the mechanics of Effrim's small smile, the downcast eyes, the aggrieved sigh for those who were not yet enlightened, and he knew his old friend was regrouping for another assault.

"This child has been through a terrible emotional ordeal," said Effrim in the tone of *Brothers and sisters, let us pray.* "His mother died when he was only nine years old. And fourteen months later, his first stepmother died."

"No good, Effrim. Psychokinesis is not my field."

Effrim rolled his eyes up in the manner of the insipid-saint school of fourteenth-century painting. "Your field is discovering new gifts and finding applications for them, is it not? This child is in the gifted category in other areas, you know. His IQ is somewhere between yours and mine. And there's some urgency to this. His new stepmother is badly frightened. It seems he's been applying his gift in a rather terrifying way."

One long and slender arm, led by five red fingernails, stretched across the back of the couch as Mallory was roused from lethargy. "So, the new stepmother is the target?"

Charles watched Effrim mentally stepping back to reappraise Mallory as a possible ally, estimating the location of her buttons, what pressure to push them with, and which buttons to avoid. This was Effrim's special gift, his art.

"I do hope not," said Effrim with exquisite insincerity. "He's been moving sharp objects around."

Charles filled Mallory's empty glass with dry sherry. A look passed between them, and in that look, a small conversation took place in which he begged her not to encourage Effrim.

He next offered the decanter to his good friend of many years, whom he would not trust with the silver. "Effrim, if you believe the boy is in trauma, wouldn't it be better to refer him to a psychiatrist?"

"Probably not," said Mallory, answering for Effrim. "How many shrinks fall into the genius category? If it's fraud and the boy is that bright, he could put it by the average peabrain."

Charles looked her way, his smile dipping down on one side to say, *I begged you not to do that.*

She was avoiding his eyes and further ocular conversation. He found it interesting that she would take Effrim's part when she was so suspicious of the man. She'd had a good instinct there.

"How did the mother and stepmother die?" she asked Effrim.

So it was only the body count that interested Mallory. He should have guessed that. She was bored with the partnership. When her suspension was over, he would lose her to Special Crimes Section. He had nothing to offer her, no dead bodies, no puzzles quite so interesting as murder.

Effrim was looking into his glass, reading his next line in the sherry. "It was tragic, really tragic.

15

The boy's natural mother died of a heart attack. Odd because she was so young at the time, only twenty-eight." He looked up to gauge the effect of the hook on Mallory, but her face was devoid of emotional cues. He stared into her eyes for too long and became unsettled by them. Turning back to his glass, he spoke to the sherry. "And then his first stepmother committed suicide. . . . She didn't leave a note."

Mallory lifted her chin slightly. Her eyes were all the way open now.

Charles stared at the ceiling. *Oh, good job, Effrim.*

"That's quite a run of bad luck in one family," said Charles.

"Only for the women," said Mallory. "We'll take it."

She didn't look to Charles for confirmation, not that he minded. It might keep her from cutting the cord of Mallory and Butler, Ltd. for a while, but the break was inevitable. Not likely NYPD would allow her to moonlight any longer. There must be limits to what she could get away with.

Effrim was edging toward the door.

Right, Effrim. Best to hit and run.

"I'll send over a check for the retainer," Effrim said. And then for his most stunning trick, the wide Cheshire smile lingered on after the door was closed behind him.

Mallory was rising off the couch, running shoes lighting on the floor at the edge of the carpet. "I'll chase down the life insurance angle."

"Ah, just a minute, Mallory. We were asked to evaluate the psychokinetic activity, not the family history."

16

"You're kidding, right?"

"Right. Lunch?"

"There's nothing in the office fridge."

No, there wouldn't be, now that he thought of it. She had trusted him with a shopping list. He had used the back of it to jot down two telephone numbers, and used the whole of it to mark his place in a book, but he had forgotten to use any part of it for shopping.

"Let's go to my place."

They walked across the hall and into the apartment that was his residence. Here, an eagle-eyed Mrs. Ortega saw to the contents of the refrigerator out of pity for the shopping-disabled Charles. Today the cleaning woman had left a note on the refrigerator door, attached by a magnet. It was a diagram of the kitchen showing all the war zones where she had set traps for the mouse. He felt sorry for the rodent, so great was his confidence in Mrs. Ortega.

Mallory was ensconced at the kitchen table. The kitchen was his favorite room. The walls were lined with racks of spices and agents for tenderizing flesh, and instruments for torturing vegetables, slicing, dicing and boiling them in oil. He was now in the process of covering the table with refrigerator finds. Mallory was picking over plastic containers, packages of meat and no less than five colors of cheese, and putting together original creations of sandwich mania. On his final trip back from the refrigerator, he offered her a new discovery in pickle labels.

"You were happier in Special Crimes, weren't you?"

"When Markowitz was alive," she said, opening the jar and sniffing, then approving the contents with a nod. "Working with Coffey isn't quite the same. If I go back, I'll be stuck in the computer room forever. He was really pissed off the last time I saw his face. He'll never let me out in the field again."

"I thought this suspension was just a formality."

"It is. When you shoot a perp, you're relieved of duty while the Civilian Review Board investigates the case."

"But you didn't kill the mugger, and he did beat and rob that old man."

"Coffey's got a different way of looking at things."

"So you don't want to dissolve the partnership?"

"No, it never occurred to me. But that doesn't mean I won't go back to Special Crimes when my suspension is over." And now she checked her watch and reached up to turn on the small television set on the kitchen counter. It was time for the news, and she did like to keep up on the city's death rate.

"But there are department regulations against moonlighting, aren't there?"

"Yes, there are." And what of it, said her eyebrows on the way up.

The news show was reporting the daily carnage with a video window on the Death Clock of Times Square. As the statistics of the dead were read by the newscaster, the numbers on the giant public bulletin board changed before an audience of a thousand cars and pedestrians, and the millions more who preferred to view cheap spectacle on television.

"I hate that thing," she said, watching the

change of electronic digits which kept the national score of death by guns.

"The Death Clock? But, Mallory, I thought you of all people would appreciate computerized death. It makes homicide so neat and efficient."

She said nothing. Her face shut him out, resolving itself into a cold mask. This was his only clue that he had erred. Why did he persist in the belief that he might ever learn to anticipate her? Who knew what went on inside of Mallory? And how could he not go on wondering?

Charles was staring at the television set, but his mind had strolled across the hall to the office where she stored her computer toys. Of course, keeping the partnership had its practical aspects. Here she had freedom from the supervision of anyone who might recognize her equipment as the electronic equivalent of burglary tools.

"This word just in," said the news broadcaster, calling Charles back to the kitchen and the moment. Now he was looking at Mallory's face on the television screen.

"We have a bulletin," the broadcaster was saying. *"A police officer has been murdered in Central Park. The victim is Sergeant Kathleen Mallory, daughter of the deceased Inspector Louis Markowitz, who gave his own life in the line of duty. Details of the murder are being withheld pending further investigation."*

Charles looked across the table at the living, solid, three-dimensional Mallory as though he needed to verify her existence, needed to be sure his eyes were not in error before he could doubt the veracity of television. Suppose she had not been with him when he heard the news?

They watched in silence. Much channel

changing told them other news programs were also carrying the story.

And now the phone was ringing in concert with the doorbell. The first of the condolence calls, he supposed. Mallory went off to answer the door as he picked up the phone.

"Hello?"

"Charles, this is Riker. Don't you ever pick up the messages on your answering machine?"

"Riker, is this about the report on Mallory's death?"

"Yeah," said Riker. "I'm calling from the Medical Examiner's Office. We've been trying to track down Mallory all day. Is she there? Could you put the little corpse on the phone?"

Mallory walked back into the kitchen, followed by Dr. Henrietta Ramsharan of apartment 3A. Henrietta's dark hair fell soft and loose around the shoulders of her denim shirt. She wore her after-hours faded jeans and the confusion of the eyes which came from having the door opened by a dead person.

Lieutenant Jack Coffey was sitting at his own desk, but the desk was in Inspector Markowitz's office. Though Louis Markowitz was dead, the old man would always be in command of the Special Crimes Section, and this would always be his office. Jack Coffey counted himself lucky that the paychecks were made out to himself. But just now, he was thinking of Markowitz's daughter, Kathleen Mallory.

Palanski's report was sitting on his desk, replete with the crime-site preliminary faxed over from the West Side precinct. The fax photos were dark, but the light hair shone through the grainy shadows, and he could make out the outline of the slender body in the familiar jeans, running shoes and blazer. He only waited on the positive identification from a friend of the family to complete the report.

No doubt Sergeant Riker would pull the pin after this one. Markowitz's death had hit the man hard. Mallory's death would be too much.

Coffey turned off the lamp and braced his hands on the desk, as though a man of thirty-six needed this solid crutch to rise to a stand. He stared at the bulletin board on the back wall of the office and wondered if a little water on his face might make him feel less dead.

Who could get so close to her that the bastard could hit her that way? No one. It could not be.

But the evidence was sitting on his desk in black and white, and her pretty face was all over the television on every channel. And when he found the cop who leaked it to the media, one head was gonna roll.

Ah, Mallory.

If he could have her back for a few minutes, he would risk the sarcasm and the look that would neatly snip his balls for caring if she lived or died. Sucker, her eyes would say. He could almost see her standing there. He even imagined that he could smell her perfume. It was time to go home where the bottle was. He turned.

"Oh, Christ!"

He grabbed at the doorframe and missed, too slow with shock to fall immediately and catching himself on the second pass at something solid, which was the chair. His stomach shot up and then slammed back to where it belonged.

Mallory stood in the doorway. Her gold hair

was backlit by the office lights beyond the door, and coming up behind her was a fluorescent, washed-out Riker.

"I know," said Mallory. "You thought it was me in the morgue."

"Well, Mallory," said Riker, "he did and he didn't. The lieutenant heard you were dead, but he knew you'd be back after sundown."

Riker ambled into the office behind Mallory and tossed his report on the desk. One beverage and two different types of food stains graced the front page.

Coffey was staring at the report and looking for his voice as she sat down in the chair by his desk and stretched out the long legs that went on forever. Riker dragged another chair up to the desk, pulled out his notebook and leaned over to flick on the lamp. On the rear wall, Mallory was casting the reassuring shadow of a living woman.

Coffey lowered himself into his chair. He was fighting down the gut flutters, one hand resting on his stomach, as though he could kill the internal butterflies by smothering them this way. "The corpse was wearing a brown cashmere blazer that was tailored for you, Mallory."

Riker looked at his notebook and nodded to her. "That was confirmed by your tailor on Forty-second Street. According to Palanski's report, you're the guy's most memorable customer."

"Can you explain the blazer?" Ease up, Coffey told himself. She was not a suspect. Softening out of the interrogation mode, he added, "It's the only lead we have."

"You'll find Riker's cigarette burn on the left sleeve," she said, and not softly at all. "I got rid of it."

22

"You trashed it?"

"No. I gave it to Anna Kaplan, Rabbi Kaplan's wife. She collects clothing for the homeless."

He looked down at Riker's report, reading through the orange sauce stains and one stain that damn well better not be beer. "According to the ME's report, this is the body of a well-nourished female in her mid-twenties. No indication that she was homeless, no head lice, no bedbugs."

He left out the feeding frenzy of maggots and beetles that would help to determine the time of death in the scavenging cycle of insects.

"So?" Mallory shrugged. "Talk to Palanski. See what else he botched besides the ID on the corpse. What have we got so far?"

Her question was well within the purview of a crimes analyst. He needed her back. How to get through this without antagonizing her, without falling into another round of one-upmanship which she always won. He scanned the lines of Riker's report.

"We know she had an abortion within ten days of death. The first wound was a frontal assault to the head. He was facing her. That could mean it was personal, someone she knew. Outside of that, we've got nothing," said Coffey. "No witness, no weapon."

"It was raining yesterday morning," said Riker, tapping the early homicide report on the corner of Coffey's desk. "The rain would have washed away any physical evidence. If Heller couldn't dig it up, it wasn't there. The weapon could have been a rock, and that rock is at the bottom of the lake if the perp has half a brain. And that's

23

assuming she was killed in the park. We know the body was moved after death."

"We don't have an officer involvement," said Coffey. "If you've got nothing more to add to this report, I'm bouncing it back to the West Side squad tonight."

Mallory sat well back in her chair, eyes half-closed, looking nearly harmless. "With no prints, it'll take them a month to ID that body—maybe longer or never. It'll be a low-priority case. So, if the park was only the dump site, they'll never find the kill site. They're gonna blow it."

"I suppose you could do it better and faster?" And yes, he could see that was exactly what she thought.

"You want me to?"

"I want you to go back to your damn computer room."

"I'm still on suspension, and I'm considering a better offer."

Mallory rose from her chair, and in the next instant, he was looking at the back of her as she walked out of the room.

"You know she's right," said Riker, leaning over in his chair, checking the door to be sure she was gone out of earshot. "The West Side dicks will lose it. The perp's gonna get away with the murder."

"It happens. Nothing I can do about it."

"Give this one to Mallory."

"Her job description is crimes analysis and computers, not fieldwork."

"But she has worked in the field."

"Unofficially, and only because I had a shortage of warm bodies. If she wants to make it official, she has to go through the paperwork and put in some time with a partner. Now, who could work with her? And you're forgetting this case is another precinct's headache."

"Well, technically it's still the property of Special Crimes. Why not give it to Mallory? Just give it to her, close your eyes and don't ask her a lot of questions."

"Like Markowitz did?" When she broke six laws a day, breaking and entering other people's computers, cutting corners, bypassing time-consuming channels and warrants—proving invaluable. "I should just let her run her own private police department? Is that the idea, Riker?"

"Yeah."

"But Markowitz didn't want her to work the field. He all but padded the walls of that computer room. He spoon-fed her every detail of a case."

"I always thought he was wrong in that." Riker lit a cigarette without asking if Coffey minded.

Coffey minded, but bit it back. He'd grown accustomed to this game they played, needling within parameters that stopped just short of insubordination. And he had not yet thanked Riker for failing to call in the false ID from the morgue.

"All this time, she could have been learning fieldwork so she could survive out there," said Riker, exhaling a blue cloud of smoke. "Now it occurs to me that she's got her own way of surviving, and it might be a better way. It's a waste of talent to keep her in the computer room."

"It was letting her out of the computer room that got her suspended."

"That was a righteous shoot."

"You know better than that, Riker. If she'd

25

killed the perp, I'd have no problem with that. But Mallory wanted to play with him.''

"Whose call is that? Are you telling me that pack of idiots on the Civilian Review Board ruled against her?''

"The Review Board commended her on restricting her use of force to shooting a gun out of a man's hand. But then, they're civilians, aren't they? I'm the one who's got a problem with the shooting. The perp aimed a gun at Mallory. She should've put that bullet in his heart. But if she'd just killed him, where would be the fun in that?''

No comeback, Riker?

Coffey mentally scratched one point for himself, but the big score would be in getting the last word. "Now I've got a backlog of cases, and she's not replaceable on the computer. That's it.''

Coffey shuffled the papers on his desk, and then bowed his head to read them. Had a more sensitive human sat in Riker's chair, he would have recognized this signal of dismissal. He was still seated when his superior looked up from the paperwork. Coffey's glare was wasted on Riker, who seemed preoccupied with his own thoughts.

"Riker, catch up to Mallory and tell her the suspension is terminated.''

Riker nodded, but remained entirely too comfortable in his slouch to be going anywhere very soon.

"If you don't give Mallory something more interesting, she'll walk,'' said Riker, spilling out his words with the smoke in an economy of effort. "She'll keep the consulting partnership with Charles.''

"That setup is illegal as hell, and it's gonna

26

stop or I'll take her badge," he said, trying the lie out on Riker first, and wondering how Mallory would take it.

"You can't scare Mallory."

He hated it when Riker was right. If the department ever did enforce the regulations on moonlighting, there wouldn't be three cops left to guard the city.

"Are you volunteering to play wet nurse, Riker?"

"Mallory doesn't need me for that. She doesn't need any human being on the planet. She came that way when she was a kid. Real self-sufficient little—"

"I thought Markowitz was your friend, Riker. Are you trying to give that dead man a heart attack by putting his kid in the line of fire?"

"If she hadn't been his daughter, he would have used her right. He would have been ruthless about it."

Riker deposited an ash on the carpet. The whole world was Riker's ashtray.

"Why should I give her this one? The guy is brutal. He's a psycho." Coffey held up the morgue photo, and Riker turned his face to the floor. "First he smashes the woman's skull in, and then he turns her head 180 till her neck snaps. How is Mallory going to—"

"If you're afraid she's gonna shoot him in the hand, I think she's learned her lesson." He lifted his shaggy head to face Coffey with something approaching serious feeling. "Give her a chance." Riker then shrugged his shoulders to show that this business really meant very little to him.

And now Coffey realized it meant a great deal to Riker.

27

"You know she'd have absolutely nothing to go on."

"That's what she likes about it," said Riker. "The first time you said that, her little monster eyes lit up like green candles. It's enough to make you believe in hell."

"All we know about the perp is that he's dangerous to women, and you want me to give him to Mallory."

Sure. Give a dangerous lunatic to the baby to cut her teeth on.

"She's perfect for this one."

"How do you figure?"

While Coffey waited on an answer, he looked down at the report on his blotter and picked up a pencil to initial it. Riker slumped low in his chair and put his feet up on the desk. Coffey's pencil snapped in two.

"You know," Riker drawled through the smoky haze, "even in the early days, Markowitz took a lot of pride in Mallory. He used to brag on her all the time. He said it wasn't every father in the neighborhood who had a kid with the psych profile of a sociopath."

Chapter 2

DECEMBER 21

He had seen the magic bullet again. In dreams, he had watched its slow float from the mouth of the gun to his gut, watched it penetrate his flesh and make the blood fly.

On his way to the bathroom, Riker's bare foot knocked an empty beer bottle to one side. He never felt the hard connection of flesh to glass, so vivid was the dream in front of his open eyes.

One day the booze would get him killed. His reflexes would not kick in when he needed them to save his sorry life. Awake or asleep, the magic bullet was always floating in the air just ahead of him.

But he and the bottle were an old married couple now. And he preferred the dream of the bullet to the vision of spiders which had come with his last attempt at divorce from alcohol.

How many years had it been? Thirteen years? At least that.

He had been going through withdrawal, strapped to a bed of delirium tremens, on the day Kathy Mallory crawled through the window of the clinic, which did not allow children to visit by the front door. The little girl had hit the floor in her rubber-soled shoes and the eerie stealth of a born thief.

For one slow blink, the strange child had blended well with the tableau of spiders which crawled all over his body, the sheets and the walls. The largest of the spiders dangled from the ceiling, madly spinning its silken line, dropping ever closer to his face in an aerial ballet of eight black dancing legs. And then it danced upon his eyes while his arms were bound by thick leather restraints.

"The spider! Get it off my eyes!" he had screamed at Mallory, who was Kathy then. (Years later, when she joined the force, she would forbid him to use her given name.) Young Kathy had come close to the bed, peered into his eyes and pronounced them free of spiders. And then, she looked at him with such contempt. She was so close, he could see his own bug-size self twice-reflected in her eyes.

He had turned to the larger mirror on the hospital wall, the better to see what she had seen: his face bathed in sweat, awash in fear, and twitching. A slick of vomit trailed from his mouth to his chin. He slowly nodded his head in agreement with Kathy. He was so pathetic—even spiders would not live in his mind with him anymore.

He remembered thanking God that Helen Markowitz had taught Kathy not to spit indoors. He could see it was in her mind to do it when she looked down at him. Instead, she only turned around and left the way she had come, disappearing through the window. Then, small hands were gripping the sash, closing the window behind her, making no sound and leaving no trace of her unlawful entry.

After that day, after all the spiders had fled for a more upscale mental disorder than his own, he had not been successful in giving up the bottle, but made a point of never again losing face with Kathy. The unpitying brat had ended his days of public falling-down, crawling-home drunken binges. As drunks go, he had become semi-respectable, rarely stumbling, never reeling anymore.

Even through his sunglasses, the light at the level of the sidewalk was painfully bright. He opened the passenger door of Mallory's small tan car and climbed inside. He leaned toward the

30

windshield, lowering his scratched green shades and squinting at the panorama of his neighborhood.

"So *this* is morning."

Dead silence from Mallory.

He had kept the punctuality freak waiting while he dressed and shaved. He was anticipating her slow burn as he shrugged down deep into the upholstery. Smiling affably, tying his tie, he waited for the sarcasm. Instead, she gunned the engine, ripped the car away from the curb and laid a streak of hot rubber on the street leading away from his apartment building.

Riker grabbed the dashboard, thinking this might keep his brains from sloshing around in his skull and stop the pain of the hangover.

"Okay, Mallory. It's gonna be a long day. Play nice."

The car slowed down to a law-abiding pace, and her voice was deceptively civil when she said, "The uniforms came up dry with the doormen on the Upper West Side. She didn't live in that neighborhood. Nobody could make the photographs."

So she had started without him. What else might she have been up to? It was only ten in the morning. Most days, he would just be opening his eyes at this hour and only *thinking* about rolling to the floor and, if he landed with enough momentum, maybe continuing on to the bathroom.

In the tone of *You got this coming to you, kid*, he said, "If you'd had a few years in fieldwork, you'd know how hard it is for most people to ID a corpse from a morgue photo, even one without a damaged face. A mother could make the ID in

31

a heartbeat, and maybe a close friend could do it—but a doorman? No way. So we still don't know that she didn't live in that neighborhood."

Mallory's expression in profile might read the venom of *I'm going to get you for that,* or the merely sarcastic *Yeah, right.* He was pretty confident it was one of those two things.

"Where are we headed?" he ventured, testing the atmosphere between them. "Going to Brooklyn?"

"No," she said. "I've been to Brooklyn. Anna dropped the clothes off at a collection center. The center trucked them into the main clearinghouse in Manhattan. Anna's bundle went to a women's shelter in the East Village."

"So we're going to a shelter? Mallory, I gotta go along with Coffey on this one. I just don't see our Jane Doe in a women's shelter."

"I've already been to the shelter. The cashmere blazer wasn't on the inventory. Somebody lifted it at the warehouse. That's where we're going now."

"How do you know it wasn't lifted at the shelter?" Oh, stupid question. She had turned the place inside out, and probably alienated every—

"A friend of Anna's runs that shelter. She opened Anna's bundle herself. No blazer. So we go to the clearinghouse and talk to everybody who handled it."

Ten minutes rolled by on the road in companionable silence. That was one bright spot of doing time with Mallory—she made no small talk. If she opened her mouth, it was to take a swipe at him or make a point. When they pulled up alongside the warehouse, he picked his own words with careful timing. He put one hand on her shoulder before they entered the building.

"Mallory, no cowboy shots this time out. I backed you with Coffey, but he was right and you know it. If you gotta spend a bullet, you do it right and you do it clean. Okay? School's out."

They passed through the lobby in a testy silence and rode up to the third floor in a gray metal box the size of a coffin. The elevator doors opened onto a single room the length and width of a city block. Irregular corridors, made of stacked packages and bundles, extended far into the illusion of converging parallels. Dust hung in the air around the forklift shuttling back and forth down the wide center aisle, picking up cartons as numbers were called out over a bullhorn in the hand of a man with bandy legs and a beer belly.

Mallory flashed her badge and fell into step with the man as he walked the center aisle. Grimy light from never-washed windows gave the place a secondhand look to go with the smell of the clothing. Riker had worn such clothes as a child, and he could never lose that smell.

He followed behind Mallory, pulling out his notebook.

The bandy-legged crew chief was alternately calling out numbers from his clipboard and carrying on a conversation that Mallory was not listening to.

"No one would touch one of those bundles," said the crew chief. "Who's gonna risk a job for a crummy secondhand rag?"

Riker smiled. He guessed the rag in question had set Mallory back at least nine hundred dollars, if not more. Nothing but the best for Mallory. Helen Markowitz had seen to that,

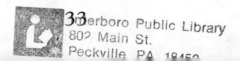

beginning in the early days when Riker was still allowed to call her Kathy. But despite the designer wardrobe Helen had lavished on the child, Kathy had gone everywhere in blue jeans, tennis shoes, and T-shirts.

Today, that wardrobe only varied in the tailored, gray wool blazer that bulged on the left as a warning that she carried a large gun in a shoulder holster. And she had traded her canvas tennis shoes for the most expensive leather running shoes God ever personally cobbled.

"Who handled the bundles when they came in?" she asked.

"Could've been any one of eight guys," said the crew chief and then called out, "Four eighty-nine," in the amplified scream of the bullhorn.

"Get them out here, all eight of them."

"Look, honey, I'm always happy to cooperate with the cops, but I ain't—"

"Did I *ask* you for cooperation? *Get them.*"

And now Riker could see that the crew chief was from the old school—no woman was going to dress him down and get away with it. The man turned on Mallory with all the indignation of a pit bull, lips parted to a display of teeth. And then, something in her face shut his mouth. Perhaps he had just remembered that he had come out this morning without a weapon.

He cleared his throat, lifted the bullhorn and barked off the names. The men came out of all the stacks with clipboards and pencils, sweat and curiosity, leers for Mallory, and puffs of cigarette smoke. They fell into a ragged line.

As she looked them over like a prospective buyer, the leers dropped away and Riker watched discomfort settle in. There was shifting of feet

34

and the small talk of eyes between them. One man was sweating more than the rest, and his Adam's apple had a life of its own. Mallory seemed to like this one with the red hair and freckles. Now she kept her eyes on him alone. His shoulders hunched, and his head lowered as he made himself smaller. His muscles were tensing, bunching through the thin cloth of his T-shirt.

Mallory turned to Riker and lifted her chin a bare quarter of an inch. She looked back to the redhead. Riker circled around to the right. As Mallory moved forward, the redhead balked and ran. Riker reached out to grab the T-shirt and missed. And now Mallory was pounding after the man, and Riker jogged behind her in the dust kicked up by her shoes.

"Jimmy," the manager screamed, "come back here, you jerk! It's only a secondhand sportscoat!"

But Jimmy was out of earshot.

Jimmy Farrow was running as fast as he had ever run from a cop, and he'd outrun a few. He looked back to see the old guy turning red trying to keep up, but the woman was almost on top of him. Every time he chanced a look over his shoulder, she was right there, four feet behind and not even breathing hard, her blazer flapping open to expose a very big gun.

Oh, Christ, was she grinning? She was.

Bitch!

She stayed with him through the narrow streets, then across all the lanes of traffic on wide Houston, and over the courtyard wall of an apartment building in the West Village.

He made the leap of his life and hooked his hands on a fire escape. He hauled his body up and climbed the metal stairs. As he gained the next landing, he looked down through the gate. She was nowhere in sight.

He was looking up to the landing above when he was grabbed by the hair and pulled backward.

Where did she come from?

A kick to the inside of his knee and he was off balance, falling to the grate of the fire escape, rolling to the edge. Blood rushed to his head as he was leveraged over the side and dangling, arms waving in circles. He was looking down at the sidewalk three flights below. Twisting his head to look up through the grate, he could see her holding the back of his jeans and kneeling on his legs. He stopped struggling. If she let go, he was gone. She could dump him anytime she wanted to.

"So you stole the cashmere blazer and . . . ?"

She eased off his legs and let him hang a little lower.

"The jacket!" he screamed. "That's what this is about? That stupid sportsjacket?"

"You stole it, right?"

He saw the pavement come up a few more inches to meet him. A winter breeze chilled the sweat on his body and made him shiver.

"Yeah, I did it! Okay?"

"Didn't she like it?"

What? Crazy bitch. What does she want?

"Yeah, she liked it! She liked it just fine!"

He wondered if he might be right side up after all, and it was the world that was upside down. The old cop was down below, snagging the ladder for the fire escape and lowering it down to the pavement. The old guy took his sweet time walking up the stairs, like it was nothing to see some poor bastard hanging in midair and pointed headfirst toward the cement.

Damn cops.

"Mallory, don't do this to me," said the old guy. "You don't want Coffey on my ass, do you?"

And the woman said, "He won't complain. I can do anything I want with him."

"You drop him, and that's three days of paperwork."

She loosened her grip. He dropped lower.

"Okay, okay!" screamed Jimmy Farrow. "I already told her I did it! Let me up!"

He was being hauled up by four ungentle hands. When he was right side up and sitting down, the old guy took out his notebook. "You wanna make a statement, kid? Is that what you're telling me?"

"Yeah, okay. My grandmother's Social Security check got screwed up this month. A neighbor bought her groceries for a few days till my mom could replace the money. I just wanted to give Amanda—she's the neighbor—I wanted to give her something. It was my grandmother's idea."

"Now let me get this straight," said the old guy, pen circling over his notebook. "First you gave Amanda the blazer, then you killed her— and your grandmother made you do it?"

Oh, God, they're both nuts.

"I didn't do anything to her. I just gave her the sportjacket."

"Were you very close to Amanda?"

"No! I go to my grandmother's building twice a week to sweep out the halls. My grandmother's the super, but she's not up to slopping all those floors and stairs anymore."

"What a good boy you are," said the old guy. "Now, about Amanda?"

"I see Amanda in the hall now and then, that's all. She and my grandmother were real tight. Talk to the old lady."

The old woman was waiting for them on the front steps of the building. Jimmy Farrow stood between two uniformed officers on the sidewalk, his head bowed and his hands cuffed behind his back. Riker climbed the steps behind Mallory and watched the old woman looking from Mallory to her grandson, lips slightly parted in disbelief.

"Police," said Mallory showing the ID card and shield. "You're Mrs. Farrow? This is your grandson?"

The old woman nodded, her eyes blinking rapidly.

Riker looked back to the sidewalk. The siren on the squad car had scattered most of the hookers like roaches, but now one came weaving back, too jazzed on crack to be afraid.

"I want access to Amanda Bosch's apartment," said Mallory.

"Do you have a warrant?" the old woman asked automatically.

That was predictable to Riker. It was a neighborhood where such a phrase came tripping to the tongue, spoken even before that all-time favorite, "I didn't do it."

"She's dead," said Mallory. "You think I need a warrant?"

Nicely worded, kid.

And the denial in the slow shake of the old

38

woman's head was also predictable. *Such a thing could not be,* said Mrs. Farrow's eyes. She pulled her thin sweater close about her neck, as though that would protect her from Mallory. She retreated two faltering steps. Mallory's long reach put a photograph in the old woman's face.

"Is that her? Is that Amanda Bosch?"

Ease up, Mallory. We don't want to kill a taxpayer.

Mrs. Farrow stared at the image of the dead woman and crossed herself. Another protection failed her as Mallory put her face in the old woman's face. "Is that her?"

"Yes, yes. It's Amanda Bosch."

Mallory made a note, and Riker knew her meticulous report would read that positive ID was made at 10:56 a.m. That would make a department record for a corpse without prints.

They followed the old woman up the stairs and down the hall to the apartment at the end of the second landing. Mrs. Farrow fumbled with the lock, but finally managed it. When the hand with the key ring came back to the old woman's side, the keys jingled with the trembling.

Riker entered the apartment behind Mallory. Mrs. Farrow hovered on the threshold for a moment and then melted away down the hall.

The first thing he noticed about the apartment was that it was clean. From where he stood, he could see through the sparkling galley kitchen and into the room beyond it. Spotless, smelling of cleansers and powders, all cleaned up for company. Or had the place been cleaned up for blood traces and prints?

The inside doorknob gleamed. He looked down and moved his head to see it from every possible angle. There might be latent prints on it, but he doubted it. Even Mallory was not so neat that she wiped the prints from her own door-knob when she left her apartment. He called through the open door to a uniformed police officer standing out in the hall with Jimmy Farrow.

"Looks like this might be the original crime scene. Ask the old lady if you can use her phone to call the techs."

"Waste of time," said Mallory, bending low to approve the polish of a small table. Every surface was gleaming. "Very neat. If our guy gets off on a psycho defense, I may hire him to clean my condo."

Markowitz had raised her right. She touched nothing, hands jammed into the pockets of her jeans as they continued the routine walk-through into the next room.

The back room was tiny, with only space enough for the single bed and the personal computer. She knew better than to touch it, but her hands pulled out of the pockets the moment she saw it. From now on, she would have no interest in anything else. She did not have her father's mania for small details.

The door to the closet was ajar. Riker's eyes adjusted to the dim light within until he made out the outline of the old-fashioned wooden cradle on the floor. So Amanda had purchased a cradle for the aborted baby, and then put the cradle away, out of sight, when the child was cut out of her.

He looked away.

He perused the bookshelf and found style guides and reference books: one on how to prepare a manuscript, another on writers' markets. In this room, too, all the surfaces were cleaned. In the better light of two windows, he could see the scallops of sponge marks high on the wall. Had there been blood on the walls? Had Amanda managed to do some damage to him before he killed her?

"Well, that tears it," he said, turning to Mallory, who was reading the label of a computer disk on the console shelf. "This has to be the crime site, and the bastard wiped it clean." He spoke on blind faith that she might be listening to him. "You know, this may be the end of the road, kid."

She was pacing back and forth in front of the computer. She could hardly wait to get at it. He knew she was only holding off for a technician to tell her what she already knew—it had been wiped clean. She was ignoring everything else in the apartment.

Not the old man's style.

Markowitz always had his investigators bring him every damned detail they could fit into a notebook or a plastic bag. She was letting every detail go by.

A uniformed officer appeared in the bedroom doorway. "There's a crew in the area. They can be here in about fifteen minutes to a half hour."

"Thanks, Martin," said Riker.

If Mallory approved the cleaning job, it was a certainty they would find nothing. She had called it a waste of time, and she had called it right. Twenty minutes later, Heller, the senior man in Forensics, was sharing Mallory's opinion. He stood in the center of the bedroom, his slow brown eyes wandering over every polished surface, and wincing.

41

As Heller pulled on his rubber gloves, the nod of his head sent another technician to the kitchen. A third man was already at work in the front room. A ricochet of flashbulb light found its way to the back of the tiny apartment. Heller, brush in hand, turned to the small nightstand by the narrow bed.

"No. Do the computer first," said Mallory. "I need it."

Perhaps another man with Heller's years in the department might have bridled at a direct order from Mallory, who was younger than Heller's youngest daughter. He only nodded, taking no offense, and set his kit on the floor by the computer.

A uniformed officer filled the bedroom doorway. "Your keystroker brought this over." He handed Mallory a leather case. She opened it to display a set of delicate tools and boxes of disks.

She turned to hover over Heller as he worked with the black powder.

"Don't get that crap in the keyboard," said Mallory. "And watch the vent—you don't want it dropping in the vent."

Riker had never seen Heller work so fast, anything to appease Mallory. And when he was done, he couldn't get out of her way fast enough.

"I'm going up to talk to the old lady and the kid," said Riker.

"Right."

She was onto the computer now. He was dead to her, as were the technicians who worked around her.

As Riker was closing the door behind him, Heller was working on the nightstand and

42

bitching about the perp being a good-housekeeping fanatic, forgetting that only four feet away from him sat just such a fanatic, and she was armed.

"Don't bag that," said Mallory to Heller as he was trying to ease the card file off the small table next to the computer. "I need it. It's a client list—all the people she did research for."

"You got your own tweezers in that kit?" Heller asked, looking down into her case of tools.

She looked up at Heller. Did he think she didn't know how to handle evidence? No. He was just doing his job. Markowitz had always coddled and petted Heller, even when he was giving the man fits, checking out details within details. And she needed this man.

"Don't worry about it, Heller. If his prints were on it, he wouldn't have left it behind." She moved her chair to one side of the screen. "Here, look at this."

Heller bent down to look at the lit computer screen of white letters on a blue field. It was a list of names. He looked back to the exposed first card in the spindle.

"You see? All the information on the first entry matches that card. You're looking at an electronic copy of the card file. Someone logged onto this computer at least six hours after Bosch was killed. Whoever cleaned the apartment cleaned up the computer, too. He deleted this file. I brought it back with a utility program. If I get lucky, that card file won't be an exact match to the computer file."

"You think the guy might have removed his own card?"

"I'd bet even money on it. Why would he delete the list if he wasn't on it?"

Heller was nodding as he accepted a plastic evidence bag from a technician. He scribbled his initials on the label and turned back to face her.

"We're done here, Mallory. I can't tell you much. The guy was tall. He's got a long reach up that wall."

"How do you know he wasn't standing on a chair?"

"You can follow the track of the sponge along the wall. No stop-and-start motion to move a chair. He was walking along the length of the wall. I'd guess his height at six-one to six-three. And he's a thorough bastard. We're taking the rugs and the mattress into the lab. If there was any blood, we'll find it. We pulled a few prints off the shoes and the belts. The prints probably belong to the victim." He looked up to the marks high on the wall. "Nobody that tall could have such small finger pads."

Heller seemed to be casting for words.

"Anything else?"

You wouldn't hold out on me, would you, Heller?

"The guy's weird," he said at last.

Heller leaned down and pulled out a drawer from the nightstand near the bed. It was empty; the contents had been bagged. He turned the drawer upside down and held it out to her. The pine-scented cleaning solvent was still strong on the wood.

"He cleaned the exterior surfaces of all the drawers," said Heller. "Now that's weird. And it's not like there was a bloodbath here. There wasn't. I'd get flecks, at least, with the light and the spray. But nothing. The guy's just weird."

"You mean I'm looking for a psych profile based on a cleaning job?"

"Could be. I saw something like this ten years back. Maybe your old man told you about it. The crime scene was already as clean as this one. They caught the bastard when he came back to the site to clean it again. There was a detective in the apartment when the perp showed up with rubber gloves, a bucket and a mop. They should all be so easy. That's all I got."

And thank you, Heller, prompted the ghost of Markowitz who sat in an overstuffed armchair inside her brain.

"Thanks, Heller."

She smiled again and made a show of taking the tweezers out of her tool kit and carefully pulling back each card on the spindle, matching it to the files on her screen.

Heller and his men were gone when she was into the H's. Missing was the card on Betty Hyde. According to the retrieved computer file, Hyde was a gossip columnist with a large syndication. Mallory didn't need the file to know that the woman also did television spots on an evening news program. Her residence was the Coventry Arms, an upscale Upper West Side condominium.

Gold.

The address was a six-minute walk from the site in the park where the body was dumped.

A quick perusal of the electronic calendar told her that Betty Hyde used Amanda Bosch's fact-checking services on an irregular basis. The notes on parties indicated something more social in the relationship.

Mallory recalled the face of Betty Hyde from

the gossip columnist's regular five-minute news segments. Hyde was vicious in her reporting of private lives. The woman would make a better victim than a suspect. When Mallory was done with the list, only the columnist's card was missing from the hard copy. The address had to tie in.

Next, she went into a set of hidden subfiles. The security would be chimp-simple to crack, but why would Bosch need that kind of lockout on a home computer? Was there someone else spending time in this apartment? It would hardly be Betty Hyde, whose tastes were radically different, judging by the address of multimillion-dollar condos.

The computer was asking for a password. Mallory flipped through her software array with the eye of a burglar viewing her selection of pry bars and glass cutters. She selected a disk and started up the program to bang down the door with a crashing cascade of every variable on a password. It was BOOK that unlocked the door, and now a novel came tumbling out.

Well, that fit nicely with the books on writers' markets and the style guides which lined the bookshelves, and which were not part of a researcher's trade.

"No, you're absolutely right, Mrs. Farrow," said Riker. "She shouldn't have talked to you that way. But you see, she lost her father recently, and she just hasn't been the same since."

Actually, there was no difference at all in Mallory.

"Oh, that poor child," said Mrs. Farrow.

Mallory was never a child.

Riker sat back in a well-padded chair upholstered in roses, and there were roses on the wallpaper and in the pattern of the rug. Roses even trimmed his coffee cup. He smiled at the old woman, who lived in the apartment over Amanda Bosch's.

"I understand you've been having problems with your Social Security checks."

"Yes. Jimmy steals them and cashes them. I thought that was why you arrested him. His mother usually makes it up to me, but this month she was a little short. I'm not pressing charges. I never do. Amanda came up with groceries and helped me out with my medication. I told Jimmy if he didn't pay Amanda back, I would put him in jail. Not that I would, you understand. So what does he give her? A secondhand sportscoat with a cigarette burn on the sleeve."

"Do you know where Jimmy was on that morning?"

"My grandson was right here in this apartment. His father dragged him over here to apologize to me at six in the morning. My son works nights, you see. Gets off at five. Well, when his wife finally told him about the check, he went crazy, my son did. And Mrs. Cramer—she's my neighbor down the hall. Oh, she's such a sweet woman. Every morning since my last heart attack, Mrs. Cramer comes by to check on me before she goes to work at the hospital. Well, she was here when Jimmy and his father came by. You can ask her—she'll tell you the same. Then we all went to mass together and sat down to breakfast at my son's house. My son drove me home at noon."

Riker looked at his notebook. It tied with what the kid had told him. He didn't take the old woman for a good liar. Her eyes gave away every thought, every fear.

"And your grandson was never out of your sight the whole morning?"

"No. Father Ryan will tell you. He'll remember. He was shocked to see Jimmy in church." She looked down at the hands in her lap, a collection of arthritic knots wrapped around a square tin box. "What are you going to do with my grandson?"

"I'll have a man drive him back to the warehouse."

"No charges?"

"No."

She pried open the box and rewarded him with sugar cookies.

"I have a few more questions about Amanda," said Riker, with one hand in the tin.

"I still can't believe she's dead. She was so young. Amanda was a good, gentle person. I can't—" The rest of her words were too weak to find their way out of her throat. She was suddenly very tired, and it showed in the slump of her back and the sag of her shoulders.

"I'd like to talk to some of the neighbors," said Riker. "Maybe they'll remember seeing Amanda with a boyfriend. Hard to figure, isn't it? Pretty young woman like that one, and no man in her life?"

Amanda had not started that baby without a man. Although it was the Christmas season, Riker required a few thousand years of distance from miracles. The old lady was keeping something back.

"Well, the neighbors wouldn't know," said Mrs. Farrow. "They're all working-class people

48

in this neighborhood. They're out of the building during the day, and all in bed at a reasonable hour. So they wouldn't know."

"And you never heard the guy downstairs on a weekend, I bet."

"Well, no."

She hunched her thin shoulders, and her chin dropped to her chest. She fixed her startled eyes on the carpet at her feet, understanding now what she had given away.

Riker smiled, and regarded the old woman as though she were made of precious stuff.

"You know," said Riker, "I don't like to speak ill of the dead either, but I don't think Amanda would mind. And I know you want to help us find the killer, don't you? So, you figure the boyfriend is married, right?"

"Amanda never talked about him, and he only came in the afternoon when no one was at home."

"But you heard them downstairs. You heard them together."

And oh, what she had heard, said the nervous fidgeting of her fingers about the cookie tin. She would not meet his eyes.

Mallory scrolled through the lines of the novel, looking for anything out of place, any sign of a damaged file. The fire escape window was at her left. Beyond the glass pane, she heard a baby crying, and then the soft thudding on the glass. She turned to the window.

Not a baby.

She was staring into a pair of slanted eyes as green as her own. The cat's fur had been white, but now it was grayed with dust and dirt, and one ear was torn and bloody. Amanda Bosch must have been in the habit of feeding the stray.

"Tough luck, cat, you're on your own."

She turned back to the computer and continued the scrolling, scanning the lines for gaps and odd characters, gleaning a little from the plot. One of the main characters lived in an expensive condo on the Upper West Side. Now that fit nicely with the missing file card bearing the address of Betty Hyde's condo. The fictional man was a married cheat. Better and better.

The cat would not shut up.

Mallory looked back to the window and tried to convey, by narrowing eyes, that the cat must stop, and right now, or she would dispatch it to kitty heaven. The animal misunderstood, its own eyes narrowing to the slits of *I love you, too*. Then the cat was on its hind legs, pawing at the glass with mewls of *Let me in, now, now, now*.

Mallory raised the sash. But before she could terrorize the small animal, it slipped under her arm and into the room, depositing cat hair on the sleeve of her blazer in passing. It ran through the galley kitchen and into the front room.

She shrugged. What the hell. Bosch was dead, the apartment was tossed, let the cat steal what it could. It was nothing to her.

It began the mewling again. Mallory looked at the cat with a new idea for making it shut up. A rare change of heart changed her mind. The cat would have enough problems out on the street without a fresh injury.

She watched it hook a paw in the closet door and open it. After a brief search, it was out again and sniffing the floor. It came back to the bedroom to rub up against her leg. The plaintive meowing ceased, and the soft roar of purring began. Mallory repressed the urge to kick it. She pushed it off with her leg. And now the cat went to the bookshelf and knocked out the bottom cartons of computer ribbon to pull out the catnip toy.

Not a stray.

Mallory got up and walked into the galley kitchen. She looked in the cupboard. All the dishes were neatly stacked, but one seemed out of place, a bowl sitting on the dinner plates. Over the blue ceramic glaze, the word Nose was printed in gold letters. The cat was staring up at her, and now she noticed the long gray marking around the muzzle, a shading she had taken for dirt. It had the comic illusion of making the cat's nose seem long and bulbous. Nose was well named.

It was mewling again. Mallory put one hand on her hip, drawing back the blazer to expose the holstered gun, forgetting momentarily that this gesture would have no effect on a cat.

The cat stood up on its hind legs and twirled in a circle, dancing with delicate, practiced steps. Done with dancing, it sat quietly staring at the bowl in Mallory's hand. And now the small animal had been further reduced in her eyes. The only thing a cat had going for it was the refusal to do stupid pet tricks. This one had copped out.

She opened a can of tuna, guessing food would keep it quiet. The cat ate as though it had been starved.

She went back into the bedroom and set the printer to spit out the cued-up files. And now she checked the closet and looked down at the cradle on the floor.

51

A cradle for an abortion?

She walked into the bathroom. In the closet under the sink was a long plastic box, the kind used for Kitty Litter. It was dusted with black powder, but there were no prints. The killer had cleaned the litter box.

This apartment was not the crime site; she knew that after a careful inspection of the other closets. She sniffed the insides of the closet doors for the familiar odor of the recent cleaning. He wasn't cleaning up after a break-and-enter. This was a place where he had spent a lot of time. He was the one Amanda Bosch had locked out of her subfiles, her novel. She might have done that if he figured prominently in the book.

But he had left the card file behind. How convoluted was he?

Of course.

He had to leave the addresses of the clients for the police, so they wouldn't have to go looking on their own, maybe asking for public assistance on the evening news. It fit. The park site where the body was found was only a few minutes' walk from Hyde's condo. It was the address he was hiding.

Now she went over the rooms of the apartment with greater care.

Details, said Markowitz from the room inside her brain, which she had outfitted with his favorite chair, a rack of pipes and a pouch of cherry-blend tobacco. *Details.*

She went through the canned goods in the kitchen pantry. Two cans of fish, but no pet food. Well, some people were a little strange about animals. Now she found the vacuum in the living room closet and pulled it open. The bag was gone. Heller would have taken it. Around the insides of the vacuum cleaner she found cat hair.

The cat was rubbing up against her leg again, depositing more hair. It stood up on hind legs, soft paws on her jeans. Mallory bent down and picked up the cat's paws.

No claws. Not an outside cat.

And that would explain the torn ear and the rest of the blood. Such a cat could not survive on the street. The animal had escaped when the killer returned. Or did he throw it out for a reason?

The cat had eaten its food with ravenous hunger, and now the bowl was licked clean. It must have gone without food for a long time. That would fit if the killer had returned to the apartment the day of the murder, the last date on the computer log.

Riker had never expected to see Mallory with a cat in her arms. Cats were the natural enemies of the compulsively neat. It had already deposited a mess of white hairs on her gray blazer. And most surprising, the cat was still alive. She set it down on the carpet beside her. The cat rubbed up against her leg, shedding more fur, and yet, she didn't kill it.

"Who's your friend?"

"The cat's name is Nose. He lives here."

"Oh, yeah?" He bent down to pet the cat. It shied around to the other side of Mallory's legs. "So, what else have you got?"

"This isn't the crime scene," she said, pushing the cat off with one leg and uncharacteristic restraint. "The original crime scene is in the park. The perp lives in that neighborhood. Not likely he'd drag a dead body home to dump it. That's where she had a meeting with him."

"A meeting? You got that off the computer?"

"No. It rained that morning, and there's no umbrella in this apartment. She had something on him, so she met him in the park and threatened him."

"How do you figure?"

"She was a free-lance researcher and fact checker. It fits. So she threatened him, and he killed her. He panicked and ran. Later, he came back, dragged her deeper into the woods and worked her hands over with a rock to get rid of the prints. That bought him the time to come down here that night and clean up the evidence of a relationship with the victim. He lives at the Coventry Arms. I'm betting he's married, and he's over six-one. So what have *you* got?"

Riker smiled and slowly folded his notebook into his coat pocket. "The kid's story checks out."

He followed her into the bedroom. The floor was littered with rolling sheets of paper which were still pouring out of the mouth of the machine on the shelf below the computer. She scanned the sheets until she found the one she wanted, and ripped it free of the rolling paper.

He read the list of names.

"First he deleted this client file. Then the jerk only took that one client address out of the card file. Bosch did occasional work for Betty Hyde, the gossip columnist. They also had a social relationship."

"So you figure Hyde is tied to it?"

"No. Hyde hasn't used Bosch's service in two months."

"Maybe Amanda was in the neighborhood picking up more work from Hyde."

"No. Look at this." She ripped another sheet free of the roll. "This is her production schedule. There's nothing on her calendar for Hyde's projects. There's even a note saying Hyde is out of the country. I checked it out with the paper and the airline. She's due back in the country this afternoon.

"Look at the billings on these accounts. Bosch logged in all her time—she never worked weekends. And she never made pickups. For the past two months, all her work was messengered in and out of this apartment."

"But the perp lives in the same building as Hyde?"

"The fool only took one card away. Yeah. He lives in that building. He didn't want the police coming back to that address asking questions. It's like he left me a map."

"When Coffey hears this, he's gonna scream like a woman in childbirth. It's a little out of your neighborhood, kid, but you know the kind of people who live in that building."

"Helen grew up in a building on that block. Her sister, Alice, still lives there."

"It's good you got those kind of connections, kid. You're gonna need 'em if you step on any toes in the Coventry Arms. I didn't know Helen came from money."

"Helen's people were well-off, but not wealthy. It's an odd mix in that neighborhood. You can have a woman on Social Security living in the same rent-control building with a society matron."

"How's your Aunt Alice's building situated?

You think she might give us some space for surveillance?"

"I don't think so. I only met her once, and she didn't like me."

"How could she not like you? What's not to like?"

She was closed to him now, lost in the scrolling action of the computer, which continued to spit paper.

"So how come you never got along with Helen's folks? I know they didn't like Markowitz, but you?"

"Aunt Alice just took a sudden dislike to me when I was a kid. She hasn't spoken to me since."

What had Mallory done to Aunt Alice?

Riker's notebook lay open in his hand as he looked around the doctor's private office. The room was thick with the scent and the green of living plants, some with delicate blooms. The doctor was also on the delicate side, and Riker pegged him for a gentle soul who trapped houseflies and released them out of doors. He felt sorry for the poor little bastard in the white coat, who was explaining to Mallory that he could not violate Amanda Bosch's privacy, be she living or dead. The doctor would not tell her if Amanda did or did not have any sexually transmitted diseases. There was a principle of confidentiality here which he could never violate.

Mallory was tensing, and Riker guessed the doctor could not read the warning signs. This poor man's career of sensitivity to women and their gynecological problems had not prepared him for this.

She was rising to a stand.

56

Too late, Doc.

Mallory slammed the autopsy photographs down on the blotter in front of the man, startling him. She leaned across his desk and pressed him deep into the cushions of his chair without laying a hand on him.

Not raising her voice, but ticking off the syllables in the even meters of a live time bomb, Mallory said, "Look at what that bastard did to her."

These were not the pretty photographs the uniforms had shown to the doormen, the shots with the head wound and the damage of insects. This was the autopsy aftermath, the hard-core obscenity of a woman hollowed out like a bloody canoe.

Mallory never mentioned that a pathologist had done this. She let the good doctor run the course of his imagination, which was draining his face of blood, bringing him to his feet and leading him to the door of the washroom.

Mallory settled down in her chair to wait out the noises of a man retching, splattering his lunch over water and porcelain. Her arms crossed and her mouth slanted down on one side to say she had expected more fortitude from a medical man.

When the doctor returned to his desk, he sat down slowly in the manner of one who had just aged thirty years and had suddenly become careful of his brittle bones. His soft white hands grasped one another for comfort.

He was Mallory's creature now.

"Did you know the father of the baby?"

"No. She wouldn't talk about him. I had the idea he was probably a married man."

"I want to know if any sexually transmitted

disease could have been a motive. I don't have all damn day to wait on lab results from the ME."

"No, nothing like that. I tested her for everything at her request. No disease of any kind. The pregnancy was compromising her health, but that was due to a physical defect of the uterus."

"Is that why she had the abortion? It was therapeutic?"

"I have no idea why she aborted the baby. She wanted that child more than anything in the world. She had enormous difficulty conceiving because of the physical abnormalities. It was a chance in a million, her pregnancy."

"You did the abortion?"

"No, it was done in a city hospital. She went into the emergency room complaining of bleeding and cramps. I got there as fast as I could. It wasn't a hospital where I had privileges. And before they would even let me see her, it was over. It was done by a bad doctor with a cut-rate education. She was butchered."

The doctor's eyes slid over to the photograph on his desk as though he had second thoughts on the definition of butchery.

"After the abortion, there was no possibility of another pregnancy. No amount of corrective surgery could have repaired the damage done to her."

"When was the abortion done?"

"It was one week ago today. She canceled two appointments with me, and I never saw her again. I called and left messages. She never called back."

"So she miscarried? Is that how it started?"

"No. There was no miscarriage."

"You think she tried to abort herself?"

"No, of course not. Nothing like that, but the

fetus was definitely in danger. She hadn't slept for days, or eaten. There was an enormous amount of pressure on her."

"What kind of pressure?"

"I don't know. When I saw her that night in the hospital, she wouldn't tell me what had brought it on. I don't know what the emotional trauma was. The doctor in attendance had given her the option of saving the baby. He said she screamed at him, 'No! Cut it out of me!' The fool never took Amanda's emotional state into consideration, he just went ahead and cut her."

"What kind of trauma would bring on the bleeding and the cramps?"

"Oh, something that would cost her peace of mind and sleep. Bed rest was important. It isn't unusual for some women with her medical profile to spend the entire pregnancy in bed."

"Give me the reasons why she might want to get rid of the baby," said Mallory. "I know she wasn't a hardship case. I've seen her bank account."

"Maybe there was some disclosure about the baby's father or his past, something that made her revolt at the idea of bearing his child. She was just entering the second trimester of the pregnancy. I have no idea when she told the father about it. He may have recently disclosed some genetic problem."

"But you would have done tests for that, right?"

"She wasn't a good candidate for amniocentesis. It was a very delicate pregnancy. I'd need a pretty good reason to put a needle into the womb to extract the necessary fluid. But Amanda never mentioned genetic problems, or any other

59

problems. She was a very happy woman—before she lost the baby."

"Can you think of any other possibilities?"

"Women will abort in cases of rape. Of course, that wouldn't apply here, but it's the fact that the man is so repugnant to them that makes them abort the issue of a rapist. The emotional trauma could have been caused by any number of things, but it would have to be something horrible to make her abort her child."

The doctor's face was set in real grief.

"I liked Amanda very much." His eyes strayed back to the autopsy photos. He reached out and pushed them off the edge of his desk. "The bank account you mentioned—that was the down payment for a house. She wanted a house with a yard for the child to play in."

At the end of the day, in Coffey's office, which was still called Markowitz's office, Riker was saying, "And the perp gets Mallory's good-housekeeping commendation."

Coffey turned to Mallory. "Did Forensics turn up anything?"

"Heller's team found a cap gun in the building trash bin. He thinks it's tied to Bosch's apartment."

"He got prints off it?"

"No," said Mallory. "That's why he thinks it's tied. The toy gun was wiped clean. It's a replica of an old six-shooter."

"I didn't know they still made cap guns like that."

"Only a few companies do," said Riker, looking down at his notebook. "But that won't help. This one was manufactured thirty years ago.

60

It might have belonged to the perp when he was a kid."

"You think he tried to scare her with it?"

"Could be," said Riker. "You gotta wonder about a grown man who keeps his toys."

A baseball with a Mickey Mantle autograph sat on the desk between them. Coffey smiled with no trace of ruffling, no rising to the bait. Riker shrugged.

"What have we got on motive—anything?"

"She had something on him and threatened him," said Mallory. "He panicked and killed her."

"Where is this coming from, Mallory?"

"She was a researcher and a fact checker. He was the father of her child—"

"You don't know that." Or did she?

"*If* he was the father of her child, it would make sense for her to check him out," said Mallory. "So she must have turned up something. It fits. No holes in it."

"But it's a lot of supposition, isn't it? Unless you were holding out on me. You wouldn't do that, would you?"

Of course she would. He looked to Riker, and gave the man credit for not rolling his eyes.

"No, I'm not," she said.

But Coffey decided she was seconds too late in saying it.

"So you made an ID on the corpse. Good job, Mallory. But the Coventry Arms address is flimsy. I can't interrogate these people based on what you've got—not without getting harassment complaints from the governor's personal guest list. We've got zip for physical evidence. If the park is the crime site, the lack of an alibi for the six minutes it takes to do a murder won't hold up in court. We've got a twenty-four-hour period where he could have gone into Bosch's apartment. He didn't even need to do the cleanup in one block of time. So we question every male in the building, and where does it get us? I can't do that just because there's a card missing from a file. We don't know that Bosch didn't toss out the address card herself. Maybe she dropped Hyde as a client."

"She didn't toss the card. There are also cards in the hard copy file for inactive clients. This woman never tossed anything."

Except a half-created baby.

"It's not enough to bring anybody in."

"I'm not asking you to bring anybody in. You could move me into the building," said Mallory. "One of those apartments has to be vacant. Somebody's out of town, somebody's relocated."

"So you think you can move into a sublet or a vacancy without alerting the suspect? We're still getting calls from people who think you're dead because they saw your face on TV."

"I know he's tied to that building. If I can't flush him out, I'll never get him."

"You can't catch them all, Mallory."

"The killer is in a circle that overlaps with Bosch and Hyde, and there are notes on a social relationship with Hyde. This woman might have introduced them, or maybe Bosch and the killer met while she was visiting Hyde. I know he's tied to that address."

"You're sure that Hyde doesn't figure in this?"

"I can place her in Australia on the day of the killing. No way she could get back in time. She's over sixty and she won't fit the height requirement."

"But it's her name on the missing card. Hired talent maybe? The MO won't fit a pro hit, but all hit men start out as amateurs."

"It won't fit at all. Amanda Bosch had a personal relationship with her killer. She went to the park that morning to meet the perp. The murder wasn't premeditated—no weapon was brought to the crime scene. He used a rock and his hands."

"Why don't we invite Miss Hyde in for questioning? We could do the interview as a request for assistance."

"No. I don't want to alert anybody to the death of Amanda Bosch. The rest of her clients are in midtown and the Village area. Her only connection on the Upper West Side was that building. It was only the address the perp wanted to hide."

"Mallory, you've got nothing solid. You don't know that he lives in the Coventry Arms."

"I know where he lives because I know *him*. He spent a lot of time with the body, working her hands over, making pulp out of them. He took his time. After he got over the initial panic, he was comfortable in that place. It was close to home."

Coffey slid a folder across the desk. It had Heller's initials on it.

"Heller's backing you up on the park as the original crime scene. How'd you talk him into going back? They found the blood splatters on the underside of kicked-over rocks by the water. He was in here half an hour ago. Says you authorized the overtime."

"That also backs up the Coventry Arms as the

perp's residence. He took the card to keep us from tracking her back to that address. Get me in there."

"Get me something solid, then we'll talk about a surveillance nest."

"If you won't do anything else to help me, at least don't release the name of the victim. If I'm going to flush him out, I need that edge."

"You got my word. Nobody gets the name."

"Yeah, right. Thanks," she said, and the words *for nothing* remained unspoken and hanging in the air for minutes after she left the room.

Mallory stopped the car in front of the Coventry Arms and let the engine idle.

The century-old building was fortresslike and forbidding. The stucco edifice was dotted with window lights that blazed and lesser lights that only glimmered. Gables and plant-choked balconies relieved the flat plane of the building and the long line of its roof, and ivy twined up the walls far past the night-black leaves of ancient trees. The character of the windows varied from squares, rectangles and circles to the great arch of the centerpiece of stained glass. This window might have graced a cathedral, but the brilliantly colored imagery was older than the church.

She worked out the ancient mythology in the glass. The years spent at Barnard had not been a total waste of time. The figure of the woman in the window must be the goddess of spring. She was being carried in the arms of her lover, the god of the underworld, as he raced toward the edge of a cliff. The lovers were frozen forever in this act of murder and suicide as they hurtled, full tilt, toward the edge of death, gateway to Hades and home.

The entrance to the building was the stone mouth of a behemoth, narrowing to a set of doors studded with copper ornamental friezes. In addition to the requisite doorman, there was a security guard on duty tonight, a recent adjunct to the age of rock stars and their building-storming groupies.

She had a badge in the back pocket of her jeans. She could enter the building anytime she wished, talk to whomever she wished. She had the power, but she couldn't use it, not yet. And she couldn't sneak in. Coffey had been right to reject the surveillance nest, but for all the wrong reasons. It was better to go in with a blaze of neon lights. It was only the covert things that people found suspicious.

She drove past the Coventry Arms and toward the less famous building at the end of the block. She had visited this place only once in her life, yet her memory of it was vivid in every detail. She double-parked the car as she always did. It was easier for her to fix the parking tickets on the computer than to mark the car for the meter maids.

She handed her business card to the doorman when he asked *whom* she had come to visit and *whom* she might be.

"Are you Mallory or Butler, miss?"

"Tell her it's Kathy, her niece."

Not strictly true. Her adoption had never been formalized. She had refused to answer questions about her past or her parents. Without a trace on relatives, the paperwork could go no further. She had kept the legal status of a foster child, and there was no such thing as a foster aunt. But though there were a lot of Mallorys in the world, Alice's only sister had only one child named Kathy.

The man replaced the house phone on its hook. He held the door open, and his smile was wide. Aunt Alice must be generous with her tips.

The night man at the desk was settling his own telephone onto its cradle and nodding tactful understanding of Mallory's importance here as she passed through the lobby.

This was a place, not of extreme wealth, but of quiet money. The lobby furnishings were good, but not museum pieces. The passenger-controlled elevator ran with the smooth hum of good maintenance.

On her first visit, there had been an elevator operator. She remembered looking up at the man from her height of ten years old. She rarely saw such people anymore. It was the human-expendable age of automation.

The elevator doors opened onto a floor of deep-pile beige rugs. The walls were papered in stripes of sedate taste. She didn't need the apartment number. Memory led her to the door at the end of the hall. On her toes, she could not have reached the brass lion's-head door knocker the first time she had come here with Helen.

The maid, the same maid, opened the door and stood back to allow her to pass into the foyer. Mallory followed the woman down the hallway, and here perception was altered again. This hall had seemed miles long when she was a child.

They passed by the music room and into wider space. The dimensions of this room had changed only slightly. It was not quite the grand ballroom of a child's memory, but close. Bric-a-brac covered every table, and family photographs hung in clusters along every linear foot of the walls. She would have bet good money that not one stick of furniture had been moved in the past fourteen years. It was all dark wood and drapes of crimson. And shadows filled the corners, light glinting in reflection off some candy dish of silver, some ornament of gold.

The photographs and portraits went back many generations, so Helen had told her on their only visit. She remembered very little of that afternoon's conversation. Alice had looked very much like her sister, and the strong family resemblance was also in the aged face of Helen's mother. But that old woman's skin was then already graying with the thing growing inside her, the same thing that would kill Helen years in the future.

The adults had bored her until they got onto the subject of Markowitz. Then she had listened, her small hands balling into fists. Markowitz might be a cop, but he was also her old man. She had risen off her chair in a burst of angry energy. Helen's eyes pushed her back down. Her small hands folded on her lap once again, and the child, who had recently been dining from garbage cans, neatly crossed her legs at the ankles as Helen had taught her to do.

"So this is the best Louis could provide you with?" said Helen's sister Alice, whose voice had been on the rise for too long. And by young Kathy Mallory's lights, it was too loud a voice to be using on gentle Helen Markowitz.

"Not even a tie of blood but someone else's castaway child, something out of the gutter."

67

Helen's mother had been quiet up to this point, and then the old woman stood up with difficulty, leaning on her cane and waving off the maid who rushed to her side. "Enough," she said, imperious in her tone, threats in her eyes. "Alice, what's done is done."

Alice began to rise, lips parting, and as Helen's mother had waved off the maid, she waved Alice's mouth shut. But too late; the damage had been done. Helen was crying, tears streaming down her face.

Kathy had gone after Helen's sister with the propulsion of a bullet, shooting her face to within an inch of Alice's. In a rush of menace, low tones working up from the gut, words carrying real weight and hatred, she said, "If you ever make Helen cry again, I'll cut you at the knees, *you cunt!*"

"Don't say cunt, dear," Helen had said then, appearing behind the child and shunting small arms into the sleeves of a new winter coat. As they followed the maid down the long hallway, Kathy heard Helen's mother laughing uproariously. She had tried to turn and go back with the intention of beating the old woman to a pulp, but Helen had restrained her. With Helen it usually took no more than a look or the lightest pressure to contain the small and continuous storm that was Kathy Mallory.

Fourteen years later, Mallory was back. Helen was four years in the ground, and she was looking into Helen's eyes in the ruined face of Alice.

"I thought you were dead," said Alice.

"Well, I'm not," said Mallory.

Are you disappointed, Aunt Alice?

"But I heard it on the evening news," she said,

68

as though she had caught Mallory in a lie. "Well, no matter. It's a bit late to be calling, isn't it? And I mean that on several levels."

"I guess it has been a while," said Mallory. "I saw you at Markowitz's funeral."

On the day they had lain the old man in the ground, she had looked up to see Alice, a ghost of Helen in her likeness, hovering near the open grave. When she looked back again, the ghost was gone.

"I thought Helen would've wanted a member of the family there," said Alice. "I thought she would have liked that."

"She would have. Thank you."

"You haven't changed so much since you were a little girl, but then, you never looked like a little girl. Your eyes were always more like an adult's. What a disturbing child you were. Violent, rude, uncivilized."

Mallory said nothing, took no offense; it was all true.

"I know where you live now, Kathy. Only a few blocks from here, isn't it? That condominium must have been very expensive. And I imagine the maintenance fees are rather high. Why are you here? You want money, I suppose."

"I don't need money."

"Then what do you want?" Alice leaned forward with a new intensity, a sudden burst of light in the watering blue irises. "What could you possibly want from me?" Her voice was rising, wavering in the high notes, close to breaking. "You took my sister away from me! Did you know she never spoke to me again? Did you know how much I loved Helen?"

Alice rose out of her chair. The effort seemed

to tax her. Was Alice dying of the same cancer that killed Helen? She looked thin and weary.

Alice's supply of venom was exhausted. She sank down to the cushion of the chair and deeper. She cried, and Mallory waited it out, neither offering aid nor withdrawing, only waiting for it to be over with.

"Why did you come? What do you want from me?"

"I need your help."

"The Coventry Arms has quite a mix of people these days. The rock stars have loud parties, and so do the political people," said the old woman who must be in her late eighties.

"There's a television personality in the building and an actor," said the old woman's husband, who had been introduced to Mallory as Ronald Rosen.

Mrs. Rosen, called Hattie, nodded. "It's true. In my day, they would never allow theater people in a nice building."

"In your day," said her husband, "gangsters were the aristocracy of the West Side." The old man turned to Mallory. "When I was a kid, we came up out of Hell's Kitchen, same as your mother's people. What a time to be alive. When I was a boy, I ran errands for Owney Madden, the Duke of the West Side. I saw two of his men shot down in the bootleg whiskey wars."

Mallory was drinking tea out of a fragile china cup and facing the elderly Rosens, residents of the Coventry Arms. Alice leaned over and replenished the tea from an antique silver pot.

"So you're Helen's daughter," said Mr. Rosen. "You must take after your father's side." Mrs.

Rosen kicked his shoe and he knew he had said something wrong, but not what. Apparently it didn't matter, for his wife resumed her good-natured smile.

"We watched Helen grow up in this apartment, didn't we, Alice?" said Mrs. Rosen. "Though we didn't see her but three or four times after she married Louis Markowitz. I was at her funeral. What's it been, Alice, three, four years since Helen died?" Mrs. Rosen turned back to Mallory. "I saw you there. I didn't want to intrude. I spoke to Louis Markowitz in the reception line. He seemed like such a . . . "She shot a look at Alice. "Oh, but I'm going on."

"Is Mallory your married name?" asked Mr. Rosen, who was again shown the error of his ways by a kick from Mrs. Rosen, who undoubtedly knew the facts from Alice.

"This is so exciting," said Hattie Rosen. "Just like television. Do you want us to use assumed names?"

"Good idea," said Mallory. "And I'll need a letter for the concierge—something to explain why I'm living in your condo."

"Of course," said Mr. Rosen. "And we should say something about it to Arthur. He's our doorman. I don't like lying to Arthur."

"Stick with the truth," said Mallory. "But keep it simple. Tell him you're leaving on urgent personal business, and I'm a friend of the family. I'll take care of the lies."

"Did I mention that Ronald snores?" asked Mrs. Rosen. "We have separate bedrooms."

"My condo is a two-bedroom with a view of the river and a twenty-four-hour doorman," said

71

Mallory. "Are there a lot of people in your building with personal computers?"

"Everyone has a computer now—even us," said Mrs. Rosen. "They wired the entire building for an electronic bulletin board."

"My wife uses the computer," said Mr. Rosen. "What do I know from computers?"

"So what's to know? You only have to know where the on-switch is. You push a button and *voilá*, there's the bulletin board for the building. You leave notes for the building management and the super, arrange for dog walking, vacation notice. You can even do your banking from the computer if you're on-line with your bank. Now don't you be afraid of it, dear. It's only a machine. And the directions are written on the door of the console. You'll pick it up easy. Oh, and the girl who cleans comes once a week. She has her own key, but you can trust her with your life. Sarah, I think. Ronald, is that her name? Sarah?"

"I can move in tomorrow?"

"Yes, but we have to be back in ten days for my cousin Bitsy's golden wedding anniversary. We've invited a hundred people, dear. You understand. Now about your condo—it's wired for cable TV?"

When the arrangements for the exchange of apartments had been completed, when the Rosens had gone, and she and Alice had said their strained good nights, Mallory was on her way to the door, passing slowly through the rooms of the apartment where Helen had grown up, taking in each detail.

She passed near the grand piano, which was covered with a tapestry throw and photographs, perhaps fifty, in small, ornate frames. All the faces were children's. The portraits to the rear were dated by the clothing, and in front were the children only recently come to abide on the piano. Mallory found Helen's photograph as a girl. It was placed toward the back with the children who had grown up and grown old. She picked it up and stared at Helen's young face.

She was setting the picture back in its place when her hand froze, and her eyes locked on a frame in the middle rows. She recognized her own likeness staring out of the sea of brand-new eyes. It was a school photograph, taken a full year after the visit.

Her own portrait had neither pride of place, nor was it hidden, but fit well into its proper station among the generations, the family.

Chapter 3

DECEMBER 22

Riker made his way up the stairs of the animal hospital and into a wide waiting room the size of an auditorium. A pet shop smell mingled with odors of cleaning solvents, and a cacophony of barks and chirps emanated from every row of seats. Pet owners crooned to their jiggling, meowing, howling carrier boxes. Others clutched leashes, holding back dogs who would rather be elsewhere. The human noises were choruses of "poor baby" and all its variations. These people, perhaps a hundred of them, were serious animal lovers.

So what was Mallory doing here?

Despite the crowding to standing room only, Mallory had half a row to herself. The cat sat on her lap and tried to lick her face. She stared down at the animal. With perfect understanding and the desire to go on living, the cat ceased its attempted licking and curled up on the legs of Mallory's jeans. One ragged ear was drooping, the point of it all but severed.

The bird people cast their eyes nervously over the cat and hugged their carrier cages. The dog people were holding their leashes with a death grip, more than a little put out that Mallory had not disguised the cat as a box. Rules of etiquette were clearly being violated here, and they were not rules that Helen Markowitz could have imparted to Mallory, for theirs had been a house without pets.

Riker watched her for a minute more. She was detached from the cat, but the cat was very attached to her. He could hear the purring four rows away. Now Mallory's head turned slowly until she was facing him, staring into his eyes.

A world-class spook that kid was. And he blamed Markowitz for that. There had been a limit to the kind of games one could play with a child who was not a child. The games Markowitz devised for her had developed ricochet vision. And he believed she could feel the rise in temperature when one more live body walked into a room.

She nodded to him. He moved past a dog and a parrot, another dog, a lizard and ten empty seats to sit down beside her.

He looked at the cat, who only looked at

Mallory. "So you think the department's gonna pay for the vet's bill?"

"Damn right. The cat's a witness."

"Hey, this is Riker you're talkin' to."

"The cat knows the perp, and the perp knows the cat."

"I think you're pressing your luck, kid."

Her eyes said, *Don't call me kid.*

"Coffey's not too thrilled about the condo switch. Might have been good politics if you'd run the idea past him first."

"It's none of his business where I live."

"Well, he had an interesting point. Amanda Bosch was your age, your style. Maybe she was a little shorter, but you're definitely the perp's type."

"I know that."

Mallory's face moved in tandem with the cat's face. Two pairs of slanting eyes stared at him.

It was too early for a drink.

"What name are you using?"

"My own name."

"Risky, isn't it? I only say that because your pretty face has been all over the television as a dead woman and a cop. Odds are he's seen you. If he hasn't, somebody's gonna mention it to him."

"Good. Just wait till he sees the cat."

"You don't know who he is. You'll never see him coming."

"I'm not dealing with Professor Moriarty here. He's a man who knows as much about computers as a secretary, maybe less. He's a liar who got caught out. And he's the panicky type."

She leaned down to the canvas bag at the foot

of her chair and extracted a manila file holder. "This is the list of tenants and their stats."

He took the file and opened it, letting out a low whistle as he scanned the names of credit card companies, insurance companies, and financial institutions. Well, this would explain the redness in her eyes; she'd been up all night breaking into computer banks. And then she'd probably been wading through that mess of paperwork pulled off of Amanda Bosch's computer—maybe five or six hundred pages she had neglected to mention in the apartment inventory.

How did she get the U.S. Army info? It sometimes took him a week or more to pull personnel files.

"What's with the military service records?"

"Physical stats—height and blood groups."

"Mallory, we didn't find anything to type his blood group."

"He doesn't know that. He drove himself nuts cleaning that place. The things he cleaned. He doesn't sleep nights wondering what we might have found."

He was looking at a list of units with more than forty-five names crossed off.

"What are the cross-offs?"

"Most of them won't meet the height requirement. And I crossed off all the single men and women. And the married man who made a fortune in software—he'd know you can delete a file, but you can't erase it. He'd know the files could be restored. Cross off the apartments owned by corporations with three-day turnover—my perp was New York based. Then the vacant apartments are crossed off. What I've got left loosely fits the profile."

"What about this writer, Eric Franz? He's single, isn't he?" He held up her fax of the vehicular accident stats dated to late November. "His wife died more than a month ago."

"The affair with Bosch started before that. A year or so—isn't that what Mrs. Farrow told you? And Bosch was more than three months gone with the baby before she aborted."

A hungry-looking sheepdog had made three rows of progress toward Mallory and the cat. His owner, an elderly woman, regained the leash and dug her heels into the linoleum to bring the dog to a choking halt.

"Got any favorites?"

"Yeah. I put stars by their names. Four of them don't keep regular hours. That would leave them free for afternoons with Amanda."

The sheepdog was gaining ground again, slowly dragging his owner behind him. Riker and Mallory exchanged glances.

"If you shoot the dog, kid, you better kill the owner, too. If you let the old lady live, she'll sue the city. Commissioner Beale won't like that."

Apparently, the cat had never seen a dog before. Nose was sitting docile on Mallory's lap, only mildly curious about the large frenzied animal which was coming to eat him.

Riker resumed his reading. Mallory had a question mark by the name of Harry Kipling. A penciled note read: Connection to Kipling Electronics?

That name might give Coffey a few bad moments. High-profile suspects were the worst. With any luck, Kipling would prove to be a computer freak, and thus beyond the pale. "How did you get a blood type on Kipling? There's no Army record."

She looked at him for only a moment, and he understood that this was not something he would want to know. And now it began to dawn on him that local hospital records must be a piece of cake after cracking the U.S. Army computers.

"Oh shit," said Riker. He was staring at two more high-profile names on the list. One was a recent appointment to the U.S. Supreme Court, and his Senate hearing was in progress. Another name was that of a prominent TV reporter who now had his own talk show every afternoon. These were two of the four bearing stars in the column.

When he looked up again, the crazed sheepdog had left the floor and was hurtling toward the cat. One of Mallory's long legs was already curling back to kick the beast into the next world.

The door to Charles's private office was closed on the low voices of moderate conversation. Mallory set the large canvas bag down on the desk in the front room. The cat stepped out of the bag and rubbed up against her arm as she opened the drawer to check the answering machine for messages.

Charles objected to the sight of modern conveniences among the antiques of another century, and so she worked around him by hiding them out of sight. He was still unaware of the security system she had installed—she was that good at wiring.

She pushed the cat away and pressed the button to hear Coffey's voice saying, "I want to talk to you the minute you get in. The minute! You got that, Mallory?"

Yeah, right.

A woman's scream pierced the door to Charles's private office. The cat flew off the desk.

She was through the door and into the next room with her gun drawn as a man's voice was saying, "Justin, don't!"

The only woman in the room was taking the quick breaths of hyperventilation. Her eyes bulged and her shoulder blades were nearly even with her ears. Her face was pale and she was shaking violently—all but her hands, which gripped the arms of the chair in the manner of a rocket pilot preparing for a maiden launch.

The man had turned from the boy and was barking at the woman now. "For Christ's sake, Sally, pull it together. It's only a damn pencil!"

"It seems to like you, Sally," said the boy, who sat between them. "Why don't you just give the pencil a name and take it for long walks in the park?"

"That's enough out of you," said the man to the boy.

Mallory looked down to the offending pencil lying in the woman's lap and up to nothing sinister. But the woman was staring at it as though it might be a living snake.

Mallory turned. She had heard the gentle rocking before she saw the vase teetering on the edge of the bookshelf. The vase fell. She shot out one hand to catch it only a few inches above that section of hardwood floor not covered by the Persian rug.

Now the man was yelling at the boy again. "Justin, I told you to stop!"

The boy shrank back from the man. He turned to look over his shoulder at the vase in Mallory's hand, and then at her gun as she replaced it in the shoulder holster. The woman with the fear of pencils was covering her mouth. Only Charles was not agitated. He was calmly watching all of them.

"I didn't do it," said the boy.

"He didn't topple the vase," said Charles. "Trains pass under this building all day long. The vibrations sometimes move objects around. That vase was very close to the edge."

Mallory stood behind the small family and stared at Charles with naked incredulity. Hands clasped behind his head, he leaned back in his chair and smiled at her as though seven thousand dollars' worth of fifth-century crockery had not nearly smashed into worthless shards.

"The trains didn't make the pencil fly," said the man in even tones that implied that Charles might be only half-bright.

"No, they didn't. May I introduce my partner, Mallory?"

She walked over to the desk and faced the small family. While Charles made the formal introductions to the Riccalos, she checked out the boy first.

Justin Riccalo's blond hair was slicked back, and his lips were parted to display two prominent front teeth. The total effect was that of a wet rabbit with freckles. He could only be eleven at the outside. He was a basic nerd in training, wearing the requisite plastic protector in the front pocket of his shirt, all lined with pens and mechanical pencils. His feet were tapping the floor, anxious to be gone, even if it meant leaving the body behind them. Electric-blue eyes danced in a rock'n'roll of what's over there, and now what's over here, and what might be up on the ceiling?

Sally Riccalo, the high-strung brunette, had been introduced as Justin's stepmother. Mallory could almost hear the tension humming through the woman's thin body, as though she were wired up to a wall socket. Mrs. Riccalo perched on the edge of her chair now, brown eyes wide and pleading, *Don't hurt me,* to everyone who looked into them.

The father, Robert Riccalo, was a former military man. That much was in his close-cropped haircut and the squared shoulders. The man was standing at attention while sitting down. He was so large in the torso, he towered over the woman and the boy, but not over Charles, to whom towering came naturally and apologetically.

When the boy faced his stepmother, his neck elongated and his eyes gave away some joke he'd told to himself. A nervous giggle was rising up in his mouth. The military man put one heavy hand on the boy's slender shoulder and caused it to dip with the weight. When Justin looked to his father, his head tucked in like a turtle. And all the while, the blue eyes danced to alternating rhythms of fun and fear.

Now, the boy lifted his face to Mallory's and a conspiracy of eyes began in silence. *I know you,* each face said to the other, though she and the boy had never met.

Charles's eyes rolled back and forth between

them, saying, *Just a moment. Have I missed something here?*

Another appointment was scheduled for the next day, and the small family trooped out, the father leading the charge, woman and boy following behind as his foot soldiers. When the door to the outer office closed behind them, Mallory turned on Charles, hefting the vase in one hand.

"About those trains."

"That's not the original. It's a cheap copy. I rigged the vase myself. And it *was* the trains."

He walked over to the bookcase and picked up a wooden kitchen match. "This primed one edge of the vase toward the natural pull of gravity. Any vibration would have knocked it down. I just wondered what the boy would do."

"And?"

"It startled him with the normal reaction time. Justin has good reflexes. But he denied all blame for the pencil and the vase. That's odd, you know. He insists he's not doing anything. That's not consistent with the profile of the average psychokinetic subject."

"And?"

"Well, it makes the whole thing more interesting. Maybe he's not the one who's doing it. There's a problem with the logic. He didn't take credit, and yet he didn't seem frightened by it. Like he's used to seeing things fly around the house, almost bored by it."

"Well, try and work it out before wife number three goes down, okay?" Mallory bent over the canvas bag on the desk in the front room.

The cat poked its head out from under the desk, whiskers twitching, testing the air for screams and other loud noises. With more assurance, it exited the underside of the desk and looked up at Charles, tilting its head to one side as though the bandaged ear was weighting it that way.

"Hello," said Charles, bending down to pet it. The cat wriggled out from under his hand. It only had eyes for Mallory. It rubbed up against her leg, and she pushed it away.

"The cat's a material witness. Now I've already been through this with Riker. You laugh and I shoot you, it's like that."

"What happened to the cat's ear?"

"I didn't do it. Can you keep the cat for one night? I'm trading apartments with the Rosens today. I can't take it back to my place."

"Of course."

Mallory pulled the cat's litter box out of the canvas bag, and then two tins of fish. "His name is Nose. Just keep him out of my office. I don't want any fur in my computers."

"I'll take him back to my place."

"Thanks. So, apart from the flying objects, how did the interview go? You know which one of them is doing it if it's not the boy?"

"I don't know."

She pulled a file out of the bag.

"The first Mrs. Riccalo died of a heart attack. But now that I've seen her husband, I have to wonder how much stress she was under and how much it would have taken to push her over the top. Here's the hospital file."

She handed it to him, and he hesitated for that moment when people are trying to decide how dirty an object might be before they touch it. Perhaps he was wrong to believe that every computer printout she gave him might be purloined.

"You stole it, right?"

"Right," she said. "But not this one."

The second file she handed him had the NYPD stamp on the cover. He scanned the information which detailed the suicide report on the deceased second wife of Robert Riccalo. He flipped through the three-page report. "Well, the files list the suicide as a nonsuspicious death."

"I may change that."

"Why?"

"When you go through the suicide files, you find most jumpers are men. Women are less messy. And there was no note. They usually like to get even with their loved ones on the way out."

"Did the first two Mrs. Riccalos have anything in common?"

"They were both professionals and carried the normal amount of life insurance through their employers. But that doesn't mean there wasn't another policy or two. I'm still working on it. Sally Riccalo is also carrying insurance through the financial house where she works as a systems analyst. According to her résumé, she and Robert Riccalo worked for the same company ten years ago when the first Mrs. Riccalo was still alive. Interesting?"

"We started out with a rather simple problem of flying objects. You don't think murder is a bit of a stretch this early on? I suppose the insurance beneficiary was—"

"Robert Riccalo. He's also the beneficiary of wife number three."

"But isn't the spouse usually the beneficiary?"

"Yes, but it's usually the wife who collects. So

now I've got one heart attack, one suicide, and wife number three looks like she's ready to explode. She wouldn't get that upset over one pencil. What else has been flying her way lately?"

"Oh, a pair of scissors, some bits of glass."

"What's the father's take?"

"Anger, disbelief. Only the stepmother seems to be a believer."

"He accused the boy of moving the vase. He sounds like a believer to me."

"No. The stepmother is the only believer in the paranormal. Mr. Riccalo probably thinks the boy is doing it by trickery."

"One of them is. Are you sure it was *your* pencil that flew at her?"

"Excuse me?"

"Charles, you're a disgrace to Max Candle's memory."

"The art of illusion is not genetic. Having a magician in the family tree doesn't vouch for talent in the rest of the bloodline."

"You have a whole damn magic store in the basement. You could make an elephant fly with all that equipment."

"Not really. Max had some brilliant illusions, but his specialty was defying death. It was Malakhai who could really make things move through the air, and nothing as clumsy as a flying pencil. He was the greatest illusionist who ever lived."

"Malakhai? The debunker?"

"Well, debunking the paranormal frauds came later in life, after he retired from the stage. Before you were born, Malakhai did an act with his dead wife. . . . You seem skeptical. No, really. She was his assistant."

"His *dead* assistant?"

"Oh yes, it was only after she died that she went into the magic act with Malakhai. When she was alive, she was a composer and a musician."

"What did he do, have her stuffed?"

"No, she never appeared to the audience in the flesh. It was always understood that she was there, and yet *not* there—dead but not entirely gone, if you follow me. Well, after the audience got comfortable with the idea that she was not only invisible but dead, things began to float through the air as she handed him one thing and another."

"He'd fit in nicely with our family of the flying pencils. So that's why Malakhai got into parapsychology?"

"Oh, no. He's the sworn enemy of parapsychologists. Every time they think they've discovered paranormal ability, he drops by to blow them out of the water and expose another scam."

"Are you thinking of calling him in for this one?"

"For flying pencils? Hardly. And it probably wouldn't be a good idea to disturb him. Malkhai's in his seventies now. He and Louisa are living in quiet seclusion."

"Louisa?"

"That's his dead wife. If you cared less for computers and more for classical music, you would know her name. Louisa's Concerto was her only composition, but it was brilliant. No classical collection is complete without it. The concerto was played during every performance. Oh, it was no act on the stage. Perhaps I should have mentioned that. No, Malakhai lived with her, talked with her, slept with her. He only created the flying-object illusions in the act so the audience could see her too."

"And this guy, this loon, debunks the paranormal?"

"Yes, as madmen go, he's quite functional. He always owned to the fact that he created his own madness. He knew there was no supernatural aspect to Louisa."

"Yeah, right. How did he get so crazy?"

"Well, Louisa died very young. She wrote this splendid concerto, and then she died. He'd known her since she was a child, and he couldn't quite let her go—so he reconstructed her."

"Again, please?"

"He re-created her from memory, from intimate knowledge of her. It's been done before, but the practice has been limited to remote Asian monasteries. The documented succubi created by monks were fashioned of pure imagination. Malakhai's creation was based on a living woman—that was one difference. He knew Louisa so well. He knew what her response would be in every given situation. Then he constructed a faithful model of her. And after a while, he could not only hold conversations with her, but see her and touch her. It was a feat of immense concentration. You see, it has to be fanatically faithful to the living woman, to react in the same—"

"But it's a trick."

"An illusion, a great illusion, and of course, delusion, but it was a piece of art as masterful as Plato's *Dialogues*. And a lot of us do it to some small extent. Don't you sometimes wonder what Markowitz would do or say in certain situations?"

She turned her face to the window, and he mentally slapped himself silly for crossing the line into her personal feelings, for he was one of the few who believed she might possess them.

"Another distinction between Malakhai and the monks was that they called up their illusions and sent them away. Louisa was Malakhai's constant companion. She still is."

Mallory turned back to him, and he watched the busywork of her good brain through the static distraction of her eyes.

"But this Malakhai—he's definitely crazy, right?"

"Oh yes, definitely. But it takes quite a good brain to go quite that crazy. When you consider the amount of concentration necessary to maintain a three-dimensional delusion—"

"And when he talked with her, she answered the way she did when she was alive, even if the question was new?"

"Oh, yes. Perversely, truth and logic were the glue of the delusion. She couldn't respond in any way that was untrue to the living woman."

"Could you do it? Could you have a conversation with a dead woman?"

"Malakhai and Louisa grew up together. What she would say, in any given situation, was predictable to him. He knew her mind, her most private thoughts. I don't know anyone that well."

Certainly not you, Mallory.

"Would you have to be crazy to create a thing like that?"

"You would have to possess, at the very least, the insanity that goes with falling in love. A woman once told me that people in love were certifiable. I believe that. Malakhai reached across all the zones of reason to bring Louisa back. Now that's the kind of love insanity is made of. He may be insane, but he's also brilliant and rather charming. Whenever I stayed with Cousin Max, Malakhai and Louisa would come to dinner.''

"Did the dead woman have a good appetite?''

"As a child, I was never sure. There was always magic going on at Max's house. They would set a plate for her and pour the wine, and during the course of the evening, the plate and glass would be emptied. The food and wine was probably spirited away in moments of distraction, I knew that, but part of me always believed in Louisa.''

"Did you ever try the three-dimensional illusion?''

"*De*lusion. No. Why would I? Why would anyone want to cross over that border?''

Except for love.

She was reaching down into the canvas bag, and then he noted the hesitation of a second thought as her hand pulled back empty. Now she turned to him. "I wish I had Amanda Bosch back for just five minutes.''

"The lady by the lake, I presume.''

"Yes, I think I've got a motive,'' she said, bending again to dip into the bag. She pulled a manuscript out and sat down behind the desk, riffling through the pages, extracting one paper-clipped section.

"I pulled this off Bosch's computer. By the log-on time, this is the last file she ever updated. She's been working on this book for almost a year. It's a novel, but I don't think it's all fiction.''

"Art is lies that tell the truth. Who said that?''

"You're the one with the computer-bank memory."

"*Eidetic* memory, and it doesn't work like a computer. I can't cross-index things the way you do with your machines."

"Here, cut to page 254 of chapter seven. Go to the last paragraph. Remember, she updated this the day she died."

He looked down at the page and read: "'He was leaving again, going through the litany of each thing he had to do, all more pressiYOU LIAR, YOU LIAR, YOU LIAR, YOU LIAR, YOU LIAR, YOU LIAR.'"

"I see what you mean," said Charles. "It's not a part of the text. More like an emotional outburst at the keyboard."

"Right. I caught that as I was printing out the file. I only had time to scan pages here and there, checking for file damage. It's almost seven hundred pages. I'm pretty sure my perp is in there in detail, but you're the only human I know who can read at the speed of light. I just don't have the time. Could you take a look at it and make notes on the parts that ring true?"

"Of course." Charles seemed only to be glancing at the pages of the manuscript as he turned the sheets one after the other, yet he was reading every word and catching Mallory in a lie. He had noted the redness of her eyes, and now he found the reason for it in the indents of thumb and forefinger which marked the base of each page she had read before him. After a few minutes' cursory reading, he looked up at her.

"I wonder what his lie was. She's characterized him as a married man from the onset. So that can't be it."

"It won't be in the manuscript. I'm guessing she caught him in a recent lie."

"That's an interesting possibility. You think he might have been cheating on the woman he was cheating with?"

"That wasn't it. I think the only use she had for this man was getting pregnant. But then she aborted the baby. I've got a problem with a lie as a murder motive, but it's all I've got. Amanda Bosch was a professional researcher. She might have done a background check on him. It's a reasonable assumption since he's the father of her baby. So she caught him out in a lie."

"Well, that won't narrow the field by much. There are as many categories of lies as there are people."

"Too bad your old friend Malakhai can't reconstruct Amanda and ask her what the lie was. If I don't wrap this up fast, the perp will get away with her murder. When you finish with the manuscript, just leave it in my office."

"All right, but I wouldn't count on this too much if I were you. I don't think a writer draws on life to a greater extent than an actor does when he fleshes out a role. The actor doesn't act his life, and I suspect, even when a writer does an autobiography, he doesn't write his life."

"And this last bit of type—the LIAR lines you call an emotional outburst? Who is she screaming at if not the character in the book?"

"All right, I'll read it with that in mind."

"Are you going to the poker game tomorrow night?"

"Of course." The poker game was the highlight of his week. He had inherited his chair in the game from Inspector Louis Markowitz, and with that chair came three friends. Each new friend was something precious to him, as though in the gathering of people he could make up for a life of isolation in academia and think tanks. "If I didn't show up for the game, they'd expect me to send them a check for the usual losses. That's only fair, I suppose. I wouldn't want them to suffer financial damage by my absence."

"Charles, one day I'll sit down with you and teach you how to beat those guys at poker."

But that would not be today. She was ticking off items in a notebook, and even at half the room's distance, he could see a great many unchecked items yet to go. He turned to the window and looked down to the street two floors below. "Actually, Rabbi Kaplan says my consistent losses speak well of me."

"Did he tell you why?"

"What? And ruin his reputation—spoil the good name of Kaplan the Cryptic? No, I think I'm supposed to work it out." His eyes were still on the street below, following the progress of a familiar figure in a shapeless winter coat. He turned to face her. "All right, you know, don't you?"

"The rabbi was complimenting your honesty, Charles. Poker is a liar's game. Tomorrow night, I want you to get something off Slope and Duffy." And now she made a check by one more item, which must have been himself. "I gave both of them shopping lists, things I need to get without going through Coffey or Riker."

"You know, Mallory, there are other police officers on the force besides yourself. They tend to think of themselves as members of a team."

"Yeah, Riker has the same idea." There was

an edge to her voice, more impatience than anger. "He thinks he's my coach."

Here, Charles would like to have said something in Riker's defense, for he liked the man very much, but there were perils to even giving the appearance of choosing any side but hers. In all their conversations, he seemed always to be seeking safe ground with her. "Why don't you come to the game with me? Rabbi Kaplan speaks highly of you as a born card shark."

"I can't. I was barred from the game when I was thirteen."

A key was turning in the lock, and as the door opened, the hose of a vacuum cleaner preceded the small dark head of Mrs. Ortega.

This precluded Charles asking any personal questions like, "What in God's name did you do to those people to get barred from the poker game?"

Mrs. Ortega stopped suddenly, eyeing the cat, perhaps with a view to skinning it and making a purse of the pelt. In her oft-expressed view as a professional cleaning woman, the only good fur shedder was a dead one. The cat rubbed up against Mallory's jeans, and now that Mrs. Ortega associated the cat with Mallory, she looked at the younger woman with surprise and something less than her former respect for a fellow believer from the Church of Immaculate Housekeeping.

Mallory handed the woman a twenty-dollar bill, with the silent understanding that she knew the cat fur would make extra work. Mrs. Ortega pocketed the bill and cast a kinder eye on the cat.

The buzzer went off, loud and irritating.

Mallory put up her hand to stop Charles on his way to the door.

"Okay, who is it?"

"Riker," he said, without the usual split second of hesitation.

He opened the door, and there stood Riker in all his slovenly glory. Mallory's jaw jutted out. Charles could see she wasn't buying this. No way could he have known who was on the other side of the door. She too could recognize the polite light buzzer style of Henrietta Ramsharan of the third floor, and the sharp raps of the musician on the first floor. But Riker had no style in any sense of that word, not in any aspect of his life.

"Hi, Charles," said Riker. He nodded to Mallory, and made an exaggerated bow to Mrs. Ortega, who screwed up her face and walked into the next room muttering something that might have been "damn cops."

"You called Charles to tell him you were coming and when," said Mallory to Riker. Then she looked at Charles for confirmation, not believing for a moment that he could've known by any other means.

Charles smiled and shook his head. There were limits to what he could discern from knocks, but in truth, Riker had never called him; he had seen the sergeant's arrival from the window. And now he had his first breakthrough in the art of poker as he decided not to enlighten her. His mind was racing on to new hopes of being the big winner in tomorrow's game as Riker was settling into the deep padding of the couch.

Riker pulled a crumple of papers from the inside pocket of his overcoat and spread them out on his lap in an attempt to smooth out the damage. The first page was a map of the park with yellow lines drawn in two areas. He looked up at Mallory, who was still glaring at Charles.

"Heller pinpointed the exact site where Amanda fell. The guy's a genius. He took soil samples down to the Department of Agriculture. The dirt in the wound was full of microscopic critters that won't live in the shadow areas like the wooded patch where we found Amanda." Riker dangled a cigarette from his lip and fished his pockets for a match. "Heller says he's gonna write a monograph and give you half the credit, Mallory. So, you ready to take a look at the crime scene now?"

"What for?" She picked up the sheet with the yellow markings. "I can read a map."

"Hey, Mallory, I'm just along for the ride, okay? But most of us like to swing by the crime scene, maybe take a look at the place where the victim died."

"Waste of time. I read the report. Forensics has been over the ground and probably ten or twelve cops with big feet. What am I gonna see?"

"You never know, kid." A match sparked in his hand; the flame died in a cloud of exhaled smoke.

"Don't call me *kid*."

Mrs. Ortega returned to the front room and was plugging in the vacuum cleaner. Riker smiled at the woman.

"You know, Mrs. Ortega, we got a suspect here you'd really appreciate. All we know about the bastard is that he lives in a luxury condo, and he can clean an apartment like a pro."

"Then he wasn't born no rich kid."

"Huh?"

"Rich kids aren't raised right. You can tell if they earn their money or get it the easy way. Mallory knows from clean." She turned to Charles. "Now your mother never let your feet touch the ground. You had live-in help when you were growing up. How do I know that? You don't know what steel wool is, or what it's for. I can always tell when you clean up after a meal in the office kitchen, and when it's Mallory. Mallory was raised right."

"But this *man* who was raised right is a killer," said Charles in a somewhat defensive tone.

"So? You think Mallory carries a gun for ballast in the wind?" Mrs. Ortega leaned on the vacuum hose and wagged her finger at Charles. "You can always tell the rich kids born with money. If the husband or the wife splits, they go off their feed for a week. You can tell how upset they are by the stock of booze and pills. But if the cleaning woman leaves them, their whole world falls apart. They go back to living like animals. So chances are, your guy wasn't born with money."

Mallory was nodding as the woman said this. Mallory deferred to Mrs. Ortega in all things regarding cleaning solvents and the chemistry of stains. Mrs. Ortega might be the only human Mallory ever deferred to.

"You can tell a lot about a person's character from the way they clean and what they keep," said Mrs. Ortega, waxing on in a rare philosophic mode.

"You know," said Riker, turning to Charles, "I asked Mrs. Ortega to clean my apartment about a year ago. She made the sign of the evil eye and turned her back on me. Now I figure I'm lucky she never saw it." A gray log of ashes fell from his cigarette and crumbled down the front of his suit as his arms shrugged out of his overcoat.

"I don't have to see your apartment, Riker." Mrs. Ortega cast an appraising eye over his rumpled suit and scuffed shoes. "You've got at least three bags of garbage piling up in the kitchen. The sheets haven't been changed in a month, and there are beer bottles under the bed. There might be two clean dishes in the cupboard. You're real comfortable with spiders, and you're seeing a woman tonight."

Three heads turned to Mrs. Ortega.

"How did you know about the woman?" asked Riker.

"This morning you used a can of cheap spot remover. I can see the powder rings around the stains from here. You don't usually get that fancy."

Mallory nodded her respects to Mrs. Ortega and headed for the door to her private office. "I have to pack my equipment. I'll be back in a few minutes."

"It's good to see you again, Sergeant," said Charles. "Can I get you a cup of coffee?"

"Is it still morning?"

"No."

"Then I'll have a beer."

The vacuum cleaner was moving slowly toward them, sucking conversation out of the air. When Mrs. Ortega shut off the machine and turned to the quieter activity of dusting, Charles handed Riker a cold beer.

"What Mallory's doing is rather dangerous, isn't it? I'm surprised you're going along with it."

"She has to do it this way, Charles. There's no evidence, no weapon, no witness, no motive.

Everyone who can hold a rock has the means. The crime scene is six minutes from the building. Even the doorman has opportunity. You see the problem? If she can't flush him out and fast, he gets away with murder."

Charles's brain was backing up in the conversation. No motive, did he say? Was it possible that Riker had not seen the manuscript that lay on the desk between them? As Riker's eyes were settling on the ream of paper, some Mallory-guided instinct prompted him to call the man's attention away from it.

"You know, Markowitz wouldn't like this at all. You'll be close by her all the time, right?"

"Like I said, Charles, I'm only along for the ride. She doesn't need me. She's not a kid anymore, and she didn't need anybody when she was one." He slugged back his beer.

"But Louis always credited Helen with—"

"Helen could only see the good in Kathy, even when it wasn't there. I remember how happy Helen was when Lou started bringing Kathy into work after school—it was the only way he could keep the kid from stealing New York. But Helen was only thinking about the positive role models of police officers."

"Apparently she was right."

"And five days a week, the kid was surrounded by off-the-wall murders when other kids were out playing games."

"Didn't Mallory ever play games with other children?"

"She used to play with Markowitz. Now she plays alone."

"What sort of games did she like?"

"I asked her once when she was maybe thirteen, what was her favorite. 'Murder is the best game,' she says. I went all clammy. It was the way she said it. I asked Markowitz if he thought the kid was capable of killing. 'Oh, yeah,' says Markowitz, like I'd asked him if Kathy could pitch a curve ball.''

"That doesn't tell me why you're so confident that she can flush the killer out without getting hurt."

"If the suspects in this condo weren't uptown taxpayers with good lawyers, we'd sweat the pack of them. Now when Mallory gets the perp, there won't be any lawyers around. He'll be under more stress than he's ever known. He'll flap his mouth with cameras rolling. The creeps always talk, even after we read them their rights. They lie, but they talk, they trip themselves up. If we don't rush this perp, if a lawyer gets to him in time to shut his mouth, we lose him. No evidence, no case. It has to be quick. She has to flush him out fast and trip him up, or he gets away."

"But the danger."

"The biggest danger is that she stumbles over someone else's dirty little secrets. You got the same percentage of scum in the Coventry Arms as you do in any tenement building."

Charles picked up a photograph that had wafted to the floor from Riker's small pile of papers.

"Who is this?"

"Amanda Bosch."

"But she looks nothing like Mallory. How did the mistake—?"

"Well, she was alive when this shot was taken. Even I had to look at the body twice after the bugs had been at her."

"Have you notified her family yet?"

"There's no family alive to notify. Mallory liked that—less chance of a leak."

"What will happen to her?"

"Her estate, whatever's in her bank account, will go to the city tax office. The landlady will sell her stuff for back rent or put it out on the street. She'll get a grave that no one will ever visit. And then she'll be gone from the face of the earth. Or maybe not. Mallory could make her famous."

The cat sat down between them, ignoring both of them and picking at the bandage on its ear. Charles was reminded of something Louis Markowitz had said: Living with Mallory was like having a wounded animal in the house.

The building had been made to last and so it had, well into the twentieth century and showed no signs of falling down at the cusp of the twenty-first. Dark wood beams and stucco facing rose for ten stories. The old West Side mansion would fit well with a gothic horror story.

Riker put down the heavy boxes to pant for a moment. Mallory had just slipped the doorman a hundred-dollar bill.

The kid has style.

Riker wondered how she was going to bury the money in the department expense account.

As Mallory talked, the doorman smiled continuously, lips parting ever wider until they threatened to escape the margins of his face.

"I'm expecting Amanda Bosch to drop by. Do you know her on sight?"

"Oh, yes," said the doorman, who was called Arthur. "Miss Hyde's friend? Pretty young woman with sad eyes? I know her." Now the smile wavered. "Is she all right?"

"Why do you ask?"

"She was acting very strange the last time I saw her."

"When was that?"

"Maybe four or five days ago. She never came to the door. She just sat over there, very quiet, like she was waiting for someone." He pointed to the wrought-iron bench twelve feet from the entrance. "I thought it was a bit odd because Miss Hyde was out of town. I've never known Miss Bosch to visit anyone else in this building. Then after a while, Miss Bosch stood up very quickly. She seemed agitated for some reason, and then she ran away. Very odd indeed."

"What set her off?"

"No idea, miss. I was busy then, opening the door, getting a cab for a tenant, people were coming and going."

"Do you remember which people?"

"No, I don't. Tenants, visitors, children and dogs. Most of the tenants have dogs."

Riker was picking the cartons up from the sidewalk when Mallory turned her head quickly, eyes fixing on an empty patch of sidewalk across the street.

Now what was that about?

He wondered if it was not too early in the game for her to be watching her back. The murderer lived in this building, and only he would make the connection between Mallory and Amanda Bosch. But it was a woman walking fast toward them on this side of the street.

He put the carton down again as a small brunette with nervous moves was looking at

Mallory and asking, "Forgive me for following you. Could I speak to you privately for just a moment?"

Mallory nodded to the doorman, who closed the door. The two women moved up the sidewalk and beyond the range of his hearing. The brunette was a tangle of loose wires. Her hands were flying. Mallory said a few words to the woman, and the brunette shook her head, eyes rolling in their sockets like startled marbles. Then the woman clutched her bag to her chest as though to fend off a weapon. She backed off a few steps and hurried down the sidewalk to a waiting cab. Mallory strolled back.

The carton was hoisted into the air once more.

The doorman had shut down his neon smile the moment Mallory turned her back. Now it was blazing again with the dazzle of every tooth exposed, and *You're my new best friend* was in his eyes as they passed by him and into the lobby.

The lobby atmosphere was piped in from another century. While Mallory handed a letter to the concierge on the other side of a carved wood desk, Riker looked around at the hanging tapestries and the oil paintings. The elaborately patterned rugs had to be a year's salary each. Plush green velvet wrapped the couches and chairs in conversational groupings. A woman passed through the lobby, wearing dark glasses on this overcast day to say, *I'm a celebrity, and you're not.* A bank of stained-glass windows lined one wall. Patches of crystal and colors of brightness. Beneath the arched center window was a mural of running deer, running blind into the cruel joke of the blank wall adjacent to the painting.

Now the concierge was leading them to the elevator. It belonged in a 1930s black-and-white movie, an iron cage of scrollwork bars on the door, and an interior of gleaming wood with inlaid designs and parquet floor. They were handed into the care of an elevator operator and rode up, watching the floors drop away from them, and each one was different from the last.

The iron door opened on the third floor, and they walked down a hallway lined by soft, glowing bulbs that would have been gaslight in the last century. The carpeting on this floor was an oriental pattern, and the walls were papered in money. Riker guessed he knew a good wallpapering job when he saw it. And money sat on a small table in the hallway, a vase holding a fortune in fresh-cut flowers. The scent of roses followed after him as Mallory fitted her key in the lock and opened the door to the Rosens' apartment.

He put the cartons down on the tiled floor of the entryway. "Okay, Mallory—the woman downstairs. Now what was that about?"

"Sally Riccalo. She followed us over from the office. She's a client with an interesting idea that her stepson wants to stab her with a flying pencil."

"That doesn't sound like Charles's style. I thought he only handled the academic bullshit. So who's whacked? Her or the kid?"

"Too early to tell. She looks scared enough."

"What did you say to her?"

"I told her to get out of town."

"And she said?"

"No."

He looked around at the Rosens' front room and wondered how the Rosens were reacting to

103

the Spartan simplicity of Mallory's apartment. In the front room was a museum of family photos. The family was everywhere, eyes of the children in the eyes of mothers and fathers, grandfathers, and on and on. And there was a toy some child had left behind on the couch. The fish in the large aquarium swam in quick schools of tropical colors. A small sticky palm print lay on the glass alongside the print of what must be the nose of a grandchild or great-grandchild. The only element out of character with this comfortable room of overstuffed furniture and silk flowers was the eye of the computer, lit and looking out through the partially opened doors of an oak cabinet.

While Mallory went exploring, Riker opened the cabinet door wide and peered at the screen. Inside the door was a simple instruction guide for computer illiterates like himself. He pushed a button, and the screen became a slow-scrolling information sheet on scheduled maintenance, and now a notice of the tenants' meeting to be held in the rooftop facility. This last item was tagged with an URGENT BUSINESS label and a request for full attendance at the meeting. More notes scrolled by, mentions of packages held at the lobby desk and the minutes of the condo board's last meeting.

The tap on his shoulder made him jump. Mallory stood behind him, smiling *Gotcha*. The games went on. The old man had taught her that one, too. For a heavyset man, Markowitz had made even less noise than Kathy when he crept up behind her. By the time she was thirteen, the old man could no longer do that. She had surpassed him in the creeping game. Between

Markowitz and Mallory, he sometimes wondered who had been the worst influence on whom.

"I found a room to set up in," she said.

He picked up the cartons and followed her into a small library. He settled them on the desk, and she began to unload the computer equipment and the Minicam, the wiring and the works he couldn't put a name to. Only the wiretap equipment was recognizable, and he averted his eyes from this, knowing there was no warrant.

Markowitz had not taught her this. Far from it—the old man had remained mechanically inept and computer-ignorant until the day he died. The less Markowitz knew about what she was up to with her machines, the more secure he had felt in the NYPD pension plan.

Mallory stepped off the elevator at the penthouse level. She had traveled only a few steps into the room when heads began to turn. She was wearing the black suit she had worn to her father's funeral. The skirt provided a rare outing for her legs, displaying athletic calves and well-shaped ankles tapering above high heels. A dozen pairs of eyes, male and female, followed after her as she passed through the gathering of perhaps forty tenants.

She paused now and then to admire a few of the art deco pieces scattered about the rooftop facility, and generally disapproved of the clutter of objects on pedestals and sideboards. But every travesty of decorators was forgiven when she lifted her face to the skylight which spanned the whole of the wide room. A waxing moon kept two stars for company. A filmy cloud raced across the glass, gaining on the moon, then killing its light.

"Death becomes you, my dear," said a cultured, dulcet voice.

"I've already heard that one today," said Mallory, turning to look down at a woman with black hair and a face that was pushing sixty, not in the wrinkles, but in the pulled-back skin of the too-manyith face-lift. "I suppose you're going to tell me how well-preserved I am for a corpse."

The older woman smiled a thin line of crimson lipstick. "You've got a smart mouth for a dead cop." And now the voice betrayed roots in Hell's Kitchen when gangsters ruled, and the woman went up one notch in Mallory's estimation.

"I'm Betty Hyde."

"Mallory."

"Kathleen Mallory, isn't it? Formerly of NYPD, currently of the consulting firm Mallory and Butler, Ltd. You're staying in the Rosens' apartment for the next ten days while your own condo is being redecorated. They're old friends of your family, and you have their proxy to vote on the swimming pool in the basement. I have spies everywhere, my dear."

But Mallory counted only two spies. The concierge knew she had the Rosens' proxy, and Arthur the doorman had been fed the rest of the story.

"And *you* sell gossip," Mallory countered. "Your column is syndicated in fifty papers around the country. You have a five-minute spot on Channel Two News. You've lived here for the past fifteen years. You have a full-size pool table in your apartment, and you change young men the way I change my blue jeans. You should pay your spies better, Miss Hyde. They have no sense of loyalty."

The woman widened her smile into a brilliant grin.

"Call me Betty. Everyone does. I like your style, my dear. May I call you Kathy?"

"No."

"Even better. Well, Miss Mallory—"

"Just Mallory. Amanda Bosch gave me your name as a reference."

She handed the woman a card, and Betty Hyde read the words aloud. "Discreet investigations? I love it."

"Our clients are government departments and universities, mostly research projects and evaluations. Do you have anything nice to say about Bosch? If we hired her services, she'd be working on sensitive material."

"I trust her with high-profile information, but I don't trust anyone with the really good stuff. I do that research myself."

"I had the impression she hung out with you from time to time."

"Well, she does—or did, rather. She's cut back on her activities for the past few months. I used to take her to parties. When I go fishing for young men, I need good bait. She attracts men nearly as well as you do."

"And in return, you introduced her to the right people?"

"Yes."

"Are any of the right people here tonight? Anyone else who could vouch for her?"

Betty Hyde's mouth curled up on one side in the attitude of *All right, let's assume I believe this charade.* Mallory took stock of that attitude, and parried with a smile to say, *Yeah, let's just assume that.*

107

"I took Amanda to several gatherings in this very room. I imagine she's met quite a few of the tenants. I don't know which ones might have used her research services. Shall I introduce you around? And perhaps later you might accompany me to another party."

Mallory was looking over the smaller woman's head, her eyes fixed on the man standing by the long buffet table.

"I think I recognize Judge Heart from the Senate hearings." Mallory nodded toward a tall man, graying at the temples and wearing a well-tailored black suit. He dwarfed the thin woman who stood next to him. Her gray-blonde hair was pulled back in a severe bun at the nape of her neck.

"Yes, that's him. And that's his wife, Pansy. See the invisible strings? She can never get more than three feet away from him."

Mallory did have the impression that he worked the woman like a puppet. Every utterance from his mouth called the woman's face up to his with a smile that was too quick, too wide.

Betty Hyde said in a lower voice, "When you get closer, tell me if that isn't a bruise under her makeup."

"You're kidding. I thought he was—"

"—riding into the Supreme Court nomination on his women's rights position? Yes. Amusing, isn't it? If I could nail him as a wife beater, I'd do it in a hot flash. If you hear anything, it's worth gold, my dear Mallory. They live in the apartment above yours. Any screaming, the sounds of a woman's soft body bouncing off the wall—I'd be interested in anything like that."

Hyde stared up at the younger woman, and

her smile became a tight line as she shifted her weight from one foot to the other in the uncomfortable dance of waiting on Mallory. For a professional gossip, that drawn-out silence would be like sunlight to a vampire.

"I've already surmised that your condo isn't being redecorated," said Hyde. "And Amanda Bosch is not taking on any new clients. If anything, she's tapering off. I understand it's a difficult pregnancy."

Hyde smiled again.

And smiled.

Mallory, from the school of Never Volunteer Anything, continued to stare down at Hyde. Her face gave away nothing.

Hyde stopped smiling, and each woman squared off against the other, making measurements and mental notes, staking out the air between them with wires of tension. Hyde gave in first.

"Never mind the research projects. You're a private detective, right? It's a logical career move for an ex-cop. Am I right?"

Mallory shrugged, and Hyde showed all of her teeth.

"Now that you've moved into the private sector, let me give you a few helpful hints." She entwined her arm in Mallory's and led her back to a corner of relative seclusion where only potted ferns gathered.

"Mallory, people in your trade carry professional habits into what should be passing for social life. You don't ask questions—you interrogate. You sound like a cop. Just smile a lot. These people love to talk about themselves. So, you're working on a case, we've established that much.

And we can definitely place it in the money set, can't we? Did Amanda put you onto something? As if I thought you'd tell me. I also know how to protect sources, if you get my meaning."

"I think we can do business, Miss Hyde."

"Call me Betty."

"Over there, by the elevator—isn't that Moss White, the talk-show host?"

"Yes, and the tan is real. He just got back from a week on location in California."

"What day did he come back?"

"This morning."

Scratch that one.

"Which one is Harry Kipling?"

"That one," said Hyde, indicating a good-looking man, black hair, blue eyes, and tall. "He's charming, but aside from his looks, he's not remarkable. His wife is really miles more interesting. There she is. See that woman over there by the bookcase? Angel Kipling is a crime against nature. All trolls are supposed to be short. She's as tall as you are."

"You mean that middle-aged woman with the bad hair?"

"I've always liked the phrase 'a woman of a certain age.' "

"The tall man with her—who is he?"

"The blind man? That's Eric Franz."

"He's blind?" *Scratch that one, too.*

"Yes. Angel took away his dark glasses and the cane because she thought it might make him fit in better with the *normal* people. He's terrified of her, so of course he never puts up any resistance. I think we're all afraid of Angel. She's one of those people who learned table manners late in life. She asks rude questions like how old you are, how much money do you make, and are those your own teeth. It's hard on the nerves. A bit like a farting gorilla ripping through your peace of mind once a week or so. You never do get used to it."

Mallory looked back to Harry Kipling. "It's hard to see her and the husband as a couple."

"Because Harry is so ridiculously good-looking? Because Angel looks like she escaped from a hole in a Grimm Brothers fairy tale? You might have something there."

"Makes you wonder what she has on him."

"I like the way your mind works, Mallory. Since you're digging around anyway, dear, you might want to share with a new friend."

"Harry Kipling—is he one of the heirs to Kipling Electronics?"

"No. Should I be wondering what these men have in common?"

"What's his story?"

"The usual thing. He lives off his wife's money and fobs himself off as an investment counselor. I doubt that he handles any of Angel's money. I believe she gives him an allowance. All the charge accounts around town are in her name. Now you have to watch out for Angel. She was misnamed. *She's* the heiress to Kipling Electronics. Her father started the company."

"And then he named it after his son-in-law?"

"Harry took Angel's family name. It was a condition of the prenuptial agreement. If you took more of an interest in gossip, you'd know that."

"What's his real name?"

"No one ever cared enough to wonder. If you're thinking he might have an interesting past,

I doubt it. Angel's father would have had him checked out, and even checked behind his ears. Oh, hit the floor, Mallory, here comes the troll. She probably saw you looking at her husband. Did you bring a weapon, dear?"

In fact she had left her gun in the apartment.

Angel Kipling was crossing the floor in a straight line of terrible sure purpose. As she neared them, Betty Hyde backed up slightly, unconsciously. Mallory didn't.

The Kipling woman had a poor understanding of personal space. Now her face was entirely too close, and matching Mallory's eye level from a height of five-ten, plus high heels.

"I understand you're a friend of the Rosens," said Angel Kipling. "Is it true they keep a baby shark in their apartment?" She looked down at the older woman. "Oh, hello, Betty."

Betty Hyde nodded to Angel and went through the introduction of, not *Miss* Mallory, but only *Mallory*.

Mallory could not take her eyes off the hairs extending from Angel Kipling's upper lip. They were long like a cat's whiskers, but not symmetrical. The body was a potato attached to toothpick legs and sausages for arms. The crown of her head was an interesting mix of three failed experiments in hair coloring, striping brown at the root into blond and then black.

A wealthy woman with do-it-yourself hair. Interesting.

"So tell me, Miss Mallory, what do you think of our building?"

"Just Mallory."

"It's an historical landmark, you know. Lillian Russel, the old time actress, kept an apartment here so Diamond Jim Brady could visit her on the sly.''

"And Dylan Thomas threw up on this rug,'' added Betty Hyde.

Angel Kipling looked down as though there might be a recent stain. She turned back to Mallory. "Let me introduce you to my husband.''

The troll put up a hand with one pudgy finger extended as though she were flagging down a taxi or a waiter. From across the room, Harry Kipling's body assumed the stance of attention and hurried toward her.

"Do you have children?'' asked Angel Kipling.

"No, I don't. Do you?''

"Oh, there's Peter, but he's away most of the year.'' The tall man entered the small circle of women. "Harry, this is Miss Mallory. She's staying in the Rosens' apartment while they're out of town. I heard Hattie Rosen was going to the Mayo Clinic for cancer. Is that true? Miss Mallory?—Kathy, right?''

"Just Mallory.'' And how did Angel Kipling know her first name? Perhaps Angel's spies were as well paid as Betty Hyde's.

Angel Kipling turned to the tall man with the dark hair and the cobalt eyes. "I was just telling Kathy about our building.''

Harry Kipling was more than good-looking. His shoulders were broad, giving him the aspect of an athlete—good baby-making material. What was he doing with the troll? If he had married for money, he could have done better.

"I use your wife's computer chips,'' said Mallory.

"I'm afraid I wouldn't know a computer chip from a potato chip. Investment is my line.'' His voice had a smoky quality, and it was seductive in the mellow notes.

Betty Hyde took Mallory's arm, and smiling at the Kiplings, she led her away, saying, "You were staring too long at Harry. Don't turn around. I think you're his type. Of course he's a little old for my tastes. I never touch a man over thirty, and he's almost forty. No, don't turn around. I'm watching his wife. She's drawing a bead on you. If looks were bullets, you'd be on the floor and bleeding from a hole between your pretty eyes."

"Excuse me," said Harry Kipling, catching up to them, sans Angel, who had gone back to terrorizing the blind man. "Didn't you die on television the other night?"

"Acting," said Mallory.

"Oh, you're an actress," said Kipling.

"I thought you were a police officer," said Moss White, the talk show host, who had suddenly appeared at Kipling's side. White was the stuff television executives swooned over. The mouth was full and sensual, and the softness carried into the liquid brown eyes. He was born for television.

"So you're an actress," said White. "God, they didn't get anything right, did they? I wonder if we could discuss a guest appearance on my television show? It might be good for your career. Just a spot where you tell the viewing audience what it's like to be declared dead by the media. They thought you were dead when they found you in the park, right?"

She turned slowly to Harry Kipling, who was arranging his features into a piano's worth of white teeth. His face had a rugged quality that

114

made Moss White seem almost feminine by comparison.

Betty was pulling her away again, and they were drifting across the wide floor toward Judge Emery Heart, the candidate for the Supreme Court nomination.

"Moss White has an accent," said Mallory. "England or Australia?"

"Indiana. He spent six weeks in London, four years ago. He's been talking that way ever since. Moss is a quick study. I paid a hundred an hour for my accent, and it took me years."

And now Mallory and Hyde were standing before an austere man who might have stepped out of an ad for middle-aged upscale clothing.

"Judge Heart, may I present Mallory, the well-known television personality?"

The judge gave off the unmistakable odor of a good politician. The smile was instant, and the brown eyes were intent. "Forgive me, I don't watch very much television, Miss Mallory. What sort of program do you have?"

"I was only on for five minutes. I played a corpse."

The smile faltered for a moment while the judge's appraising eye was reassessing her importance in the scheme of things. Now the smile was back with full force. "Well, they say there are no small parts. This is my wife, Pansy."

Mallory turned to the small anxious woman at his side. And yes, there definitely were strings that tied her to her husband.

"Isn't that right, Pansy?" the judge prompted. "No small parts?"

The woman nodded automatically, stiffly. She smiled too quickly, and the sudden display of teeth was startling in the context of her eyes. And yes, there was a bruise below a heavy layer of makeup.

"Do you have family with you, Miss Mallory?" asked Pansy.

"Just Mallory. No, do you?"

"Well, Rosie's been gone for a while—oh, don't get me started. I cry whenever I think of our little Rosie. She's such an angel. Emery taught Rosie to shake hands. Didn't you, dear? Rosie is such a clever little thing, isn't she, Emery? And she can sit up and beg."

"Rosie is a dog," said Betty Hyde, after drawing Mallory away with explanations of introductions promised elsewhere.

"I think I worked that out," said Mallory.

"Now let me introduce you to our resident Pulitzer Prize winner." Betty Hyde paused by a bookcase to retrieve a pair of dark glasses and a cane. "He's marvelous with a cane in his hands. I just thought I'd give him a sporting chance to run for it before Angel comes back."

"I wonder why he doesn't deck her."

"Unfortunately, Eric was well brought up. I thought you might find him interesting. He's one of my best sources. People think nothing of what they say in Eric's presence. They seem to lump all handicaps into one, taking him for deaf and learning-disabled, too." Now Betty Hyde placed one hand gently on the man's arm to announce herself. "Hello, Eric. I'd like you to meet Mallory, a new resident."

"How do you do," said Eric Franz.

The man's voice was cultured, but in this crowd, that told her very little about his background. The lack of cane and glasses had the opposite effect of aiding the blind Franz to blend in. Here was a man with eyes out of focus and staring at nothing.

Betty Hyde slipped the cane into one of his hands and the glasses into the other. In the tone of conspirators, he asked, "What's between me and the door?"

"Four people I never cared for. Hit them with the cane if you can manage it."

Dark glasses in place, he made a courtly bow to Mallory, missing her general direction by two feet. "It's been a pleasure."

He walked across the crowded floor with the confidence of a sighted man and hit no one on the way out. And there was time for Mallory to wonder if he wasn't navigating entirely too well, and how he had been blinded, and how much insurance money had been involved, and if he had carried insurance on his dead wife.

"He isn't all the way blind, you know," said Betty. "He spots fakes and sharks in the dark— all the survival skills necessary to make it in New York City."

Mallory knew Harry Kipling was watching her. She could see his dark hair in peripheral vision and saw his head turn as she crossed the room with Betty Hyde. She turned back to look at Kipling's wife, who was following her husband's every move. There was an expression of bitterness in the woman's eyes. Now, all things flashed across the woman's face—hate, anger, suspicion and hurt.

Not a happy marriage.

"I know the lawyer who drew up their prenuptial agreement," said Betty Hyde, nodding to the Kiplings. "They have one child. The estate passes over the mother and goes to the son when he comes of age. I've only seen the boy once."

"I haven't seen many children today."

"Most of the year, you won't see any children at all. Children from this building are a new class of wealthy homeless people. They only come home from boarding school during the holidays. But if you really dislike your children, you can pay the school extra to keep them away from you for the entire year."

"Do the Hearts have children?"

"Judge Heart has one child by another marriage, a daughter. I've never seen her in the flesh—only in publicity photos that ran in the Sunday supplement before the Senate hearings. I suspect they rented the girl for the photo sessions."

"Is there anything wrong with her?"

"Like drug addiction, shoplifting? Oh, Mallory, that's so common among this group, I wouldn't stoop to writing about it."

"Could there be another reason why you never see her—something radically wrong with her?"

"You mean something like a lockaway child, an embarrassment in the public eye? That's an interesting angle. Leave it to me, dear. I'll get back to you. It's something you can only dig out of the right people. You won't find it on any records, not with the money behind the judge."

"And the blind man? Eric . . . ?"

"Eric Franz? No, he and Annie never had any children, unless you count the guide dog. And the dog is such a sweet animal, it would be hard to believe it was Annie's natural offspring."

"A bad marriage?"

"It was no great love affair. Her idea of sport

was to rearrange the furniture so he'd trip over it. And Eric used to tell their friends that Annie was feeding him dog food. Now that was his idea of a joke, but she probably did. She had a great sense of humor."

He was a late visitor to the kitchen, and alone. He pounded his hand on the cutting board, and a bowl of fruit jumped and tilted over, rocking its apples to the table.
That bitch.
She knew what he had done and what he was. She knew things.
An apple was still rolling on the board, red as her lips were red. He held the ripe fruit in one hand and fumbled in the drawer for a paring knife. He stabbed the skin and watched the juice flow out. He stabbed it again and again. And now he sliced off the skin in slow peels, imagining the screams emanating from the mutilated fruit in his hand.
Bitch.
All women were bitches.

She was sitting in the Rosens' library, facing her computer screen. It had taken five minutes to break into the guts of the building computer system—so much for security. Now she scrolled through the files on the tenants and made notes on access routes to bypass all but three computers.
She set up a dummy screen, and in the area of PERSONAL MESSAGES, she typed her own message, tailored only by the three different names, and otherwise the same. If her suspects didn't check the bulletin board tonight, they

would do so in the morning. Once the computer was accessed again, the fake board would disappear with no trace of tampering.

She picked through the building's list of fax numbers. Two of the suspects had fax machines. That would come in handy. After a glance at the building schematic for the best route to the basement room where the phone lines were located, she picked up her flashlight and telephone kit.

Thirty minutes later, the elevator operator was carrying her up and out of the basement. The iron cage stopped at the lobby floor. A boy got on the elevator. He might be fourteen years old.

If Harry Kipling had played around, his wife had not. The boy had the same blue eyes and black hair, the same stocky build as the father. And now the boy was looking her up and down. His slow widening smile was more of a leer.

She stared at the boy in the wordless disbelief of *You're kidding, right?*

The boy's face went to a high red color, and he got off on the next floor, though it was not where he lived.

She wondered if womanizing might be genetic.

She continued on, watching the floors drop away. Looking up through the iron grill of the doors, she saw the tip of the white cane at the blind man's feet. Eric Franz was standing by the elevator when the doors opened on the Rosens' floor. As she stepped out of the elevator, he inclined his head. "Miss Mallory? I've been looking for you. Oh, I'm sorry, it's just Mallory, right?"

"Right," she said, after a hesitation.

"It was your perfume," said Eric Franz, in

response to the question she was about to ask. He shrugged and smiled. "When you lose your sight, nature gives you another gift, a heightened sense of awareness. Betty Hyde tells me you have an interest in the judge. So do I."

"Also professional? I work for a research group. I assume she told you that, too."

"Yes, she did. But my interest in the judge is personal. I'm curious about an old incident. Being blind has its drawbacks, you know. There's always missing information on some level. Take the day the medical examiner's people showed up for the death of old Mrs. Heart, the judge's mother."

"Are you saying it wasn't a natural death?"

"Supposedly, it was a heart attack. Maybe it was, but I did wonder when the police detective came a half hour later. I was in the lobby when he said to the doorman—just the one word— 'Homicide.' "

"That wouldn't make sense if she died of a heart attack."

"It is interesting, isn't it? And now I expect you'll want me to describe the police officer?"

Mallory smiled. *Yeah, right.*

"He was tall and thin." And as though Franz had read the expression on her face, he hurried on to answer her next unasked question. "He made long strides. He knocked into me. I remember saying to him, 'What are you—blind?' I never miss an opportunity to use that line. When he knocked into me, there wasn't much bulk to him. He apologized, and judging by his accent, he was originally from Brooklyn. Oh, and he wore too much after-shave. It was a very expensive brand. And his coat was made of leather."

"You mentioned the ME investigator."

"Oh, that man was already up there in the judge's apartment. The Hearts' family doctor was there too. I was sitting in the lobby waiting for a friend who was detained in traffic. All of them trooped past me."

The detective could only be Palanski. Palanski again. He was the closest thing NYPD had to an ambulance chaser.

The mouse crept silently across the kitchen floor, mindful of the giant's blue pajama legs. Its small eyes were filled with the reflected crumbs of a golden croissant. It snatched up the bread and scurried back to its hiding place beneath the refrigerator, where it sat feeding in the dark, insanely pleased with itself.

Charles watched the cream bubble over a blue gas flame and wondered how many days the mouse might have left in this world. Mrs. Ortega had tried repeatedly to murder it with traps, to break its back with a broom, and to poison it. So far, the savvy city mouse had eluded her with supernatural skill, and gained Charles's respect. But Mrs. Ortega was also a mythic creature in her own right. However quick the mouse might be, Mrs. Ortega was sure to be close behind it, broom held high.

The mouse was as good as dead.

The coffee dripped its rich brown juices down into the carafe. The heady aroma wafted high up to the fifteen-foot ceiling of the kitchen and beyond the appreciation of the mouse and the man.

Charles carried his coffee into the front room

and set it down beside the bulky manuscript. He cleared his mind of all but the task at hand.

One thing became clear to him in the first twenty pages of text: If Amanda Bosch was the female character, she had no capacity for self-delusion. He ceased to speed-read and slowed down to a human pace, for this was very human material—Amanda awakening from a bad dream and finding it there beside her in her bed.

The male character of the novel seemed not to know or care about the rules between men and women when they became lovers. The woman wondered why he came back time and again. He showed so little interest in the affair once the conquest of her had been made.

The excuses he gave to explain his infrequent need of her were insulting. Yet she did not end the affair, telling herself it was better to be touched by this cold and dispassionate man than never to be touched at all. This, she realized, must be what it was like to feel as a man did when he separated the act from the partner. She never asked about his wife, fearing that he had never felt anything for her, either, nor for anyone. He could make love to a woman better than any man she had ever known, yet he did not like women.

When they were together, in warm weather and cold, the bedding would always be soaked with sex and sweat. They went swimming in the fluid off their bodies, plunging down and rising up in the water that streamed off their flesh. He would make her come first, insisting on it, manipulating her body. And when she came, he took a technician's pride in this job well done. There was a perverse coldness in the very heat of the act.

He would be dressed when she came out of

the bathroom, where she had been emptying out his sperm and flushing it away to the sea. She would watch his back as he walked to the door, reciting the litany of excuses, not turning to say goodbye, and never a kiss, as though to teach her not to set too much store by this attachment which was detachment.

She would strip the wet bedding off the mattress and lay it out to dry in the air—the heat of July the first time, and the winter now. It was better than nothing, she told herself, knowing it was not.

Charles looked away from the manuscript to a clear place on the wall beside his chair. Eidetic memory called up the photograph of Amanda Bosch which Riker had shown him only once. His vision was a perfect reproduction, even to the smudge and crease at the upper left-hand corner of the print. Her sad eyes stared at him. The expression was in the very shape of her eyes, a sadness fashioned in her mother's womb.

He felt that he knew Amanda Bosch so well, he might have had a dialogue with her and predicted the answers to nearly every question.

If he only had her back to life for a minute's work.

But only Malakhai could have pulled off that stunning trick—to blend the device of dialogues and the illusion of a woman with uncanny, unerring faithfulness to life.

He had often thought of Malakhai over the years, the elderly magician and his strange creation. What a mad idea.

And yet.

The manuscript did promise an exquisite problem in mental construction. It could be done. The manuscript's narrative was no mere imitation of life, it was Amanda's mind at work. With only the manuscript and the photograph, the old man could have done this. But the old magician was insane, and far from here in mind and body.

It was a lunatic idea, and he must let it go.

He turned back to the manuscript, but the face of Amanda would not leave him. Eidetic memory had called it up, and his mind's eye could not send it away. It swam over the text. His thoughts ran strongly with Malakhai now, as he stared into Amanda's eyes.

Oh, Malakhai, how do you like your last days, old man? Are you still in love with Louisa? Still crazy? And does that dead woman share your bed tonight?

He stared at the telephone. With one call he might have an audience with the greatest magician who ever lived. Cousin Max had said there was none better, cracked brain or no. What would he say to Malakhai? "Excuse me for presuming on family connections, but I have a small problem with a dead woman of my own. How do I go about becoming as mad as you are? Or am I half the way gone already?"

He shook his head slowly from side to side. This was no kind of dabble for an amateur in the art of illusion. He must not forget what the mental construction of a succubus had cost Malakhai, who was a master. He turned back to the manuscript. It was that time of night, he supposed, when mad ideas seemed the most wonderful.

He was an hour into his reading when a noise called his attention away from the pages. He was unaccustomed to company at this hour. He had forgotten about Nose. Now he watched the cat a scant few inches from his slippers.

The fact that Nose was declawed had hampered the animal only slightly. A small brown mouse had wriggled free of the clawless paws only to be captured more firmly in rows of sharp white teeth. Charles silently rooted for the mouse. The cat's teeth crunched down on small bones. The mouse cried. It was not a squeak; the tiny animal was crying.

The cat looked up at him, very Mallory in the color and the aspect of its eyes.

He reached down with the good intention of taking the mouse away to kill it quickly. The cat emitted a low warning growl, and the tail began to switch and threaten as his hand hovered near the mouse.

Back off, said the cat's eyes. *It's my toy, not yours.*

Angel Kipling gathered the quilted silk of her robe closer about her person, as though the room might be cold. It was not.

She sat before the computer, transfixed by what was written there in the personal-message file. She could see her husband in the reflection of the dark screen behind the green letters. A tiny replica of Harry floated toward her from deep inside the box of glowing letters. Now she could feel the heat of him standing close behind her chair.

"Angel, what's wrong?"

"Oh nothing, Harry." She continued to stare at the screen. At last, she said, "It's a personal message. I think it must be for you."

She rose from her chair and walked slowly in

the direction of her own bedroom, where she slept alone. She turned to see him bending over the computer monitor, reading the message which filled the scrolling screen and repeated endlessly: YOU LIAR, YOU LIAR, YOU LIAR, YOU LIAR . . .

He only wanted to be where the cat was not feeding on the mouse. He unlocked the door of the office across the hall from his residence, and at the touch of a button, the reception room filled with soft colored light from antique shades of stained glass. The ancient woodwork of furniture and tall arched window frames gleamed and lustered.

He wandered into the back room which was Mallory's office and another planet. The wall switch filled this room with harsh light, bright as day, and brought him rudely and solidly into the age of electronics. Machines gleamed and stared at him with dead, gray terminal eyes. The beige metal knights of the New Order formed a row of perfect symmetry. A wall of manuals faced a wall of equipment, and no speck of dust dared light in this place, for fear of Mallory the Neat.

The corkboard which lined the rear wall was an even more ruthless departure from his own world of antiques and all things civilized. If murder be Mallory's religion, the ghastly collage of this wall was a shrine to Amanda Bosch, a Madonna without a child.

When had Mallory accomplished all of this? Did she never sleep?

There were photographs of Amanda's apartment, her person, and samples of her handwriting. Mallory's precision in the neat placement of every item was overridden by the softer personality of Amanda. The shot to his heart was the picture of the old wooden cradle Amanda had purchased for her unborn child.

He looked at the autopsy photos and looked away. The crime-site photos were more palatable. But every artifact of the death had become intensely personal, for now he knew this woman as few people could have known her in life.

The best of the death photos was centered on the board. The damage to the skin of her face he overlaid with a memory of the photo Riker had shown him when she posed as a living model. He superimposed the rosy live flesh over the white and the dead. When the living image lay over the death mask, it had the unsettling effect of the photographic woman suddenly opening her eyes.

His mind did a little dance and jog away from reality and then came back to it with caution, tripping all the way, falling now as the wound to the side of her head bled through the double image. He winced at the living expression juxtaposed with the clotted blood. The brown blazer she died in bore the drippings of the wound in a great bloody stain draped over one shoulder.

She was smiling. That bothered him. He found he could alter the smile to a more appropriate expression and still be true to the likeness. Now her facial arrangement seemed only friendly and slightly inquisitive. *What now?* it asked. He held this new image of her for too long—so long that it would remain in memory for years.

He scanned the items of the apartment inventory and found a bottle of her perfume on the list. He found it again in the photograph of her bathroom counter. She wore the scent of roses.

The perfume bottle bore the logo of an old and prestigious house. He remembered seeing a bottle of that scent among the sequined costumes and the makeup boxes in the cellar where the illusions of Maximillian Candle were stored.

Her husband was staring at the computer screen when she walked into the room.

Pansy Heart came up behind him softly. Noise of any kind irritated him. Over his shoulder she read the words YOU LIAR, YOU LIAR, YOU LIAR. The words filled out the entire screen. She looked up to the slot at the top of the screen, which labeled this file as a personal message.

He turned on her. His face was red with anger.

"Don't you ever sneak up behind me again!"

She backed away quickly, stilling the hand that rose almost of its own accord when it sensed an oncoming blow. But he only turned his face back to the screen. He pounded on the console and sent the books and papers flying. She knelt on the carpet and began to crawl on all fours, retrieving every fallen thing.

"Get out of here!" he yelled. "Get out!"

She backed away from him, still on her knees, then stumbling to a stand, now scurrying off down the hall. As she entered the bedroom, she was met by her own reflection hurrying toward her. She stopped before the full-length mirror and fit her fist into her mouth to keep from crying out loud.

When had she dropped so much weight?

With her hair pulled back the way he insisted she wear it, and with the new thinness of her body, and now that expression of a hunted animal, she had come to be a living likeness of Judge Emery Heart's dead mother.

The braille printer scrolled out the message, filling sheet after sheet with two damning words.

Eric Franz sat very still, eyes fixed on a scene inside his head, a horror movie that never ended. A bright snowfall cascaded by the wide front window, large flakes illuminated by the building's exterior lights. He turned from the window and ripped the scrolling sheets from the printer.

And now it snowed outside and inside as he created his own small storm of white flakes of paper being torn into ever smaller bits. He worked in the dark.

His hands were full when he returned to the front room of his apartment. Charles unloaded his small cache on the coffee table. Of the ingredients for making a woman, Riker's contribution had been half a pack of cigarettes left behind this afternoon. According to the medical examiner's report on Mallory's wall, Amanda had been a smoker. There were no cigarettes on Mallory's meticulous inventory. Amanda might have given up the habit when she knew she was pregnant, but her manuscript was filled with imagery of smoke, matches struck in the dark when she woke alone to hug her knees and rock her body and hold herself in her own arms through the long night into a morning of filled ashtrays and dust motes swirling in the blue smoke and the gray light.

Cousin Max's contribution had been the bottle of rose scent from the old wardrobe box in the basement. Old Malakhai's Louisa had gone everywhere in the scent of gardenias. Amanda Bosch had gone about in roses.

He called up Amanda's face on a patch of wall, the eidetic images of life over death, which were fixed in memory.

Now what was Malakhai's recipe?

He should have started with a massive head injury like the one Malakhai had sustained in the Korean conflict. Such a wound was definitely concomitant with all the most bizarre aberrations, such as the stigmata.

Well, if he had no physical trauma, he certainly had his own injuries to the heart and the mind. And perhaps this was Mallory's contribution to the unholy stew.

Next on the list would be the years of Malakhai's solitary confinement in a Korean prison cell, the terrible isolation he had suffered, emerging finally from that cell with a phantom Louisa.

Charles reflected on his own years of isolation. A sprawling university campus was as close to the six-foot-square cell as he could come. He thought of his years of being the freak child among the tall students ten years his senior. And then came the years of isolation in the sheltering womb of Effrim Wilde's think tank before making his escape into real life and his own consulting firm.

For most of his life, he had been a thing apart, an alien in a culture of socially adept people. All of this would nearly approximate Malakhai's isolation from the world. But he needn't go back so far in time. There was the ache of loneliness each time Mallory quit a room.

Another contribution, thank you, Mallory.

If anything should happen to Mallory, she

could never be reconstructed as Malakhai had done for Louisa, as he would attempt to do for Amanda Bosch. No one had access to Mallory's thoughts and feelings. Nothing must ever happen to her.

Oh, fool.

He had forgotten the music. The concerto had been a prime ingredient in Malakhai's creation of Louisa. In childhood, it had been the trigger of his own imagination. His copy of the concerto had been worn to shreds. But the music was so much a part of him he had never thought to replace the recording. There was an old 78 vinyl record in the basement somewhere, as well as the old turntable for that period of technology.

Ah, but wait. If Amanda Bosch was to be a mental construct, perhaps he should practice first with the music. He had only heard the piece a thousand times in his life.

Now he had all the ingredients of Malakhai's madness. The music, the scent, and the loneliness.

Yes, he could manage it.

He lit one of Riker's cigarettes and set it to smoking in the ashtray. He concentrated on Amanda's face, re-creating the image he had composed in Mallory's office, the pictures of life imposed on death. And now the eyes of Amanda Bosch stared into his own. Photographic memory assisted him with every detail of those sad eyes. She had only the flatness of any photograph he could call up, for he was no Malakhai. But even in this poor translation, she was compelling. The eyes communicated much of her, even in the poverty of only two dimensions. Mystery was there, and profound loss.

And now with an inner ear, he searched for the notes of *Louisa's Concerto*.

He had been a child of seven the first time he heard the work performed as the overture to Malakhai's performance of magic and the madness of dead Louisa. Cousin Max had taken him to the show as a treat for his birthday.

He could find many of his own features in his adult cousin, but Max had been a handsome translation: a nose not so great, and eyes with a more normal proportion of white to the colored bits.

He and Cousin Max had found the way to their seats by the glow of flickering candle footlights. The conductor's baton was rising as they settled down to the red velvet chairs in the concert hall.

There had been no gentle beginning to *Louisa's Concerto*. The instruments had welled up and rocked him with an explosion of opening chords, and the music rolled over him, powerful and eerie, then calmer, subsiding into echoes of music within the movement, metaphors of empty corridors. The music rose again to crash down upon him with a passion. And then, at the most unexpected moment, there was a lull, bleeding into an empty silence that caused angst among all the listeners. It was a vacant space which the ear strained to fill with echoes from the refrain which were not heard except in the mind. It was a true vacuum, and the imagination of every independent listener had rushed to fill it with phantom notes to end the terrible, unbearable silence.

And then, the real music of solid instruments had resumed with an intake of breath which emanated from every quarter of the hall, relief from the audience that they were not lost. The music was back and flooding over them, making them all new again as though they had been cleansed, not by fire, nor by water, but by passage through the void.

The curtain rose and the music had begun again in accompaniment to the magic act. Malakhai had created Louisa on stage as a real presence. Then he sent her out into the audience, and here and there, a gasp was heard as one person and another imagined that Louisa had touched them. The scent of flowers was everywhere for a time, and then it was gone away into the dark of a child's imagination.

And this time, in the void, the magic silence where the listeners placed the phantom notes rather than endure the emptiness, there he had heard a woman screaming.

Long after the hall emptied of its audience, and only the concerned stage manager remained, Cousin Max had sat in the front row, holding the hand of a badly frightened child.

Max had once told him the best of music kept to the natural rhythms of the heart. *Louisa's Concerto* was such a piece. He had the basic structure of it now, and he strained to find the subtle places where Louisa had placed the most delicate constructions. He sat still for an interval of time which might have been an hour or four, and finally, he had recreated the music, note for note, just as he had heard it that first night so long ago. And in that void Louisa's genius had created within the music, he re-created the scream, just as he had heard it as a child, but not to the same effect. Now he welcomed the sound of another voice, even a scream, to fill the empty space he had come to recognize as loneliness.

He lit another cigarette to replace the one whose coal had gone dark. The smoke spiraled and wafted around his face without odor or sting to the eyes. He could only smell the roses.

Perhaps the perfume had been a mistake. The scent in the small gold bottle retrieved from the basement had the life span of all things with living ingredients. It filled his senses with the tainted aroma of decayed blooms which had died long before young Amanda was born.

The strains of the concerto were in his mind in vivid detail, interior music, corridors of sadness, and then—Amanda.

She was only the two dimensions of his called-up photographic image, but there was a palpable energy to the woman before him. Expressive eyes could create that illusion in any number of dimensions.

Now, in the manner of adding pinches of pepper and dashes of salt, he put liquid and gleam in the soft blue eyes, and he gave her a luster of Mallory's sun-gold hair which could thieve light from shadow.

Ready now.

He leaned forward. "Amanda?"

The photographic image bowed its head in response. It was more like a sheet of paper bending to force, an awkward attempt at animating the flat image of a dead woman.

"Why were you killed, Amanda?"

She responded with Mallory's voice. He created it for her with only the silk of Mallory and not the sarcasm, only the soft notes for Amanda, and with this voice Amanda said, "He lied to me."

Her soft mouth had opened and closed in a

135

succession of jerking photographic images—a poor approximation of life, a bad joke on God.

There was a wounding to the eyes, as though he had offended her. And he had. His eyes went away from her, and she died off to the side of peripheral vision.

"I'm so sorry," he said to no one, for there was no one there, not Amanda certainly, nor even her after-image anymore. What a grotesque puppet show this had been. How pathetic was he.

He capped the perfume bottle, but the death of killed roses hung in the air. When he passed into the other rooms, it hung in memory, this smell of death. And when he was in his bed and most vulnerable, hands and feet bound by sleep, floating helpless in the dark—Amanda came back.

All the night long and all about his dreams, fresh young roses were being killed. Even the small, sleeping buds, still closed in tight balls of soft petals—they were also dying.

Chapter 4

DECEMBER 23

For a full minute, Charles Butler had been standing by the door, listening to the scuffle of shoes in the outer hallway. By the light-footed pacing to and fro, he knew his visitor was a small person. And just now, somewhere between acute hearing and Zen, he detected the sound of someone standing on one leg and then the other. He politely waited until his visitor had resolved the hesitation and the door buzzer sounded.

Charles opened the door with his smile already in place, a genuine smile, for he liked small children.

"Hello. So you've come early." A full hour early.

"Yes," said Justin Riccalo, rocking on the balls of his feet. "I'm supposed to meet my parents here. My piano lesson was canceled, and I didn't know where else to go."

Not home? Was it possible he wasn't welcome there?

As though the boy had read his mind, he said, "I don't have my own key. I could go somewhere else. I'm sorry—"

"Don't apologize. I was just on my way to the basement. I'd be happy to have some company. Do you like magic tricks?"

Justin's response was not what he had anticipated. The rocking ceased, as though his store of nervous energy had escaped from a hole which had suddenly deflated the boy. He was a slender child, and if he deflated any more, he would be altogether gone.

"Do I like tricks? Mr. Butler, is this your subtle way of asking me if I can make a pencil fly?"

"Not at all. I think you'll like the basement."

With only the lift of one slight shoulder, the boy made it clear that he didn't care one way or the other.

Charles locked the office door, and they walked down the long hall toward the exit sign which led to the staircase. The boy looked back over his shoulder to the elevator, and Charles explained that stairs were the only way to the lowest level, and he hoped that Justin didn't mind the walk. Justin trudged along at Charles's side, walking as though his legs weighed fifty pounds, each one.

Apparently, stairs were a novelty for a child raised in a luxury high-rise. When the door opened onto a spiral staircase of black iron, Justin held on to the rail and leaned far over the side. He seemed hypnotized by the winding metal. Bright lights glared at him from bare bulbs at each floor and twisted the shadows of the curling iron.

"Awesome," said Justin, approving the tortured shapes of light and shadow. "This is a great old building."

"You haven't seen anything yet."

Charles led the way, and the boy followed, reluctant hesitance gone from his steps.

"So what are we going to do down there, sir? You have some kind of spook meter you want me to stick my finger in?"

"No, nothing that sophisticated. Usually, I just sit around and talk to the subject. Sometimes we do written tests."

"What kind of subjects do you specialize in? UFOs?"

"Nothing that entertaining. Sorry. In my work, the subject is always a person with a unique gift. I find a way to qualify it, quantify it, and then I find a use for it. Lots of people are overdeveloped in some area of intelligence. Take my partner, Mallory. She has a natural gift for computers."

"Computers are only mechanical devices." Justin's pronouncement had the peal of middle-aged absolutism. "Anyone with a manual can operate one."

"Well, Mallory doesn't need manuals. She does things the designers never thought of. You would not believe the things she accomplishes at a computer."

Oh, wait. Perhaps Mallory was not such a good role model for a small child.

"But your partner's gift already has an application."

"Yes. In most cases, I find people with gifts that have no apparent application, and I project the area they'll do well in. Then I find them a place in a research project. Sounds dull, doesn't it? But it creates a window for developers of new technology."

"All right, Mr. Butler. Do you want to start without my parents?"

"Oh, no. This excursion is just for the fun of it. I was on my way down here to look for an old record album that belonged to my cousin. He was a magician—Maximillian Candle. Have you ever heard of him? No, you wouldn't have. It's been a very long time since he was on the stage. Are you interested in magic? You didn't say."

They had reached the last floor, and Charles was working the lock on the door. Once inside, he felt at the top of the fuse box for the flashlight. He clicked on the beam and motioned for the boy to follow behind him.

They made their way through a canyon of shadowy boxes and crates, old furniture and picture frames. He trained the flashlight beam through a myriad of draped furniture, ghosts of castaway items, boxes and mazes of trunks and cartons.

The pleated back wall was a paneled screen which ran the length of the basement. Charles inserted a key into another lock and this wall began to fold back on itself, a gigantic, silent accordion.

The cavernous space beyond was dimly lit by a wide back window high up on the basement wall. The bars on the window were Mallory's work, as were the pick-proof locks installed throughout the building. She would have put bars on every window if he had allowed it. It had taken a long time to explain to her that he would rather be burgled than jailed in his own house.

Now the beam of his flashlight shone on a collage of bright satin and silk gleaming through cellophane wrappers. Sequins and rhinestones sparkled through the dust of garment bags which hung in a wardrobe trunk. A portion of the room was obscured by a large fire-breathing dragon on a tall rice-paper screen. A rack of sturdy shelving lined one wall with satin masks, top hats, a silver dove-load, giant playing cards, ornate boxes and small trunks each containing its own magic.

If it was the boy who made the pencils fly, this might be the outlet. The world could use a little more magic.

"I'll have a light on in another minute." Charles touched one finger to the top of a glass globe and the orb came to life, glowing with eerie pulsations as though light could breathe in and out.

He turned back to the boy, whose attention was focused elsewhere. "Oh, that's Cousin Max."

"How do you do," said the boy to the severed head which perched on the wardrobe trunk. Justin looked from Charles to the waxwork. "It looks like you."

"I only wish. He died when I was about your age." Charles removed the head from the trunk and held it in one hand. It stared back at him with lifelike eyes and the expression of amazement Max always wore when he lived.

"Cousin Max saved my childhood for me."

"How?"

"Magic. He was a wonderful magician. Of course, the greatest magician who ever lived was Malakhai. He did an act with a dead woman, a ghost."

"Sure, Mr. Butler. I think I see her coming now."

"No, really. Her name was Louisa. She died when she was only nineteen. She was one of those people I was talking about with extraordinary gifts that—"

"Louisa Malakhai? *Louisa's Concerto?*"

"Apparently you've learned something at school."

"No, I try not to learn anything at the Tanner School. It's too risky. I'm not sure they know what they're doing. My first stepmother used to play *Louisa's Concerto.* Did you know her? Louisa, I mean?"

"Well, yes and no."

"Do you know why she named the concerto after herself? Was it like a self-portrait in music?"

"That's not bad, Justin. In fact, it's a good theory, but she had given the concerto another title. It was Malakhai who changed it after she died. So you're familiar with the music."

"Not really. I only played the album once after my stepmother died. It was an old record that you played on a turntable like—like—"

"Like in the olden days?"

"Yes. It's probably on discs now. But what we had was the record. My stepmother—the crazy one who killed herself—she loved that album. She used to listen to it all the time."

"Did you like it?"

"I never heard it all the way through. She played it when she was alone. She'd turn it off if anyone else was around, or she'd listen with the earphones. She said the concerto was haunted."

"Haunting?"

"No, *haunted*. She said she could hear someone moving around in the music. Crazy, huh? Anyway, after she died, I was playing the record and Dad ripped it off the turntable and destroyed it with his bare hands. When I backed out of the room, he was breaking the pieces of it into smaller pieces."

Was it the screaming both man and wife had heard in the music? In that magic empty space, a different effect was worked on every ear. Once, he had heard Louisa screaming. Another time, after he had fallen into puppy love with the phantom woman, he heard her laughing. But all of that had taken place in the stage-dark atmosphere of a magic act. The air had been primed for the imagination to make whatever it would.

"Louisa died young. The concerto was her only composition, all that Malakhai had with him when he came walking out of the end of the Korean War. He used it as the theme of every performance."

"Performance with a dead woman."

"Yes, an invisible dead woman. She handed him objects and did everything an assistant would do. When she handed him a prop, you watched it float from her hand to his. You never saw her

142

hand, yet you believed, that's how good the floating illusions were."

"Tricks. Wires and stuff."

"Ah, but Malakhai also knew how to create terror."

Now he had Justin's full attention.

"He sent Louisa into the crowd. Members of the audience swore they felt her passing by them, the brush of her dress, the rush of air. Some recounted the scent of her perfume."

"How did he do that? What kind of gadgets did he use?"

"There were no physical devices involved. By the time he sent her out among them, they had come to believe in her."

"The whole audience?"

"Actually, it's easier with a lot of people. Mass hypnosis to psychosis, the more the better. You can do quite a lot with that much energy in the room."

"But no one really saw her?"

"Yes and no. He described her in such great detail I can see her now. She wore the dress she died in. It was blue but for the red bloodstains."

"How did she die?"

"No one ever knew. That was part of Louisa's mystery. Some people said Malakhai had killed her. Other rumors had her shot for a spy. It was all very romantic. When I was your age and younger, I was in love with Louisa."

"So you were as crazy as Malakhai."

"I suppose I was. And you're right—Malakhai had gone insane. It's truly amazing what people will do for love—to keep it, to kill it, or avenge it. And some people even die for it."

In the distraction of his compartmentalized

brain, Charles speculated on what Amanda had done. "Cut it out of me," she had said to the surgeon, she who loved children. She had cut out the child that was barely begun.

"So, I gather," said the finished child who stood before him now, "that falling in love is not the bright side of growing up."

Charles smiled. "The love of a child also leads to pretty strange behavior at times. The things people will do for their children."

"Or *to* their children."

"Yes, there's that, too.

Amanda, why did you cut your baby away from you?

Now he dragged his brain back to the case at hand. Had Justin been abused? Was that the link Mallory saw in the boy? There was something between them.

And he had his own common cord with the boy: Justin Riccalo did not have the conversation of a child. So he too had been raised among adults and shunned by the children who would have provided him with the bad habits and speech patterns of the normal boy Charles had never been either.

He located the old record turntable, leaned down and blew away the worst of the dust. Now where were the records?

Ah, there they are.

He pulled the crate of old record albums out from under a table, sat down in the dust, and began to sort through them. The boy hovered over him, always in motion even when he was standing still.

"So, Justin, when the pencils aren't flying, how do you get along with your stepmother?"

"I don't know her very well."

"I had the idea that your stepmother had known your father for quite a long time."

"I think they worked together once. I'm not sure. I think my real mother was alive then. I didn't know her very well either."

"Pardon?"

"I was at school most of the time. I started the usual progressive school crap when I was four. My parents realized that farming me out to after-school programs was more cost-effective than a nanny and less paperwork. Some nights I don't get home till eight or nine o'clock. How did Malakhai make those people believe Louisa had touched them?"

"The audience did it to themselves. They only had to know she was among them to complete the illusion, right down to imagining the tactile sensations."

"You think my stepmother is filling in the illusions? But the pencil—"

"The pencil was not her imagination. But after the trick is done, the imagination takes over. In Malakhai's act, all the real magic was in Louisa's music."

Charles slid the record out of its ancient cover, and with the practiced handling of the audiophile from the age of dinosaurs and turntables, he slipped it onto the spindle.

Justin sat down on the backs of his heels. Nervous energy made it seem that he was set to spring, to push off from the cement floor and into flight. "You can get that on CD, you know."

"So you said. Hush. Listen."

The volume was set too high. When the music rose up in a tidal wall, the large room was dwarfed by it, too small to contain it. Charles lowered the volume to a normal setting, but the concerto was undiminished, Louisa's raw talent defying laws of physics to increase the power of her music in the lower registers of sound. This was truly magic.

And now Charles was lost again in childhood memories of Louisa in the blue dress with the red stains. The bloodstain turned his thoughts back to Amanda Bosch and the events of last night. Louisa and Amanda became entangled in his mind. Out of old childhood habit, his eyes closed as the music rolled over him, for Louisa was always created in darkness.

Justin's stepmother had described the music well. It was haunted. Someone did move through the music, and in the empty space—this time she was crying.

Before the music could swell up again on the other side of the void, he opened his eyes and looked down at the boy, who was doubled over. Justin's hands were pressed to his ears.

What do you hear in the void, Justin?

And now Charles was also frightened.

Amanda Bosch was standing over the boy.

She was rounded out in all three dimensions of his self-induced delusion, wearing the bloodstain on her brown blazer and the wound at the side of her head. She was reaching down to the boy curled at her feet.

Charles's hand flashed out to knock the needle off the track. The record made a screeching noise as the needle tore across its surface, ripping the vinyl skin and ending its song.

Amanda was gone.

★ ★ ★

Well, if it isn't the homicide dick to the rich and famous.

Riker grinned when he saw Detective Palanski, a beanpole in a black leather jacket and dark glasses. Palanski must think he was a damn movie star, wearing his shades indoors. The detective was sticking his pointy finger in the face of Martin, a uniformed officer with orders to keep everyone away from Jack Coffey's office.

Well, no hotshot from the West Side was gonna take that from a uniform, said the jabbing finger in Patrolman Martin's face.

It didn't register with Palanski that Martin was a decade younger, more athletic, that he was squaring off, planting his feet like a boxer, not liking the finger in his face, not liking it at all. The young patrolman was holding his own bit of turf with a confidence lent him by Jack Coffey, who was in the habit of backing up his people. To his credit, Coffey had even backed Mallory when she was dead wrong.

Riker walked up to the duel of "I outrank you" versus "I don't give a shit." He tapped Martin on the arm and nodded him away. Martin backed off to the door of Coffey's office and folded his arms. Palanski turned on Riker with the wrath of an unnaturally tall nine-year-old.

"My captain wants to know why your lieutenant is keeping this homicide case—the stiff in the park. You got no officer involvement."

"You don't know that," said Riker, pulling out a cigarette and searching from pocket to pocket for matches.

Could Palanski have gotten wind of the Coventry Arms angle? Yeah, that was it. Now that the case was high-profile, he wanted it back to cover ass on the botched job at the crime scene. There was no other explanation for a cop asking for more work when there was no shortage of dead bodies and open cases.

"The stiff wasn't Mallory," said Palanski. "I know that much."

"But you didn't know it when you rolled the body." Riker lit his cigarette and let the barb sink in. He knew it had to be Palanski who had leaked the premature identification to the press. Information was currency in New York City, and he figured Palanski was too ambitious and on the edge of dirty, if not gone over. He dressed too well for a cop supporting a wife, an ex-wife and two kids. Riker only supported the bottle, and he could not afford the pricey salon where Palanski had his hair, not cut, please, but styled.

"So, Palanski, if *you* thought it was Mallory, maybe the perp did too."

Palanski lowered his sunglasses and leaned into Riker's space. "You'll have to do better than that, Riker. I'm not buying it."

And wasn't it just a little strange that Palanski had been the first one on the scene when Amanda Bosch was found? A quick check of rosters had confirmed that the man was off duty that morning. Palanski must believe that uptown territory of wealth and fame was his own private preserve.

"I could have Mallory talk to you if you like," said Riker, smiling amiably at this man whom he loathed.

"No, I don't—"

"No problem. It's her case. You just tell her why you want to take it away from her."

"Listen up, Riker, I don't—"

"Well, if it isn't the devil in drag. Here she comes now."

Palanski's eyes did a little dance, and his head snapped around to see what might be coming up behind him. Mallory was indeed walking toward them and growing larger in the reflection of Palanski's dark glasses. In place of her sheepskin jacket, a long black coat whipped around her heels. And, Riker noted, she was wearing her formal-wear black running shoes today.

What had Mallory done to Palanski? He must ask her sometime.

She was still advancing on them.

"Never mind," said Palanski, turning back to Riker. "I'll tell my captain you think it's tied to one of your operations. He'll buy that."

And Palanski had managed to get all of that out as Mallory came abreast of them and stalked past with only a nod to Riker, leaving behind a suggestion of eighty-dollar-an-ounce perfume. Palanski's head swiveled after her. When Mallory was four steps beyond them and her back safely turned, Palanski made the sign of the cross to ward off evil that could not be killed by bullets.

Mallory stopped suddenly, as though this little act of heresy had been spoken aloud. She turned on one heel to face the man down, and Palanski's finger froze at the last station of the cross.

Riker shook his head slowly. He had known Mallory for so long, and he knew her not at all. In her kiddy days, Markowitz had once described her as a short witch with the eyes of a mob hit man. All these years later, she still had the eyes of a killer. Innocent men, Jack Coffey among them, had stared into those eyes and thrown up their hands in surrender, assuming there must be a gun.

She only stared at Palanski for a moment before turning around and walking on, but his face paled as though she had found a way to suck the blood out of him without the necessity of sinking in her teeth.

Riker looked down at his own spread hand and wondered if a drink might stop that tremor.

Jack Coffey sat back and counted noses. Mallory was her punctual self, not a second before nor a second after the hour, and Dr. John J. Hafner was late.

"What have you got, Mallory?"

"Harry Kipling lied on his credit application at the bank. He's trying to get credit in his own name. The banks keep turning him down because he keeps lying."

"Everybody lies to banks. That's penny ante. What else have you got?"

"He lies on his tax returns. He files as an individual and not with his wife. IRS nailed him for an unreported income last year. And he has a growing stash of capital in a foreign bank."

Coffey covered his face with one hand. "I hope we're doing the background checks quietly?" Translation—*You steal the information, right? You never talk with humans, only machines, right?*

"Yeah, real quiet."

He had to wonder whose computer she was accessing now. Had she found the back door to Internal Revenue? He would never ask. It might come in handy one day. The ghost of Markowitz was laughing at him as he framed this thought.

150

Wasn't corruption just awfully damned easy when Mallory was involved?

"And the other suspects? What've you got now? Four altogether?"

"I'm down to maybe three. My perp is tall. Harry Kipling is six-one."

"I'm afraid to ask how tall the judge is."

"Six-three, and he's in the running."

"If you screw up with Judge Heart, you're going to be lying under an avalanche of influence and called-in favors, you know that. What have you got on him?"

"He beats his wife."

"Oh, great, just great. The President's hand-picked champion of women's rights. Shoot me, Mallory, shoot me now."

"Fits well, doesn't it?"

"If I may interject?" Dr. Hafner, the NYPD psychologist and the mayor's golf buddy, walked into the office with no knock and no apologies for the lateness.

Coffey glanced up at Hafner, who went everywhere with the same insipid smile that said, *I have all the answers and you don't.*

"A wife beater fits this case better than you know," said Hafner, unbuttoning his suit jacket and pulling on the legs of his pants, prelude to sitting down without creasing his expensive suit. The tailoring and material were only rivaled by Mallory's long coat and blazer.

Hafner's glasses were sliding down his nose; they always did that. Hafner was always pushing them up, always picking imaginary lint from his clothing and tapping his feet. And Coffey was always resisting the urge to lean across the desk

151

and swat the man each time he had to suffer one of these appointments.

How was he going to keep Hafner from annoying Mallory? How to get Mallory to play nice as long as the mayor's close friend was in the same room.

"The judge is a Supreme Court candidate," said Coffey, smiling pleasantly. "I don't want him to fit."

You useless, pompous little twit.

Hafner adjusted his glasses. "You will note that Amanda Bosch carried no purse, no wallet. I don't think it was stolen from the body. I've looked at the inventory of the apartment. Her credit cards and driver's license were lying loose in a drawer, and she had no purses whatever. Women usually own a number of purses, one for dress, one for—"

"Get to the point," said Mallory. It was an order.

Hafner pushed his glasses up, and the constant smile was even more patronizing, as though he thought this was an unruly child he was dealing with. "This lack of a purse is significant in the interpersonal dynamics of the relationship. People who don't carry identification on their persons lack identities of their own. A woman of low self-esteem would gravitate toward a man who was habitually abusive to women."

"According to Mrs. Farrow," said Mallory, leaning in for the first shot, "Bosch stopped carrying a purse after she was mugged three years ago. The robbery report is on the record. I sent it to you with all the rest of the paperwork. Do you read the reports we send you? And there are lots of women who prefer pockets to purses."

Coffey watched Hafner's eyes drop down to note that Mallory did not carry a purse. Now Hafner was scrutinizing her face, evaluating Mallory like a specimen. His eyes were gleaming, as though he had discovered a unique life form. He had.

"Dr. Hafner," said Coffey in his best damage-control tone, "Do you think he's likely to kill again?"

"Oh, definitely. He may have killed many times. We don't know that this is his first murder. I don't think he'll be able to stop himself."

Coffey was thinking, *Bullshit*, and Mallory's eyes were framing stronger language.

"Go on, Dr. Hafner," said Coffey.

You idiot, personal friend of the mayor or no.

"The immaculate condition of the apartment is an example of ritualistic, compulsive behavior, the ultimate cleansing. Such compulsively neat individuals always have severe personality disorders."

Coffey concentrated on Mallory. Her lips parted. For her, this was tantamount to an emotional outburst. And now he wondered what Hafner would make of Mallory's compulsively neat and well-ordered environs. The computer room was spotless and kept that way by a civilian keystroker who feared for his life if dust should settle on the computer equipment.

"So you think our man would fit the profile of a serial killer," said Coffey.

"Highly probable. And I would be very interested in the formative years of all the suspects." Hafner was staring at Mallory as he said this. "Was there trauma? Abuse? Abandonment? Maybe a history as a runaway."

Coffey sat back and studied Hafner. The man was just too damn fascinated by Mallory, openly examining her face as though gauging the effect of every word on her.

Hafner pushed his glasses up again. "The cleansing ritual may go hand in glove with compulsive punctuality."

Coffey leaned forward.

Punctuality? Where was that coming from?

Perhaps Hafner had seen Mallory's computer room after all, and more. Hafner could have accessed Mallory's psych evaluation, which had been mandatory following the discharge of a weapon in the line of duty. This was not about the suspect. This pumped-up twit thought he was going to play with Mallory, to bait her like a lab animal.

Coffey looked to Mallory's face, and he could see that everywhere he had gone with this idea, she had been there before him. Coffey sat well back in his chair and well out of the loop. Let the twit fend for himself. Whatever she did to Hafner, he had it coming. He communicated all of this to her with the slight inclination of his head.

Sick him, Mallory.

"Perhaps a visual aid would be useful," she said, her voice assuming the soft, deceptive notes of a civilized member of society.

Coffey watched her gun slide easily from the shoulder holster, and then he ceased to see it in the lacuna that was part of the cop's blue wall of silence. He was blind to the gun—no, the damn cannon, not a police-issue revolver, but something that made substantially bigger holes.

"Listen, fool," said Mallory, bringing her chair

154

closer to Hafner's, closing in for the kill, and not a neat kill either. The gun that Coffey could no longer see was in her hand.

"This was a spontaneous act," she said in even syllables. "The weapon was a rock. You had that information."

She raised the gun, touched the metal with one long red fingernail and the revolving chamber swung out of the armature. Her voice rolled on in velvet octaves which contrasted sharply with the deadly thing in her hands.

Hafner was a study in rigidity. A black fly whined past his head. He seemed not to notice. The glasses slid down his nose. He did not correct them.

"He didn't bring a weapon to the crime site," said Mallory. "He didn't plan to kill Bosch that morning. When he did kill her, he panicked and ran. It took him more than thirty minutes to get his nerve back. You would have known that if you'd read the ME note on the body being moved."

She emptied the bullets into her lap, and then inserted one bullet back into the gun and swung the chamber back into place with a click.

The fly landed on Hafner's cheek. He never moved to swat it, he never moved at all.

She smiled.

Coffey was fascinated by Hafner's new role as Mallory's mouse.

The fly whined off and landed on the wall beside Hafner's head.

"I figure he was more your type, Hafner— comfortable in a controlled situation. Prone to panic when things got out of his control. Like when he used that rock."

She pointed the gun at the fly crawling about on the wall; the barrel was aiming over the bridge of Hafner's nose.

She fired.

Hafner jerked backward. The click of the empty chamber had the effect of an exploded bomb. A wet stain was spreading out from his crotch. It took seconds for the man to adjust to the fact that he had not been hit and need not fall down, that he had merely wet his pants.

The fly was gone.

Coffey stared at the bare wall with wonder. Had the fly winged away, or was it lying at the baseboard, dead of a heart attack?

She dangled the gun for a moment and slowly brought it back to rest in her lap, the barrel carelessly pointing toward the sweating man in the chair close to hers.

Coffey could hear the man breathing. The glasses, greased with sweat, slid further down Hafner's nose, off his face and landed on the floor at his feet.

"He didn't stalk her—he knew her well," said Mallory. "That's why he came back to destroy her fingers, her prints. He figured it would buy him the time he needed to clean the apartment, to get rid of his own prints. A learning-disabled twelve-year-old could have worked that one out."

She leaned forward now, holding the gun casually, her arms propped on her knees. Her gun seemed only incidentally pointing toward the doctor's crotch.

"You're an inept jerk, aren't you, Hafner?" She was nodding her head slowly, and he mimicked the motion, nodding his own head in agreement. His eyes twitched back and forth between her face and her gun.

"And you're not going to submit a bill for this crap, are you?" She shook her head slowly from side to side, and in this way, she worked Hafner's head in the same motion.

"Good. You can go now."

Hafner never moved or blinked.

"Thank you for coming by, Dr. Hafner," said Coffey in the manner of a wake-up call, rising, dismissing the mayor's close personal friend. He was averting his eyes from the dark stain on Hafner's trousers. He was not seeing the gun, which he had never seen, sliding back into the holster.

Now Coffey was smiling at Hafner's back. Mallory was going to get clean away with this. What were the odds that Hafner would ever tell anyone she had made him pee in his pants?

The man was not quite out the door when Mallory was rising to her feet saying, "I'm getting my own shrink. The department's paying for it with what I just saved you on that idiot."

"Sit down. I'm not done with you yet." Before she could give him any grief, Coffey said, "I don't care what kind of a busy day you have planned. Sit!"

She sat.

He had learned a lot from Riker. Anything passing for a polite request would have been considered a sign of weakness.

"Let's start with the cap gun Heller found in the trash. If it's tied to the perp, then he might have premeditated the act. It's possible he used it to threaten her into a private location to kill her."

"It was a—"

"Shut up, Mallory. You only take the bits and pieces that support your pet theory. You can't know for a fact that he didn't plan to kill her. The real facts are barer bones."

"Hafner doesn't know—"

"I have no use for Hafner. I'll sign off on your own shrink. But you open up to the possibility that the perp planned the kill, and maybe he's killed before. And what about motive? She caught him out in some kind of a scam? Is that the story you want me to take to the district attorney?"

"She was a researcher. If you've got the skills to check out the father of your baby, you do it. She got something on him. If she could find it, I can find it."

"You don't even know that he was the father of the baby. You see what you're doing?"

No, she didn't see, didn't hear. He was talking to the air.

"You underestimate a perp and you're dead. You're hanging out there on your own." And that took guts, or maybe not. Perhaps she was merely fearless, and it was that which would get her killed—the lack of a healthy sense of fear.

"Are we done?"

"No, there's just one more thing. Be careful you don't shake out the wrong tree, Mallory. You may have more than one of them coming after you. I can see the lawsuits piling up now."

Charles sat back in his chair and waited out the family ritual of Robert Riccalo admonishing the boy and the woman.

He didn't like Riccalo.

The man craved a spotlight and a stage so he

could strut up and down all morning and display his mind, his maleness, his ruthlessness. And then, after lunch, he would want to rule the world. The man's eyes were black water. God only knew what was really under the surface, and God had probably shuddered and looked away quickly, only checking briefly to maintain His reputation for omniscience.

Now the man was leaning close to Justin, denying the child any possession of personal space. The boy turned to the woman. No help there. Sally Riccalo always avoided looking directly at Justin. And that was interesting.

"Justin, this nonsense will end!" the man was saying, booming, threatening.

The cat was backing away to a corner of the room. Nose didn't like Robert Riccalo either. Charles smiled at Justin, and the boy seemed to take a little heart from that.

Mallory walked in, and all conversation stopped. The cat trotted up to her, eyes fixed on the one it clearly adored.

Mallory cut the small animal dead with a look. In tacit understanding, the cat backed up a few steps to sit down and love her from a safe distance. The purr was audible all over the room.

The purring stopped when the square wooden pencil caddy on the desk began to rock. The cat was under the couch before the caddy fell over on its side. A fury of color flushed Robert Riccalo's face. His hand gripped his son's arm, and the boy winced with the pain.

"Not so fast," said Mallory, walking over to the desk. It was a command, and Riccalo seemed stunned to see his hand obey her, as it released the boy's arm and fell back to his lap.

Mallory picked up the pencil caddy and righted it. "We're accustomed to objects flying around the office. Aren't we, Charles?"

And now a pencil came flying out of the caddy and aimed at Charles's throat. Mallory's hand shot out and intercepted it.

Charles swallowed. "Well, some of us are more accustomed to that sort of thing than others." Oh, fine. Now Mallory had added flying pencils to her private arsenal.

"It happens all the time." Mallory was staring at the boy, who only showed curiosity. She walked behind Charles's chair and another pencil flew out of the caddy and neatly into her hand. "Nothing to it."

The boy was showing no reaction anymore. Apparently he had grown bored with airborne pencils.

"So it *is* a trick!" said Riccalo, turning on the boy with a look which promised something nasty when they were alone again.

"Not necessarily," said Charles. "But you see, so many things in the area of psychokinetics can be duplicated with illusion. That's why it's so difficult to test for a gift. It's going to take a while is all my partner meant by that demonstration."

He looked up to Mallory, willing her to nod and smile in agreement. *Fat chance,* said her eyes. He turned back to Riccalo. "We're looking for something we can test. Come back after Christmas, and we'll get into this in more detail."

When goodbyes were said, a new date set, and the Riccalo family was through the door and gone, Charles turned around to find Mallory standing close behind him. And this was another trick of hers that unsettled him. There was never any warning noise of footfalls. Sometimes he wondered if she just liked to see him jump outside his skin for a second or two. Nose trotted into the room to sit at her feet. When Mallory was around, he could at least keep track of the cat by the purring.

Mallory ignored the sound of the small, contented engine, and settled into a wing-back chair with dancing Queen Anne legs. She nodded to the couch, beckoning Charles to sit down with her. "Aren't you going to ask me how I made the pencil fly?"

"No, let me guess, all right?" He was smiling as he sat down. "Every now and then I see a street vendor who still sells the Wonder Widow, a black rubber spider on a nearly invisible nylon string. When the vendor works the string, it looks like the spider is crawling along by itself. When a large crowd gathers, he makes the spider fly to the face of a victim, who invariably screams and then buys ten of them. Did you ever have a spider like that?"

Mallory nodded. "Riker gave me one when I was a kid. He said it was a souvenir from his last round of the DTs. And if I liked that one, he knew where he could get a million more."

"So you took a nylon thread from a stocking, attached it to something sticky, but not too sticky—maybe a small bit of tape dusted with lint or talc. Then you attached this sticky sliver of tape to the pencil. When you jerked the thread, the pencil was aloft and the sliver of tape came loose. So whoever picked up the pencil would find no evidence of the method. You maneuvered the direction of the pencil by angling the thread around my chair."

"Right. So now at least we know how it's being done. A kid could do it."

"Mallory, you'd make a terrible paranormal investigator. When I accepted the case, I let go of my preconceptions. Just because you duplicated the flying pencil, that doesn't mean that was how it was done. This type of investigation must be conducted by gathering facts, and with no preconceived ideas about guilt or method."

"You'd make a bad cop, Charles. While you're dicking around with empirical evidence, someone is going to get hurt or dead."

"Now you see, you're doing it again. You develop a hunch and hang the evidence. Damn anyone who gets between you and your preconceived solution."

Charles watched the cat curl up in a patch of sunlight at her feet. "However, you're probably right about one thing. There's an unhealthy dynamic in that family. I have no idea which one of them is doing it."

"Well, yesterday the pencil flew at the stepmother. That's something."

"It is easiest to make the pencil fly in your own direction, isn't it?" Though Mallory had rather neatly sent a pencil toward his own throat.

"I wouldn't rule out the stepmother. But with two women down, it seems more likely that she's the new target. Either that or she wants to frame the boy."

"But for what reason? What a mess."

"What are you complaining about? You started out with a set of suspects and a walking, talking victim. I had to work at the park murder."

"Solved it yet?"

"Yeah, right," she said, rising to a stand and

placing one hand on the hip of the blue jeans, the soft material of the blazer falling back from the gun. "When is Henrietta coming?"

Before he could respond, the cat stood up on its hind legs. Charles watched Nose turn gracefully in a perfect circle, and then another. From Mallory's expression, he gathered she had seen this trick before.

"I think you're supposed to give Nose a reward when he dances. He might have been trained that way. The dancing is in the novel."

He walked over to the reception room desk, pulled the thick manuscript from the center drawer and quickly thumbed through the first chapter. "Here—'He taught my cat to dance.' Seems he did that during a four-day weekend, early on in the relationship. You can't take a work of fiction literally, of course. But the cat does dance."

"Four days? I thought it took longer to teach an animal tricks. Especially a cat."

"Not if you know what you're doing and you don't mind being ruthless with the animal. I expect he withheld food from Nose."

Mallory turned her back on the cat, which was dancing still. "Well, he doesn't have to do that for food anymore."

The cat dropped softly to ground, as though she had commanded him.

"So, Mallory, you were also right about the manuscript. It's a matter of weeding the truth out of the fiction. Listen to this:

'When New York is covered with snow, it's beautiful for all the minutes before you're mugged, shot in the crossfire of a drug war, run down by a drunk, attacked by a psychotic who

163

has forgotten to take his medication, sued by your landlord, threatened by the tax collector, bullied by the mouthy neighbor, bitten by the pet pit bull, surprised by rats running across your path with full-grown house cats clenched in their teeth, divebombed by pigeons, infested with mice and roaches, shorted by a payroll clerk. . . . When the baby comes, I will take her away from here to a safe place where it's beautiful all the time.'

"The baby is in the last few chapters of the book. The female character doesn't seem to have any emotional involvement with the man. The child is everything to her, all she cares about."

Mallory nodded. "The baby might argue for Harry Kipling or Judge Heart. They're both fertile. Maybe I should scratch the blind man off the list."

"You're not serious? A blind man?"

"He was blinded on the job. He was working for a newspaper then—huge settlement."

"I understand your love of the money motive." For this was her father's influence at work on her; Markowitz had loved this motive best. "But the man is *blind*."

"Charles, I always took you for the politically correct type. I hope you're not suggesting that blind people are too handicapped to kill right along with the rest of us."

"A blind man would never have returned to the crime scene. He'd have no way to know who might be watching."

"Suppose he panicked and did the murder, and then an accomplice came back and cleaned up after him?"

"Seriously?"

"No. I don't think a blind man did this. You're

164

an expert on gifts. Tell me about the gifts that come out when a man loses his sight."

"Oh, that's a myth," said Charles. "The blind do not have more acute senses of smell and hearing, if that's what you mean. They merely have fewer distractions without the sense of sight. And there's more dependence on the other senses, so they tend to pay more attention to them. Does he have a Seeing Eye dog?"

"Yes. Everyone in that building has a dog."

"It is true that blind people are less likely to walk into plate-glass walls—the cane or the dog prevents that. A good dog will also watch traffic and lead the blind away from obstacles. The dog is the truly gifted partner in the relationship."

"What about a really good adaptation to blindness?"

"Well, some people do make an art form out of it. They look directly at you when you speak to them, trying to create the illusion of being sighted."

"Eric Franz doesn't do that. But he does come across as the bastard child of Sherlock Holmes and Mrs. Ortega with his *acute* senses bullshit. And he can find his way across a crowded room without touching anyone with his cane."

"Interesting."

"I think so. So I'm keeping him. Now I've got a blind man, a wife beater, and a beauty-and-the-beast combo."

Charles stared at his hands. He had his own beauty-and-the-beast problems. He looked up to the antique mirror by the couch. No, his own story would be beauty and the clown. Her reflection moved behind his own. That incredible face did not belong in the same gilded frame with his own ridiculous ensemble of features. And if he didn't get to the barber soon, his longish wavy hair might take on the character of a clown's fright wig.

He turned to face her, and waved one hand toward the door near her chair. "Would you mind opening the door for Henrietta?"

And only now, the buzzer sounded.

Mallory stared at him. "One day, you must tell me how you do that."

"When Henrietta's working, she's nearly as punctual as you are. She's joining us for lunch."

Mallory opened the door to the psychiatrist from apartment 3A. Today Henrietta was dressed in her work clothes, a neat tailored suit and soft pastel blouse.

Charles left them to their business of the park murder and wandered into the kitchen. The cat followed him, knowing this was the place from whence all food flowed. Mallory had stocked the office refrigerator anew with all the makings of sandwiches. He pulled out a tray neatly prepared with every imaginable condiment, cheese and meat.

Henrietta walked into the kitchen as he was bending down to feed the cat a piece of pastrami. In the last twenty-four hours, he had learned a lot about the cat's likes and dislikes.

"Hey, Nose, how are you?" asked Henrietta.

Charles looked up. The cat did not.

Ten minutes later, Charles and Henrietta were seated at the kitchen table, drinking coffee to the music of purring which originated at Mallory's feet. Mallory stood at the chopping block on the counter, slicing cheese. She looked down at the cat and seemed to be weighing the knife in her hand against the cat's potential value.

Charles turned to Henrietta and asked, "Can you explain why the cat is so attached to Mallory? Nose won't dance for me, and I'm the one who's been feeding him."

"Does the novel tell you how the cat was trained?"

"No. I just assumed it was food."

"Nose may have been trained with pain, and it could also be tied to visual cues. What happened to the cat's ear?"

"I didn't do it," said Mallory, setting a plate of four varieties of cheese on the table alongside the rest of the sandwich makings. "It happened when Nose was loose on the street. The vet said the cat was otherwise well cared for."

Charles nodded. "If the female character in the novel is Amanda Bosch, I don't see her allowing the cat to be tortured."

"Her lover trained the cat to dance in four days," said Mallory.

"*If* we can believe the novel," said Charles, to his immediate regret. Mallory didn't like that. He could feel the tension crawling toward him from her side of the table. He filled Henrietta's coffee cup. "The novel was started over a year ago. Signs of abuse might be gone by now."

"Then most likely the cat dances to avoid pain." Henrietta was loading her sandwich with pastrami. "It's like child abuse. The child may cling to the abusive parent. That's why I wondered about the cat's ear. Mallory bears a general resemblance to the victim. She's probably triggering a memory."

Charles took a string of beef from his own

sandwich and dropped it into Nose's open mouth. "But surely the cat knows its owner from Mallory." The cat returned to its steady occupation of shedding fur on Mallory's jeans.

"Animals can respond strongly to visual cues," said Henrietta. "I got my own cat from an animal shelter. I was walking by the cage and the cat went berserk, paws reaching through the wire, crying nonstop. They told me the cat did that every time a woman with long dark hair walked by. So I went there for a dog and came home with a cat. It was instant love. Same as with Mallory and Nose."

"What else is in the novel?" Mallory asked, pushing the cat away from her with one leg, love apparently always being one-sided with her.

"Nothing that would isolate one of your three suspects," said Charles. "He doesn't particularly like women, though he likes to make love to them. I don't suppose that helps much. I have no idea what the lie might have been. There's no clue in the manuscript."

"All three of the suspects could fit the profile of liars," said Mallory. "And they've all got something at stake. Judge Heart has a career to consider. Other nominations have failed because of reefers and illegal nannies. If she dug up something in his background, it wouldn't have to be much to cost him the appointment. Harry Kipling has a rich wife and a brutal prenuptial agreement. Eric Franz was with his wife the night she was killed in a traffic accident. He might have had something to do with that."

"So what have we got?" asked Charles. "A novel we can't use in court and no physical evidence. There was nothing else turned up at the park site?"

"Heller's the best. If he can't find another forensic detail, no one can."

"Well, there's the cat", said Charles. "But unless you think we can train Nose to bite the suspect on the leg in open court, the cat is worthless."

"No it isn't." Mallory was staring down at the animal with an expression that gave her nothing in common with animal lovers. "I can use the cat and the book to flush him out. The tricky part is where I get him to incriminate himself."

"Any confrontation with this man is dangerous to you," said Henrietta. "If your theory is correct, he's demonstrated his willingness to kill in order to protect himself."

Mallory seemed unimpressed. "So? The perp I'm dealing with doesn't have the nerve of the average psycho. It was a one-shot crime to cover another crime—all fear and panic."

"You can't know that," said Henrietta. "It doesn't matter that the murder wasn't premeditated. He may have killed her a thousand times in his fantasies. He may be someone who knows her only as a service person, a maintenance man. And you can't tell a sociopath from his appearance or public behavior. This man may very well have a dangerous pathology and still pass for a normal member of the community."

"A sociopath can't pass for normal, not with everyone."

"Well, yes he can," Henrietta said with rare insistence.

"No," said Mallory, with finality. "He can't."

Charles watched the sudden shock of understanding come into Henrietta's eyes as she realized she was talking to someone with an inside view.

"So now that we've established what he isn't," said Mallory. "How much weight can I put on a lie as motivation? If I went into the lives of all the tenants in that building, I could dig up something on every one of them. What kind of lie pushes that kind of button? He panicked once. I want to make him do it again."

"It would depend on the lie," said Henrietta. "A person's entire life can be structured on lies."

"What kind of buttons should I push? How do I scare him into talking?"

"Fear might make him close up. Better to get him angry. A disclosure in anger is worth more. If we can assume he taught the cat to dance, we might consider control issues here. It's the fount of the hatred of women and the most violent crimes against them. In that case, getting caught in any lie might have set him off. Which one would you say was most prone to lying as a pathology?"

"Everybody lies," said Mallory.

"Surely not everyone," said Charles.

"No, Charles. You don't. But then you can't lie, can you? You don't have the face for it. Wait, I take that back. There's the vase you rigged. That's a lie by omission, isn't it?"

"It's a common test situation."

"And?"

"A lie by omission. I'll bet Helen never lied."

"Well, Helen only lied out of kindness, but she was kind to a lot of people."

"Markowitz never lied."

"Oh sure he did. He lied like crazy. The old

man was the best. I've heard him lie to the mayor, the commissioner. He lied every time he held a press conference. He lied—"

"All right. Everybody lies."

As she carried the cat down the sidewalk between the garage and the Coventry Arms, she caught sight of the doorman reading the newspaper. A cab pulled up, and Arthur quickly removed his glasses, tucking them into the fold of the paper which lay on the shelf beneath the house phone. Arthur was smiling and opening the door of the cab when Mallory slipped through the door. As she passed by that shelf, she flipped back the fold of the paper.

Bifocals. An ugly little man who was too vain to wear his glasses in front of the tenants. Interesting.

She walked over to the wide lobby window which overlooked the sidewalk. Another tenant was walking toward the building. As Moss White, the talk show host, came abreast of the bench twelve feet before the door to the building, Arthur put on his wide smile.

Well, at least the man's field of vision included the bench where Amanda had been sitting the day before she died.

Thoughts of Amanda Bosch rode up in the elevator with Mallory. What had the woman seen that day? What had upset her and made her run off? And how much value could she put on Arthur's testimony if she needed him in court? She and Arthur must have another little chat, and soon.

When she walked in the door of the Rosens' apartment, she had the feeling that there was someone else close by. Nose felt it too. The cat in her arms ceased to purr. It was kneading its clawless paws into her coat, looking everywhere.

Something in the bedroom was being moved. Now she heard the sound of the vacuum. She walked into the room to see the cleaning woman who must be the Rosens' Sarah.

"Oh, hello, miss." The woman switched off the vacuum, and now Mallory heard the sound of the flushing toilet in the bathroom. The door opened, and Justin Riccalo was standing on the threshold and looking up at her. He began a small smile; it died off as Mallory turned her back on him to face the cleaning woman.

"I hope it's all right, miss," said Sarah. "He was standing out in the hall waiting for you. He needed to use the bathroom. It is all right, isn't it?"

"Sure." Now she looked at the boy again. Lately, he was always in her mind on some level. She felt a tie to him without being able to name it, as though they had been through something together. It nagged at her, this feeling that occurred each time they met—a bizarre and twisted notion approaching déjà vu. She knew where he had been, for she been there before him.

"Well, I'm done in this room," said Sarah, coiling the cord around her vacuum cleaner. Mallory and the boy continued to stare at one another in silence until the cleaning woman had shown herself out of the bedroom.

"How did you get past the doorman, Justin?"

"I walked in behind a man and a woman. I guess the doorman thought I belonged to them."

"How did you know I lived here?"

"I looked it up in the phone book."

No, said the slow shake of her head, *that could not be.*

The vacuum cleaner began to drone and toil across the carpet of the front room.

"Okay, I was with my stepmother when she followed you the other day."

"So that was you." She had felt him but not seen him. The stepmother had not explained the watcher who had occupied the space on the opposite sidewalk, a space which had been empty by the time she had turned round.

"I gave the elevator man your name, and he took me to this floor. I ran into the cleaning woman in the hall. She was just going into your apartment. I told her you were expecting me."

Now he seemed to be waiting for praise. She let him wait.

He jammed his hands into his down parka and rocked on the balls of his feet as he looked around the bedroom with its frilly four-poster canopy bed, the chintz and the bric-a-brac. "It's not what I expected of you."

All his confidence ebbed away in the ensuing silence.

Mallory was listening to the hum of Sarah's vacuum cleaner. Mrs. Ortega always cleaned one room at a time, and the front room already had the furniture-polish and ammonia smell of a finished job.

The boy opened his mouth to speak. Mallory moved one finger up to silence him. He closed his mouth and turned to the sound of the vacuum in the next room.

When the vacuum stopped and the front door finally closed on the departing Sarah, he said,

173

"I've got to talk to someone, but no one will listen to me."

"I'll listen if you're straight with me. Has your stepmother missed any nylon stockings recently?"

"How did you know?"

"Did she accuse you of taking it?"

"Not yet. I found a mangled stocking wadded up in my dresser this morning. I didn't take it, and I don't know how it got there."

What was the connection she felt to the boy? Something old. Half a memory. He was a liar—that might be part of it.

"When you're ready to tell me the truth about what's going on, I'll help you."

"You think I'm making the pencils fly, you and everyone else. Why? What do you really know about me? Nothing. Only what my father tells you."

"Oh, I know a lot about you, Justin. I know you're smart enough to figure out how the tricks are done. But you won't tell, will you? Either you do the tricks yourself, or you're afraid of your father, or both. Or maybe your stepmother is doing it. Maybe you keep quiet about it because you like the idea of driving your old man straight up a wall."

She looked at his clothes and his unmarred pink face, his unskinned knees. His running shoes were not new, but they weren't dirty, either.

"You're a loner. You have no friends, no sports to play."

He stood very straight, shoulders pinned back.

"You attended a military school." Good guess. His head was nodding. "And you're holding out on me. If these stunts with the flying objects are your doing, I'm gonna find you out. You got that?''

"What reason would I have to do it? You don't know everything. You don't know that all my mother's money—"

"—was left to you in trust. And your father controls the trust."

"He controls me, too."

"So you're ratting out your father, is that it? You know, if I'd been in your place, I would have targeted your old man. That bastard wouldn't have lasted six seconds with me."

"He *is* a bastard. I really worry about my step-mother."

Mallory only stared at him in silence to tell him she knew he was lying again.

"Okay," said the boy. "She's a dweeb."

"What was your real mother like?"

"She was like my second mother, and my second mother was like my third. She was afraid of everyone and everything. My father has a type. Each one is just a copy of the last one."

"Was your real mother afraid of you too?"

The boy's hands dove deeper into the pockets of his parka. She watched the frustration welling up in his eyes, and it was in the hunch of his shoulders and the rabbit teeth pressed down on his lower lip—frustration growing and growing, finally culminating and escaping in a sigh.

The cat padded into the room. It started toward her. She looked at it once to warn it away. Nose stopped a respectful distance from her and sat down beside the boy. Now two pairs of eyes were on her, both needy.

"Don't let the cat out when you go," she said, and turned her back on both of them, leaving the bedroom to walk down the short hallway to the den where her computer was waiting.

Too bad the cameras hadn't been running. Maybe she should run a continuous tape against the possibility of another intrusion when she was not home.

The front door closed softly.

"Charles, let me fix you a drink. No, really. Have one with me."

Effrim Wilde opened the dark glass doors of a chrome-trimmed cabinet to gleaming glassware and a fully stocked wet bar. "Eleanor's forbidden me to drink alone. She says it leads to alcoholism."

He turned his back on Charles as though the recipe for whiskey and soda might be worth guarding.

"Eleanor came back?"

"Yes," said Effrim, rimming each glass with a twist of lemon and a loving smile. "She felt guilty about abandoning me to my cigarettes and whiskey and good food. She's a saint, that woman. This past weekend, I didn't have a single meal that didn't taste like low-cal library paste."

He handed one glass to Charles and carried the other to his own chair, which put three yards of plush carpet and four feet of dark glass desktop between them.

The office had been recently redecorated. The walls were a sickly yellow green. How did Effrim stand it? Of course, he only spent a few hours of the day in this place. The rest of the time was spent in three-hour lunch seductions of grant committee chairmen and other sources of funding. The lines of the furniture were sharp.

Every surface was cold metal and glass. The four wall hangings, all done by the same brutal hand, were abstracts of angry red shapes and a nervous, manic energy of black lines. Not Effrim's style. This private office said more about Eleanor than Effrim.

"Does Eleanor know you're dabbling in bad magic acts?"

"So you pegged the boy for a fraud?" Effrim feigned surprise, but not well. "I hope the experience hasn't been entirely worthless."

"It's not entirely done with. I need some data from the research group."

"Ask my assistant. He'll get you whatever you need. I suppose you're shopping for a little something in the line of flying objects? You were right about the Russian data and the Chinese. Their methodology is a bit lax, isn't it?"

"I want the Chinese data on the succubus experiments."

"Is the boy branching out?"

"No, but he's led me along another line of investigation."

"I thought you were put off by the bizarre stuff. Anything in particular?"

Charles's memory called up a page from a journal and displayed it on the wall by Effrim's head. He scanned the lines. "There's an experiment with an Asian monk who created a succubus under lab conditions. I want that one. His profile fits the stigmatic. The succubus, in front of witnesses, was seen to bruise the man's flesh."

"Come back to work for me and I'll get you all the cuckoo material you like."

"You still get the lion's share of funding from sources like Riccalo's employers? In addition to sitting on grant committees, Mallory tells me his other duties include real estate scams which bilk the elderly."

"Ah, but no arrests, indictments, or convictions. By New York standards, this makes him a model citizen. Oh, Charles, we just never seem to agree on the Institute's funding, do we? I'm stealing money from the bastard's company. I should get a community-service medal. But I can be flexible. Come back to work for us, and I'll track down alternate funding."

"Thanks, I think I'll just take the succubus material and run."

"You're losing your mind out there among the tiny brains. But I'd be willing to trade any four good brains at the Institute for what's left of yours. Come home, Charles. Come back inside where you belong. I'll triple your project funding."

"I don't think so."

"It's cold out there, Charles."

By "out there," Effrim included all of real life beyond the isolation of the think tank. Charles surmised that Effrim had daily anticipated his prize freak would return home, beaten by the ordeal of making his way among people who found him eccentric and out of sync with the rest of them—which he was.

"Will we be able to give a good report to the boy's father?"

"The boy's father could very well be orchestrating this. I don't trust Riccalo. And I have my doubts about you, too."

An hour later, Charles was seated in his own front room and closing the file of succubus material. So it was true; there was a link to the stigmata phenomenon exhibited by fanatics. The mental aberration of the succubus could work its effects on the body as well as the mind.

In the darkening room, a memory from his childhood came back to him in striking detail which included the succulent brown flesh of a roasted fowl. It was a goose, and it held a prominent position on the white lace tablecloth spread with fine china, gleaming silver and candlelight. Malakhai was seated at the dinner table beside the empty chair which belonged to Louisa. The adults had been drinking wine and laughing with one another, accompanied by a lively recording of Mozart. The small child he had been was staring at Malakhai in the moment when Louisa kissed him. He had seen the imprint of her lips on the man's face. Charles had rubbed his eyes with small hands, but not rubbed away the kiss which made the depression, the contour of her lips in Malakhai's flesh.

Well, Amanda Bosch had created no physical phenomena yet. She was merely an image like a holograph. So he had a ways to go before he became truly damaged. Amanda was not solid stuff, and he was not yet mad. He'd only made a clever moving picture, an odd extension of his eidetic memory.

Right.

The red light was flashing on the system alert box. So the judge was using his fax. The rewiring diverted the fax to her own machine. It was an application form for a new bank card. She scanned it into her computer and reset the type with a few alterations. After the lines for name and address, she typed in her own questions.

179

Then she copied the letter for Harry Kipling, who also had a fax machine.

Now that she was getting to know them, she could tailor the terror to fit the man. What should she do to the blind man? According to the building super, his computer was rigged for a braille printer, but did he use it? She typed his message into the personal files: I'M RIGHT BEHIND YOU. CAN YOU HEAR ME? CAN YOU SEE ME? CAN YOU SEE?

The purring at her feet annoyed her. She looked down at the cat, her eyes matching threats with the cat's contented slits. And now a crash came from the kitchen. She felt for her gun, and the cat's nose went up as it tested the air for what it could not see.

Gun drawn, Mallory walked into the kitchen and found the floor near the table littered with shatters and sparkles of glass and water. She checked every closet and room and then returned to the kitchen. She felt along every wet inch of the tabletop, searching for any small object which might do the job of the wooden match Charles had used to prime the vase in his office. There was nothing.

Well, the boy was smart, but not supernatural. So, the glass had simply fallen.

The unbeliever knelt down to the tiles with a dustpan and swept up the glass, and then mopped the floor and carefully wrapped the shards of the glass in plastic.

A barrage of soft thuds came from the next room. When she walked in, the cat's body was arched, ears flattened, eyes round. It had knocked the bowl of fruit onto the carpet. An apple was rolling toward Nose, and the cat was backing up on tender feet as though the carpet might be on fire. Mallory snapped her fingers at the cat to get its attention. The cat ran the length of the room and leapt into her arms.

Another trick?

She put the cat down again and snapped her fingers once more. And the cat was in her arms.

What else can you do?

She dropped the cat, and crawled along the carpet, picking up the fallen fruit. The cat stayed beside her, loving up against her, mewling for some small attention, anything at all.

Mallory poured the wax fruit back into the bowl. Nose licked her hand, and she drew it back. Now she scanned the carpet and its recent proliferation of white cat hairs.

House-proud Helen Markowitz would never have allowed an animal in the house, yet she had fed every stray that came through the yard. And for ten days of winter, a mongrel had lived in their garage, lapping up leftovers and licking Helen's hand and adoring her with its great brown eyes.

Helen had shown young Kathy each scar of abuse on the animal's pelt. *You can learn a lot about people from their animals,* said Helen. She had learned so much about the mongrel's owner that she made no attempt to find him. Helen lost the tag on the dog collar and found another home for the animal with a family on the next block.

It's not the dog who is lost, Helen had said. *The one who abused this animal is lost.*

Helen had never used the words of Kathy and Markowitz's shared vocabulary: dirtball, scumbag, scum-sucker. The bastard who had split the dog's pelt with kicks and broken its ribs, he was only *lost* to Helen.

Everyone has a dark side, Helen told her. *When the dark kills off all the light of the soul, this is a lost person.*

Small Kathy had figured, *Naw, he's a scumbag*, and she knew the dog's former owner deserved a few kicks to his own ribs. Her young sense of justice was very dark, and it had an elegant simplicity that was not much changed over the years. But for Helen's sake, she had tried to behave as though the light shone for her, too.

Mallory reached out one hand and gently stroked the cat's head. Helen would've liked that.

The cat closed its eyes in contentment.

Duty done, she quickly withdrew her hand, wiped it on the leg of her jeans, and left the cat sitting in the middle of the living room, its eyes wide open now and looking everywhere for the vanished Mallory.

The Amanda Bosch file had an honored place in the top layer of the mess on Riker's desk. He was fumbling through the contents of a lower drawer, fingers grasping what he thought were recent park-site photos. But he had gone too far in his haphazard method of filing, and now he held the snapshots he had taken at Kathy's graduation from the police academy.

There was Helen Markowitz, smiling broadly, not realizing the cancer in her body was already planning to cut her life short in one more year. Markowitz had never really recovered from the loss. If not for Kathy, he might have followed Helen years sooner.

It had always angered Riker to think back on Helen's death and how quietly she had gone to it, sedated, unprotesting. The hospital gurney wheels had whispered Markowitz's wife into that sterile operating room, and only the body had come wheeling back to them. She had slipped under the surgeon's knife and slipped away.

There should have been more noise to mark the event. In low tones, the doctor had told Markowitz and Kathy how sorry he was. Unspoken were the words *The show's over*. And so Markowitz and Kathy had sat together on a cheap plastic couch in the terrible silence of that waiting room, two unimportant people in the aftermath of an event which had not been properly called to an end. It was a play which tapered off to a mumble and had no curtain to tell the audience it was time to go home.

Riker understood what Kathy had meant when she turned to him then and said, "This is a rip-off." It was.

Now someone was standing before Riker's desk, not wanting to interrupt a thought, only politely waiting with just the minimum of shuffling noise to announce himself.

Riker knew only one person who was that polite. It was no surprise to look up into the smiling face of Charles Butler. And this was another reminder of an old friend. Markowitz's smile had no such loony aspect, but, as with Charles, one tended to smile back, regardless of grim thoughts and small heartaches.

"Pull up a chair, Charles. You waiting around for Mallory?"

"No. Jack Coffey invited me in for a little chat about Amanda Bosch."

"He probably thinks Mallory's holding out on him. She probably is. But then, to be fair, Coffey holds out on Mallory, and I hold out on both of

183

them. We're a very dysfunctional family, we three. You didn't rat her out, did you?"

"Of course not."

So Mallory *was* holding out.

"What can I do for you, Charles?"

"Coffey tells me it was your idea to give this case to Mallory. May I ask why?"

"Because of Amanda Bosch. When a kid dies young like that one, there ought to be some fanfare, you know? Sicking Mallory on the perp was the worst thing I could think of doing to him."

"But it's dangerous."

"If she's right about him, she only has to flush him out. If she's wrong, she may have to shoot him."

"You're not worried about her?"

"No," he lied, because he really liked Charles.

"But the way she's going about it, she might as well—"

"We can't put anybody in jail without evidence. Sometimes we know who did it, and we can't touch him. People do get away with murder—I won't tell you how often, but it happens. Now I'm betting this bastard doesn't get away from Mallory. I've got a hundred bucks riding on the kid."

"But she's hanging out there like a target."

"She *is* a target—she's a cop. And she won't give it up, either. If you're thinking she'd be safer with you in civilian life, just get rid of that fairy tale. This job gives her a rush. Now she's got a lock on this case, and she's flying. And what can you offer her, Charles?"

"Nothing. I know that." Charles stared at his shoes for a moment. "But you're looking for court-supportable evidence against this man. Her methods aren't strictly within the law, are they?''

"I know she'll break rules to get him, and this is what I've come to. I'm following Markowitz down the slow path of corruption. I'm copping to it, okay? You can have me arrested for it.''

"Suppose she gets caught breaking the rules? What about her career then?''

"Charles, you must know how Markowitz used her. I know the old man liked you and he trusted you, but I don't think he shared much of the department dirt. If we did everything by the book, the results would look pretty poor. Mallory could get things for him, impossible things. He never asked how many laws she broke in a day. What she got by illegal means wasn't evidence, nothing admissible in court, but it was stuff Markowitz could use to finesse a perp into a nervous break-down. Mallory knows things about this killer. She has under-the-skin intimate knowledge. When she's done with him, he'll think she was there in his pocket when Amanda Bosch went down. Mallory will get him. I'm counting on it. She is a thing to behold.''

"She's a breakable human being like the rest of us.''

"Charles, we've all fallen into that trap. She's so young, isn't she? Just a kid. Of course you want to protect her. That perfect, unlined face— eyes like an angel.''

Charles was still nodding in agreement as Riker leaned forward and shook his arm to call him back to the real world, the scary one that Mallory inhabited.

Riker raised his voice to say, "She's got the coldest eyes I've ever seen. She gives normal people the shakes—even if they don't drink as much as I do. She packs a monster gun, and you don't. She's a great shot, and you probably couldn't load a gun without an owner's manual."

Now Riker leaned back in his chair and put his feet up on the desk as he watched Charles trying to make logic work in tandem with the blind psychosis of having fallen in love with Kathy Mallory. He'd had occasion to wonder if Mallory understood how Charles felt about her. He was inclined to think she knew it and used it.

In a softer voice, he said, "I'm glad you stopped by, Charles. I hope this little talk has put things into perspective."

As Charles pulled up in front of Robin Duffy's house, he nearly put the car up on the curb, so startled was he by the lights of the menorah and the Christmas tree in the house across the street. The former occupants of that house, Louis and Helen Markowitz, were dead.

Robin, his host for the evening, was standing in the warm light of an open doorway. Charles crunched new snow as he crossed the narrow band of earth that lined the recently shoveled sidewalk. He hurried up the flagstone path to the door, and his hand was grabbed in a warm handshake. Robin had been Louis's neighbor for more than twenty years.

Done with hellos, Charles turned round for a last look at the house of bright holiday lights.

Robin grinned. "Lifelike, isn't it?"

Together, they walked into the warmth of Robin's house, and the smells of pine needles warring with floral air freshner.

"I can't get Kathy to sell the place," Robin

was saying as Dr. Edward Slope stood up from the card table to clap Charles on the back.

"Kathy's the only Upper West Sider with a summer home in Brooklyn," said Edward. "I think she enjoys being perverse."

"But it's not like she ever uses the place," said Robin. "She never comes by anymore. So, I try to make it look like someone lives there. Lou put up a Christmas tree every year since Kathy came to live with them. It didn't seem right with no Christmas tree."

"A Hanukkah bush," Rabbi David Kaplan corrected him as he entered the room from the kitchen, carrying a tray of sandwich makings. "Louis swore to me it was a Hanukkah bush."

"It does make the house look like a family lives there," said Charles, staring out the wide window of the front room.

"I trimmed the tree with the original ornaments from that first Christmas," said Robin.

"And the ornaments Kathy stole from the department store?" asked Edward Slope as he cut the deck of cards.

"Well," said Robin, who had been Louis Markowitz's attorney as well as a friend, "Helen went back and paid for those, so technically—"

"Never mind," said Edward. "Pull up your chairs, gentlemen. Robin, tell him what else you did to the place."

The four were seated around the card table, picking up the dealt cards and swapping mustard for mayonnaise, passing around meats and pickles, slices of white bread and slices of rye. The caps of beer bottles were pinging off the tabletop as Robin delivered a lecture on the technical intricacies of electronic lighting devices.

"I bought timer lights for the lamps in all the rooms," said Robin as he threw down one card in hopes of drawing a better one. "The lights go off and on automatically at different times. I rigged the kitchen light to go off at seven forty-five. That's when Helen usually finished cleaning up."

"Robin's really into this," said the medical examiner, dealing out Robin's card and two for the rabbi. "The Harvard Law School graduate finally found a set of timer lights with directions he could understand."

"My favorite is the light that goes on in Louis's den after the evening news is over. It's that window under the gable," said Robin, pointing his beer bottle toward the picture window of his living room to indicate the dark gable of the house beyond the glass. Now he picked up his new card and fitted it into his hand.

Charles had no way to know if Robin had bettered his hand any. The man's face gave away nothing. Yet everyone seemed to know what was in his own hand. Edward laughed out loud when he raised the ante on a bluff. Folding his cards in humiliation, Charles stared out the window at the row of blinking colored lights which trimmed the porch roof of Louis Markowitz's house. "You know, for a moment I thought Mallory had done it."

"The lights? You mean as a gesture of sentiment?" Edward was studying Charles's face over the tops of his cards, perhaps checking for signs of a fever.

Charles nodded, and Edward looked to the ceiling. "Charles, I'm telling you this as a friend—you've got to let go of this strange idea

188

of the gunslinger with a heart of gold. I'm a doctor, you can trust me on this one. She has no detectable heartbeat."

"She loved Helen." Rabbi Kaplan perused his cards, and his sweet smile dissolved into the mask of the veteran poker player.

"Okay, you got me there. She even loved Louis in her bizarre way." Edward folded his cards.

"This speaks well for a heart," said the rabbi, laying down his cards next to Robin's splayed hand, and simultaneously raking in the first pot of the evening. "Robin, the electric menorah in the window was a nice touch."

Robin was dealing the next round of cards as Charles was asking, "Was she was raised in both religions?"

"Kathy has no religion," said Edward as he gathered up his cards. "We think she works for the opposition."

"The way you talk about her," said the rabbi. "She's not a criminal."

"The hell she isn't." Edward slammed his cards down on the table. "Now she thinks I'm going to steal for her. She wanted me to raid my investigator's personal notes and give them to Charles. Too many leaks in the department, she says. You know she's just bypassing Jack Coffey."

"Coffey should be grateful she works around him," said Robin. "If he learned anything from Markowitz, he'd never want to know what she was doing. You're doing him a favor."

Edward pulled a fold of papers out of his back pocket and pushed the wad across the table to Charles. "These are the investigator's notes. No police request would have turned them up. If an investigator gives his notes to a case detective, he can wind up spending a few days in court defending things that were just idle thoughts and speculations. It's a bit like reading a diary."

Charles was looking down on a straight flush. The other players followed Edward's suit and folded. How did they always know? The four quarters in the pot might represent his only win of the evening. "Did you find anything interesting?"

"Not really. She wanted a report on the death of Judge Heart's mother. I told her we don't send ME investigators for a natural death if a doctor's in attendance. She said look again. Turns out we did send a man out, but it was a mistake of an inexperienced dispatcher. I also found ER hospital records for injuries to the old woman. Two broken bones were set in a one-year period. Old bones break easily. There's nothing solid there. Tell her I'm not going to move for an exhumation on Judge Heart's mother until she gets real evidence of foul play. You tell her that, Charles."

Robin Duffy put an envelope on the table by Charles's hand. "That's the dirt on Eric Franz. It's a transcript of the court session for the traffic accident that killed his wife. The Franzes were having an argument at the time of the crash. But according to witnesses, he didn't help her into the path of the car, if that's Mallory's angle. He was at least three feet away from her throughout the argument and right up to the moment the car got her."

"I would have thought she'd be more interested in the accident that blinded Franz," said Charles.

"She was," said the doctor. "Eric Franz was blinded in an accident three years ago. The settlement was in seven figures. There was no apparent restoration of sight immediately following the corrective surgery, and he changed doctors before the next exam was scheduled. I have no idea who the new doctor was. His records were never forwarded."

"Is it possible that his sight was restored at some later date?"

"The surgeon gave an eighty/twenty possibility, but it wasn't in Eric Franz's favor."

"There wouldn't be much point in faking it," said Robin. "He was definitely blind when the court awarded the settlement. Even if the surgery had restored his sight, he would've kept the court award. And his wife's life insurance benefit was donated to charity. I'd say the guy is squeaky clean. I don't know where Kathy thinks she's going with this one."

"So, Charles," said Edward, "do you know why Kathy didn't drop by to pick up her own dirt?"

"She said she couldn't come tonight because she was barred from the poker game."

Edward smiled. "Is that the story she gave you? She's not here tonight because she wants to be legally one person removed from these records."

"Smart kid," said Robin with some amount of paternal pride. "She learned that trick from Markowitz. No time lost with warrants, no paper trail for opposing counsel to follow."

"But she *was* barred from the poker game, wasn't she?"

The other three players stared down at their cards. There were no volunteers.

"Why was she barred from the game?"

Robin raised his head. "I'm still holding a

grudge from her kiddy days. Markowitz used to bring her along if Helen was going out for the evening. The kid used to win so big Markowitz had to buy her a little red wagon to carry home all the loot."

The rabbi turned to Charles, "Her biggest win was thirty dollars in a penny-ante game. The legend grows."

Charles shuffled the deck and dealt the first card to Rabbi Kaplan. "What was the real reason, Rabbi?"

"Charles, such suspicions."

The second card was dealt to the doctor.

"I knew Mallory would be a bad influence on him."

And the third to the lawyer.

"She can't play. It's not fair. The little brat was born with a poker face."

Charles sat in polite silence, holding on to the rest of the cards and waiting on a better answer.

"Okay," said Robin. "Kathy was attending a private school, a girls' school with young ladies who had never played poker. Kathy taught them the game."

Charles dealt out the second round of cards.

"She was bringing home three bills a week when Helen and Lou were called in for a little chat with the principal," said Edward.

And now all the cards were in play.

"We thought it was great." Robin rearranged his hand. "The kid was champion poker material, and we took a lot of pride in that. But it upset Helen."

"And worse," said the rabbi, hardly looking at his cards.

Edward folded his hand and pushed the cards

to one side of the table. "Lou didn't want Kathy thrown out of school, so he took the fall for her. He told the principal it was a bad joke that had gotten out of hand, and Kathy couldn't be expected to understand that what she was doing was wrong after he'd put the idea in her head."

"Louis was a gifted liar," said Robin. "He was so good that Helen bought the lie. It was the only rift between Helen and Lou, ever. Kathy knew it was her fault, but she didn't understand why. And you know, it was a semihonest racket. It wasn't like she marked the cards or anything."

"She was just light-years ahead of every child she fleeced," said Edward. "You never knew Helen. You don't understand how it was between her and Lou. They held hands under the dinner table. They sat up and talked until two in the morning."

"So, suddenly," said the rabbi, "there's silence in the house. Helen believes that Louis had damaged Kathy. Louis was devastated, but he went on taking the blame for Kathy's racketeering. Kathy felt the rift between them, the terrible silence. She came so close to understanding the difference between right and wrong."

"But then it slipped away from her," said Edward.

"But she wouldn't play poker again," said the rabbi. "Kathy barred herself from the game. It was her version of penance."

"You credit her too much. She's a heartless little monster. She corrupts every—" Edward was interrupted by the loud jangle of the telephone.

Robin answered it and handed the receiver to

Edward. When the doctor put down the phone, he turned to Charles. "My wife says Kathy left a message on our answering machine. She'll pick up the folder herself."

"Kathy's coming here?"

"Yes."

"When?"

"Eight-thirty."

"It's five past that now," said Charles. "Odd, she's never late by even one minute."

"Oh, God, the lights!" said Robin. "Kathy doesn't know about the lights."

And she was never, never late. They turned in concert to the window. Mallory's small tan car was parked at the curb.

It was Edward Slope, her greatest detractor, who flew out the door, without his coat, to fetch her. He was down the flagstone path before the others could rise from the table.

Now three men congregated in the open doorway, unmindful of the chill night air. Charles stared at the back of the man running across the street.

Later it would hurt him to remember this small event with such great clarity. But there was a crystalline quality to a cold winter night. Even from the distance of a road's width, no detail was lost to him, not the line of her cheek, nor the lamplight on her hair, nor the terrible stillness, the eerie quiet broken only by the footfalls of the doctor.

There was Mallory, alone on a small field of new snow. But for the frost of her breath on the air, she was a statue in blue jeans, standing in the yard of the old house across the street. She was staring in the window at the Christmas tree and the menorah. And now her face turned upward as a window came to life on the second floor where Louis's den was.

Slope came up behind her and put his hands on her shoulders. His voice was low, near a whisper. She never moved nor spoke to him, but only stared at the second-floor window, so entranced was she by the light.

An ex-partner was like an ex-wife, even if the partner had been a man—which Peggy was not, most definitely not. He missed her sorely since her early retirement via a bullet in the lung. He missed her, though he saw her at least once a week as though a night in the bar were a sacrament.

Riker's eyes were on Peggy as she left him to run her white rag over the wet ring on the mahogany and pocket the change left by the last customer.

Age had hardly touched her, but only because she fought it off. Her hair was dyed a honey blond to cover the gray, and her figure was only a little fuller at the hip and thigh. In the dim light and from the distance of the other end of the bar, she had changed not at all.

Oh, all those years ago when she was young, and he was younger, when he was still sober most of the day, when Peggy packed a gun and a shield. Now that was a time.

The matron draped on the stool next to his might be the only civilian in the bar tonight. The woman had that soft look, and she was staring at him with the disapproving eye of a taxpayer. Even in peripheral, the civilian was annoying him with her waving arms. The woman was making a damn point of waving the smoke away from her, and she had to reach into Riker's own personal piece of the bar to do that.

"Did you know that secondhand smoke kills nonsmokers?"

"Good," said Riker.

The woman picked up her purse and moved to the other end of the bar, and Peggy came back to him with a broad smile and a fresh beer.

"So where were we, Riker?"

"The early warning signs."

"Right, the early warning is in the money area. That would be a natural for Mallory. Have her check the credit card accounts for favorite bars and restaurants. A gym membership is a good giveaway. They like to keep in shape for the new one. Is the guy buying his own underwear? Something with a little flash? That's another one."

"If there's so many signals, how come the wives don't catch on?"

"They do. The husbands aren't too quick to spot a cheating wife, but the wives always know what the husbands are doing. Even when they come in here and tell me that for years they had no idea. They knew what was going on—they knew from the beginning. It's the blind spot that won't let them acknowledge it. That damn blind spot. They're staring straight at it, they can describe everything around it, but they don't see it."

"Ah, Peggy. I can't buy—"

"They rationalize it away. The amount of rationalization these women do is in direct proportion to what they've got to lose. With no kids and no mortgage, a woman can be pretty cynical about a cheating husband. With eight kids, she will sit down with the man and help him work out the lies she can believe in."

Riker pulled out his notebook. A silver ornament on a chain was entangled in the spiral. It freed itself and dropped to the bar. Peggy picked it up. "So what's with the Star of David? You're an Episcopalian."

"No, I'm not. I'm an alcoholic."

"Ah, Riker, you're dreaming those social-climbing dreams again. If you want to be an alcoholic, you have to go to meetings." She handed him the six-pointed star.

"Okay, I'm a drunk with aspirations." He stared at the star in his hand. "Lou Markowitz used to carry this around with him. Mallory thought I might like to have it."

"You sentimental slob."

"That's what Mallory calls me, but she doesn't think I'm sentimental." His pen hovered over the notebook. "Okay, markers for the runaround husband. Suppose he's not a regular cheat, suppose it's a first-time fling?"

"He'll start changing his habits. Maybe he walks the dog without being asked four times. Or he takes up a new sport for two—like tennis. Look for out-of-town trips that don't match up with his job description, late hours at the office as a change in routine."

"Is he a good liar?"

"Oh, they all think they're great liars, but the wives have probably caught them in more lies than they can remember. It's a pity you can't just ask the wives. And a pity that most of them wouldn't tell you."

In Riker's notebook, it said only "dog walking."

"So, Riker, you think Mallory's right about the perp? He panicked and ran?"

"I think she underestimates him. She thinks the guy is a wimp who'd run if a mouse screamed."

He liked it when they screamed. But he loved it when they howled.

Bitches. All women were bitches.

Did she think he would not recognize her as an enemy? How transparent and stupid she was.

He stood in the shower and let his hatred of her wash over him with the water. She was the enemy. He stepped from the shower, and water pooled at his feet as he rubbed a clear place on the glass. He stared at the mirror until his eyes seemed to float independent of his flesh.

What intelligence lay therein, what quickness of thought, thoughts running to the color red. But that insect in the background of his reflection crawling on the tiles, it marred his serenity. Better step on it quick. He did, and each time he did this, his enemy screamed and died. He beat her face in as he beat his pillow, and then wondered why he could not sleep. When sleep did come, his dreams were all of death, angry death. Now the cancer of hatred was all, waking and sleeping. He was complete and invincible.

Mere humans had never proved a match for cancer. There was no cure.

With one long red fingernail, Mallory tapped the wad of papers which had traveled from Edward Slope's hand to Charles and thence to her. She stared into the troubled face of a young investigator from the Medical Examiner's Office. The man would not meet her eyes. His hands were worming around his coffee cup, which had grown cold. A waitress was standing near them. Mallory waved her away.

"Slope doesn't figure you're dirty, but I do. I know how much you have in your bank. I know every transaction in your stock portfolio, and I know your salary."

"Your old man never ratted on anybody."

"No, he didn't. He just transferred them to hell. Most of them quit. They decided they'd rather live than do hard time in death precincts. I know that because I did the computer work for him. And what I did to them, I can do to you— and more. I can send you to a worse hell than early retirement on a partial pension."

Ease up, Kathy, a memory of Markowitz cautioned her. *If you scare them too much on the first go-round, they go for a lawyer. You don't want that.*

She sat back in her chair. "I just wanted to give you a little something to think about over the holidays—give you a little time to go over your notes on the Coventry Arms visit. Merry Christmas. I'll get back to you real soon."

Nice touch, kid, said the memory of Markowitz which would not go to that part of the mind reserved for the dead.

Pansy Heart lay in her bed, watching him rise and walk back into the bathroom. She was imagining, for a few moments of quiet horror, that her husband crawled along on eight legs.

She was quiet for all the bathroom noises and the sheet rustling and the click of the bedside light switch. She sighed in the dark and wondered if he heard. And then she felt she could breathe again, breathe but not sleep. Not till she heard his own regular breathing and knew he would not wake until morning. And even so, she lay awake until the exhaustion of fear overtook her in the dark.

Angel Kipling looked up as Harry walked into the kitchen. His face was still dazed from sleep. He hovered in the doorway as though debating whether this was safe ground or battleground. Between coming and going, she nailed him with the first shot.

"So what have you done now, Harry?"

"Nothing," said Harry Kipling, opening the refrigerator and pulling out the leftover chicken from dinner.

She stared into his smiling face, and she wanted to hit him with a closed fist.

Pansy woke with a blow to her head. It was not a sharp blow but glancing. In the dim light of the bedroom, she saw the fist flying in the air, and her hand moved out to fend it off. It fell back to Emery's side. She turned on the bedside lamp, and the pearls of night sweats glistened in the light. The longish hair was an aureole of gray spreading on the pillow around a face of eyes-closed anguish.

"Emery, wake up!"

The brown eyes snapped open and looked into hers. She detected a wince, and she shrank back as if from an unkind word. He had trained her in that behavior, much the same as the dog had been trained. And what had he done to the dog?

And why did he have to lie about it? What had he done?

"Having a nightmare, Emery?"

Were you dreaming of Rosie or your mother?

"Yes, a nightmare. I look in this hole and it's alive with maggots, and I'm going into it. It's all coming undone. Who's doing this to me?"

If Pansy had believed in ghosts, she might have had an answer for that. It was the face of Emery's mother she saw in the mirror across the room, and it was her own face.

The bouncer and the bartender each had the frowzy redhead by one flabby arm, and even so, she was giving them trouble as they led her out the door. The two large men had loud, hollered words with the woman on the sidewalk and out of Betty Hyde's earshot.

Hyde looked around her, noting the rodent droppings on the floor. Definitely not an A rating from the Board of Health.

Reminders of her less accomplished relatives were on the faces of every drunk at the bar. Her glass had lipstick stains from the previous customer. The slatternly waitress had actually seemed amused when she complained, but a dollar bill had bribed the girl back to the table with a clean glass, and Hyde had slugged back the whole shot. With enough whiskey, anything could be borne.

She leaned forward as she spoke to the younger woman who sat on the other side of the small table.

"Mallory, how do you find these places?"

Of course, she understood the logic. No one from the Coventry Arms was likely to wander in, not without their own private security. The bulge under Mallory's coat could only be a gun. Now that was comforting.

"Tell me more about Eric Franz," said Mallory.

"Anything specific?" And what did Eric have in common with a judge and a gigolo?

"Are you sure he's blind?"

"Dead sure," said Betty Hyde.

"How so?"

"If the blindness was fraud—the wife didn't know. How does a man keep a thing like that from his wife?"

"Maybe she did know."

"No, Mallory. Annie believed he was blind."

"How can you be so sure?"

"Well, I did tell you his wife had an interesting sense of humor . . . for a bitch. She used to flirt with men in front of him. Nothing spoken—only the rubbing up, the nuzzling. What Annie did with other men were the sort of things Eric couldn't see or hear. It was quite a show—the two of them in public. And there were other jokes at his expense, the faces she made, the obscene gestures. It was the darkest humor. You couldn't look away. You couldn't tell her to stop. You were a prisoner to every exhibition."

"Why did she hate him so much?"

"Because he loved her so much—too much. If only he'd been rude to her occasionally, it might have gone a long way toward improving the marriage. She was that type."

"And his type? He was a doormat?"

"A nice guy. But you're right. She had nothing but contempt for him in all the time I knew them."

"Is that why they never had children?"

"You know, there was a time when I could've sworn Annie was pregnant. She had that certain aura of impending motherhood. That special glow that comes from vomiting every morning. But then, when I saw her again, she was her old self—drop-dead gorgeous and frighteningly awake."

"You think she got rid of it?"

"Abortion? Yes, I do, but there's no way to confirm it. I pride myself in being a hard case, but I can't ask a blind man if his wife aborted their only child. Well, I could if it had the makings of a good story. Does it?"

"Did you tell Eric I was a cop before I joined the consulting firm?"

"No, dear. I only told him you might be interested in any little tidbits about the judge. But it was all over the news. Every channel said you were a dead cop."

"A fireman was killed on Monday. Do you remember the news story?"

"Yes, he died saving an old man. It was a long story."

"What was the fireman's name?"

"I don't remember. . . . Oh, I see. Yesterday's news—who remembers the details, the names and faces? But you, my dear, have a memorable face."

"And Eric Franz is blind."

When she returned home, she hung up her clothes in the closet as Helen had taught her to do. The cat had already sensed her presence and was pounding its hello on the bathroom door with the soft thuds of paws. She pressed the play button on her answering machine, and went into the kitchen to open a can of tuna for her star witness.

It was Riker's voice on the machine.

"Mallory, do any of the suspects have a dog?"

Charles dimmed the lights of the front room and settled back on the couch, long legs splayed out in front of him. An early Christmas present from Mallory lay in the midst of its green velvet wrapping paper.

He was staring down at yet another of Mallory's attempts to lure him into the current century. He had a remarkable record collection and the finest turntable money could buy, but he was a dinosaur in her eyes. It was not the music that counted with her, but the technology. Every old thing be damned, technology ruled.

He picked up her gift, the portable CD player. Did she really expect him to go about the streets wired up to the age of electronics?

How perverse was their gift giving. He gave her jewels in antique settings, which she never wore. She gave him expensive high technology, which collected dust between visits from Mrs. Ortega.

He pushed the button to open the top of the machine, just on the off chance she'd had the plastic cover inscribed with a sentimental message. He gave the same odds that two moons might appear in the sky tonight. A disc lay in the machine, ready to play at a touch. It was only a mild shock that it should be *Louisa's Concerto*.

Could she have known about the ruined record in the basement? Probably not. More than likely, she had noticed the concerto was not included in his record collection, after he had made a point of saying it was a popular recording for any classical music buff.

Earphones grew out of the small dark box in his hand. But he didn't actually need the earphones, did he? The concerto was locked in his memory now and running through his conscious mind.

What had happened this afternoon had stunned him in the way cattle are stunned with a bat before they go into the slaughterhouse blades. He understood how it had happened. The music had always been a trigger in his childhood fantasies of Louisa. Now the concerto was keyed to his eidetic re-creation of Amanda. She was archived in his freakish memory, and she would probably live there forever.

He didn't want to touch on this again. The fear was real. It was no ghost story this, but something threatening to his mind.

Mallory would not be frightened so.

And what exactly was he frightened of? It was only an illusion, wasn't it? Something he had made with a child's memory of a magic act and nothing more, a mere holograph of remembering. Malakhai's magical insanity had been a gift of sorts, and that was his field, wasn't it, exploring gifts. Furthermore, he had actually found a practical application for the old magician's delusion. If Amanda was true to life, if he was faithful to her in creation, she might be able to tell him something useful to Mallory's investigation. If Mallory could face bullets, he could face Amanda. It was not so insane. A mere conversation in the mind.

Memory led him back through the setup for the act.

He was a child again. The conductor's baton was rising as the concert hall quieted to heart-stopped silence. The concerto had begun. The inner music fled the confines of his braincase and rose around him in a wall of sound which opened onto bleak corridors filled with the scent of roses. The lull of music was the warning of the great dark hole which sprawled out before him. In that magic silence where the listeners placed the phantom notes rather than endure the emptiness, there he heard a woman keening, wailing for a death, softer now and coming toward him into the light.

She wore the clothes she died in, the blazer, the blue jeans and running shoes. His memory had faithfully re-created the stain on the material and the uglier stain of the golden hair where the wound matted it to wisps of red strings.

How did Malakhai begin? Oh yes. So simple.

"Good evening, Amanda."

She gave him a shy smile as she sat down in the chair opposite his own. There was a moment of relief when he realized his creation did not have the substance to make an impression in the plush upholstery. She rested her hands on the arms of the chair. He looked to the wall, more relieved because she cast no shadow to sit with his own.

"Good evening, Charles."

Her voice might be borrowed from Mallory, but in Amanda's throat, the words were gentled. And gentle were her eyes.

"Amanda, when I saw you this morning, standing over the little boy—"

"He was in pain," she said, looking down at the soft white hands folded in her lap. "I couldn't bear it."

"You only wanted to comfort him."

"Yes. Such a troubled little boy. I love children."

"I know. It's difficult for me to understand why you changed your mind about the child you were carrying."

She looked down to the floor for words, and not finding them there, she looked up with tears that were all too real to him. Her hands raised in a gesture of helplessness.

"You wanted that baby very much, didn't you?"

"Oh, yes. I planned my life around that child. The baby was the world to me, all that meant anything at all."

"Then why? Why did you do it? You asked the doctor to cut the child out of you. What was it about this man that was so horrible it made you abort his child?"

She rose gracefully and walked away from him, back into the shadows. Her gait was listless, tired. It had been hard work cutting a much wanted baby from her womb, her life, her future—when she had one. Too hard on her.

Chapter 5

DECEMBER 24

Angel Kipling scanned the bulletin board, her bright eyes rocketing across the scrolling lines, seeking out the evidence of fresh lies and wondering how much it would cost her this time. Perhaps it would cost her one husband in addition to the fees for keeping her name out of the press.

Each time he kissed her cheek, she recoiled, wondering where he might have been, wondering what he might have done, *had* to wonder, couldn't stop herself. His lies were unnerving, and her logic was relentless in puzzling out each one.

Early-morning sun obscured only a few of the lines which repeated endlessly. Angel glared, but the lines would not go away.

"Don't panic," she whispered. "You always panic."

It was probably a shakedown. If it wasn't a shakedown, it would have exploded all over the media.

So, nothing's going to happen for a while. We wait for a connection.

She looked to her reflection in the glass of the monitor. "See how simple things can be, if you only let them be?"

She wished sometimes that he would die. As

long as he lived, he would be within harming distance. Would that he might die, and she could be done with him instead of always listening to his lies and his excuses and his endless apologies. He had apologized very nicely for illegally putting up the condo as loan collateral. But then he apologized for clearing his throat. He apologized to the dog, and then he apologized to her in the same tone.

The concierge surveyed his world, the lobby of the Coventry Arms, and found nothing amiss. Perfectly attired people went to and fro in their designer dresses, tailored suits and handmade shoes. He paid more attention to the clothes than to the faces, and the faces of the occasional children registered not at all.

His toe tapped to the quick, bright notes of a Vivaldi mandolin concerto which played throughout the lobby at a tasteful level of background music.

Less tuneful, downright disruptive music of high-pitched barks and guttural growls was coming from the elevator in its descent to the ground floor. The doors opened and the dog fight overflowed from the elevator and into the lobby.

The concierge waved his hands at the porter, but the porter was hanging back a safe distance from the fray. Of course, no job description required the man to be torn to shreds by a pit bull and a mastiff. The owners were displaying the same common sense. And now the doorman had abandoned his post and entered the lobby to cheer on the mastiff. The porter displayed a five-dollar bill and placed a silent bet with the doorman, his money on the pit bull.

Well, something had to be done.

The concierge, who had never been invited to a dog fight before and didn't understand the rules, found himself standing too close, and now he was wincing with a bite from the mastiff, his own scream chiming in with the barks.

All comings and goings had stopped, and twelve people gathered to watch. Between the blood flow and the betting, not one of them noticed the key being taken from the rack behind the desk, and then being replaced with a key similar to Mallory's.

"Did you like the CD player?"

"Yes, thank you. And the recording of *Louisa's Concerto* was a nice touch."

"You have to change to CDs, Charles. You might be able to transfer most of your records. They're in good shape."

"For artifacts, you mean? I like the records. I like the turntable." He did not want any more technology invading the house.

"Your record collection can't grow with obsolete technology. And you can't replace worn-out records anymore. I noticed you didn't have a copy of *Louisa's Concerto* in your collection."

"I wore it out ages ago. There was another one in Max's collection downstairs, but I'm afraid I ruined that one. The timing of your gift was perfect."

"Whatever happened to Max's friend, crazy Malakhai?"

"Oh, he's living a quieter life these days."

"I suppose he *is* pretty old."

"Yes, he's getting on in years." Since when did Mallory make small talk?

"And Louisa? She's really still with him?"

"Oh, yes. But Louisa would still be young, just nineteen, forever."

Charles watched her pinning more printouts to the corkboard which spanned the wall of her private office. "Are you quite sure you're onto something with the business of the lie?"

Mallory tapped the printout from the real-estate-agency computer, and he did not ask if the real estate agency had donated this material by consent or by a hijack on the midnight rail of the electronic superhighway.

"Four days before the abortion, she made an offer on a small house upstate. According to her agency file, she was concerned with local school systems and area playgrounds. During the next four days, according to the doctor, she hardly ate or slept. I'm guessing this is where he told her the lie. So it worked on her and then she had it out with him."

"The outburst at the keyboard was just before her death, wasn't it? Could we have this wrong? Might that be the day she caught him in the lie?"

"No. The lie made her abort the child. It worked on her. Maybe she just couldn't take it anymore. She snapped late."

"There's a flaw in the logic here."

"You can't always go by logic. You have to get into the perp's skin. When you know him, you know how and why. All I'm missing now is who." She turned to him. "How well do you think you know Amanda?"

There was only a subtle shadow across his mind. She couldn't know what he was doing with Malakhai's magic madness. But the timing of her gift of music was entirely too perfect. Had she made a trip to the basement and seen the ruined record? No, of course not. That was paranoid.

"Based on the manuscript, I might know Amanda well enough to guess her reactions to events, but not the events themselves, not the lie that was told to her. I can only tell you it had to be something monstrous. She had a gentle personality, a wry sense of the ridiculous. I rather liked—"

"Nothing in the monster category in their background checks. But she had to turn it up with the usual research avenues. If she found it, I can find it."

"Not necessarily. And you have to consider that this might not have been his first kill, that he's done it before and gotten away with it. That might be what she uncovered. It's better logic—"

"If there was no record of it, how did she find it?"

"Mallory, these two people had very intimate knowledge of one another. This was no great love story—but they shared a bed; there was conversation. If he lied to her, she may have caught it in the untechnological way the rest of us catch lies. When you tell the truth, it's always the same truth. When you lie, you must have a superb memory, or it will be a different lie in every telling."

And now his eyes took on some pain as he clearly understood their separate roles in this business: Mallory could crawl into the mind of a killer with disturbing ease. She had left the difficult job to him, the job of identifying with a frail human being who had no pathology or defenses in a brutal landscape peopled with those whom Mallory best identified with.

He wished he could wire Mallory into his delusion of Amanda and remove himself from the game. And a game it was to Mallory. Murder was the best game.

Now she was unloading a pack of tapes from the morning's scavenging. "Something on television could have tipped her. The judge had a lot of airtime in the past two weeks."

Could it be that simple? A clue in Amanda's last days? They were spent in the upheaval of the lie: lack of sleep, anxiety and guilt from the abortion.

He walked the length of the cork wall at the back of the office. This was not Louis Markowitz's style. All the tiny little detailing was missing. Mallory's quick brain could not stop for the minutiae which had been Louis's obsession. He had to keep reminding himself that she was not obliged to be a copy of her father. Now he read the interview with the doorman.

"What's this about?"

"It looks like that's the day she finally snapped. The doorman said she was agitated. Then she went home, obsessed about it, and that same night she logged onto her computer. Maybe she was working late to get her mind off it. But the book was about him, wasn't it? That's when the YOU LIAR outburst occurred."

She fed one tape to the VCR. "These are all the broadcast cuts from the past two weeks."

The first tape was a press conference. Judge Heart's stage presence was commanding, and he seemed to know it. He singled out women reporters for questions, and looked into the eyes of each one as though she might be the center of his universe.

Even more entertaining were the tapes on the Senate hearings for Judge Heart's nomination to the highest court in the land. Mallory's candidate for wife beating was rambling on and on about his concern over sexual harassment in the workplace. The senator from Maine was nodding in approval of each lie he fed her on his empathy for women and the need to protect them.

Charles was wondering what might draw Amanda to this man. Power had its attractions, he supposed, and fame. And Heart's intelligence was undisputed.

"The judge is always in the paper. Pretty dry stuff—coverage on the hearings, pictures of candidate and family. Did I mention that I think he killed his elderly mother?"

"Slope ran that by me at the poker game. He's not convinced. There's no evidence. It's pure speculation."

"Sometimes speculation is all you ever get to work with, Charles. And you did ask me to keep an open mind about the possibility that he had killed before. A mother killer. You think that might put a woman off having a baby, just on the off chance that matricide was genetic?"

"Perhaps. By your description, Harry Kipling seems harmless enough."

"And he's just the type to panic. All the testosterone in his marriage is Angel's."

They sat in silence throughout an hour of Mallory fast-forwarding tapes and stopping the action to have a closer look. Over the two weeks of tape, he noted a growing tension in Heart.

"Now watch the judge lie to this reporter."

A young woman approached him, smiling brightly, and the judge beamed down on her with his most avuncular smile. He was the man every boy and girl wanted for a daddy.

"I'm going to wrap this up on the twenty-sixth," said Mallory. "And this conversation is between us, not us and Coffey and Riker."

"How can you orchestrate the day? You don't even know which one it is."

"Oh, not just the day. I can even plot the moment roughly."

"How?"

"I was always in charge of him, Charles. When I get him on camera, I start pushing his buttons. I've got the usual buttons for Franz and Kipling. I'm going to get the judge in motion by telling him that I'm going to get the paperwork to dig up his mother."

"Slope won't support—"

"I don't need Slope's permission to dig up a dead mother."

Indeed, she didn't seem to need anyone. "You have a favorite, don't you?"

She ignored this.

"I'm going to wrap him up for the DA on the day after Christmas."

"Is it me you're wrapping up?" asked a small voice behind them.

Justin Riccalo stood in the doorway. The boy was staring from one to the other. "Is it me?"

"Does that worry you?" asked Mallory. She didn't wait on his answer, but turned her back on the boy. "Charles, when little kids can just walk into the building, I'd say we had a security problem."

Charles looked down at the boy. "How did you get in, Justin? Why didn't you use the intercom?"

"I walked in with an old man on crutches. He

dropped his package, so I carried it in for him. It seemed kind of silly to go back outdoors and use the intercom. It's cold out there."

"Mugridge let you in?" Mallory seemed skeptical—and with good reason. The elderly Mugridge was the most security-conscious person in the building.

"Yes, ma'am. I did knock on the office door. You probably didn't hear me."

"There's a buzzer on the door," said Mallory.

In an effort to ward off any further interrogation by Mallory, Charles ushered the boy into his own office and pulled the door shut.

"Mallory hates me, doesn't she, Mr. Butler?"

"She's suspicious of everyone, even me. Don't take it personally. What can I do for you, Justin?"

"I wondered if we could go back to the cellar."

"I didn't think you would want to. Not after—"

"Yes, I would. I think I do like magic after all."

"Your parents don't mind you missing a morning of school?"

"School's out. It's Christmas vacation."

Of course. It was Christmas Eve. Where was his mind?

"Well, I'll just give them a call to let them know where you are."

"I wish you wouldn't do that. I'm supposed to be at the Tanner School right now."

"But you just—"

"I *am* on Christmas vacation. The Tanner School is warehousing me for the day. It's a holiday program for working parents. My parents are doing the cocktail circuit this afternoon. Every corporation in town is having their Christmas parties. So they think I'm at school."

The boy sat on the edge of the straight-back chair, his wriggling feet not quite touching the carpet. His hands gripped either side of the wooden seat, as though unsure of the chair's intention to remain stationary.

"I see." How would Robert Riccalo react to his son's truancy? Not well. "You know, I did want another chance to talk to you alone. I have an idea that your parents make you a little nervous."

"You have a gift for understatement, Mr. Butler. They both drive me right up the wall. Your partner makes me nervous too. She thinks I'm doing it. You don't believe in this levitation crap, do you?"

"Oh, I don't believe anyone is levitating anything. Humanity has enough bizarre problems without dragging in the occult. Parapsychology is a nonscience as far as I'm concerned. But I do think one of you is rather good at illusion." Or maybe not. Even if it was a slipshod job, who looks for the obvious thread when a sharp object is flying toward them?

"I'm betting on my stepmother."

"But she seems to be the target."

"I think she's using this to turn my father against me. He doesn't even like me anymore. He avoids looking at me. And she's already gotten to your partner. One day, I saw Sally talking to her on the street. I know she turned Mallory against me."

"Where was this?"

"In front of her apartment house, the Coventry Arms."

"Your stepmother followed her there?"

"Yes. She made me wait in the car down the block, but I followed her. I know what she's trying to do to me, and no one will believe me."

"Justin, I really am on your side." The boy seemed unconvinced. "I know something that will cheer you up." Charles gathered up his house keys from the drawer of the desk. "Let's go down the basement. But no music this time—only magic."

As they walked into the hallway, Mallory was disappearing into the elevator with no goodbye, no *I'll see you this evening*. She was not usually inclined to unnecessary words. But she never missed appointments. The sun might not come up in the morning, but Mallory would come back at eight of the clock for dinner.

Now, in some part of his brain, he was recalling each bit of small talk on the subject of Malakhai, and wondering what to make of this deviation in her.

He and the boy walked down the hall in the silence of their separate thoughts. Charles looked down on Justin, who was clearly miserable. But not frightened. This time, the boy led the way down the winding staircase to the room below, drawn along by the stored remains of Maximillian Candle's Traveling Magic Show.

When the wall partition was pulled to one side, Justin was first in, not waiting for the light of the globe to go exploring. The dull light caught up to the wandering boy and cast a fuzzy moving shadow on the trunks of props and costumes.

"Oh, cool!" said Justin from the other side of the tall Chinese screen. And he knew the boy had discovered the guillotine. But as Charles rounded the panels of rice paper, he could see it was the knife set that had Justin's attention. Charles touched another globe, and another light came to life as the boy was staring at the rack of knives.

He looked up at Charles and then to the old, much punctured red-and-white bull's-eye which was propped on an antique easel. One hand reached out to the knife rack, hovering tentatively, as his eyes shot up to Charles to ask permission.

He nodded. "You will be careful with them, won't you?"

Justin picked up the first knife and missed the target, though it was large and close.

"Don't feel bad. It takes a bit of practice. Max had many years of practice."

"I can tell," said the boy, approaching the target, which was pocked with scars. His finger traced the outline of a human body surrounding the area free of knife holes. "That was where his assistant used to stand, right?"

"Right."

"He cut it close, didn't he? I can see the holes of the knife points between the fingers. Can *you* do it?"

"Yes I can. Once, when I was your age, I stood in the target center. It was a birthday present from Max."

"You're kidding. Weren't you scared?"

"No. Then Max gave the knives over to me, and he stood in the center of the target."

"So you *can* do it. Really?"

"Really."

The boy moved into the center of the target and flattened out on the rings of the bull's-eye. "Do it. I trust you. Go ahead."

"Actually, you would only have to trust me not to let go of the knives. The blades come out of the target, they don't go into it. You pretend to throw the knife, but you really drop it into this pocket."

He turned a small table so Justin could see the black velvet bag which hung just below the tabletop. He pointed to the black lever by one leg, and the wire trailing away from the table and toward the target.

"The trigger for the knives is in the foot pedal. See? Then the hilt of the blade springs out from inside the target with a spring-load. But the audience sees what it's conditioned to see. A knife is thrown, and a knife appears on the target. It would take me a few minutes to set the springs. It's perfectly safe once you know how the trick is done."

If Justin was the one who rigged the flying objects, this might be a practical application for his gift. He was wondering how he was going to sell a future in the magic trade to the boy's father, when Justin walked away from the target, all interest in it lost.

The boy looked up to the guillotine. "And that's only a trick too, right?"—as if he were asking if this was only another lie, a cheat.

"Yes, sorry. It has a fail-safe mechanism. It's wicked-looking, but harmless."

As a child, Charles remembered being enthralled by the trickery, not the danger. Justin was of an opposite bent. He seemed disappointed at the lack of danger. Perhaps the magic trade was not the right area for Justin's intellect. Whose, then? The stepmother? The father?

"Justin, I know you've been told what your IQ

is. Have you given any thought to the future, what you might do with it, how you might develop it?"

"What's to develop? A brain is a brain. And if you believe me when I tell you I don't make things fly around the house, then I don't have any talent, either."

"Well, you might have a talent for observation and deductive reasoning. That's something we can test for. And it might even be fun. Suppose I help you figure out how the objects fly. Then you'll know what to look for. So you work with me for a while, and we'll help each other. Deal?"—as Mallory would put it.

"Deal," said the boy, his small hand thrust into Charles's for a handshake.

"Good." He was lifting a black ball with holes in it from a box at his feet. "This was one of the few floating illusions in Max's act. It only takes a few minutes to set it up." Where was the fluid container?

He found the bottle he sought in a neighboring box covered with dust. While Charles pondered the shelf life of chemicals, Justin was examining another box, and apparently he had tripped the spring, for now bright-colored scarves exploded from the box, shooting straight up and then billowing out, flowing onto the floor in a loam of silk.

Justin was trying to smash the scarves back into the box as quickly as he could pluck them from the air. He looked over his shoulder to Charles, guilt and apology on his face, and fear was there too. "I'm sorry, I'm sorry."

"It's all right, Justin. Just let them be. There's no harm done, really."

221

"You're not angry with me?"

"No, of course not."

"You know your partner hates me."

"Oh, I doubt that." He trained the beam to another dark quarter of the basement, searching out a track-line post. Ah, there it was, and it was still set with the running wires. "Now why would Mallory hate you?"

"My father says people hate other people for what they hate in themselves."

"Well, I suppose that's sometimes true. But what might that be in Mallory's case?" Matches? Oh, yes. He pulled an old box from the chest of drawers in the open steamer trunk.

"I don't know. I don't know much about her."

"Well, she's a loner, like you," said Charles, disappearing into the dark at the edge of the globe's small circle of light, and then reappearing with empty hands. "She doesn't mix well with people."

Other qualities in common? He had to wonder. There was something between her and the boy, a mutual understanding he could not understand.

"All right, Justin. Ready?"

The boy nodded.

Now there was a bright flash of light, and a glowing ball of flames was hurtling straight toward them. It stopped three feet short of its targets, man and boy, and then rose over their heads and was extinguished in the darkness beyond them.

Justin whistled and clapped his hands.

"Now *that's* a flying object," said Charles. "And miles more fun than pencils, don't you think? It runs on a track of wire. It's the only floating illusion I know, but there are crates full of books on magic if you want to look through them."

"I don't know. Maybe the less I know about this stuff, the better off I am. Why did everyone assume I made the pencils fly?"

"Well, when teams go out to investigate the odd ghost story or some other instance of paranormal activity, they usually discover the origin of the event behind a neighbor's garage in the form of three small children laughing their tails off."

"But this isn't funny. Sally's gone nuts. I can't sit in the same room with her, she's such a basket case. And she's always staring at me. It just never lets up. Every time something happens, we're all together, but I get the blame." Justin kicked at a box. "It isn't fair. I need somebody on my side. Somebody has to listen to me."

As Charles was facing the boy, they both heard the noise to the left. Charles turned to see the knife sticking out of the target, the blade still wafting with the vibration.

Justin's eyes were wide this time. This was no flying pencil, no ball on a wire.

"Now you'll never believe me," said the boy. He turned and ran in an uncoordinated, jagged stagger, out of the circle of light and into the dark, hitting against cartons and trunks in his mad flight, his wild search for a way out, for the light of an exit. His thin, flailing arms were poor versions of moth wings.

Memory guided Charles through the darkness and swiftly to the door. He opened it to a rectangle of bright light. In a moment, the boy was through it and flying up the stairs, shoes slap-dashing the ironwork. On the top landing, Justin fell. Charles lifted him to an upright stand and held him by the shoulders.

"Are you all right?" No, he could see that the boy was not all right. Justin's eyes were filling up with tears. The child slumped against his chest, and Charles held him until the racking stopped.

Captain Judd Thomas of the West Side precinct sat dead center in the hierarchy of arranged chairs in Jack Coffey's office. The captain was wearing his diplomatic smile, just enough teeth showing to say he wanted to keep this meeting friendly, no blood drawn, not today.

"Palanski wants in on this case."

"I don't think so, Judd," said Jack Coffey, who was overworked, understaffed, and only wanted the meeting done with. All of this was in his face, the shadows of too little sleep, the lines of too much stress.

"Palanski has a way of getting information from these people."

"Don't I know it," said Mallory.

Captain Thomas's tiny eyes became even smaller as he turned on her. "And what's that supposed to mean?"

Mallory rose from her chair and left the room so quickly there was no time for Coffey to threaten her with a look that promised charges of insubordination, charges that would have meant nothing to her.

Riker smiled.

Coffey was looking at Captain Thomas with something approaching temper in his eyes, but not crossing the line with the words.

"Who told Palanski she was working that building?"

"He's got sources in that crowd."

Riker leaned forward. "And I'll bet his sources don't stop with the doorman. He can work those wealthy people like street weasels. Is it just me? Am I the only one in this room that finds that interesting?"

Coffey shot Riker a look that said, *Shut up.*

Captain Thomas ignored him and looked at Coffey with raised eyebrows, clearly asking if Riker was housebroken and leash-trained. "Palanski is one of the best detectives I have. He'd be an asset to any investigation."

"It's Mallory's case, Judd. You don't get squat. That's it."

"Commissioner Beale and I go back a long ways, Jack."

"As far as Beale is concerned, the sun only shines on Kathy Mallory this week. The little bastard's grinning like a ghoul. She's the only cop ever commended by the Civilian Review Board for shooting a citizen. She can do no wrong."

"But what about you, Jack? You're in line for promotion. This is a high-profile case—big money, big names in that building. Palanski's got sixteen years' experience. Mallory's a kid. You don't want her to blow that promotion out of the water, do you?"

"Judd, if I thought you were threatening me, I'd have Mallory blow *you* out of the water, 'cause I just really hate that."

Riker sat back in his chair. If Coffey kept up this insubordination with superiors, then one day he might have to stop ragging the kid and show him a little respect. Then what would he do for fun?

"Tell Palanski to back off, Judd."

The captain sighed. "You know, Jack, with all the moonlighting and the free food and discounts for cops, all the little fiddles getting worked all over town, if we ever enforced the rules, we wouldn't—"

"I don't know where you think you're going with this, Judd," said Coffey. "You got something on one of mine, you spit it out! Now!"

Thomas put up his hands to say, *Okay, enough*, and he lifted his bulk out of the chair and left the room.

And Riker knew that was too damn easy. He was wondering what the captain's own fiddle might be, when Coffey turned on him, angry.

"Do you know what Mallory has on Palanski?"

"No idea. She'd never rat out another cop. She might shoot him if he gets in her way, but she'll never rat on him."

"You went too far with Judd Thomas."

"It's her life on the line. You know Palanski is dirty and I know it. He's responsible for all the damn leaks. One of those leaks could get her killed."

"You went too far, Riker. Thomas finds Palanski useful the way I find Mallory useful. If all she's got on him is flashy clothes and fifty-dollar haircuts—Mallory's clothes are tailor-made, for Christ's sake, and she doesn't cut her hair over the bathroom sink, does she? Right now, we're real lucky the captain got his new job with politics instead of brains. But let's not count him a complete moron. Let's not push our luck, okay?"

Riker hated it when Coffey was right. "You want me to see what I can turn up on Palanski?"

226

"No. I've got someone else working Palanski undercover. So just table that, okay? No more speculation, even if your lips don't move."

"You didn't put it through Internal Affairs?"

"No, no IA men. I want to keep this one in the family. When you see Mallory, tell her to get her ass back in here. I think it would be nice if she went through the formality of handing in reports—just to be polite."

"You know, this might be her version of professional courtesy. Maybe she thinks you'd rather not know what she's doing and how she's doing it. She might have something there. Think about your pension."

"I've already got a problem with the way she's handling the case. She's trying to cover three suspects by herself. It's a scattergun approach for one cop. If she doesn't get him soon, she'll lose him."

"Oh, I think she knows which one it is. If she tells you she has three suspects, you can figure two of them for smoke. She thinks you don't trust her to run her own investigation, and that's wise on your part. I haven't trusted her since she was ten."

"It's nothing supernatural, I promise you," said Charles.

Justin was deathly quiet, his small face turned to the cab window, to the fall of snowflakes silently crashing against the glass.

"When I get home, I'll go back down to the cellar and have a close look at the target. I'll find that the old mechanism was triggered by accident. You probably jostled it when you leaned on the target. It's that simple. In fact, I don't even need to look. And I won't look, that's how much faith I have in you. There's no other explanation, Justin. The knife came from the other side of the target. No one made it fly through the air. All right?"

The boy turned to him. In that small face, there was clearly a will to smile.

When they exited the cab in front of the school on the Upper East Side, Charles stayed awhile to watch Justin join the other boys who were standing about the yard in groups of threes and fours. But Justin did not join them. Hands in his pockets, head down, he stood alone by tacit agreement of the yard.

Charles winced, for he was watching a living memory of his own school days. Now a bell called the boys back into the building, two by two, and three by three, and Justin on his own.

Charles unfurled his umbrella against the hard drive of snow and stared at the park on the other side of the wide street. Mallory would be a straight shot across the park and a jog in the road north. Perhaps he would visit her if she was at the Rosens' apartment. Also just the other side of the park was the crime scene.

Cabs passed by him, empty of passengers and ripe for the hailing, but he liked to walk in the snow. Over the years, he had acquired a taste for all the solitary occupations. And so would young Justin.

On his foul-weather meanderings closer to home, Charles would frequently encounter others in this select club. He was on a nodding acquaintance with fellow rain-walkers and snow-walkers, and they would smile at one another in passing, recognizing the secret sign—the gait of no pressing business, while all the other pedestrians were hurrying along, anxious to be out of the wet and the cold.

He crossed the street and took a path that wound down from the sidewalk and into a pristine valley of new snow. Only his footsteps marked the way until he came to the road which wound through the park. He walked along the road, wondering what Mallory was up to, wondering if he would actually want to know that.

Now a horse-drawn carriage approached him. The snow ploffed on his umbrella, and it suddenly occurred to him that his shoes were not meant for snow. It crossed his mind to hail the carriage driver. But no. He let the carriage pass unhailed. New shoes could be got, new snow was not so easy to come by. He continued his solitary tracking.

What would Markowitz have said about Mallory's negligence in failing to visit the crime scene? What might she have missed? Nothing probably. Her refusal was most likely only an overreaction to Riker's lecture on procedure.

Suppose he visited the scene himself, and possibly noticed something useful? How would she react to that? Well, they were partners, weren't they?

"You're living in a fool's paradise," said a voice which had come to shelter under Charles's umbrella. "Behold a pale horse," said the man who materialized at his side to hold a conversation with a third person, who was not visible to the naked mind.

Charles felt an involuntary shudder. He looked down to a shiny bald spot in the center of the smaller man's matted swirls of gray hair. The old man's coat was dirty, but good wool. A scarf was wrapped around his neck and trailed behind him on the ground. It was the longest scarf Charles had ever seen, and with all the colors of an unwashed, unkempt, unraveling rainbow. The man continued to walk along with him, accepting the shelter of the umbrella as though it were his due.

Charles knew he could never look on madness in the same way again. He had done his own time with one who was not there. And he had to wonder how often Malakhai had done that trick before the damage became permanent, before it became impossible to send Louisa away. Each thought changed the configurations of the very brain itself.

"I am Alpha and Omega, the beginning and the ending."

"I'm Charles Butler. Good day." He moved the umbrella to one side, the better to protect his gray-haired companion from the driving snow that dusted the old man's sloping shoulders.

"And lo, there was a great earthquake; and the sun became black as sackcloth of hair," the old man intoned.

"Well, perhaps it hasn't been a good day," said Charles.

"A woman clothed with the sun, and the moon at her feet."

What is Mallory's day like? What is she up to right now?

"And there was war in heaven."

That might not be far from the mark.

Now the old man parted company with Charles, as the invisible partner in conversation led the man down another path of revelation and gravel covered over with snow.

When Charles came to the site of the murder, the yellow strands of tape were still in evidence, stake-tied by their broken ends and waving in the white wind of snow.

He walked to the place confirmed by Heller's map as the original murder scene. He stood by the water and looked around in all directions. So far he had learned nothing that Mallory might not have gleaned from the map. The site was within view of the path along the water. That fit nicely with Mallory's theory of a spontaneous act. There was not sufficient cover to do a murder undisclosed.

The murder had taken place on a rainy day. Few people walked in the rain and the snow, but those who did were habitual in their defiance of the elements. He stared up at the towering building on Central Park West. The upper floors reached above the treeline of bare branches. Mallory might be looking out one of those windows at this moment.

He walked around the leg of water to the path lined with benches, and then he sat down to wait. He had not been sitting there for very long before the one he waited on came walking along the path—the other walker in the snow.

He nearly missed her, though she was close. The bright snow had strained his eyes, and he had to work to pick out the particulars of her, the white face, white hair covered by the white woolen cape. She was as close to invisible as one could be without being a figment of the mind.

Cora pulled the hood of her white cape close about her face.

Too late.

He had seen through her camouflage. The man was very tall, but not threatening in his stance. She squinted to focus on his face, which became clearer as he walked toward her.

Well, with that silly, wide grin, she might assume that he was one of the more docile lunatics who roamed the park at will. No, he was not dangerous.

Her hands went past the layers of sweaters beneath the white cape, and into the deep pockets of her white woolen trousers, looking there for a few coins.

"Excuse me," the man said, standing before her now and bowing down to her so the wind wouldn't take his words, and no matter if it did, for she read the words off his lips.

She drew the coins from her pockets and offered them to him. "Now promise me you won't spend this on wine."

"Oh, no thank you. It's not money I need."

And now her suspicions were aroused anew. He didn't want money? Well, he must be crazy, and perhaps dangerous as well. She turned away from him. He circled round to the opposite end of the path, but kept a courteous distance. There was an apology in the way he stood, and a foolish hopeful look to his eyes, the pair of which had entirely too much white around the irises.

Oh yes, he was quite mad.

"I need your help," he said. "It's about what happened there on the morning of the nineteenth." He turned to point to that place across the dark water where the broken yellow tapes were waving in the wind. He turned back to face her before speaking again. He had already picked up on the fact that she was a lip-reader. That spoke well for presence of mind.

"Ma'am, I don't suppose you were out walking that morning?"

He seemed sane enough now. The shape of the words on his mouth had a good neighborhood to them, without slang or slur of form, and she could find no fault with his manners.

"Yes, young man, I was out walking that morning."

"Did you happen to notice two people, a man and a woman, standing over there?"

He must be speaking of the young lovers, Blue Legs and the tall umbrella. Oddly, she felt protective of the young couple. Who was he to pry into their secret meeting?

"Why do you ask?"

When he was done explaining that the lovers were murderer and victim, she felt the need to sit down. He sensed this and guided her to a bench a few feet up the path. He dusted it for her with touching chivalry and sat down beside her.

Now the man's face was all concern. Was he reading the new horror that was setting in behind her eyes? She had taken Blue Legs' wound for a flower. What a fool she had been. A rose in winter? Why hadn't she known the young woman was on her way to dying? Perhaps she could have—

Oh yes, she could have. If only she had not had the fool's idea to go out without her glasses and her hearing aid. And now she bowed her head with the weight of a dark understanding. In the same way she had prevented the carnage twixt

233

a beetle and a spider, with only the flick of her wrist, she might have prevented a murder.

So a bug survived, a woman died.

Blue Legs, I am so sorry.

He touched her hand lightly to call her face back to his so he might ask another question. Had she seen anything else, anything out of the ordinary?

Well, no. The young lovers had taken all her attention.

A speeding blur of red cap and jacket with churning blue-jeaned legs ran past them in a boy's whiff of spearmint gum and wet wool. A dog was fast on the heels of the boy. Dog and boy left the path and put new tracks in the virgin snow of the incline behind the benches. Then they were gone.

"Oh, the dog. Yes, there was a dog racing up that hill, and he caught his leash in the brambles. I suppose I should have thought it odd to see the dog with the leash and no human attached to the other end. But you know, people will let the dogs run wild in the park, though it is against the law."

"There's someone I'd like you to meet," said the man. And now she found his smile quite engaging—though still a bit loony.

When they stopped to speak with the doorman at the Coventry Arms, the man's friend, Mallory, was not at home. The doorman checked the name against a list on frayed, creased paper. He smiled broadly and invited them to wait for Miss Mallory in the lobby.

"Mallory, just sit down and shut the hell up."

To Coffey's surprise, and he hoped it was concealed surprise, she sat.

"Don't you ever walk out on a meeting again.

I don't want any more grief from you. Don't you even think about irritating me anymore, no more insubordination, none of that crap. I've got Riker for that. If he thinks you're stealing his song and dance, he won't like it."

"I'm not going to work with Palanski."

"No, you're not. But that was my decision, not yours. And now about that other little job I gave you. Did you pull the records for me?" *Did you steal them for me?*

She said nothing and he had to make what he could of the silence. He was operating by Mallory's rule book now.

"I hope you're doing this discreetly." *Don't get caught.*

Silence.

"I've got an idea Palanski does a lot of overtime." *He's on the take.*

She only nodded, but that was promising.

"He seems to have some kind of radar for homicide scenes within smelling distance of money—even on his days off. He was on vacation time when the body turned up in the park. Oh, sorry, Mallory. I'm telling you what you already know. That's rude, isn't it?"

He was close to joy when the side of her mouth dipped with annoyance. So even Mallory had buttons. "Did you bring me the records?"

"You don't want to see his records," she said.

"Mallory—"

"Markowitz never turned on a cop."

"Shut up, Mallory. Granted, I'm no Markowitz, but neither are you. Your old man was a detail fanatic. He'd take any information he could get, from anywhere, anybody. You should have learned more from him when you had the chance. Your lone-cowboy attitude isn't something I expect to cure in a day, but I do want to keep you alive long enough to bring you up on charges the next time you cross me. Someone at the Coventry Arms tipped Palanski to the activity. It might be your perp, or it might be you rattled another cage and its unrelated. If I'm going to plug the leaks, I need the dirt on Palanski."

Her arms folded across her chest. *No,* she was telling him, she was not going to roll over on a cop.

"I'll handle Palanski," she said. And then she threw in, "If you like," as a concession. It was a small gift from Mallory, a consolation prize as she was telling him to go to hell. Another round was lost.

"Okay, you handle it." Was he losing his mind, loosing her on Palanski, giving her carte blanche? "Don't do anything Markowitz wouldn't ask you to do."

"Understood."

Later, in the washroom, he saw a ghost in the mirror over the sink. It was Markowitz—no, it was Jack Coffey wearing Markowitz's old worries over Mallory and what she did and what might come back on him. Breaking laws to keep them was the norm now.

He was so easily seduced by her.

He was going to kill her. It was the only way. But first, a little fun. He would make her pay for torturing him, and she would pay slowly.

Thoughts of her came and passed. When she was in his mind, she brought with her a burning sensation, inflicting a hot, red flush all through his body and his brain. When he thought of her, it was her eyes he saw before him, the bright lanterns of an onrushing accident, running mindless, relentless, along a single track, no one at the wheel, no way to stop her.

And each time that moment of helpless fear and panic passed on, he was left to exhausted humiliation and anger. Now his hands balled into fists so tight, his nails left red indentations on his palms. One of those indents was filling with blood.

He looked down at the bleeding flesh. She had reached out and done this to him. She had drawn first blood, and she would be sorry.

A fat gray bird strutted along the ledge by his open window. It was still there when he returned from the kitchen with the bread. He crumbled a slice in his hand and slowly reached through the window to lay a line of crumbs for the bird.

It jerked and started and cocked its head to look at him with one eye only. It was a city pigeon and unafraid of humans, who had failed in all their pathetic attempts to annihilate its entire species as a defecating public nuisance. Contemptuous of the hand only inches away, the bird concentrated on the meal of bread crumbs which brought it ever closer to its death.

A young woman stood at the desk in the lobby. Something was concealed behind her back, and concealed quickly at first sight of the couple being pointed out to her by the man behind the desk.

Formal introductions were made to Cora by her new friend, the man with the foolish smile, and now the small party moved up through the floors of the tall building to the spacious apartment which did not fit the personality of the young woman called Mallory.

"Mallory, you were right," said the man whom Cora now called Charles.

He was well mannered in the way he kept his face toward her so that she should not miss any part of his conversation with the young woman.

"Amanda was meeting him in the park that day. It was a spontaneous act, as you said. And the murder occurred at seven forty-five. We have a witness. Mrs. Daily, may I introduce my partner, Mallory? Mallory, this is Cora Daily who likes to take long walks through the park in bad weather."

"How do you do," said Cora. The child before her was so lovely, but there was an aspect to the girl that was inhuman. Eyes like a cat she had. Well, that was all right; in fact, that was fine. In seventy-eight years, Cora had outlived many cats and had no fear of Mallory.

"What did you see?" asked the young woman, who was also quick to pick up on the lip-reading. She brought her face low and close. "Did you see the murder?"

"No, I'm afraid not."

"Did you see him strike her? The first blow?"

"No. But I did see the meeting between them."

"So you can identify the killer?"

"No, you see I wasn't wearing my glasses. But I know he was a tall man."

And now Cora could tell this was not news to the girl. She felt she had let down the charming Mr. Butler. "I saw the red wound to the side of her head after he struck her. There was an umbrella in the way when the blow must have been struck. But he was holding on to her before and after the wound appeared. Is that helpful to you?"

"Tell me more about the perp."

"Excuse me? The—"

"The perpetrator—you said he was tall. How tall?"

"He was taller than the woman."

"How much taller?"

"Hard to say. The umbrella was an impediment most of the time. And I suppose the way he held it made him very tall, but—"

"Do you think I'm very tall?"

"Oh, my, yes."

"Are you even sure it was a man? Or did you assume that because you thought they were lovers?"

"You're quite right, of course. I shouldn't have assumed that. I haven't been very helpful, have I?"

"Of course you have," said the young man, gallantly jumping into a breach of uncomfortable silence. He looked up and exchanged expressions with the young woman. His face said, *Play nicely.* And her face said, *Why the hell not.* And now the young woman smiled.

"You were better than most. I have nightmares that any case will hang on an eyewitness. Eyewitnesses are never any good. Their testimony is the worst evidence you can bring into a courtroom. But you confirmed the scene of the crime. That's useful. You placed the time of the murder—that's helpful. You saw the first blood. I like that. All in all, a good job."

And now the smile evaporated, and Cora could read nothing in the young woman's face anymore.

Charles leaned forward, still careful to include

Cora in the conversation by not averting his lips as he spoke. "Mallory, do any of the suspects have dogs?"

"Everyone in the building has a dog. Why?"

"Cora tells me there was a dog running through the park that morning. He was dragging a leash. Maybe one of your suspects walked the dog that morning and then lost track of the animal while he was doing a bit of murder."

Mallory turned to Cora. "You saw the dog?"

Cora nodded.

"What was the breed?"

"I'm afraid I couldn't say. My glasses—"

"What size was it?"

"Oh, a standard size, not awfully big or very small. I'm sorry, I can't—"

"What color was it?"

"I don't remember, but I think it might have been dark—but not black, not that dark—Maybe a brown dog."

"Maybe?"

She had no answer for that. She had underestimated the young woman, and now she was wondering if there had been a dog at all, or a pair of lovers. Could they have both been women? Might the dog have been—

"Well now," said Charles, lurching once more into the silence. "You place a dog on the scene, and you've ruled out toy poodles and Great Danes."

The young woman nodded. This was useful to her, which seemed to please Charles very much. Any fool could see he was in love with the girl. Well, at least he was happy. Good job. She had come to like this man.

When she rose, announcing that she must take

her leave of them, he escorted her down in the elevator and handed her into a cab. He insisted on paying her fare to the driver. As she shook hands with him, she said, "You were born in the wrong century, my dear."

When he returned to the apartment, it was difficult to miss the sharp knife lying on the coffee table next to the canvas duffel bag. As if she didn't own enough weapons. First there was the very large gun bulging under the blazer. She removed this now and took it into a back room. Then there was the gun she ought to be carrying, the one the police department actually approved of. He supposed she kept that one at home. And last, there was Markowitz's ancient Long Colt, which she kept in the desk of her office at Mallory and Butler, Ltd. He would never have pictured her with a knife.

He picked it up and turned it in his hand. On the reverse side of the blade was the crest of Maximillian Candle.

"It's probably none of my business," said Mallory, walking back into the room and nodding toward the knife, "but I wondered what was going on in the basement. I just came from there. The door was unlocked, and the partition for Max's equipment was wide open."

"My fault—I left in rather a hurry. You didn't by any chance pull that knife out of the target, did you?"

She nodded.

Charles stared down at the knife and forgot to ask what brought her to the basement, so great was his surprise. It was the wrong knife, of course. All the blades that came from the interior of the target were partial blades without points, and fixed to the mechanism. They could be pushed back into the compartments but not drawn out, and not with a full blade and a point.

When he had explained it to Mallory, she asked, "Could anyone else have been in the basement with you and Justin?"

"Well, it's possible, but I doubt it."

"Did you tell the parents what happened in the basement?"

"Yes, of course. I called them from the office. It took me forty minutes to track them down to a cocktail party. The child had been in trauma. They had a right to know he was upset."

"Well, you also left the basement door open. Has the boy had time to go back and change the knives, the boy or one of the parents?"

"But the front door of the building wasn't unlocked. It's self—"

"And we both know that a kid can bypass that security. How tough do you think it would be for an adult?"

"I just can't picture one of them—"

"Easier to picture that scenario than a knife flying through the air on its own. Someone has gone to some trouble here, and this is quite an escalation from flying pencils. This business has got to be cleaned up, and it's up to you. I've got my hands full with a murderer."

"You truly believe someone in the Riccalo family is going to get hurt?"

"Oh, sure. It's coming. Count on it."

"There's no supportable argument for that."

"So?"

So, when did logic ever interfere with her train of thought? It was her method first to settle upon a target hypothesis and then to move toward it with great velocity, and let nothing get between her and it.

An eye-blink ago, the space by Mallory's feet had been empty, and now it was full of cat. Nose was picking up her bad habits.

"Are you still planning to wrap up Amanda's death by the twenty-sixth?"

She nodded. "If I don't move on it now, I'll lose him. If I string him out too far, he might get to a lawyer before I can nail him."

"Lucky for you, all three suspects are spending the holidays in town."

"If one of them had left town, I would've crossed him off the list."

"But logically—"

"Logic only works on paper."

"Jack Coffey seems to think—"

"You talked to Coffey? You didn't tell him about the novel, did you?"

"No. Why didn't *you* tell him? Why all the secrecy? You work with these people." *No, wait, fool. She doesn't. She works alone.*

"A cop is leaking information. I'm not taking any more chances."

"But you're taking terrible chances. Suppose you've underestimated the murderer. Coffey says you underestimate every—"

Mallory's posture was ramrod-straight. Her chin lifted only a little.

"I *know* this man. He cleaned that apartment over and over again. He cleaned things he couldn't have touched. He had to be absolutely sure he wouldn't miss anything. And so he can never be sure he didn't miss *something*. He's the only one who can tie me to Amanda Bosch, because he's the only one who knows she's dead, and that I was mistaken for her. He wants to run, but he can't. He figures I know something, but he doesn't know how much. It's driving him crazy, me being here. Every message I leave on the computer puts him closer to the edge. He can't leave. He was my prisoner the day I moved into this condo. He's waiting for me to come and get him. Every knock on his front door is the end for him. When he can't stand it anymore, when he snaps, he'll come to me. And I will pick that moment."

For the duration of her soliloquy, he could swear she never blinked her eyes. There was an edge to her voice. It was the sort of edge fools like himself were prone to falling off of, crashing as they fell, and proximity made him nervous.

"Jack Coffey's right, you know."

Nose locked eyes with him as though asking how he could have said such a thing out loud.

"Coffey is?"

"Well, yes, I think he is right about a few things."

The cat looked away, giving him up for dead.

"And I'm wrong?"

The measured weight of her words also carried the second question: *Whose side are you on?* For it would always be that way with her, this demand to choose up sides—her side versus the balance of the planet.

"Mallory, if you string out all the facts, just the bare facts, they don't amount to much of a portrait, certainly not what you've extrapolated. You can't bet your life on it."

It was Nose who picked up the warning signs first, with an animal's radar for the impending storm. He bristled and crept under the couch. And Charles was suddenly reminded of the old man in the park quoting from Revelations—warnings of earthquake, the dark of the sun.

The long red fingernails disappeared into the duffel bag on the coffee table and emerged again with a small bundle of printouts sectioned off with paper clips. She selected one clipped bundle of sheets and held it up to him.

"Okay, Charles. Let's take a look at your own little problem with the flying objects." The light sheaf of papers hit the coffee table with real force. Her face was rigid.

"These are the *facts*—my contribution to the partnership. Two women died. Two insurance companies paid off. A third woman is frightened, or at least she acts that way. The kid's trust fund is down by a full third. The father is the executor of the trust. You might assume he just made bad investments, because his own portfolio and accounts are also depleted, but that would be supposition, and I'm sticking to the facts. The stepmother is a computer programmer with a financial background. She has a fax origin number, access to the executor's signature and documents. She knew Robert Riccalo for ten years before she married him. Per your own notes, nothing flies unless the three of them are in the room. A pencil flew at the stepmother. Now it's easiest to make the pencil fly to the person pulling the thread, but I made it fly to you, didn't I?"

Her voice was entirely too civilized, prompting the cat to stick its head out from under the couch.

Where was all this background information coming from? As quickly as he framed that question, he filed it away among all the other unspoken, unanswered questions that were suspended from the rafters of his brain like bats sleeping in the dark. When she got information for him, he had ceased to ask where she got it, and he tried not to speculate on the source, setting his ethics adrift—becoming more like Markowtiz.

Another printout hit the coffee table with a hard slap. The cat was gone again.

"The boy used to keep normal school hours. He had one after-school program to fill out the parents' workdays," she said. "Now his hours at the Tanner School are longer. He sometimes goes six days a week without eating a single meal at home. The new stepmother arranged that. And Justin was right about all the wives being copies of one another. They all favored extended after-school programs. None of them wanted the kid around. The kid's trust fund is down, and Dad's in a hole. The new stepmother is top-heavy with insurance from her job. The natural mother had a history of heart problems. The suicidal step-mother had a brief psychiatric history. These are facts."

"I suppose the one with the psychiatric history saw things flying through the air?"

"No way to know. It's a *fact* that a shrink was observing her for signs of paranoia during a brief hospital stay. She didn't leave a suicide note. The ME investigator tried to do the workup for a postmortem psychological autopsy. He said the family never discussed flying objects with him. There's the file on the woman's death. There are personal notes in there about the kid. The word 'spooky' is mentioned twice. I'm only repeating the facts."

There was a restrained violence to the words,

a force being held in check. Though her anger was increasing in pent-up energy, there were no signs in the cool mask of a face.

"Well, the suicide rules out the insurance motive."

"No, Charles, *in fact* it doesn't. Riccalo went to court to make them pay off. There was no suicide exclusion, and she had no psychiatric history at the time she took out the policy."

"And Robert Riccalo was the beneficiary."

"That's a fact. The settlement was deposited into the boy's trust."

"That sounds sinister."

"Let's stick to the facts, Charles. The settlement barely covered the amount lost in bad investments the previous quarter. If that trust fund had dropped too low, it would have triggered a bank audit. He didn't have much choice about depositing the money back into the trust. So, just at the right time, a heavily insured woman dies. I call that interesting."

"You have nothing to indicate foul play. As I understand it, there was no one in the house when it happened."

"That's speculation. The department won't check an alibi unless the case is written up as a homicide. If you stick to the facts, you have a logical case to fit any one of them. But, if instinct counts for nothing, how come I know the perp from the next victim, and you don't?"

The air between them was chill to dangerous. Even Malakhai in his debunking days would have found her quite unnatural in the world. All the good logic of his good brain excused itself and went off to keep the cat company under the couch. Too late, he had come to believe in her as others might believe in magic.

"Which one of them is doing it?"

"Too bad I can't tell you. I didn't figure it out with logic, so it doesn't count, does it?"

"Which one? Who do you think it is?"

"Oh no, Charles. I've seen the light, I've got religion. I'm only a cop, a detective. You're the genius, and now that you have it trimmed down to logic and solid facts, the rest should be easy for you. Let me know if you ever work it out."

"But there's a case to fit any of them. Logic—"

"Logic is your handicap, not mine. If logic is king, how come I know and you don't? Have fun, Charles. Don't forget to duck. Send postcards."

She began unpacking new boxes of disks from the duffel bag.

"You make it sound like I won't be seeing you for a while."

"I've got things to do."

He only turned his back for a moment, looking for something to say to her. When he turned back to face her, she was gone. The door to a back room was closing behind her, the cat was padding after her, and he was left to show himself out.

"So, we're still on for this evening, right?" he called to her through the door to the back room.

Silence.

As he walked to the front door, he had to examine another set of facts. She had been right about the manuscript being autobiographical, certainly to the extent of the pregnancy and the dancing cat. And right about the meeting, the spontaneity of the act. He had closed the door behind him and was standing at the elevator when he thought to go back, to pound on her door and demand to know which one of them made the pencils fly.

She knew.

And only now he remembered the knife was still sitting on the coffee table. Why had she brought it back to the Rosens' apartment? What had *she* been doing in the basement?

Robert Riccalo still managed to dominate the large room, though he had retreated behind the financial pages of his newspaper, which obscured all but his trouser legs and the green leather of his chair.

The chair was positioned like a throne and elevated above the cushions of the couch where his wife perched. Justin sat in a small wing-back chair which might have been made with a child's size in mind.

The rustle of Robert Riccalo's newspaper could be heard above the television chatter of a commercial for fabric softener. Every grunt or sigh from the throne called Justin's eyes up and away from his book. Each time he looked up, he would catch his stepmother staring at him, finding Justin a hundred times more interesting than the television set, which played on to no one.

All three heads turned in the same direction when they heard the crash of glass in the next room. Robert Riccalo looked at his son, who scrunched down in the chair. Sally Riccalo was rigid as a board, sitting ramrod-straight at the edge of the couch cushion, eyes fixed in the direction of the noise, her long, thin nose pointing to it like a compass for things that went bump in the night.

Robert Riccalo was first into the dining room. Pieces of blue glass lay on the marble tiles. Four of the longest shards were lined up in a row pointing toward the room he had just left. Now he turned quickly at the sound coming from his wife, who stood behind him. It was from deep inside of her, a squeak that escaped. Her eyes fixed on the bits of broken glass.

Justin was last to enter the room as the first shard of glass was inching along the floor toward Sally Riccalo. She stood there paralyzed, unmoving. Now she broke formation and pointed at Justin. "It's him, he's doing this to me. He's trying to kill me! It's him!" Her finger pointed at the boy, and Robert Riccalo turned to his son, thunder brewing in his eyes.

Justin fled the dining room and ran down the hall to his own room. He turned the lock and strained to move furniture across the door.

"Justin!" his father bellowed. "Justin!" The yelling was coming closer. "Justin!" almost at the door now. The doorknob moved as the lock was tried. He listened to the large man turning on his heel, footsteps fading off to get the key. Then Robert Riccalo was back and fitting a key into the lock.

Justin backed up to the far wall as the door cracked against the dresser and that heavy piece of furniture was being moved slowly, relentlessly out of his father's way.

It was the five-year-old who caught her attention when he yelled in anger, "I want to see the body!" And now Mallory wanted to see it too. She walked toward the group of pedestrians clotting the side-walk in front of the next building. The boy kicked the leg of a woman who held him by one arm. The woman of a different color, and by her uniform, a different piece of the planet Earth, one closer to the ground than the high-rise strata where the child dwelled.

"I will not go inside!" said the child, balling his tiny fists.

Now she noticed the long black coat of outstanding tailoring, even by Mallory's stan-dards. It was draped on the man who was pushing at the body with the tip of his umbrella.

"Is he dead?" asked the woman next to him, drawing back. "Is that why he smells?"

"No," said another woman. "They all smell like that."

Mallory pushed through the small group to see the umbrella successfully rolling the stiff body of a man. The eyes were closed as if in sleep, and there was no trauma to the grimy face, no trace of insult at the prodding umbrella, for he was dead. The bottle by his side, the spill of vomit, and the ragged clothing told his story. He had crawled into the bushes late at night and frozen to death, too far gone with booze to seek better shelter. Or perhaps he had choked to death in the vomit. The third-shift doorman, whose job in life was to drive off the poor, had probably been sleeping on duty or reading his paper when the man had taken refuge from last night's snow beneath the slim cover of a bush.

The child was looking up at Mallory, having ferreted out some authority in her. "Is the doorman gonna call the roadkill wagon, like he did for the dog?"

"What dog?"

In the glee of a really great conspiracy, the boy said, "I saw a dog murdered. It happened right there." He was pointing to the curb. "I was upstairs—"

"How far upstairs?"

The nanny stepped forward. "He lives on the tenth floor. He keeps going on about the dog, but I don't know if he could have seen—"

"I did too see it! And I wasn't on the tenth floor. She just says that so my parents won't find out I was *unsupervised*," said the child, giving care to this last word, which was obviously a newly acquired tool to blackmail the nanny. That would explain why the nanny wouldn't fight back. The kid had something on her.

"I was standing in the hall on the third floor," he said. "I looked down, and the man was murdering the dog."

"How?"

"He strangled it. The dog pulled on the leash, and I guess he didn't like that. He lifted the dog up by the choke chain. He lifted it right off the ground, and the dog was kicking and kicking. And then it stopped moving. It was dead. He kicked the body into the street. I wanted to go see the body, but the doorman wouldn't let me. He said he was waiting for the roadkill truck."

"When was this?"

"I don't know."

Mallory looked to the nanny now. "When did it happen?"

The nanny shrugged. "It never happened. He makes these things up."

"I don't, I don't!" said the boy, with another well-placed kick to the woman's leg.

"Maybe I should talk to the doorman or his parents," said Mallory.

"It was on the nineteenth," said the nanny, with instant recall. "The day it rained."

But neither doorman nor boy had been able to describe the dog. And Mallory knew the world would be a better place without the clutter of eyewitnesses.

The door was open. Mallory shifted the bag of groceries to one hip and pulled out her gun. With the gun concealed by the bag, she pressed through the door and into the apartment.

The concierge was standing in the front room when she came through the foyer. Now all of the room was exposed and she could see Angel Kipling opening the closet door.

"Looking for something?"

The concierge spun around.

"Oh, Miss Mallory, pardon the intrusion, but Mrs. Kipling was sure she heard a scream coming from this apartment."

"It must have been the cat," said Angel. "Yeah, that's it. Had to be. You always keep him locked up in there?"

"It's a big bathroom. I don't want him shedding on the Rosens' furniture."

When the concierge had excused himself and closed the door behind him, the woman turned on Mallory.

"We got your message."

"What message?"

"Don't be cute. I saw the setup in there." Kipling nodded to the door of the den, which was wide open. "Most of us only have the one computer. All the harassment comes over the computer. It explains a lot. So what do you want? How much?"

"To keep quiet?" Too good to be true. Pity the cameras weren't rolling, but whatever Angel gave her couldn't be used against the husband. "I'd rather deal with your husband."

"You're dealing with him. I'm the husband in this relationship."

Advancing on Mallory, Angel Kipling opened her mouth to say more, but then she either lost her words or thought better of them. The woman backed up in the way of the cat when Mallory's glare said, Enough. Kipling stiff-walked to the door and slammed it behind her.

Mallory walked into the kitchen and set down the grocery bag. She laid the gun alongside of it on the counter and put the perishables in the refrigerator. The phone rang. She let it. She put the butter away, and closed the door on the second ring. She walked into the front room in her own time with no hurried motions. The cat was pawing at the glass of the aquarium, maddened by the swim of fish, unable to get at them.

"I know just how you feel," said Mallory.

On the fourth ring, she picked up the receiver. "Mallory."

"It's me, Justin. It wasn't me that made the pencil fly."

"What?"

"It wasn't me. Will you help me?"

"You know the conditions. When you're ready to tell me the truth, I'll help you."

She heard the child's sudden intake of breath, and then the connection was broken abruptly.

Justin was forgotten in the next minute.

Through the open door to the back room of the Rosens' den, she could see the vase falling from the small table, bouncing on the plush carpet, strewing yellow roses and water.

Damn cat.

But now she heard Nose mewling from the room behind her. She stared at the roses until she was distracted by the warning light from her computer system. Another fax was coming in.

She brought the fax up on her monitor. It was addressed to Judge Heart. The logo bore the name of a law journal, and the text was a request for permission to reprint one of the judge's papers in an upcoming edition.

She fed the fax into a graphics file, where she cut and pasted the logo and signature onto a clean page. And then she typed her own text: "The journal is considering a manuscript, and we want to cover ourselves for libel. There are only a few little things to clear up. Is it true that you beat your wife on a regular basis? Is it true that your mother died of a savage beating?"

Then she sat down to a quiet hour of computer terror, tailoring new messages for the building bulletin board.

"Oh sweet Jesus," said Riker as he approached Mallory's door. Was that what he thought it was?

It was the genuine article, all right. He pressed the buzzer and pounded on the door. "Mallory! You in there?"

When she opened the door, he grinned. Mallory would never know the relief that was washing through his system, shutting down all the reflexes that would have broken in the door if she hadn't been quick enough to answer it.

He pointed to the large scrawled X on her front door. The marking could only be blood. They could both tell catsup from death.

"Nice touch, Mallory," said Riker, walking past her and heading toward the phone on the table by the door. "A little ostentatious, but I like it. The perp knows your name, and where you live. That wasn't enough? You thought he might lose his way?"

"Definitely a squirrel," was all she said, still staring at the X.

"Now let's have another little talk about your pet theory. This guy's stalking you. It doesn't square with a frightened perp who kills in a panic and runs away. It's a different game."

"Maybe it is. Or maybe somebody's working with him?"

"Okay. Two of the suspects are married. Say one of the wives is a different type of personality. More like yours. Either she's a ballsy monster in her own right—"

"Or she does whatever she's told."

"Still an open game, huh? Or maybe you're shaking out too many trees. You had to scare all three of them? It never occurred to you someone else might come after you, maybe with a multimillion-dollar lawsuit against the city?" Or a weapon. He looked back to the door. "How long do you think it's been there?"

"It wasn't there an hour ago when I got in."

Riker was on the phone now, saying, "Ask Heller if he can get down here. Maybe we'll get lucky. If the blood is human, it might be his." He put down the phone and turned to Mallory. "Time for backup, kid."

"Don't call me kid. And I'm the low-budget case, remember?"

"You can't stay here alone anymore."

"I don't have that high an opinion of the perp. Look at this." She pointed to the center of the bloody X on the door. "Feathers. Our fearless perp murdered a bird. So no backup. I'm not letting anybody screw this up for me."

They were still playing "backup, no backup" when Heller arrived with his kit and began to scrape the samples off the door. Riker was worn down to "okay, no backup" when Heller left.

"When do you figure to bag him?"

"Maybe on Sunday."

It figured that she would pick the day when God was resting, not looking—if she wasn't lying to him again.

The cat was purring around Mallory's legs as she holstered her gun. Mallory picked the cat up in her arms. Nose nuzzled her face, licking her skin with a pink sandpaper tongue, eyes closed slowly in the cat's idea of a smile. Mallory walked to the door of the bathroom, held the cat out at arms length and dropped it on the tiles. The cat stood up and began to dance.

Riker whistled low. "Has he ever done that before?"

"No."

Kneeling down, she took the paws in her hands and put them firmly on the floor.

The cat purred at her, half closing its eyes again. She stood up, and now the cat's eyes were open hurt as she was closing the door. *What did I do wrong?* asked a confusion of rounding eyes and the jerking starts of the small head, the paws rising.

The door shut.

If only she had been a woman of standard intelligence and ambition. If only her countenance had not been the beautiful antithesis of his own clown's face; if only she had been normal, he would have given her everything he had. But she was abnormal and deviant, and if she wanted it, he would give her everything he had.

He had known she wasn't coming at only five minutes past the hour. Now he measured the passage of time by the ice melt in the silver bucket. The red wrapping on her gift looked pathetic to him now. Stupid box, ridiculous thing, sitting there all dressed up for a woman who didn't care to open it. For an hour more, he stared at the door she would never knock on. And then, he was pulling on his coat and opening the front door, which he would not remember locking behind him, because he hadn't. He passed through the halls and down the stairs and into the dark to walk and think.

The night was crisp and cold. To the north he could hear the bells of the convent on Bleecker Street, and to the west the bells of St. Anthony's. He was such a fool that he found the night romantic, though he had no one to share it with, and perhaps he never would.

Mallory was everything Riker said she was: no heart, no soft places he might reach. Of course she thought him a fool. Of course he was one. He always said the wrong thing. If only there were some aspect of her that was conventional, a bit of sure ground that he could understand.

The CD player slammed on his thigh from the deep pocket of his coat. He had thanked her for the gift, but never used it. Well, perhaps this bit of technology was the bridge to Mallory. He pulled it from his pocket, set the earplugs in place and pushed the play button. Music poured into the center of his skull and seemed to be coming from everywhere at once. It was *wonderful*. It was all new again, this music he had carried in his head since childhood.

And something new had been added to his homemade madness.

For a moment, he forgot to breathe as he listened to that sound that was not music, and neither car horn nor church bell. He knew it was Amanda's footstep behind him, even before she came abreast of him. A delusion with audible footfalls. Her tread was too light and a bit off stride, an as yet imperfect imitation of a living woman. He turned away from her and turned the music off.

The footsteps vanished.

He kept his eyes other-way directed and focused his concentration on Mallory.

She knew who made the pencils fly. Perhaps she also knew the dynamics of his small telekinetic family in a way that he could not. Was it signs of abuse she recognized in Justin? Or, as Justin had said, something she saw in the boy that she did not like in herself? Or was it something simple that allowed her to see what he could not? Something simple—the absence of a heart?

"Sometimes they can't love back," Amanda said, keeping time now with his own footsteps. His delusion had a near-human persistence. Amanda had come back to keep him company for a while. He looked down at her sad face, and fear of her turned into curiosity.

"You weren't loved back either, were you?"

"No."

"And when you came to know this man, contempt killed what feeling you had for him. Am I right?"

"Yes. But you will never have contempt for Mallory—it's not the same. My contempt was for his weakness. She has a terrible strength that's not quite in the normal scheme of things, and frightening sometimes, isn't it? You're lost, Charles. I was better off than you. It's better to have a definite end to the loving."

"In the end, it was only the child you cared about."

"Yes."

"Why, then, did you ask to have the child cut away from you?"

"He lied to me."

Her footsteps made less noise now, as she walked along beside a lonely man who cast one shadow for both of them. He had gone to no trouble to create her this time, and this should have worried him, but he was oddly glad of her company.

"Do you know why she gave you my manuscript?"

"So I could give it a thorough read, maybe find something of value to the investigation."

"You know she read every page before she gave it to you."

"Of course she did."

"It was the love of the child she couldn't fathom. She couldn't understand how I could want to build plans for a lifetime around the future of an unborn baby."

"But Mallory was a much loved child. Helen and Louis were devoted to her."

"Yes, after the damage had been done to her out on the street. What about Mallory's own mother? How was a child so quick, so beautiful, left wandering the streets? She was the child women pray for. How was she let go? If you're still looking for the link to the boy, it might lie in her history. What do you really know about her early days?"

Charles sighed. "Mallory is an intensely private person. Her history was never open to discussion."

"If you could bend your mind outside the parameters of fact and logic, you might reach the conclusion that Mallory's mother is dead, perhaps murdered."

"I think that's a bit farfetched, Amanda."

"Is it? She's predicting violence in the Riccalo family. You see a link between her and the boy. They've both lost their mothers. Doesn't it make you wonder? What sent her into the street, a small child on the run? What was she running from?"

"Perhaps she was abused as a child?"

"By her mother? No. She loved Helen on first sight. Someone taught her to trust women like Helen Markowitz the nurturer, healer of scraped knees, lover of children. Suppose Mallory saw her mother killed?"

"Oh, this is absolute rot. There are no facts to support that line of reasoning. Next you'll be telling me that Justin saw his mother die, and *that's* the common bond, as though Mallory could read that in his mind."

"Maybe they read one another's eyes. Don't they both have the look of damage? Justin doesn't behave much like a child, does he? He doesn't have a child's conversations. There's another commonality. Mallory was the same way, wasn't she?"

"The purpose of creating you was to find out who killed you."

"Yes, but was that your idea? She only gave you my manuscript when she realized that once you had this intimate piece of me, you could do the succubus illusion."

Could she be that convoluted? Mallory? Certainly. All those prompts about Malakhai? What else could that have been about? He'd been had.

Amanda nodded her understanding and walked ahead of him.

"And what about you, Amanda?" he called after her. "Who killed you? How could you be killed that way, and why?"

"He lied to me."

He was too tired to sustain her and thus restrain her. Unable to keep her with him, he watched her go into the shadows. She was of such frail substance, she was killed by the first patch of darkness she encountered.

To be abandoned by two women in one day.

He stared at his shoes for a moment as he walked on, in and out of the light. Lost for a while in thoughts of Mallory, he meandered south and east for too many blocks into territory he was unsure of, unsafe in. When at last his eyes were looking outward again and he realized this, he found he didn't care. And he was only dimly aware that the time was passing from Christmas Eve into Christmas morning.

He shuffled through the pile of newspapers close to the brick of a building wall, and then he went sprawling. The cement came up to meet his face with a hard hello. Something small and alive was squirming out from under his splayed legs.

She was standing in front of him now, and wearing a little red coat.

Oh, dear God, he had tripped over the body of a child. She must have been sleeping under the newspapers. He was staring into the smudged face of a little girl with matted hair and the biggest eyes he'd ever seen. She might be six or seven. The child was extending a cup to him. It was torn and jingled with change. It took him a moment to grasp the idea that the little girl was begging for money, that she was thin and shivering.

"Where's your mother? Why are you—"

Now the child was backing away from him. Bright eyes, quick with intelligence, had sized him up for a nondonating type, and maybe an authority type, and possibly even a cop, or worse, a social worker. As quickly as he realized all of this was going on behind her eyes, he was watching the back of her as she slipped away in the dark.

He found his feet and gathered himself up to a stand and ran after her, pounding down the sidewalk, in and out of the black and bright zones of streetlamps, intact and broken. In one of these dark patches, she had disappeared. He stopped to listen for her soft footfalls.

Silence.

Now a jingle.

He looked up to see her straddling the top of a chain-link fence, and he held his breath as she monkeyed down the links with amazing speed. He came up to the fence in time to see the small red coat flapping around a corner in the distance.

And now the child was altogether gone, and with her, a ghost of Mallory's Christmas past.

Oh, fool.

His head bowed into the cold metal of the fence. His eyes closed tightly. His heart was breaking.

Fool.

Her eyes were not a Christmas green, nor the green of living things, but cold and, just now, eerie. The lights from the dashboard made them glitter in the shadows. They seemed lit from within, as though Mother Nature had thought to do something different with the makings of Mallory—to break up the monotony of stereotypes and throw an occasional scare into Riker.

"You know, Mallory, if I thought you had a heart, I'd think you were worried about me offing myself for the holidays."

Yeah, right, said the dip of her mouth on one side and no words necessary.

He closed the passenger door of her small tan car. "I won't be a minute—just a few things to pick up for breakfast." He turned and walked toward the dim glow behind the plate-glass window of the bar. He peered in and waved one hand. Peggy leaned her broom against the bar and waved back to him. He ambled toward the front door.

The beer he'd already put away had numbed him. He was only dimly aware of the teenage boy thirty yards to his right. Now he looked casually toward the boy. The kid was looking in all directions, probably waiting for someone. Riker looked back to Mallory, who was lost in the darkness of the car. The bartender opened the door, and he walked in.

"Who's your friend, Riker?" asked Peggy, looking over his shoulder.

Riker slowly turned his head to see the teenager behind him. Peggy was not so slow, not drunk at all, and she was backing up to the bar where she kept her shotgun.

Too late for that now.

He was watching the boy reaching into his jacket, hand closing on the gun in his belt. Riker wondered if it would be the fast reflexes of youth that would kill him, or could he put it down to his own slowed reaction time—too much booze. Either way, the young thief would have him. All this was calculated in the second it took for the boy's hand to pass into his jacket, just another second out of sixty.

The boy never got a chance to pull the gun.

Suddenly, a rush of manic energy with bright curls was pushing the boy through the open doorway, slamming him into the near table so hard Mallory nearly cut him in half at the gut level. She reached into the jacket and pulled out a .22 revolver. Now she was cuffing him and hustling him out the door. Momentum, stunned wonder and pain had made the boy docile.

Riker never said a word to Peggy. He lifted his hands to catch the brown bag with his breakfast six-pack on the fly as he followed Mallory and her new pet out to the sidewalk.

Hey, what's the deal here?

Mallory was pressing down on the boy's head to ease him into the front seat of the car on the passenger side. Any kid who watched too much television would know the perp rode in the back of the car. What was she up to?

She opened the back door of the car for Riker and said, "Sorry about the inconvenience, sir. I'll get rid of him as soon as I can."

Since when did Mallory ever call anybody *sir*? She hadn't called him that even when he'd held the rank of captain. But that was one wife and how many bottles ago. He nodded and settled into the back seat to play out her game.

When Mallory was in the driver's seat, she leaned over to the boy and said in a low voice, "It's too bad you had to witness the deputy police commissioner drunk in an after-hours bar. I guess I'll have to kill you. You understand, don't you? It's politics and nothing personal."

As Mallory drove the streets, Riker watched the boy's face. The kid was sweating, and his mind was weaving between *This is crap* and true believing.

"It's a damn shame you had to pull this stunt on a night when a top cop is drunk in the back of my car. Yeah, I guess I'll have to kill you."

It was ludicrous, but now Riker realized that this boy was so young, it had not been so many years ago that he had bought into Santa Claus and the Tooth Fairy. And then the kid had additional proof in Mallory's eyes, the eyes of an assassin.

Yeah, the kid was buying it.

Riker felt a worry coming on in the pit of his stomach where he kept his ulcer. She hadn't waited for the kid to pull the gun, to commit the crime. She hadn't read the suspect his rights.

266

She'd broken every rule, and now she was making up new ones to break.

Well, he could relax a little. She wouldn't actually kill the kid, because Markowitz wouldn't have liked that. In the absence of a normal sense of right and wrong, good and evil, Mallory was much guided by what would have pissed off Markowitz and what wouldn't.

Now they were in the Wall Street area, deserted on Christmas Eve. She pulled into a blind street closed off by construction signs. Her eyes roved over the bins of debris left on the site.

"No, not here," she said. "Sorry it's taking so long, sir. I'll get rid of him on the next block. Okay?"

"I won't tell!" screamed the kid.

Mallory said nothing as the minutes rolled by slow with the creep of the car, stopping in dark places, shaking her head and driving on.

"I gotta wonder where that gun came from," she said at last, "and I gotta wonder what you've done with it."

Riker found it interesting the way her expensive education fell away at warm moments like this one. Her voice had a rough edge that would scare any sane person into backing off with no sudden movements. He could only guess at what was going through the kid's mind. His own body was pressing into the upholstery of the back seat.

Mallory and the perp looked so young to him. With their unlined faces and blond hair, they might have been brother and sister. But he could almost feel the car dip to one side with the power on the driver's end of the front seat.

"Are you in a lot of pain?" asked Mallory, her voice switching gears, all mother love in her tone.

"Yeah, my gut hurts something awful," said the boy.

"Good. I noticed there weren't any bullets in the gun. That's not too bright, is it?"

The kid looked from the gun to Mallory and back to the gun, genuinely startled.

"So you stole the gun, but not the bullets? When I wash this registration number through the computer, am I gonna find out that some taxpayer was burgled by a moron who thinks the gun makes its own bullets? What else did you steal?"

"Nothing, I didn't—"

Riker jolted forward as Mallory slammed on the brakes. The boy didn't fare as well. With hands cuffed behind him, his head hit the dashboard. The boy moaned and Riker looked away, the better not to see Mallory drawing first blood of Christmas morning.

Wall Street was a ghost town after the financial houses' end of business day. You could do what you liked in this neighborhood without fear of another pair of eyes.

Mallory leaned over to grab the boy by his shirt collar. "You *are* stupid. When I run the gun through, you think they won't mention the rest of the stuff?"

"It was nothing. There was a ring and a bracelet, but it was junk. I took it to a jeweler. He said I'd be better off selling it at a flea market, and that's the truth. I've known him all my life. He wouldn't lie to me."

Riker shook his head and smiled. A baby felon who took stolen goods to his neighborhood jeweler. The criminal class was getting dumber every year. And no bullets. Didn't these kids learn anything in school?

He listened as Mallory called in on her car phone to run the dates and the jewelry description. But she neglected to mention that she had the suspect in custody, and she never mentioned she had the gun, and at the last, she said, "Sorry, it doesn't match up," and closed the call.

"It checks out," she said to the boy. "I'm gonna cut you loose. But you never tell anyone you saw the deputy police commissioner drunk in an after-hours bar. Deal?"

The kid nodded his head like a trick pony. Yeah, whatever she wanted, so long as she didn't hurt him anymore.

Riker stopped smiling. He sat still in the dark at the back of the car and tried not to lose the glow of the previous six-pack of beer. No good. He was becoming unwillingly sober as he crept up on Mallory's mind.

Of course. It all fit.

It was only the thief's gun she wanted. He rolled his eyes up to the ceiling of the car.

Ah, Markowitz, you bastard. How could you die on me and stick me with your kid? Can you hear me, you son of a bitch? Look at what your baby's doing now. She's robbing another baby.

"If I don't see you when I count to ten, I don't shoot you. Okay?"

She leaned across him to open the door on his side of the car. Riker listened to the metallic mechanics of Mallory unlocking the irons. She sat back. But the boy was tied to the upholstery by fear, and she had to finally cut the cords with "*Get out,* you idiot!"

The boy did his dumb-pony nod again as he

was half falling, half stumbling from the car. He staggered in a weaving line for all the seconds it took to understand that he was free, and then he ran.

Riker got out of the car and slid into the front seat.

"I'll take the gun, Mallory."

"No, it's mine."

"You never planned to take him in, and that wasn't to save me the embarrassment of showing up at the station house drunk. Everyone already knows I'm a drunk. No, you wanted his gun for a throwaway piece. You wanna save it for the perp in the condo. Now if I've got this wrong, just stop me."

But he wasn't about to let her stop him, and he went on with the relentless energy of a train running at her full speed, because it was the only way to deal with her—if he lost his breath, he lost his turn, and the train would turn around and crush him.

"You figure the perp's weapon of choice is his hands. If you have to kill an unarmed man, the Civilian Review Board will get you. But if you pull another gunslinger stunt, let's say you get him in the knees, Coffey will get you for it. He'll lock you up in the computer room, and you'll never see the street again. Almost seems like you can't win. But if the perp has a weapon lying on the floor beside him, if it looks like he brought his own gun to the party, you can't lose, can you?"

She wouldn't look at him.

"Markowitz never carried a throwaway piece, not in all the time he put in on the force. He hung out there in the breeze with all the rest of us. He played it straight, and that took guts. Maybe you don't have the stuff, Kathy. Did you learn anything hanging out with the old man? Anything at all? . . . Kathy?''

"Mallory to you," she corrected him.

"You're going to give me that gun, or I'll beat the crap out of you and take it. I loved Markowitz longer than you knew him. I'm not gonna let his kid screw up. Give it to me. You know I don't bluff. Never have, never will.''

Nothing.

She was rigid, deaf and blind to him.

"*Now*, Mallory, or it starts to get real ugly.''

She handed him the gun. "And Merry Christmas to you too, Riker.''

The device on his belt gave off the annoying beeps, the mechanical, nagging request to call in, and quickly. He picked up the car phone and dialed the number for Special Crimes Section.

"Yeah," he said into the receiver, "I know him. . . . No, it's no problem, I'm on my way.''

To Mallory, he said, "Charles is at the station. He needs something and says I'll vouch for him. You coming?''

"No, I'll drop you off.''

"Trouble between you and him?''

"Charles asked for you, not me. He doesn't need my help. He made that pretty clear.''

When he stepped out of her car ten minutes later, he leaned down to say softly, "Have you given any thought to the toy gun on the inventory sheet?''

Her eyes shone with sudden understanding.

She smiled slow and sly. He really hated it when she did that.

Charles sat on a yellow plastic chair too small to accommodate his long body. His legs crossed and uncrossed, tucked in and splayed out, looking for a way to look unfoolish.

At three in the morning, there was a constant activity under the bright fluorescent lights. A woman, wrapped in a blanket and screaming, walked past between two uniformed officers. A dazed and docile teenager was led along by a plainclothes detective Charles knew slightly. Two tourists came in yelling. By the snippets of their conversation, he deduced that they were minus their luggage, wallets, and jewelry. Next in the parade, two young men in handcuffs were escorted by four officers.

Merry Christmas, said the bright-silver paper letters strung over the desk of the civilian clerk who had taken his report.

Charles looked down at the lines and pock-marks on the floor until he saw the familiar scuffed pair of worn brown shoes, topped by a bad suit and a cloud of beer that was Riker's breath.

Riker nodded to him and walked on in the company of the two officers who had tried to reason with Charles and failed to communicate that there was no way to catch a kid who didn't want to be caught. They had no problem catching grown-up felons, they told him, but kids could fit into hiding places they had never dreamed of. Then, in desperation, Charles had resorted to the crime of name dropping. One phone call from the desk sergeant and only minutes later, here was Riker, the improbable knight.

Now Riker was sitting down at a desk and nodding amiably as the two officers leaned down to tell him all their problems with his friend the lunatic. Riker picked up the phone, and Charles watched him make three calls in quick succession. On the fourth call, Riker smiled into his telephone, eased back in his chair and put his feet up on the desk. His hand waved to tell the officers they could go on about their business. In parting, one officer put a friendly grip on Riker's shoulder.

Riker set down the phone after another minute and motioned Charles over to the desk. He picked up the sheet of paper which Charles recognized as his report, and began to read it aloud.

"So, your small friend had a little red coat that didn't quite fit, right? Mismatched shoes and socks, matted brown hair, and light-colored eyes?" Riker did a double take on the next line. "She was unwashed, malnourished, but excellent motor skills, good reflexes, three feet, six inches tall, approximately seven years old, and in a big hurry?"

"Yes, that's her."

"And she had head lice, Charles. You left that out. I found her. You done good. You scared the little brat right into a shelter for runaways. They know this kid as a regular. She came in with big eyes and gave them this fairy story about being chased by a giant. I guess that was you."

"I didn't mean to frighten her."

"Good thing you did. She'll get a hot meal and a bed."

"What else can I do?"

"Nothing, Charles. You'll never see that kid

273

again. You'll never find out what happened to her. I won't even give you the name of the shelter, because a deal is a deal. Normally, they won't tell us anything at all. You see, we hold the legal position that the kid belongs to the parent. The shelters sometimes take the view that the kid will live longer if we butt out. But this supervisor owes me one. So, with the understanding that we never had this conversation, I tell her about my crazy friend who wants to turn NYPD upside down to keep a kid off the street on Christmas morning—and she asks me how tall you are."

"I'm a fool."

"Don't ever change."

"I've ruined your holiday."

"My wife left me on Christmas Day. It isn't much of a holiday for me. Let me buy you a drink."

"I insist on paying."

"No, my treat. I'm gonna get you the best scotch money can buy. Come with me."

They passed through the swinging doors that led down the familiar corridor on the way to Special Crimes Section. When Markowitz was alive, Charles had been this way many times— up the narrow staircase and into the cavern of dimmer lights and dead quiet, broken now by the plaintive ringing of a single telephone. Two detectives sat alone in separate pools of light on the other side of the wide room. One lifted his head and waved to Riker.

Riker opened the door to Jack Coffey's office, which had once been Markowitz's office. He sat down in the chair behind the desk and seemed at home as he pulled out a wire, jiggled the lock on the bottom drawer of the desk, and extracted a bottle and a half-empty package of plastic cups.

Charles folded his long frame into the opposite chair, smiling and utterly companionable in this small criminal activity. He accepted one of the poured shots and lifted his paper cup in a toast. "Merry Christmas, Riker."

"Merry Christmas, Charles." Riker downed his shot and smiled. "So what's the problem between you and Mallory? Anything I can help you with?"

"We had an argument at the wrong time. She's not speaking to me. Did she tell you about the Riccalo boy?"

"Flying objects, and no hands in play? Yeah."

"There's something she sees in the boy that I can't see. Something like a memory, a kinship or a likeness. I need to know what the link is. But she's not talking to me anymore. What should I do? Apologize?"

"Oh no. Worst possible idea. You don't ever want to lose face with her. Never show a weakness."

"Then what do I do?"

"What makes you think there's a tie?"

"Well, it's not logical of course, I've got nothing to support the idea, but I do believe she sees something of herself in the boy."

"You mean the kid's a monster?"

"I was thinking along the lines of abuse. Do you know what her past was like before she went to live with Louis? Any clue at all?"

"Markowitz did wonder about it. He spent a lot of time trying to trace her. Helen was hot to adopt the kid. But Mallory wouldn't cooperate, not even for Helen. She would have died for

Helen, but never told her a thing. After a while, Markowitz and Mallory came to an understanding. It was her history, not his. And he backed off."

"Did he ever speculate on it?"

"He respected the kid. Whatever he figured out, he never let on, never shared."

"You think child abuse could've been a factor in her early history?"

"If anyone had tried to abuse her, the bastard could've figured on losing an arm. ... No, Charles. You only think I'm kidding. I watched her grow up."

"But surely—"

"When Markowitz pulled the kid off the street, he recognized her position on the food chain— she was a baby predator. Mallory may rack up suspensions, but she'll never lose her job with NYPD. None of us could stand the strain of having her on the other side. All you need is a few simple rules—don't ever let her down, don't ever rat her out, and don't ever trust her."

Was Riker changing the subject, or was this his imagination?

"I need her connection to the boy. This is very important."

Riker pulled out his wallet, which was falling apart at the creases, and slid a photograph out of the cracked plastic holder. "Maybe you've seen this before. It's the one Markowitz always carried. That's what the brat looked like at ten. See anything familiar?"

Charles stared at the photograph. She had been so defiant when she posed for it. Yes, there was an unsettling aspect of the boy in Mallory, that same look of damage.

"Riker, do you think it's possible that Mallory witnessed a murder when she was a child?"

Riker spilled a portion of his drink, and it was not from lack of coordination. Wasting liquor was a breach of Riker's religion.

Curious.

Riker reached down into the drawer and pulled out a brown bag, upending it and spilling a passel of deli napkins on the desk. He kept his eyes down as he mopped the desk with the napkins, buying the time to recompose. Now he shrugged as he looked up at Charles. "She was out on the street for years. She could've seen a murder, I guess. She never said."

"Perhaps I should ask Edward Slope. He's known her as long as you have."

And now something in Riker's face said he wished Charles wouldn't do that.

What might Riker be holding out on him?

Charles looked down at a roll of paper in the path of the spreading puddle. He picked it up. It was a computer printout, and scrolling on forever, the words said: I PROMISE TO SHOOT TO KILL. I PROMISE TO SHOOT TO KILL, line after line. Charles held the roll up to Riker.

"What lunatic did this?"

"Mallory," said Riker. "Turns out the kid has a sense of humor after all. Coffey reamed her out, and she dropped that on his desk the next day."

"Why is Coffey angry with her for not killing the mugger? He was holding a gun on an elderly man, and she—"

"Coffey figured she was playing with the perp, and she was. I backed her on that one, but Coffey was right. She screwed up. When you draw a gun to shoot an armed perpetrator, you're trained to shoot for the widest part of the body, the best shot you can place to stop the perp cold."

"That sounds pretty brutal."

"It is. You may only have that one chance to save your life. And every civilian in the area is in your care when you draw that gun. From the moment she arrived on the scene, that old man, the victim, was in her care. If she'd blown the shot, the old man would've taken the bullet after hers."

"All the people on the Civilian Review Board—"

"Yeah, the Review Board, the city's grand experiment with amateurs. So this week, Mallory's a hero. But if the perp isn't happy with the crook of his little finger after the surgery on his gun hand, he'll sue the city for a million dollars. It happens. Your high-minded civilians will remember they're also taxpayers. They'll turn on her. Every one of them will curse her for not killing the perp, because dead men don't sue. I *love* this town."

"What am I going to do about her? She knows something crucial about Justin, but she won't talk to me."

"Learn to think like Mallory."

"How can I? I don't have an underprivileged childhood to draw on, and I still don't know much about hers."

"Charles, you're a very smart man. I think that's why Lou asked you to look after her. Now think. She's too old to need a nanny, right? The old man figured you were the only one with a prayer of outsmarting her. He left her to you, not one of his old cronies like Doc Slope.''

"Yes, he would have been my choice. Edward Slope is a very intelligent man.''

"True. He's a smart old bastard. So why not him, you wonder. You always hear him bitching about her defects. He can see every scam coming, right?''

"Right.''

"In case you hadn't noticed, she walks all over him. He'd break his Hippocratic oath for Mallory. And the rabbi would take her side against God's.''

Riker finished his shot and poured another. His red eyes rolled up to Charles with a question which could only be *And what would you do for Mallory?*

Chapter 6

DECEMBER 25

All women are bitches.
Only death made them beautiful. That stunned look, when they knew death was coming, when they could see it, hear it coming for them. Only then did he respect them for this experience, this knowledge which had eluded him. To be dead, to be nothing, never to be challenged again.

To actually watch life leave the body was his obsession. But this too had eluded him. For in death, they might only have been asleep. The women had taken the secret with them. Bitches, unwilling to share. Perhaps one day, one of them would tell him what it was like as it was happening to her. Perhaps the next one.

He plotted against her as he opened his drawer to find his socks, as he pulled on his pants, as he buttoned his shirt. He schemed as he ate his morning meal and it went sour in his stomach. He kicked a small animal and heard his enemy screaming. He looked at sharp knives with longing and stuck one into a piece of fruit . . . many times. He killed her a hundred times a day, and the animals, the fruit, and the insects all suffered for it.

Sandstone carvings graced the elaborate structures extending as curving arms from either side of the wide staircases running down into the plaza. The vast public space was presided over by a bronze angel high atop the Bethesda Fountain. Her wings were unfurled, her robes were rippled, and there was debate as to whether she danced or not.

From the cover of high ground and stonework, Mallory looked down at the man in the plaza. He was the only one walking the paving stones, casting a weak shadow from the morning sun riding low in its winter orbit. He checked his watch and sat down on the edge of the fountain's wide pool. The Angel of Bethesda loomed behind him, some twenty feet or more above his head. The waters of the ancient biblical Bethesda were said to have healing powers. Mallory figured those waters would be wasted on a sick bastard like Palanski. The things she suspected him of were a crime in every philosophy under heaven.

Mallory lifted the antique opera glasses to her eyes. Bored silly by opera, she had finally found a practical use for this gift from Charles. She cared nothing for the delicate settings of tiny pearls and precious stones; it was the resolution of the lenses she approved of. She could pick out the mole on one side of Palanski's face. And now she scanned the rest of the plaza. The sky was overcast, blunting the sun and giving its light an eerie quality as it flooded the stone floor. There were only occasional moments when the sun could create a shadow, and then the clouds would thicken and uncreate it.

Now a woman passed near Mallory's position. Mallory turned to see the back of her walking along the path leading to the wide staircase. The woman's carrot-red hair was piled on top of her head. She was small, only five foot—if that—and thin. A short, leather hooker skirt rode high above the bare gooseflesh legs. The backs of her knees bore the bruises of the needle, another trademark of a hooker.

The woman passed behind a bank of decorative stone which obscured half the staircase, protecting her from Mallory's view. As the small prostitute cleared this facade, Mallory raised her binoculars to her face.

Not a woman.

Beneath the penciled dark eyebrows, the eyeliner and the smear of red lipstick that was her mouth, was the face of a child. How old could she be? Twelve or thirteen years? The light brown eyes had the look of a stunned animal. Her face was in a junkie sweat, though the air was cold and her thin, close-fitting jacket could offer little warmth.

Mallory slipped the opera glasses into her pocket and wondered how long it had been since the baby whore last had a fix of the needle.

Palanski rose to a stand as the girl made her way down the stairs and along the wide stone floor. Her hand rose in a vague gesture of recognition and then fell back to her side.

Mallory slipped along the footpath leading down into the plaza on Palanski's blind side. She was in the open now with no cover as she silently walked the stones. Skirting the fountain, she was moving faster now.

The little prostitute took no notice, legs in motion, but mind in limbo, eyes blank and staring at nothing, moving slowly toward Palanski, whose hand delved into his pocket and produced the lure.

In a sudden cloudbreak, the bronze angel cast a long shadow across the pool of water, the tips of its wings lighting on the stone under Mallory's running feet. The little girl was within two yards of Palanski when Mallory rushed the child and gripped her by one arm, which was bone-thin beneath the light material of the sleeve. When the girl looked up, a badge was thrust in her face. The girl, body and soul, crumpled under Mallory's hand in the same dispirited resignation of her older peers, her sisters, the adult whores. For this was part of the job, wasn't it?—the arrest.

Palanski was gaping at Mallory as she pocketed her shield. His eyes were panic-wide and disbelieving. He took one step forward. Instinctive reflex sent her free hand to the holster inside her jacket. He stopped dead. She watched his darting eyes and knew he was framing the story to explain this away. As his mouth opened, Mallory said, "Don't even think about lying to me. I know what you did."

Palanski turned, willing his feet to move at first, trapped on his toes for a full second, then breaking into a jog and now sprinting across the plaza.

Three packets of jettisoned white powder floated on the fountain's waters.

"You *better* run, you son of a bitch!" Mallory's scream echoed off the stones of the cold and desolate plaza, wherein she kept company with a blind bronze angel and a small child with faraway eyes.

Betty Hyde waited by the entrance as Arthur opened the door for an elderly tenant and her dog, then a woman with groceries and a man with a briefcase, the last stragglers of the morning. She looked across the street to the place which had been bloodied more than a month ago on the night Annie Franz was run down by a drunken driver.

Now there was no more traffic through the door to the Coventry Arms. Arthur had his smile in place as she walked over to him.

"Good morning, Miss Hyde."

"Good morning, Arthur. Lovely day, isn't it?"

A fifty-dollar bill found its way from Betty's purse into Arthur's pocket in the New York sleight of hand which out-of-towners mistook for a handshake.

"Yes, ma'am, it is indeed a lovely day."

"Correct me if I'm mistaken, but didn't you switch shifts with Bertrum on the night Mrs.

Franz died? I seem to remember you were on duty that night."

"Yes, Miss Hyde, you have a good memory."

"So you must have seen the whole thing."

"I saw everything, every detail. I was able to give the police a complete description of the drunken driver and the numbers on the license plate. They caught him within the hour, you know. It happened right over there."

Arthur pointed to the park side of the street and continued in the well-worn patter of a tour guide. "It was two-fifteen in the morning, and Mrs. Franz was a little unsteady on her feet. I'm not saying she was drunk, mind you."

No, Arthur would never say that. Betty nodded her encouragement to go on.

"Well, they were arguing again."

There had been no argument in Eric's version when she gave him shelter from the press and the police. She had called her own personal physician to treat him for shock. In Eric's version, he and Annie had been discussing the first draft of his new book.

"*She thought it was the best thing I'd ever written.*"

And that same line had found its way into subsequent interviews with Eric on the talk show circuit—circus—following the death of his wife.

"So the argument's getting pretty loud by now," said Arthur. "She stumbled back a bit. And then she was standing in the street."

"*Annie said she had dropped her purse in the street. She went back to get it,*" Eric had told her, tears streaming down his face. Behind him was the $1.5 million view from her apartment, the skyline and the blue-gold spectacle of dawn, as he described the sickening sound of his wife's body hitting the car.

Arthur was now slipping into the mode of a broadcaster describing a sporting event instead of a death.

"So, he's still on the sidewalk. He's looking straight at her, and right into the lights of the oncoming car. I remember the look on his face with the headlights shining in his eyes as the car is coming to kill his wife. It would have been so weird if you didn't know Mr. Franz was blind. He was three feet away, but that was close enough to pull her back, or at least warn her. But he couldn't know the car was coming, because he couldn't see."

"Did the police ever ask you about it?"

"Yes, ma'am, a few questions. I talked to the uniformed officers, and then later, a detective—tall, thin fellow. But at the time, they were all more interested in the hit-and-run vehicle."

And the police had not paid him for the entire monologue, the blow-by-blow account on the death of a woman Arthur must have hated as much as he liked Eric Franz. Everyone liked Eric.

"Later, the detective came back to ask if I could corroborate the statements of the other drivers. You know, there were three vehicles in all. But of course the papers got it all wrong. Well, she had her back turned when the drunk's car ran her down. She flew about twenty feet in that direction."

Arthur pointed north. She wondered if he was aware of the fact that he was smiling as he warmed to the subject of the flying body.

"Mrs. Franz landed on a southbound van. The van driver put his vehicle up on the curb and wrecked the awning support for the building next door. She fell off the van, and into the path of a vintage silver Jaguar. Her dress got snagged up in the rear wheels, and the Jaguar dragged her for maybe fifteen feet before he stopped."

Very confidential now, just between the two of them, "She was still breathing, Miss Hyde. That wasn't in the papers either. She didn't die until just before the ambulance arrived."

Betty nodded. Of course it would take at least three vehicles to kill Annie Franz. And it was so fitting that the last one was shaped like a silver bullet.

"Did Mrs. Franz say anything before she died?"

"I don't think so. You'd have to ask the police department, or maybe that detective could help you. He was the first one on the scene. 'Piece of luck,' I think he said. He was just passing by, I believe. He gave her first aid while we waited for the ambulance."

"And what was Eric doing while this was going on?"

"He was just standing there. He was in shock, of course. One of the uniformed police officers was trying to take a statement from him, but I think he was having trouble making sense of the whole thing. And that was when you came down and took him away from the policeman."

"Yes, he was in shock. Poor Eric," said Betty. "It must have been so hard on him. If only he'd been able to see—"

"—he could have saved her."

★ ★ ★

286

Mallory leaned down to the driver's window of the cab. "This is police business. I'm commandeering the cab."

"No English," said the driver.

"*Police!*" Thrusting her shield and ID into the cabby's face, she said, "*Badge.* So, now you know English."

As she was handcuffing the girl to the handle of the cab door, the cabbie was protesting in his native tongue, which had many accompanying hand gestures, and one of them was obscene in any language.

Mallory crossed the street to the pay phone. After five minutes of conversation, she was back at the cab door, undoing the cuffs and giving directions to the driver.

"No English," he said.

She opened the door and, jerking on the material of his coat, she spilled his short body out onto the street. "You want to ride in the back seat or the trunk? If you don't tell me now, I'll decide for you. Oh, and I noticed the hack license picture isn't your face. Maybe this is a stolen cab."

"I guess I'll ride in the back seat," said the driver, rising to his feet and reaching for the handle of the back door. But Mallory and the girl were already in the front seat, and the cab was pulling away from the curb.

"Why didn't you call for a police car?" said the girl, who had been silent till now.

"Paperwork," said Mallory. "If we go through the paperwork, I have to turn you in. You're already dope-sick. If I turn you in, you'll be in custody when the real misery comes on. Is that what you want?"

287

The girl turned her face to the window.

"I didn't think so," said Mallory. "I want to know what kind of business you do with Palanski. He wasn't meeting you in a public place for sex."

The girl kept her silence, pressing angry lips together—a prelude to a tantrum, and taunting evidence that this was still a child.

"If you're thinking Palanski will get you out, he won't. He'll be keeping a low profile for the next few days. And if you're thinking he'll kill you for talking, you've got good instincts. But I won't let that happen."

"I suppose you want my life story, too. What's a kid like me doing in a—"

"No, I know your story. All the stories are the same. You can't go home again."

Nothing passed between them until Mallory was taking the cab out of Manhattan through the twilight lamps of the Lincoln Tunnel.

"It wouldn't do any good to tell on him," said the girl. "No one would take my word against a cop."

"You're right about that. Palanski would say you were just an informant. He'd get off with a reprimand for not turning you over to Juvenile officers—unless there was someone else to corroborate your testimony."

"The johns would never talk. That's nuts. Rich bastards, they'd—"

And now she shut her mouth again, knowing she'd said too much. Mallory smiled. "Okay. Let's see if I can work this out. Palanski lines up the johns for you. He does the background work, shadows them, gets to know their habits. Then he tells you where to plant yourself so they'll run

288

into you. Does he feed you lines, too, or do you know how to get them to take you home?"

The girl's head lolled to one side as she closed her eyes. "I give them all the same line—'It's cold, mister. Do you know how I can get out of the cold, and maybe get something to eat?' Sometimes they just give me money. One of them tried to flag down a cop car, and I had to run for it. Palanski screws up sometimes. But you'd be surprised how many men want to take me out of the cold."

"Then Palanski shows up at the john's door the next day, right? He shows them a mug shot and the date of birth. How old are you?"

"Thirteen."

"And the johns pay up, and they pay well."

He wouldn't even need to solicit the bribe. This was New York City, and they all knew the drill. The wallets had flown from their pockets, the money had spilled into Palanski's outstretched hand, and he had tipped his hat and smiled on his way out the door.

"Where are you taking me?" The girl's eyes were open now and looking out the windows on a landscape that was not Manhattan anymore.

"Someplace safe. A friend of mine arranged for you to spend a few days in the country. A few days is all I'm gonna need."

"I can't go three days without a—"

"I know." Mallory reached inside her jacket and pulled out the three bags of white powder she had retrieved from the waters of Bethesda. She showed them to the girl and put them back in her pocket.

By the time the car pulled into the circular drive, she knew the girl's name was Fay, and Fay could never go home. If she did, her mother the drunk would beat her to death. Or perhaps the mother's new boyfriend might get first dibs on the girl's young body. Mallory pulled up in front of the large and graceful old building with a white Georgian facade. Edward Slope's car was parked near the freestanding wooden sign.

"Mayfair Research Facility? What kind of a place is this?"

Mallory kept silent until she and the girl were in the lobby, which might have passed for the ground floor of a fashionable hotel. When the girl saw the first white-coated attendant, she tried to bolt. She pulled at Mallory's hand, which would not release her. Now the attendant had Fay by both arms and was forcing her down the hall and away as she screamed out to Mallory. "You said you wouldn't turn me in! You promised, you promised!"

She broke free of the attendant and ran to Mallory. "We had a deal. You promised."

She was crying now, the garish makeup washing down her face like yesterday's Halloween mask. She was stripped to childhood again. She wrapped her arms around Mallory's waist as the attendant tried to pull her away.

Dr. Edward Slope was glaring at Mallory. "I told you to prepare her for this. You never listen to me—or anyone else."

He sat down on his heels and gently turned the face of the child toward his own. "You think it's going to hurt. It won't. I want you to go with this man. You're already feeling sick, aren't you? Yes, I can see that. He's going to give you something to take the pain away. It'll never hurt you again. You have my word on that."

She loosened her grip on Mallory, but the look of betrayal remained. A deal had been broken. Nothing would change that, and they both knew it.

When she was gone down the hall with the attendant, Slope turned to Mallory. "There's a limit to my influence here, but I pulled every string I could. I just hope you know what you're doing. An underage Jane Doe is illegal as hell, so I'm passing her off as a relative incognito. She's in the program, but only for the three days of detox. What then?"

"I hadn't thought that far ahead. I just need her off the street for a couple of days. Oh, and I need a Polaroid of the kid. Can you manage that for me?"

"Yes, of course. But what happens to the child when the three days are up?"

"I don't know. I've got enough problems right now."

"Kathy, sometimes I think you're growing into a real human being, and then you exasperate me this way. You got her this far, that's good. But after the detox—what then? You can't just dump off a little girl like she was a sack of potatoes."

"Doris does all the cooking in your house— that's her job, right?"

"What?"

Mallory's hands went to her hips. Her words had a cautioning edge. "If you'd ever tried to prepare a meal, you'd know what an art form it really is, making every dish come out at the same time." Her voice was on the rise now, and angry. "Well, I'm cooking! I've got six dishes going at six different speeds, and they all have to be done at exactly the same time or the whole thing falls apart on me." One long fingernail jabbed at his chest. "You go do your own damn job! Get off my back!"

And the cook with a gun walked through the lobby and out the front door.

Today Mallory had only one message for each of her suspects. She blocked out the bulletin board they would access on their screens and tapped in the code to call up the dummy board. It displayed only one sentence repeated over and over again: I HAVE A WITNESS.

And that was no lie if cats counted.

Though the hallway was generous in width, Pansy Heart pressed her body to the wall as her husband walked by. His face was red, his eyes hard, and he walked heavy on his feet, sending one fist to the wall a scant few inches from where she stood. In the room he had left, the computer screen was blank once more. What had been the message this time?

A door slammed at the other end of the hall. She jumped as though she had trodden on a live wire. She gripped the edge of the hall table, feeling empty and airy inside, believing that she might fly upward without this solid anchor of oak. Her heart was knocking on the wall of her chest.

It was natural to be thinking of her mother-in-law on that last day of the old woman's life, in that moment when the organs were shutting down one by one. There had been an inner knowledge of impending death in the ancient eyes. Only minutes before, terror had lived in that deeply lined face. Then the lines had smoothed out, and in the eyes was, not peace, but triumph. And then her mother-in-law had died—escaped.

Angel Kipling paced up and down the carpet before her husband Harry. "Don't tell me you don't know what this is about." She held up the printout from the computer. A single sentence repeated one hundred times across the sheet. "A witness to what? What have you done?" Her voice was in the whining mode and threatened to climb into a scream.

Harry Kipling was buttoning his shirt in front of the mirror. Now he sought out her reflection behind his own. "It's not addressed to me, is it?"

Angel's lip was curling as he turned around to face her in the flesh. She placed her hands on her wide hips, and her robe fell open to display the ponderous breasts sagging against the thick body. His eyes dropped to the opening in the robe, and he quickly turned away from her. She winced as though she had been slapped.

As he left the full-length mirror to examine his tie rack, Angel stood alone in the glass, staring at her reflection. She had not yet put on the armature of makeup, and her hair was wild with snarls.

She closed the robe quickly and addressed her husband in a smaller voice this time. "It's not another bank card scam, is it, Harry? You're not having trouble living on your allowance money, are you?"

It had cost her a fortune to clean up after his last foray into creative banking, that or face the scandal and the stockholders. And she had never believed the stolen money was gone, spent. Was he amassing capital for a getaway? No, he would never leave her. He would never stray far from the source of unlimited wealth.

He ignored her and continued the business of tying his tie, an odd and useless preoccupation for a man who had no occupation, no business to conduct. And now she forgot that she was ugliest in the morning, most vulnerable without her magic makeup.

"Answer me, you prick. You don't want me to cut off your allowance again, do you?"

"Angel, I have no idea what's going on. It's probably a prank. Some kid in the building."

"It's another bank swindle, isn't it? I thought I made it very clear what would happen if you tried this one more time. You won't like being poor again, Harry."

"I haven't done anything."

She pulled a crumple of computer paper from her robe pocket and thrust it at him.

"This was faxed yesterday. It's an application for a credit card, and the form is addressed to you."

"I haven't applied for any credit cards."

"Read it!"

He accepted the ball of paper and made a small production out of smoothing it over the surface of the bedside table.

Under the heading of pertinent information, it read: First, tell us why you did it. Please print or type your confession in the space provided.

He picked up the sheet of paper, bringing it close to his eyes, examining the logo of the credit card company, which appeared at the top of the page.

The next line read: Does your wife know what

you did? If so, we have provided additional space for her comments.

Now he stared at the short list of questions:

1. Why did you lie?

2. Would you do it again if we gave you the chance?

He lowered the page and then looked up as Angel paced back and forth across the rug with barely contained fury.

"And now this message on the building bulletin board!" The words exploded from her mouth. "What does it mean?" She looked down at the most recent message, clutched in her hand. " 'I have a witness.' A witness to what? Talk to me, Harry, or I'll cut off your allowance, and then I'll cut off your balls!"

Eric Franz was slow to answer his door. Betty Hyde could hear him walking toward the foyer, a shuffle of hard soles on marble. When the door did open, he was looking over her shoulder, as though just missing her with his eyes. A sheet of paper was wadded in his hand. His face was a mask. The room behind him was dark but for the constant glow of the computer's ever-open eye.

"If she knew you were digging into her past, it could end your friendship," said Rabbi David Kaplan.

"I only want the connection between the boy and Mallory," said Charles Butler.

The rabbi's den was a place where books lived. They were not kept to the shelves, but quietly gathered in stacks on every surface of the room, perched in groups of agreeable subjects. A single leather-bound volume lay open on the desk, patiently awaiting the rabbi's return to the interrupted business of scholarship.

"Perhaps the connection between them is only a simple commonality," said the rabbi.

"The difference in their backgrounds doesn't leave room for much in common."

"All children have a commonality in innocence."

"I wouldn't describe either of them as innocent. The boy talks like a forty-year-old man. And Mallory . . . is Mallory."

"Perhaps they share the innocence of good and evil."

"That's the first time I've heard the word 'innocence' so connected with evil."

"Take Helen's view of Kathy. Helen could see nothing bad in the child. Helen always said no one had ever explained the rules to Kathy, and she was close to the truth. These concepts of good and evil, right and wrong, heaven and hell— what is that to a child on the street, living by wit and theft? When she first came to live with Louis and Helen, her behavior sometimes bordered on that of feral children raised apart from humans."

"What about the natural mother? Is it possible she abused her child? Perhaps that would explain a lot of the damage."

"Charles, I know nothing about the natural mother. Kathy has never once spoken about this woman."

"Suppose you had to speculate on her parents. Just based on what you know of her, what would you say?"

"We assumed Kathy had been on the street for three or four years before Markowitz arrested her. She was a ten-year-old thief. She tried to lie her way to twelve, and Markowitz let her get away with eleven—but she stole that year.

"Now we know she'd never been to a formal school. Helen had her evaluated at the Learning Center. But someone had taught her to read and write at a very early age. She also had an astonishing natural aptitude for mathematics. That was why Helen and Louis spent more than they could afford on private schools. They were afraid her gifts would wither in the public school system with one teacher to every fifty children."

The rabbi went to the shelf and took a box from among the books. From it he withdrew papers. "This is a sample of Kathy's handwriting at ten. It's not the hand of a child. Someone took great care with her, and very early on.

"And then Helen evaluated her religious education. One day we took her with us to meet with Father Barry at the parish in the neighborhood. It was that time of year when we joined together to feed and clothe the poor. When Kathy saw the crucifix above the altar, she automatically made the sign of the cross. Helen took this as an omen, and she gave the Christians equal time in Kathy's spiritual guidance. So someone had taught the child to make the sign of the cross.

"From only this, I may deduce that someone spent an enormous amount of time with her. She was not unwanted or ignored, not considered a burden to her mother, but the focus of attention. And that person enabled Kathy to love Helen at first sight. I like to believe she must have been rather like Helen Markowitz, this special someone. Can you see this woman abusing her child? Or allowing anyone else to go it? I can not.

297

This woman I know nothing about, I remember her in my prayers."

"May I take that to mean you think the woman is dead?"

"What else could separate such a woman from her child?"

"I'm going to bring down the judge."

She thought that might make his little eyes spin around.

Mallory stared at the ME investigator across the same table in the same coffeehouse where she had first hooked him. She had left him just enough time to let his own imagination do all the work for her, and then she had reeled him back in. That was the old man's style, and it had worked well.

Thank you, Markowitz.

"Heller lives for his work, and there's none better. If he knew you were walking evidence out of the crime scenes, he'd hunt you down and put a bullet in you. So you walk the evidence. You give it to a cop, and you're one person removed from the crime of blackmail."

"You've got nothin' solid, Mallory. If you did—"

"I've got reports on three suicides with no notes left behind. That's what tipped me. You were the ME investigator on all three scenes. Who did the notes implicate? What embarrassing details were in them? Suicides just love to unload before they cross over. I imagine you've carted out other souvenirs, maybe a few photographs of married men? Love letters? What else? In the case of the judge's mother, you obstructed a homicide investigation. You kept quiet about evidence of

298

murder. Palanski showed up because you called him in. You had to. No way you could hand him the old lady's body. So now I've got the two of you in the same room of a dirty operation. But this time you covered up a murder."

"No, it was battery maybe, but not homicide. And the battery wasn't all that recent. She had a split lip, but it had healed some. Maybe it was a day old. And there was a bruise on the side of her face, but it was at least two days old, and that didn't kill her either. Her own doctor was there. You can ask him. She did die of natural causes."

"But the marks would've been embarrassing to the judge, right? So Palanski shows up, and he takes over and works the judge. Am I right?"

The ME investigator would not meet her eyes. She looked down to the paper napkin in his hands. He was shredding it to moist confetti. He opened his mouth to speak, but she dared not give him time to say he wanted a lawyer. She slammed her open hand down on the table, and his mouth closed as he jumped in his chair, nerves shot to hell.

"Your biggest problem is that your partner is stupid. He buys stocks, bearer bonds, and the idiot thinks nobody can trace them because the deals are cash. Every cash transaction is logged just like the credit transactions. All his financial activity is on computer. Did you know that Palanski's been cheating you on the cuts?" No, she could see he hadn't known.

"The way you handled your cut of the payoffs was only a little brighter." She thumbed through the sheaf of papers on the table till she found the one she wanted. She set this in front of him. "This is a record of all the cash deposits you made into your mother's bank account. But you have power of attorney on that account, so you're tied up by computer transactions too. Your mother's entire legal income is Social Security, and yet she has this fantastic bank account. Still, Internal Affairs would never have tipped to that. Oh, but that fool Palanski."

"You won't get anything on him without me testifying on the payoff."

"I won't hurt you. A deal is a deal. I'm going to let you rat on yourself *and* Palanski. You know the drill. The first one to turn state's evidence gets immunity."

Nose was paroled from the bathroom for the evening. He purred around her legs as Mallory put the bullets into the speed-loader for her revolver.

She faced the foyer mirror and thought of visual cues. She looked down at the cat and closed her long and narrow eyes to suspicious slits. Nose began to dance.

The cue for the dancing, what was it?

A muffled noise called her eyes up to the ceiling. The sounds upstairs were unmistakable. Plush carpet and thick insulation could not block out the scream. Now furniture was being turned over. Feet pounded into the front room above her head. She followed the sounds, eyes to the ceiling. She stopped by the phone in the living room.

She tapped keys on the building computer and scrolled through the list of tenants until she had Betty Hyde's number. More furniture was moving. A dial tone. Another scream.

"Hyde residence," said a foreign voice.

"Put Hyde on the phone. Tell her it's Mallory and it's urgent."

Telephone pressed between shoulder and ear, she opened the closet door and pulled out the heavy sheepskin jacket to hide the bulge of the gun. The jacket was bulky enough to interfere with action, but she was not ready to show her hand or her gun in public, for this was the visual cue to call the lawyer. She was slipping into the sleeves of the coat when Betty Hyde came to the phone.

"Mallory, darling, I thought you'd never call."

"Meet me at Judge Heart's apartment. I'll be there before you. Stay back, all right? Stay the hell out of my way."

She took the stairs three at a time. She noted the three locks as she neared the door. Most people only used one lock until they were in for the night. It was early yet. The main lock was the flimsiest. But the thick door was too formidable to break down. She banged on the door with her fist and pressed the buzzer.

"Open up!"

Now there was dead silence within. And maybe a dead woman?

She banged on the door again. "Open up or I'll call the police!" Magic words for the man in the public eye.

She heard heavy footsteps on the tiles of the foyer beyond the door, and then the sound of the lock being undone, the latch chain being slipped into its notch. The door opened a crack, and she was looking into the cold eyes of Judge Heart just above the length of brass chain which bound the door to its frame.

She smiled politely, stepped back and kicked

the door at the center, breaking the latch chain and knocking the man off balance. She pushed past him and entered the apartment.

Pansy Heart was in the corner of the front room, trying desperately to crawl into the pattern of the rug and disappear. Her nose was bleeding, her lip was split, and the side of her face was already beginning to swell.

Behind her, the judge was screaming, "You have no right!"

Mallory turned on him. "I'm taking her out of here. Don't give me any trouble."

His face had gone to purple rage as he advanced on her. With a quick, sure kick, she put her foot into his groin and watched his skin drain of color as his eyes bulged out with surprise and pain. He slipped down to one knee.

Pansy Heart was crying softly. Mallory pulled the woman up and walked her toward the door, one arm supporting the smaller woman about the tiny waist.

Betty Hyde stood in the doorway. Her eyes were fixed on Pansy Heart's ruined face, and her mouth was suppressing a smile.

"I'll take care of her," she said, putting her arms around the crying woman as Mallory stepped back. "Come with me, Pansy. You need a doctor, dear."

The judge was getting to his feet. He was clumsy and slow about it, as both hands were clutching his groin. Mallory tucked a foot under his unbending legs and tripped him, sending his face into the corner of a heavy oak table and giving him his own bloody nose.

Pansy Heart looked back at her husband as though awaiting further orders. Then she yielded to the gentle force of Betty Hyde, who was propelling her through the door and into the hall.

The gossip columnist was on her way to an interview with this battered woman, and nothing but a joint act of Congress and God would have stopped her. Mallory wondered if she had done the judge a favor by preventing him from getting between Hyde and his wife.

Mallory set a tray of teapot and cups down on the table, and then she let her eyes roam the generous front room of Betty Hyde's apartment. It was a copy of the Rosens' only in the architecture. The decorator had been a pro. She knew Charles would have appreciated the American and British antiques masterfully woven with the modern pieces. The front room was open and airy, without bric-a-brac. It was gracious living without souvenir or sentiment or any heart to it at all. Mallory approved.

The judge's wife was sitting in an early-American rocking chair, holding a cold compress to her swelling face. Betty Hyde sat on a footstool and gently pushed on the armrest of Pansy's chair, rocking, lulling the crying woman. Entangling her gaze with Pansy's, Hyde crooned soft words, smiling, eyes gleaming, playing the good nurse.

Mallory handed a cup of tea to the judge's wife. The woman smiled her gratitude and accepted the tea with a nervous clattering of the china. She seemed even more fragile than the delicate Old Willow teacup.

Mallory leaned down until her eyes were level with the woman, who had ceased her crying and now looked up at Mallory with absolute trust.

"Mrs. Heart, were you at home the night the judge beat the crap out of your mother-in-law?"

The woman's eyes were startled wide, and it seemed that her thin shoulders were being pressed to the back of her chair. Then her head dropped to her chest, and her entire body wilted. Now Pansy had been assaulted for the second time in one night.

Mallory eased back, lifted a cup from the near table and began to stir her own tea.

"Did that old woman scream as loud as you did?"

The sobbing began again, racking the smaller woman's leaf-light body.

Betty Hyde rolled her eyes. She rose from the footstool and led Mallory back to the kitchen.

"That was brutal, Mallory. One day we must have a long talk about your style—I think I could learn from you. Are you just fishing, dear, or do you have something more on the bastard?"

"I've got copies of the hospital records during the years Judge Heart's mother lived with them. There's another file with his wife's hospital records. He probably didn't kill the old lady with a beating, but if you want to get to the judge, I would suggest applying a little pressure on his mother's doctor—you might want the old woman's body exhumed. The DA is a good political animal. You might approach him with the word 'cover-up' and then explain that a high-profile case might be good for his career. And leave my name out of it."

"Understood. And what can I do for you, Mallory?"

"Milk Pansy for everything you can get. At the

tenants' meeting, she said her dog was gone. Is it dead?"

Betty turned to the woman in the other room. Pansy had ceased her crying now and sat quietly staring into her teacup. Hyde raised her voice to ask, "Pansy, you still have a dog, don't you, dear? Rosie, isn't it?"

Pansy Heart turned to face Betty with a look of mild surprise. "Yes, Rosie is at the animal hospital. I don't know when she'll be coming home. She's very sick."

Mallory found something familiar about the tone of voice. It was the practiced way the woman said the words. She was lying.

Well, everybody lied.

Mallory strode back to the front room and leaned down with both hands on the arms of the rocking chair. Pansy looked up, and her hand started to rise to ward off a blow. It was an instinctive reflex.

"Your dog is dead, isn't it?"

The woman was flying apart from the center. One hand flashed out and sent the teacup and saucer crashing to the floor. Her eyes were slipping into shock.

"When did the dog die?"

And now the words came out in a gush of hysteria. "I don't know! I haven't seen Rosie for days. My husband took her out for a walk, and she never came back again. He said she was at the vet's."

"But you called the vet and the dog wasn't there, right?"

Pansy was nodding. Quiet now. Shock was doing its calming work.

Mallory turned away and left Hyde to clean

up the damage, this puddle of a woman in the middle of her floor.

Edward Slope took his seat at the table. "Stop apologizing, Charles."

"But I only meant to leave a message on your office machine. I would never have dragged you away from your family on Christmas night."

"But I wasn't with my family, Charles. I was catching up on a backlog of autopsies. Christmas is my busy season. So why the secrecy? Has the little brat asked you to break the law?"

Charles had never been able to win at poker. He didn't have the face to run a bluff, or so Edward Slope had reminded him once a week. So how to begin this foray into lying, which was Mallory country and an uncharted place he had never been to.

"I had a few words with Riker last night," said Charles. "I know Kathy witnessed a murder when she was a child." And that was true, wasn't it? Riker's reaction had confirmed it, certainly. And his reaction to discussing the matter with Edward Slope had suggested that Edward could tell him what Riker would not.

The doctor sat back in his chair and went through the stalling mechanics of removing his glasses and cleaning them. "So Riker told you about that?"

Charles nodded, and in that nod he told his first lie of the evening. He was practicing at Mallory's religion of Everyone Lies.

Forgive me, Edward my friend, for my trespasses against thee.

Slope restored his glasses to the bridge of his nose. "When I asked Riker, point-blank, if he had ever seen any of the films, he denied it. You haven't mentioned this to anyone else, have you?"

"No," said Charles, with the sudden realization that somehow he had just betrayed Riker.

Forgive me, Riker, for I'm about to trespass some more.

Charles settled the napkin on his lap, not wanting to meet the eyes of the man he could not beat at poker. "Riker wouldn't go into any detail about the film."

And that was true. No, it was not. It was deception.

"I'm sure he wouldn't. He's not supposed to know the film existed. But apparently Riker did know about it. There's no other way he could have known about the murder. I gather this is important, or he wouldn't have hung himself out to dry that way."

"It's very important." If he was right about the connection between Mallory and Justin, a child was at stake.

"Markowitz swore to me that Riker had never seen the film. And we destroyed it that night. It wouldn't make sense for him to tell Riker after the fact, not if you knew Markowitz's style. Do you understand that, technically, this knowledge could make you an accessory?"

Charles nodded. *Another lie. No, I don't understand. And only a second has gone by and now I've somehow betrayed Markowitz, too.*

"Markowitz would never have shown it to anyone else. This was Kathy's history, and he protected it. He wouldn't have risked the feds seeing Kathy on tape, interrogating her. He only showed it to me because he wanted to close out

307

the case. He needed a positive identification based on a scar. The original wound was on the film. Did Riker give you any background on the case?"

"Not much."

"The FBI came into Special Crimes Section when a body turned up in Manhattan. The remains had the trademark wounds of a pair of serial killers operating up and down the Eastern Seaboard. Markowitz turned up a lead on one of the killers, and the feds botched the arrest. They sent five men to arrest the suspect, and the man was killed in a shoot-out."

"Markowitz must have been furious."

"He was. He flushed the feds out of Special Crimes as though they were so much vermin. He took over the site of the shoot-out and recovered a cache of film. It took him a long time to go through all the reels. He did it himself. It was so brutal, he said, he didn't want to burn out his detectives. But really, he was a bit like Kathy, always keeping something back. All he shared with the others was a splice that showed the face of the second killer.

"I know you've heard the story of how Markowitz took Kathy in. Well, he did arrest Kathy for breaking into a car. And Helen was adamant about keeping the child—that was all true. But the real reason he wouldn't turn Kathy over to Juvenile Hall was because he recognized her. She'd been several years younger when the film was made. But who could forget that face?"

"So she had seen the murder, and he wanted her as a material witness?"

"No, they'd already found the location of the film set. Several years had gone by, and the site was cold. It was another four years before Riker made the arrest on the second man and killed him."

"But it was in the line of duty, wasn't it?"

"That was Riker's story. One thing that worked in Riker's favor at the hearing was that the FBI had killed the man's accomplice during an arrest. Markowitz took the position that Riker had done the same thing it took five agents to do—no more, no less. And Markowitz swore under oath that he had been the only one to view the films. So IA couldn't take it as a case of a cop cracking up and taking vengeance for the victims. And since Riker had killed the suspect with his fists and not his gun, Internal Affairs and the DA came to the conclusion that death was not premeditated, that it occurred while resisting arrest."

"That would seem reasonable."

"At the time, it did. I backed their conclusion. To my knowledge *at the time*, Markowitz was the only one who knew the personal connection of the film. So now it seems that Markowitz lied to me. Well, that was typical. He wouldn't have told me the truth if it made me an accessory after the fact. And he was probably feeling part of the blame for what Riker had done. You know, personal detachment is everything in police work."

And Riker loved Kathy.

"Kathy doesn't know about the film. Markowitz wanted it that way. You can never tell her about this evening. That's understood?"

"Of course."

"Markowitz warned me, said I didn't have to sit through the entire thing. He told me I'd regret it if I did. But I was so confident in my own

309

professional detachment, I took it for a challenge. I had to view the film because Riker had made such a mess of the man's face, Markowitz couldn't identify the victim from the driver's-license photo, and there were no prints on file. He asked me to make the ID based on the scar from a wound the victim received in that film."

"Tell me about the film."

"After I tell you, you will wish I hadn't. I guarantee that. Shall I go on?"

This was his last chance to be an honest man, the man Edward Slope thought he was dealing with.

"Yes, go on."

"Do you know what a snuff film is?"

"No."

"It's a film of the torture and murder of a human being. A little something for the ultimate film buff—the freak. Most of the victims are children. Any child you see on the streets of New York can be turned into some kind of currency."

Slope waved down a passing waiter to order a double scotch. He turned back to Charles. "I can't do this sober. Are you sure you want to hear all the details?"

"Quite sure."

Not at all sure. I have nightmares enough. No. Go on. I deserve this.

"When the film opened, the children, a boy and a girl, were asleep on the floor of a cage. It wasn't a fancy production. It was shot in a warehouse with only one set. I believe the children were drugged. The little boy was just coming out of it. Maybe that's why they took him first. The little girl wasn't moving at all. It was Kathy, of course. You knew that."

Charles nodded.

Another lie, and another bad dream due for penance.

"She could only have been eight years old when the film was made. She'd apparently been on the street for a while by then. She was wearing a grimy T-shirt and jeans that were miles too big for her. I remember her telling me once that she'd always stolen the jeans closest to the door of the shop, so she didn't always get a great fit."

A waiter hovered over the table to deposit a glass, which Edward grabbed up at once. He drank quickly.

"She was only wearing one shoe, and one foot was bare. Well, they took the boy out of the cage and started to work on him. I made Markowitz turn off the volume, but I can still hear the child screaming. You don't need to know what they did. But he lived quite a while before they were finished with him. And all the while, the cage was in view to one side of the screen. Kathy never moved, never opened her eyes. I watched her the whole time they were torturing the little boy."

Oh, God. No, wait. I'm a visitor in Mallory's church tonight, and God is not here.

"Then it was Kathy's turn."

I don't want to hear any more of this.

"One of the men opened the door of the cage and lifted her out. She was dead weight in his arms." Edward ran one hand through his hair, and then drank from the glass as though with a terrible thirst.

"You know what I remember most vividly? The one small shoe and the little bare foot. Isn't that absurd? Kathy slept on as he laid her down on the mattress that was bloodied from the body

311

of the little boy. They had just rolled him off to one side. So much blood."

Charles watched the rapid movement of Edward's eyes and realized that the man was watching the film all over again. Edward's hands covered his face for a moment, and his next words were muffled.

"Oh Christ! Isn't it just a wonderful world for children, Charles?"

Charles began to rise from his chair, leaning toward his dinner companion. Edward put up one hand.

"No, I'm all right. Sit down, Charles. I'm sorry."

And after another moment, the reel in the doctor's eyes rolled on again.

"And then the man bent over her. Suddenly, Kathy was awake. Not just coming around from the drug, but wide awake. She'd been shamming sleep—that was obvious—waiting out the murder, picking her moment. And then she was all over the man and all teeth and snarls like an animal. Her little thumbs stabbed at his eyes. That one veered off with both hands to his face. Blood was streaming out between his fingers. You can guess at the damage she did there. And then the cameraman was on her. She closed her mouth on his bare arm and bit off a chunk of the flesh. A *chunk of flesh*, Charles. And she spat it out on the floor."

Charles looked into the shattered lenses of Edward's eyes. The doctor was in the moment. It was happening all over again.

"And now the men are screaming, lights are being overturned, the camera is lying on the floor. The closing shot is Kathy hightailing it down a dark hall and away from the light, running like the devil, with one shoe off and one shoe on."

He had liked that stupid look of surprise in the moment she realized she would die. Best of all, he liked the look of her when she was dead, all lines of hostility smoothed out. The only good bitch was a dead bitch. Mallory would be no different.

The two grapes were squashed beneath his thumbs, but slowly, in the delicious destruction of the orbs, the breaking of the skin, flattening of membranous flesh therein, the feel of the cold destroyed tissue. Each was a green eye to him. And now he drew his thumbs back from the cutting board. Staring at them, mashed, split, she was blind to him.

"She wouldn't press charges," said Betty Hyde, setting her coffee mug on the countertop in the Rosens' kitchen. "I don't suppose you have any more proof on the beating of his mother? I've got a very vague column for the morning edition. My editor won't let me use any names till we exhume the body—and that's in the works. I also have a young reporter waiting to ambush the judge outside the building tomorrow. You know the sort of thing . . . 'Is there any truth to the rumor that you beat your elderly mother to death?' "

"Did Pansy give you anything?"

"No. Poor Pansy. I've never seen that kind of pain up close. She's gone back to him."

"She's up there now? She's crazy."

"She says he's always very contrite after he beats her. She's not afraid of him right now. She thinks she can work this out."

"You know he's going to kill her the next time."

"Does she have to file the complaint? Couldn't you do it? In addition to the humane aspects, I'm thinking of libel laws. An editor won't touch it without a police report, and there isn't one."

"I didn't witness the beating. If she says she fell down, the law agrees with her."

Mallory's face was devoid of all expression as she folded her arms and looked down at Betty Hyde. Hyde fought off the startling illusion that Mallory had grown taller in the passage of seconds. Now Mallory leaned down, and Hyde stepped back until she was pressed against the kitchen counter.

"You're holding out on me. What have you got on Eric Franz?"

It was late to be calling on the neighbors. But then, she had taken Eric in on the night Annie died. It was late then, too. *Tit for tat, my dear.*

When Eric answered the door, he was pulling his robe closed about his waist, and staring into the air over her left shoulder.

"Eric, it's Betty. Can we talk?"

He stepped back from the door and waved her into the room. It was black until he said, "Oh, sorry," and pressed the light switch. She shouldn't have been surprised to see the room unchanged. It had been little over a month since Annie died. Although gone was the bad joke of their framed wedding portrait with crayon cuckold's horns drawn on the head of his likeness.

They were hours and bottles into the wine rack when Eric lost control.

"Are you crazy? Annie would never have stayed

314

with me those last three years if not for the blindness. No, actually it was the insurance money that changed her mind about divorcing me. And then I had the success of the books and the prizes. But if I had been sighted, she would have left me in a minute and taken a large settlement. But she couldn't leave a blind man, could she, not a socialite like Annie. What would the neighbors think?''

The latch lowered, and the door opened with a gentle push. He prowled through the dark rooms until he found her. Her long slender body was stretched out on the bed. Her hair had a glow to it, as though she had found a way to trap sunlight, to bring it indoors with her and keep it alive in the night.

He lay down beside her with animal stealth and rolled onto his back and into sleep, four feet paddling the air, chasing mice across his dreams.

It was the cold metal of the gun against his nose that woke him to the bright light of a lamp. He looked at the tip of the gun, and it was necessary to cross his eyes to do this. Weary and unsteady on the bedding, he rose to his hind legs and began the dance. But she was already gone, having slipped from the bed and into the dark of the next room, preceded by the gun in her hand.

He thudded down to the floor and padded after her as she searched behind each door. She stopped awhile by the bathroom door. He rubbed his head against one of her bare feet, which did not love him back but pushed him away. Her hand depressed the latch on the door. She pressed on it again and again.

She looked down at him and whispered, ''Are

you that smart?" which he, more or less, correctly interpreted as "Good boy," and he began to purr.

Now he was being picked up in her arms, luxuriating in the warmth of her skin. And then, he was falling toward the tiles of the bathroom floor. The light went out, the door slammed, and he sat alone in the dark, wondering what he had done wrong this time.

Mallory, the consummate liar, had barred herself from the poker game for the damage of a lie. How perverse and convoluted was her code of what passed for honor.

Charles had learned to lie and betray in one night. Oh wouldn't Mallory be proud of how far he'd come, how low he'd sunk.

No, no she wouldn't. One did not do such damage to people in Mallory's orbit. But she would never know what he had done. Even if he was in the confession mode, he was bound by Slope to keep silent. A lie of omission.

As Riker had once explained to him, her history belonged to her alone. She would hate this intrusion, this conspiracy of knowledge. Slope would never discuss this evening with Riker. The lies and betrayal would go unnoticed. And so there were more lies by omission.

He didn't have the luxury of barring himself from the poker game. Questions would be asked, she would ferret out the answers, more damage would be done. Once a week, he would be reminded of his crimes, sitting across a card table from Edward Slope.

And he could not confess to Riker, either, not without the web spreading. He only wished he were a practicing Catholic so he could confess to someone.

The pattern of his web had become too intricate. Sleep was lost in the tangle of the weave. But finally, sleep did come for him, all in visions of a little girl running in the dark, pursued by things which were darker still and might be spiders. And when she slipped in the blood of his dreams, he snapped awake.

His mind flooded with music to kill the images and thoughts created by a night of lies, and now his penance was in the room with him. He shut his eyes and tried to end the music. But he could hear the light steps of Amanda's feet all around his bed.

"Interesting, isn't it," said Amanda. "She was able to pretend sleep while another child was being murdered."

No, please. I don't want to think about that.

"Oh, Charles, you'll never stop thinking about that. It wasn't the reaction you'd expect from a small child, was it?"

Since when was Mallory predictable?

He kept his eyes closed, his hopes of minimizing the damage to his mind. He didn't know how to send her away. Perhaps the delusion would pale without the reinforcement of sight.

But no. She continued to pace, footsteps growing heavier, waiting on her answer as a solid woman would do.

Addressing his words to the ceiling, he said, "It wasn't Mallory's mother who was killed in the film. You were wrong about that angle."

"Was I?" Amanda's pacing stopped for a moment. "She never moved the entire time a child was being tortured. She played dead."

317

"She might only have been paralyzed with fear. There are not facts to support—"

"Logic and facts have failed you, Charles. You had a qualified medical examiner as a witness to the film. She was playing dead. Where did she learn that? Maybe she'd had some practice witnessing another bloody murder. Maybe that's what happened to her mother, and to Justin's mother."

He rolled over to face her, this woman who was not there, yet he kept his eyes closed. "Amanda, this is ludicrous. Justin's mother died of a heart attack. That's a fact. Now the aspect of child abuse makes more sense. That's what Mallory would see in the boy. She would recognize the signs of an abused child. Even Mallory could not divine a murder through the boy's eyes."

Strains of the concerto meandered through his brain. He recited the Greek alphabet in a whisper. The music fled; Amanda remained to pace the floor around his bed. Her footsteps were heavier now. He opened his eyes to faint moonlight and the stronger light of street-lamps pouring through his bedroom window. He turned his face to the opposite wall, where his ultimate nightmare was moving across the wallpaper.

Amanda had learned to cast a shadow.

Chapter 7

DECEMBER 26

She had been unsuccessful in her efforts to bully the maid. Perhaps it was true that Betty Hyde was not at home this morning. And neither was Eric Franz answering his telephone. But the judge was in, and so was Harry Kipling.

She picked up the plastic evidence bag and held it up to the camera to visually record the chain of evidence written on the seal, and then the breaking of the seal. She pulled out the cap gun and set it down on the table in the front room.

Back in the den, she ran a test of the camera equipment which had just made her visual record of the evidence. On her way to the front door, four gilded wall mirrors caught the swift passing reflection of her T-shirt, shoulder holster and jeans. She was pulling on the new brown cashmere blazer, a twin to the garment Amanda Bosch had been wearing when she died. The tailor had reproduced it exactly. Not that most people would appreciate the detailing.

She had been tempted to re-create the cigarette burn on the sleeve, but the ghost of Helen Markowitz wouldn't let her do it. And Helen would have been the first to comment on the bulge the gun made in the line of the blazer.

Mallory stopped at the mirror in the foyer, checking the giveaway bulk with a critical eye.

She called the cat to her, and it came. She snapped her fingers, and the cat made a leap into her arms and nuzzled her neck. She looked back to the mirror. No, it wouldn't do. The squirming cat wouldn't hide the bulge of the gun unless she killed it first and pinned it on like a furry corsage.

She dropped the animal on the floor at her feet, shrugged off her blazer and removed the shoulder holster. She slid the gun into the drawer of the small table beneath the mirror. Putting the coat on again, she snapped her fingers for the cat.

With no self-respect, no pride, Nose jumped back into her arms.

She made her way down the hall wondering that doors didn't open to inquire about the racket of purring. She stopped at the door to Judge Heart's apartment, and knocked. It was a repeat of last night; the chain had apparently been replaced. The door only opened a crack. The judge was staring at her.

"I want to see your wife," said Mallory.

"Go away."

"I could be discreet or not. Up to you. I want to see that she's all right. I want to see her *now*!"

The door closed to the sound of the newly installed chain slipping off the latch. Now the door was opening, and the judge was calling out, "Pansy! Pansy!"

Pansy Heart entered the room. Her face showed only the damage of the previous night and no fresh marks.

"Just checking," Mallory said, turning to go. She stopped and looked back over her shoulder at the judge. "I know what you did, and I'm going to get you for it."

Judge Heart's face was in rage-shades of red as the door slammed.

When she knocked on the next door, one flight up, the Kipling boy opened it. There was no leer on the boy's face this time. He stepped back to make room for Mallory, and she walked in. Harry Kipling was seated at the table. He looked at the cat and rose quickly to his feet, but not quick enough.

A springer spaniel was bounding across the carpet and heading for the cat, jaws wide and joy in his eyes.

The apartment was still, with no current of air or sound to indicate an animate being, not even a cat. Then the quiet of no-one-home was broken by a pair of feet crossing the foyer and dragging a shadow along by the heels.

The intrusion was short-lived, for the revolver lay in the first drawer opened. The gun metal gleamed for the moments between the drawer and the dark of a bag. Stepping softly, the thief quit the apartment.

When Mallory slammed the door behind her, the Kipling boy was yelling, "Look what she did to my dog!"

Mallory returned by way of the stairway. The door to the Rosens' apartment was open. Could she have been that stupid?

This time, the cat didn't cry when she dropped him. He was even prepared for the fall. Nose had grown accustomed to this game of holding and dropping. He padded away, yawning.

She opened the drawer of the table by the door.

The drawer was empty; her Smith & Wesson revolver was gone.

Nothing else had been disturbed. The cap gun lay on the table where she had placed it.

What now? She couldn't call in for backup and admit she'd lost the gun. Neither Coffey nor Riker would let her live that one down. A rookie would not have lost her gun.

A crash came from the direction of the bedroom.

She passed through the kitchen and slipped a wine bottle into her hand. Now she entered the bedroom. The cat was standing over the remains of a broken lamp. There was no mystery to the breakage. A fringe of the lampshade was tangled in the cat's paw.

But there was still the problem of the gun.

She picked up the phone and dialed Charles from the bedroom. "I'm in a big hurry, Charles. Go to the center drawer in my desk and get the old Long Colt. And bring the box of ammo with it. You'll have to turn off the—" She lowered the phone at the sound which may or may not have been the cat. Now she set the receiver back on its cradle to stifle Charles's loud repeated "Hello?" coming from the mouthpiece.

She left the bedroom, quickly, silently gliding down the short hallway to the den. She flipped the array of switches for the cameras, backup tapes and audio.

She entered the front room to find the cat crawling under the couch and Harry Kipling standing in the center of the room. The cap gun was lying on the coffee table.

How much time would it take Charles to get to her with the real gun?

"You left your door open," said Kipling. "That was careless."

She had meant to make his access easy, but she had planned to have a gun in her hand when he came through the door. It was an odd moment to be thinking of Riker's I-told-you-so grin. Too late for backup, and Charles was miles from here.

The cameras were rolling.

There was time to wonder if Coffey would catch her in this screwup, or could she lie her way out of it.

Max Candle's knife lay on a shelf of the bookcase behind Kipling. Had he seen it? Originally, she had planned to steer him to it, so he would have a weapon in his hands in the event the cameras should catch her blowing away a taxpayer. But that plan had been contingent on having a gun in her own hand. And where was he hiding her gun?

Kipling was still staring at the cap gun on the table.

"You recognize it, Harry? It's the same toy gun you used to teach the cat to dance. Now Nose only has to see a gun and he dances. Was it the noise of the caps? Did you fire that toy close to his head to make him dance?"

And now the cat began to snore.

Charles was closing the door to his apartment. So that was it? *I'm in a hurry! Bring me a gun!* How many weapons did she need all at once? She had a rather large gun and a sharp knife in her possession now. But who was he to question

Mallory, he who kept company with a dead woman.

He was crossing the hall to the offices of Mallory and Butler, Ltd., wondering which of all the stupid things he had said, which had made her the most angry. He had accused her of lack of logic, and of underestimation of—

Oh, fool.

She had questioned him about a blind man. Not too quick to underestimate that suspect, was she? And now she was gathering more weapons. No lack of caution there. Where was his own logic?

Perhaps he had gotten everything wrong, genius that he was. What had possessed him to take Coffey's side in this? At the time, it had made some sense, but now? Maybe Coffey had only feared she was too fixed in her knowledge of the suspect. Riker had been right to caution him. He should have shown her more respect. He must not let her down now.

He unlocked the door to Mallory's private office and strode quickly to her desk. The center drawer was locked.

Now that was a snag. He had no keys for drawers. Mallory must assume that everyone was as gifted as she in the art of breaking and entering. He picked up the letter opener he had given her. It was the only object in the room not manufactured in the current decade. In fact, it dated back to another century. He only hesitated for a moment, hefting the irreplaceable piece in his hand. Then he inserted it into the space above the drawer and used force to pry the metal open.

An earsplitting squeal was the first warning, followed by a cascade of bells, giant bells, gongs in hellish amplification. This must be Mallory's idea of accommodating his aversion to high technology. She had wired the office for an alarm, and in place of an annoying beep or a siren, she had worked in his recordings of church bells. And now he was inside the bell tower, inside the bells themselves.

He put up his hands to cover his ears. He would altogether lose his ears if he stayed much longer. He could turn it off, but there was not time enough to hunt the wiring from the drawer before serious damage was done to him. And the speakers might be anywhere in the myriad of electronic equipment. There could be no direction to sound when one's head was itself the clapper of a monster bell.

He opened the wooden case nested in the center drawer, and there was Markowitz's old .38 Long Colt, gleaming with Mallory's good housekeeping, which extended into the barrels of antique guns. He picked up the revolver and the ammunition box and ran for the door. The peal of the church bells from hell followed him down the stairs and into the street, where every window had a head sticking out of it.

He put out his hand to flag down a cab, silently begging forgiveness from the neighbors.

Kipling walked back to the front door and locked it. "I don't think we want to be disturbed right now."

What would Charles do when he met with a locked door? He had the size to kick it in, but he would not know how.

"How did you get onto it?" Harry Kipling

lowered himself to a straight-back chair and motioned her to another.

She remained standing.

He leaned back in the chair, lifting its front feet off the rug and rocking on the two back legs, staring absently into space. His face was drawn, dramatic in the hollows below the high cheekbones where afternoon shadows followed the contours. He seemed tired, at the point of giving in or giving up. "What mistake did I make?"

"You made a lot of them," said Mallory. They had been tap-dancing for ten minutes now. Where was the gun? It could be hidden in his belt at the small of the back. He had not yet looked directly at the knife with the crest of Max Candle.

"How much do you want?" Kipling smiled. "This is a simple case of extortion, am I right?"

"What's it worth to you, Harry?"

"What's my marriage worth? Call my wife's accountant. I don't have all day for this. How much do you want to keep it quiet?"

"Why did you do it?"

"Desperation. If you want the sordid details, you're not getting them. Just tell me how much money you want."

"I'll get back to you."

She would not allow her eyes to travel back to the knife, to give it away. But she knew she could have it in her hand in a heartbeat if she only had the advantage of position. The chair and the rocking Kipling blocked the way.

Moving in slow silence, she angled around Kipling, who was holding the cap gun in his hand, examining it as a curiosity. She could see him in profile now. There was no gun concealed in the small of his back. He was dressed in a polo shirt and close-fitting slacks. There was no place on his person to conceal a large weapon.

So where was her damn gun?

"So I had a relationship with Amanda Bosch— Now how much do you want? How much not to tell my wife?"

"Well, there's a bit more to it than just the relationship with Amanda."

"You've only got me on one woman. If you believed there were others, you would have said so before now. I'm not going to pay the moon for this. Now how much do you want?"

"Did I mention that I knew Amanda? I know you lied to her, and she caught you on it."

"But there were so many lies." By the way he smiled, he seemed to take some pride in that.

"I'm talking about the lie that made her abort her baby. Does that narrow it down for you?"

"That particular lie isn't worth any cash to me. I don't think you did know her. I think you're a crooked cop. The news said you were a cop, and the daughter of a cop. Was your father crooked too? Does it run in the family?"

"Let's say I learned a lot from my old man. If I never knew Amanda, how do I know what tipped her off to the lie, what made her snap?"

She had not been a world-class poker player for nothing. Helen always wanted her to have a fine education, and now the weekly poker games of childhood were paying off.

"Amanda was sitting on a bench outside the building on the day before she died, the day before she called you on the big lie. She never went up to the door, she just watched. It was a busy day for the doorman. People were coming and going, tenants, kids, dogs. Then she saw—"

"Let's not get too dramatic, shall we? She saw Peter and she knew he wasn't adopted. You know, until then, I always thought it was a blessing that he looked like me and not Angel."

Still holding the cap gun in the palm of his hand, Kipling stood up and crossed over to the bookcase. He leaned against the shelf where Max Candle's knife was sitting. He was only inches from it.

"So it *is* a shakedown. If you know her, you know she was only using me for genetic material. She didn't ask me if I wanted to make another brat, did she?"

"She didn't know that she could make one. It was a miracle pregnancy according to her doctor. So then you lied to her."

"Yes. I told her the genetic stew was botched. What of it? I told her it would be a monster, that all my children would be monsters—things growing on their outsides that really should be on the insides, missing their little eyes and little hands, little things like that. So what? That's not a crime. A cop wouldn't have any interest in that. This is a shakedown. Now how much do you want to make this nasty little business go away?"

"It was a stupid lie, wasn't it? You had to know she'd catch you in the lie when she saw your son."

"What were the odds they would ever meet? Most of the year, my son is away at school. There are camps in the summer. My wife has no maternal instincts. Peter looks so much like me, Angel hates the sight of him. He's rarely around."

"But Amanda saw him. That's why she forced the meeting in the park."

"I don't know what you're talking about. We only met at her place."

"I know you met her in the park. You don't have to talk to me. You could remain silent. If you say anything, it could be used against you in a court of law."

"Are you reading me my rights? Still playing cops and crooks, are we? Next you'll be telling me that if I can't afford an attorney, one will be appointed for me. You're no more a cop than I am. Did they kick you off the force? You're a cheap little hustler, aren't you? There's no law against cheating on your wife. Maybe the two of you are thinking in terms of a multimillion-dollar civil suit? Well, forget it."

Mallory shrugged. His constitutional rights were recorded on camera. His arm leaned on the shelf of the bookcase, close to the knife, only inches from it. It was working so well. The only snag was that she didn't have the gun. What had he done with it?

"You met her in the park. She called you on the lie. She had just killed her child, thinking it was a monster, but it wasn't. She aborted it for nothing. She was so angry. You panicked when she threatened to tell your wife what a monster you were. She was going to do it then, wasn't she? Right that minute. Then you killed her."

"So Amanda was the woman in the park killing. No wonder you thought you were going to score big. Cheating and murder. Has it occurred to you she knew more than one man in this building, that someone else killed her?"

"No. It never did, not from the beginning."

"If it was me, I'd take the subway," said Amanda, taking a long drag on her cigarette.

Charles stared at her. There was no music in the cab. Perhaps it was the stress that had triggered the delusion this time.

Now he realized that there were flaws in his construction, glitches in the mechanics of freak memory, for every now and then, Amanda's blue eyes would slip into Mallory green.

"Amanda, you're not allowed to smoke in this cab. See the sign? Perhaps you—"

"I ain't smoking, buddy," said the cabdriver. "And the name is Fred."

Amanda smiled and continued to hold the cigarette. "One of the perks of being dead—no fear of lung cancer. But if it bothers you, I'll put it out."

He couldn't smell the burning weed, and neither did the swirling blue smoke sting his eyes. That was a good sign. He was not altogether crazy. The gun pressed into his leg, and he removed it from his pants pocket and shifted it into his coat.

"So, what's with the gun?"

"Mallory needs it."

"What did you say?" asked the cabdriver.

"Nothing."

"Take the subway," said Amanda. "Just on the chance that she needs it in a hurry. This traffic is the pits." She stared out the back window at the still life of motionless vehicles trailing behind them.

330

"I'm sure we'll get moving soon," said Charles, waving his hand at the phantom smoke swirling around the interior of the cab. "You know, the cigarette smoke does bother me. The cab is full of—"

The cabdriver turned around to say, "For the last time, pal, I'm not smoking."

And now the cab was filled with smoke that was not real, but which obscured every real thing. He was engulfed in the smoke, panic was rising.

Steady now. It's not real.

But then he turned to Amanda, who was blurred by the thickening blue clouds of his delusion, and he realized he was getting lost in this very cramped space which was his mind.

"Please stop! Stop it!"

"Okay, that's enough," said the driver. "Out of my cab, fella. Now!"

"Cheating on my wife doesn't make a good motive for murder."

"Oh, sure it will. *I* like it. Money motives are the best. According to your father-in-law's will, you don't inherit if your wife dies. Smart old man, your father-in-law. And you don't get alimony if she divorces you for cause. And that, incidentally, is the clause that hangs you—you couldn't afford to get caught in the act."

"You can't possibly base a murder motive on the possibility that she wouldn't overlook one small indiscretion. You'd be laughed out of court. Everybody cheats."

And everybody lies.

"You mean the way she overlooked your embezzlement? I found the transactions in the company computer. She covered the sale of the stock you didn't own, and she covered the collateral loan on the condo. She wouldn't haul you in court for that. It might make the stockholders nervous to find an embezzler in the family. But I'm betting she'd haul you in for adultery."

"The threat of divorce is still a weak motive for murder."

"Is it? If Angel divorces you, you get nothing. You even had to agree to give custody of your own child to another relative in the event of your wife's death. That's how much the old man trusted you."

Kipling was backing off in the body language, regrouping for another tack. "My wife is rather cold. She never lets me touch her anymore. I had to have a woman on the side. But I certainly didn't kill Amanda."

She had always known it would be something simple, and disappointing. Now there was only the tedium of letting him flap his mouth, catching him in the lies while the camera was rolling. He was exhibiting all the signs of the liar. He explained too much, emoted too much. And now he was going on and on about the tragic death of Amanda and his own, more important tragedy.

All his life, he'd been waiting on opportunity, which had arrived in the shape of an heiress. And now, when he was set for life, it was all falling apart on him, everything unraveling, and he could not, would not see it. The lies didn't work anymore, and yet he kept on lying.

"Amanda made the decision to have an abortion," he said.

Butchery, Mallory silently translated.

"It's unreasonable to blame me."

She was going to tell your wife.

332

"Eventually, Amanda saw it my way."
Stunned with a rock, and bleeding.
"I loved Amanda. I love all women."
To death.

And here, Mallory interrupted him. "Your blood type is B positive."

Kipling tightened all the muscles of his face.

"You killed her by the water, and then you ran away. You came back later and smashed up her hands. You took some time with that."

"I suppose you were there when this fantasy supposedly happened?"

Mallory smiled.

At a dead run, Charles took the stairs leading down below the level of the sidewalk. He was half falling down them, as others were shouldering up the narrow stairway. At the booth, he made a frantic exchange of coins for tokens. The man behind the bulletproof window busied himself with some bit of paperwork and then began to slowly count out a packet of dollar bills. He never looked up, never responded to the crazed knocking on the glass, which sounded the panic of the oncoming train which Charles would miss without the token. The train pulled in as the token clerk was pushing a coin under the partition.

Charles turned into the crush of disembarking straphangers to plant his coin in the slot and hurry through it. He ran at the train. The doors were closing, and he put his hand inside and pressed them open again with the aid of an electronic eye which had not kicked in until Charles felt real pain. He squeezed in among the press of other passengers, who looked up at him as though his size were something he was guilty of.

Now the train was in motion and the public address system was making an announcement to the passengers. He couldn't make out the individual words among the garble of mechanics and the garble of a man who was eating his lunch as he addressed the riders over the loudspeaker in what was obviously his second, and recently acquired language.

"What is he saying?" Charles asked a woman who had the bored look of having been this route many times. The woman only shrugged.

It was Amanda, by his side, who answered his worst fears. "He's saying what they always say. No matter where you're going, you can't get there from here."

When the train did stop again, he discovered the local had turned into an express. Guessing by the lynch mob attitude of other passengers, who were far more irritated than the shrugging woman, this change of route was a whim of the engineer. When he saw the light of day and the first street sign, he knew he was miles out of his way, and he began to run.

"You were standing down by the water when she nailed you on the lie. She was going to give your wife all the evidence she needed to divorce you for cause. You panicked and grabbed her by the arm. First you stunned her, and then you killed her. Then you ran away . . . like the dog."

"My dog—"

"You were walking the dog that morning. That

was your excuse for going out to meet her in the park. The dog was running loose. While you fought with Amanda, he got his leash caught in the bushes when he was heading north over the rise. You're probably wondering how I know that. So you found the dog and took it home. Then, about thirty minutes later, you came back to drag Amanda's body into the woods—"

"You couldn't—"

"—and you smashed up her hands, her finger-prints. You made so many stupid mistakes, Harry."

He moved toward her and away from the knife. Good. Now she was circling around him. The way to the door was almost clear. His hands were rising now, the hands which had snapped a woman's neck. It was panic time again for Harry Kipling. He was rushing toward her. She reached out to grab his outstretched hand, struck one long leg across his path, and pulled hard on his hand to guide all of his weight to the floor.

Big he might be, but not terribly graceful.

He was looking for his large feet when she kicked him in the groin to double him into a fetal position. Then she rolled him on his stomach and pulled one arm up behind his back until he screamed.

"You're going to break it!"

"Then hold still!"

With her free hand, she reached for the heavy drapery cord and yanked on it, bringing down drapes and curtain rod.

His running was hampered by the dense crowd of people on the sidewalk. It wasn't fair—the streets should be deserted. Couldn't all these people have waited one blessed day before racing out to return their Chistmas gifts and exchange them for the right sizes?

Charles dropped the gun, and an old woman kicked it out of her way. He wondered if she could not see it over her packages, or did she think it was commonplace sidewalk debris for this part of town? He leaned down and picked it up. He began to make better time now, suddenly not bothered by the crowd anymore. In fact, people were hurrying to get out of his way.

Well, this was more like it.

And now it occurred to him that this sudden show of public courtesy might have something to do with the naked gun in his hand. Well, of course they were all being polite.

Fool.

Harry Kipling was hog-tied. Hands tied behind him and roped to one leg, he was pulled back in a bizarre bow. He looked ridiculous; he was ridiculous, a pathetic bastard who had struck out in childish fear, in anger, and then tried to clean up his mess, the death of a human being named Amanda.

He was so disappointing, an unworthy opponent who made so small a noise in the world he had failed to wake the cat.

The camera was rolling on to the music of cat snores and Kipling sobs. With a critical eye, Mallory looked at both her hog-tied trophy and her weak criminal case. An assault on a police officer was not hard evidence for murder. There were loose ends to be tied, better evidence to be gotten, something with more weight for a DA who chickened on every case with less than a complete set of prints and a smoking gun in evidence.

Whatever she might have to do, Kipling wasn't going to get away with this.

"Stop crying. It's not like I really hurt you. What did you do with my gun?"

But he would not stop crying, and she was not taking much satisfaction in this.

She lifted her head and turned toward the door with the first sound of metal on metal. The door was being unlocked. Charles? No, it couldn't be.

It wasn't.

Someone else was standing in the foyer, alone but for the long shadow extending back into the outer corridor.

Now this was more like it. This was walking death.

She was staring into mirrors of her own eyes above the barrel of her stolen .357 revolver. "Murder is the best game, isn't it?"

"Yes, it is," said Justin Riccalo, leveling the gun at her head. Now he pulled the barrel up slightly. "Oh, that's wrong, isn't it? You're supposed to aim for the widest part of the body." And now the barrel dropped to the level of her chest, her heart.

Perversely, she smiled. He didn't like that. She knew he wouldn't.

"Kill the bitch!" yelled Kipling, not sobbing anymore but frantic in the eyes.

"All women are bitches," said the boy in the monotone of a litany.

"Yes, yes, they are, all of them," said Kipling with the fervor of a television evangelist playing the crowd. "Kill her now!"

"Lighten up, you idiot," said Mallory to the man at her feet. "He's going to kill you next. I thought you understood that."

Kipling's mouth hung open, and no more words came out.

All the words she heard were toward the back of her mind where Markowitz lived with Helen. *Get him to talk to you, kid,* said a memory with a Brooklyn accent.

"Tell me, Justin, what kind of a bird did you kill to make the bloody X on my door?"

"It was a pigeon," said Justin with a hint of a query at the end of his words.

"I love all the little details," said Mallory. "How did you rig the glass of water in the kitchen?"

Prime the pump, get him talking and he won't be able to stop.

Justin smiled. "I set the glass near the edge of the table, and then I put pennies under the back legs to make it slant, but only a little. The glass was leveled on a sliver of ice. When the ice melted, the glass crashed and the evidence was gone."

He looked up at her with the expectation of being petted and admired for this.

"Nice job, Justin. Same thing with the vase?"

"Yes, it had to be something with water to explain away the slick of the melted ice."

"I thought your best trick was the knife in the target. You even fooled Charles, and that's not easy. I'm betting you rigged the spring-load."

"Yes. I was surprised to see that old carnival prop in the basement. As you may have guessed, I have a passing interest in magic. The spring was easy. It was old. You could see the rust, even in bad light. After I pulled the spring over the edge

338

of a gear, I only had to keep Mr. Butler talking until it broke and released the fake knife.''

"Then later, you went back to the cellar and pushed the fake blade back into the target compartment, right? Then you stuck one of the real knives into the face of the target.''

Justin nodded.

"How could you count on getting back to the building in time to change the prop for the real knife?''

"It was easy. He goes everywhere in cabs. I've watched him from the street. I gather he doesn't like subways, and probably has so much money it never occurs to him to take one. I took the subway back to SoHo after he walked into the park. I had all the time in the world to change the knives.''

The gun was heavy in the child's hands. He corrected the dip of the barrel which aimed at her heart.

"Don't you have any questions for me, Justin?''

"You weren't surprised to see me, were you?''

"No.''

"When did you begin to suspect me?''

"From the first. Violence was coming, I knew that. You'd gone to a lot of trouble to set it up. You were the brightest one in the family. I always knew you'd be the last one standing.''

Justin moved the gun to point at Harry. "If you like, as a last request, I'll kill him first.''

"He is annoying, isn't he?''

"No! I can help you,'' he said to the boy.

"You're trussed up like a hog,'' said Justin. "You can't even help yourself. Do you have any idea how silly you look? They're going to find your body that way. Does that disturb you?''

"Listen to me, boy. I can help you. I have an idea. It's foolproof. I'll back you up if the cops get onto it. She wants to arrest me for killing a woman, a bitch. You need me, and now you have something on me. I can't tell on you, can I?"

Justin looked to Mallory. "Did he really kill someone?"

"No. I don't believe he'd have the nerve. Do you?"

"Why did you tie me up, then? Explain that one to the kid."

The boy looked to Mallory for his answer.

"I tied him up because the twit pissed me off, and the Civilian Review Board won't let me shoot him."

She made a mental note to edit that out of the videotape.

"You heard about the unidentified woman who died in the park?" Kipling raised his head and yelled, "Well, I killed her!"

Mallory shook her head. "We call this a confession under duress. It's worthless." And now she turned her eyes down to Kipling. "I don't think Justin's buying it either. You're a documented liar, Harry. Now this kid is smart. He's probably going to make it look like he was trying to defend me against you." She turned back to the boy. "Right, Justin?"

The boy nodded. Mallory looked down at Kipling, who was squirming on the floor. "Harry, I just don't think you've got a handle on the situation. You're an adult, you're bigger than he is, or to put it briefly, a dead man. Right again, Justin?"

"I'm afraid so."

"Damn straight. Not too bright, is he, Justin?"

"I did kill her! I killed Amanda Bosch because she was a bitch," said Harry, in his best attempt to pass for a fellow disciple in the hatred of women. And the boy who believed all women were bitches seemed to be weighing this.

"Well," said Mallory, "let's have some details that weren't in the papers. In my case, it's professional interest. Now Justin's killed twice before. We can't call him an amateur. But you are, Harry. Details. Did Amanda cry? Or did she take it like more of a man than you are?"

"Hey, it was her own fault. If she hadn't threatened me, it wouldn't have happened. The bitch brought it on herself."

"All women are bitches," said Justin, in the descending note of an *amen*.

"Details, Harry."

"I hit her with a rock, and then I snapped her neck. That wasn't in the papers."

"Did you grab her by the throat and strangle her?"

"No, I twisted her head until her neck snapped."

"How long did it take you to teach the cat to dance?"

"Four days! Okay, kid? Now untie me!"

"No," said Justin, "I don't think so." He pointed the gun at Kipling, and the man froze. Then the gun turned slowly back to Mallory. "It *would* be more logical to kill Mallory first. She's the dangerous one. You, sir—you're pathetic. You didn't even hate that woman, did you?"

"No, he didn't. It was a panic kill," said Mallory. "And then he ran away. Not your style, Justin."

It was like Markowitz was in the room with

her. *They like to talk, Kathy,* the old man had told her. *Even after you read them their rights, you can't shut them up.*

The boy giggled, clearly enjoying this power over two adults.

"I'd bet even money you put more thought and planning into your murders," said Mallory. "Or maybe I overestimated you. Your mother and stepmother died alone. Maybe *you're* blowing smoke here too."

"You know better than that. You were close, weren't you? You must have been. You were planning to dig up my mother. I heard you say that to Mr. Butler."

"If I had dug up your mother, what would I have found?"

"You might have found out that I replaced her heart medication with vitamin pills the same size and color. The absence of medication might have been noticeable."

"Why did you kill her?"

"Well, let's say I never miss an opportunity for fun."

"So she died for lack of proper medication? That's pretty boring."

Arthur was holding the door for a tenant, when he saw the large man running at him, clutching some object to his chest and then concealing it in his pocket. Now the man was close enough to identify as Miss Mallory's friend. And as the man drew closer still, Arthur could see the twenty-dollar bill extending out from the man's hand. The bill hung in the air as Charles shot past him, and Arthur clutched the twenty before it hit the ground.

"No time to be announced—I'm late!" yelled the large man in passing. "She'll kill me if I'm any later." The words trailed behind the man as he ran past the occupied elevator and pushed through the side door and into the stairwell.

Arthur nodded his understanding at the closing stairwell door as he pocketed the twenty. He would not like to cross Miss Mallory either.

"Oh no. I killed her," said Justin.

"She died of a heart attack," said Mallory. "I've seen the death certificate."

"Yes. I suppose you could say I scared her to death. Once she was weakened by the lack of medication, it wasn't all that difficult. I did the sort of things that would make her seem crazy if she told anyone. She was hardly going to tell my father she saw things flying through the air. You've met my father. A bit intractable, wouldn't you say?"

"You are an interesting kid, I'll give you that much, but this still sounds very tame as murders go."

"Oh, it wasn't tame at all. She crawled from room to room following that bottle of worthless pills. I walked along beside her kicking the bottle out of her reach. She screamed, she cried. She was terrified. It was glorious. You should have seen her face as she was dying. She just could not believe this was happening to her."

"And what about her replacement, the first stepmother? I suppose you killed her, too?"

"Yes. I also made things float through the air for her. She never told anyone, either. She thought she was going crazy. In my opinion, she was half-crazy when I started to work on her."

"But there was nothing wrong with her heart."

"No. But with her brief stay in the psychiatric hospital, the suicide was quite believable. They should have had a child guard on that window, you know. It's the law."

"According to the ME investigator's reports, both women were alone when they died."

"School was in session both times. I'm afraid the Tanner School doesn't keep very good track of children. They're very progressive—attendance is on the honor system. But I don't think anyone bothered to check. They just assumed I wasn't in the apartment. They also assumed neither death was all that suspicious."

Amanda was less the thing of solid stuff as she floated up the stairway beside him. "It's three more flights. You should've taken the elevator, Charles."

"Now you tell me."

His side hurt from the unaccustomed exertion. He could feel a searing in his lungs, as though he had swallowed fire.

"Did you keep any trophies, Justin? It's just professional curiosity on my part. All the big names in serial killing kept trophies of every murder."

"I kept the bottle of doctored pills, and the tricks I used on my first stepmother."

"How did you get her to jump out the window?"

"Well, she didn't actually jump. I had the window open. It was a large window. Then I took the knife and ran the cord to follow the bars of the track lighting system that runs across the ceiling. I only had to maneuver her into line with the window and make her back up. When you see a knife floating toward you, you do tend to back up in a hurry. When she was at the window and off balance, I only had to run at her to give her a push in the direction she was going in. That was the tricky part. There was a moment when she understood what was happening to her, and she was reaching out to take me with her. There was a bit of a risk in that one."

"But your new stepmother told your father about the floating objects."

"Yes, and I blame myself for that. I should have spent more time with Sally, gotten to know her better. I had no idea she was one of those pathetic New Age freaks, a paranormal obsessive. But it's working in my favor. Now she's a documented hysteric."

"So you're still planning to kill her."

"Well, of course. You can kiss that bitch goodbye. And now I'm going to kill you. It's been fun, Mallory. Really it has."

The boy was raising the gun.

"Look, kid, the gun won't fire," she said. "The safety is on."

"A revolver doesn't have a safety. Good try, Mallory. What else have you got?"

"Have you ever heard that old standby, 'Look, someone's coming up behind you'?"

"Once, I think. It was a television rerun from the seventies."

Charles Butler was standing in the foyer on the far side of the room, which seemed miles wide to her now. Markowitz's Colt was in his hand. His head was turned to the side and down as though he were distracted by someone or something unseen. What was wrong with him?

Charles, don't fail me now.

"So if I tell the guy behind you to shoot you, there won't be any hard feelings?"

Charles was staring at her now, eyes wide, head shaking slowly from side to side.

Charles, don't fail me.

The boy was smiling. "They're your last words, Mallory. Say what you like."

The barrel was rising, aiming at her face, when she yelled, "Charles, shoot him!"

Charles raised the Colt and fired on the boy, not once, but pull after pull on the trigger, walking the length of the room on shock-slowed feet, firing and firing.

The boy's head had turned quickly with the first click of the empty gun, and now he stared at the crazed giant with the wide eyes, sad eyes, advancing on him, clicking and clicking and clicking.

Mallory moved and the boy's head snapped back. She watched his eyes making choices. He was opting for the larger threat. The barrel was turning to Charles as the cat ran out from under the couch and stepped lightly, delicately on its hind legs, dancing up to the gun. The boy stared. Mallory dived for the gun. It went off. The bullet spun the cat in a wicked turn, and blood splattered the rug.

Kipling's body went limp as his eyes rolled back, lids closing, chin falling to his chest, mouth hanging open, all still now.

Before she and the boy hit the carpet, she had the gun in her hand.

"Nice going . . ." she said, pinning the boy neatly under one leg and looking up at Charles.

His gun hand dangled by his side, but his grip was tight and the trigger finger continued to spasm and click the misfires. And then the ammo box fell from Charles's other hand, seal unbroken.

"You've never loaded a gun, have you, Charles?"

"No, no I never have."

So he had gone up against the boy with no bullets in the gun, no cover, and no hesitation. And the empty gun had to be the explanation for the lack of hesitation. He couldn't have fired so fast, not looking at the child in his sights. Civilians were not constructed that way. Charles was the soft and civilized type; such things were not done in his world. So, with his own peculiar courage and backward thinking, he had risked his life to draw fire and buy her time.

Now Riker and Martin were coming through the door, Martin first, Riker panting behind him, guns drawn. They stared at the hog-tied Kipling and the boy pinned under Mallory.

Riker hunkered down beside her, panting from the run upstairs, fishing for his irons. In another moment, the boy's hands were cuffed behind his back.

"How did you get here so fast?" She said. It was an accusation.

"Well, Charles caught my eye when he streaked by the car." Riker pulled a small device from one ear. "Oh, I've been listening in. I planted a highly illegal bug in the apartment the last time I was here. I've learned a lot from you, kid." And now he fingered the fallen drapes on the floor. "Very messy, Mallory. This is so unlike you."

Martin holstered his gun. "The reception kept going in and out. Most of the time, all we could hear was this noise like a little engine. So Riker tells me it's a cat snoring. He thinks I'll buy anything."

Riker nodded her attention toward Charles. "You think you could stop him from clicking that thing? It's getting on my nerves."

Mallory stood up and moved quickly to Charles. She used force to pry his fingers off the gun, and then she closed her hand over his to stop the finger from its spasmodic firing of a gun that was no longer there.

Charles's eyes were locked with the boy's. Justin was still and quiet, turning his eyes away from Charles to look inward. And it was only a little disturbing that he pouted like a real child, an angry child.

Martin was standing over the hog-tied Kipling. "Is he dead?"

"No," said Mallory. "He fainted when the gun went off."

Riker and Mallory exchanged words without words. *Do I know my perps?* she asked with only the lift of her chin. *Damn straight,* he said with one thumb up.

Martin was fishing out his cuffs.

"Naw," said Riker, putting up one hand to stay Martin. "I don't think the cuffs could improve on Mallory's knots. Let's carry Kipling out through the lobby like that."

Martin grinned. "Yeah, I like it." Now Martin stabbed his finger at the blood splatters on the carpet. "So, who took the hit?"

His answer was crawling slowly across the rug, pulling itself along by its front paws, crying and making its way to Mallory. At last, it lay at her feet, bleeding on her white running shoes.

"What happened to the cat?"

"I didn't do it," said Mallory.

"Mallory, you're going to love this."

Betty Hyde slipped the videocassette into the VCR. The picture was of the judge on the steps of the Coventry Arms. He was flanked by an escort of two uniformed police officers. A young woman reporter was thrusting a microphone in his face and asking him if it was true that the district attorney was planning to exhume the body of his mother.

Then the judge advanced on the woman. One fist knocked the microphone out of her hand and the other fist was flung at the cameraman. The camera lay on the sidewalk shooting the feet of the officers scuffling with the feet of the judge, dragging him back from the feet of the woman reporter. The audio portion was a woman's screams of "You're hurting me, you son of a—"

"About that police escort with the judge," said Hyde. "I don't suppose you could explain that?"

"I'm not sure," Mallory lied. "I heard a rumor that some ME investigator implicated a detective in an extortion racket. I think they just wanted to ask the judge if he had any information on the case. But you didn't get that from me."

"Of course not. Thanks for the judge on a platter," said Betty Hyde. "Not that I'm greedy, but did you dig up anything else that was interesting?"

"No," Mallory lied again as she continued her packing.

"Well, I did. You were right, Mallory. I was holding out on you. Eric Franz is not blind."

Mallory pressed out the wrinkle on a T-shirt before she folded it into her duffel bag. "Eric Franz told you that?"

"Oh no, he denied it for several hours. Actually, he spent most of that time getting drunk and reminiscing about Annie. That's the strange part—he really did love her. But the accident was certainly murder if he was sighted, and he didn't—"

"If Franz didn't confess to you, then where is this coming from?"

"I told you I have spies everywhere."

Mallory folded a pair of blue jeans into the duffel and slowly zipped it shut. "Arthur, right? He was on duty the night of the crash. Is he the one who told you Franz killed his wife?"

"Well, no. Arthur doesn't know Eric can see. He only said that if Eric had been able to see, he could have saved his wife. But Eric's version of the accident doesn't match. Eric lied."

"How much did you pay Arthur?"

"Fifty dollars."

"Well, you probably got the full treatment. I only gave him twenty." Mallory opened the flap pocket of the duffel and rummaged until she found the file she was looking for. "Arthur told you he gave the plate number to the police, and they caught the guy in an hour, right?"

"Right, but—"

Mallory held up a sheet of paper. "This is the accident report. He did give them a plate number, but it was the wrong plate. And they didn't pick up the hit-and-run driver until seven a.m. The driver was parked outside of his own local garage, sleeping off the drunk, waiting for the shop to open so he could have the dent removed from the fender. There was still blood on the car. A meter maid caught him."

"But Arthur described—"

"And did he tell you the part about the little silver Jaguar? It was a gray Ford. Nothing like a Jag, but it makes a better story for the money."

"He saw a fight between the Franzes."

"Across the street? I don't think so." She selected another sheet of paper from the file. "This came off his optometrist's computer. Arthur does fine for the first twelve feet—without his glasses. So all you've really got is a case of the blind contradicting the blind. But even if Arthur's vision had been twenty/twenty, it probably would have been the same story. Any cop could have told you eyewitnesses are the least reliable evidence you can have. If your case hangs on a witness, you're dead meat in a courtroom. And the testimony you have to pay for is the worst. I don't think you'd make it as a detective. Don't give up your day job."

"I've been had, haven't I? You steered me into Eric Franz to keep me away from Kipling, didn't you?"

"You've got the judge's head, and you've got an exclusive story on Amanda's murder. So you don't have anything on Eric Franz. Two out of three isn't bad."

"I owe you one, Mallory."

"You owe me a lot more than that. If you'd printed any of that crap on Franz, you'd be in the middle of a lawsuit and looking for another job.

Out on the sidewalk, Eric Franz stopped a moment to talk to her. He lowered the dark glasses and stared at her as a sighted person would do. His face looked sleep-starved and pained.

"I understand we have some business to transact. I gather the computer messages were yours? You'll be contacting me again?"

"No," said Mallory. "We have no business, you and I. I don't think we'll ever meet again." She pulled out her shield. "I'm only a cop, and you didn't break any laws." None that she could prove. He was just a little crazy. Charles could explain it better—he was good at guilt.

She had neglected to mention to Betty Hyde that the doorman had been wearing his glasses that night. Arthur had only made all the mistakes of the average eyewitness with good eyesight.

The doorman had seen the lights of the oncoming car shining on Eric's face. In that bright light, the doorman would have seen the proximity of the man who watched his wife cut down in the street. Like Cora, Arthur had witnessed a murder without realizing it.

But it was not the cold-blooded murder that good cases could be built around. It had been a crime of passion just as surely as if he had caught her in bed with another man and shot her dead. There were moments in everyone's life when they should not have a gun in their hands. She had understood the moment of the kill. Eric Franz had been presented with two thousand pounds of speeding metal. And for lack of a warning, Annie Franz had died.

Mallory watched the faux blind man walk away with his dog. She would always wonder what it was like to live in that charade of darkness, unable to leave it for an unguarded hour. It had crossed her mind to finesse him into a breakdown, but what would be the point? What fresh hell could she have added? And what for? This man was doing his own version of hard time.

Markowitz would have let Franz walk away. She wasn't sure how she knew that, but she knew.

Epiloque

NEW YEAR'S EVE

Jack Coffey had seen the tape version of Judge Emery Heart attacking a reporter. Who had not? It had run continuously on all the news channels for the past five days.

At that moment, the real live version of the judge was cooperating nicely with Internal Affairs. The judge was singing to IA and the DA, ratting out Palanski for an extortionist, and supporting the allegations of an ME investigator.

The exhumation order for the body of an elderly woman was the currency for the judge's testimony. Exhuming the judge's mother would not have led to a murder charge according to Mallory, and unlike Riker, Coffey did trust her— now and then.

And with only the prompt of a photograph from the ME's office, Palanski was confirming that the judge was a woman beater. Palanski was also taking revenge on his ex-partner in extortion—the ME investigator who was sitting in yet another room, happy in the ignorant fairy tale that immunity as a state's witness might protect him from a charge of tax evasion. It wouldn't. Once the trial was over, the treasury agents would be waiting for him in the wings, their mouths hanging open and sloppy with saliva. And when

Palanski finished a long sentence for extortion, the T-men would get him, too.

And nowhere in this chorus of singing rats was there any trace of the music director. One day he would teach Mallory to trust him, and then he would ask her how she had pulled that off— and she would tell him to go to hell.

Coffey looked down at the snapshot in his hand, the one that had so frightened Palanski. It was an innocent picture—a sweet kid with wavy tumbles of carrot-colored hair. She was standing in front of a Christmas tree in the chief medical examiner's home. The protecting arm of Doris Slope was draped across the girl's shoulders. The photograph had come to him with a brief, cryptic note from Dr. Edward Slope and no mention of Mallory.

He lit a match under the photograph—per Slope's request. Now Special Crimes was completely out of the loop, and Mallory had never been in it.

Later in the day, when Riker caught the news on Palanski, he would only know that Mallory had held out on him.

Well, everybody held out. Everybody lied.

He and Riker would never discuss the possibility that Mallory had brought down another cop. She had covered her tracks, always one person removed in the chain of evidence.

And in his hand, awaiting his signature, was the final paperwork to wrap up no less than three homicides. It was a rare, sweet day.

Like Malakhai's delusion, his own had required him to be faithful to the logic of his creation.

Amanda would not come back again; he knew that. She was a woman who loved children.

How mad was he? He touched the button to the CD player, and the real and solid music which Mallory had given him swelled up and out from the center of his consciousness. His eyes were cast down at the desk, and his head slowly bowed. When the music ended, he sat quietly in the gloaming, the after-dinner hour when the office shadows were the deepest.

But now, in sidelong vision, he saw the woman taking shape in the darkness, coming to life for him, walking toward him into the light.

Mallory.

She sat on the edge of his desk and waited until he lifted his face to hers.

"Justin is going to a funny farm for the very rich. I thought you'd want to know."

"You think it'll do much good?"

"No. I think he was born that way."

"Still, he's only a child."

"A killer."

A child.

"What did the district attorney think of your camera work?"

"He was thrilled. Two killers, and three murders on one roll of tape. What a saving for the taxpayer."

He couldn't make out her face in the gathering darkness, but thought she was smiling.

"The Civilian Review Board might think *I* shot the cat," she said. "But they haven't charged me yet."

He smiled too, though against his will and against his state of mind.

"Well, you've got the video."

"I don't have those last few minutes on tape." Which was Mallory's way of saying she had erased the part where he had opened fire on a little boy, and therefore, it had never happened. Every now and then, she surprised him with unexpected insight and delicacy.

"That took balls, Charles. Faking him out with an empty gun."

She eased off the desk and padded out of the room, followed by the cat, which made more noise on its feet, less graceful now with the weight of its new bandage. A trace of perfume lagged behind, and it was a few minutes more before Mallory was altogether gone.

In the romantic literature of another age, a woman might have asked, "Wouldst thou slay a dragon for my sake?" But the world had changed, was changing still, and the monsters were cruelly deceptive in their different faces. In the bizarre romance near the edge of a new century, Mallory might ask, "Wouldst thou slay a child for my sake?"

She had a code of sorts, and never would she ask, but the question would always hang between them. And if he could ever bring himself to it, he would tell her yes—for he had believed the gun was loaded when he shot the boy, and shot to kill—for Mallory's sake.

IF YOU HAVE ENJOYED READING THIS
LARGE PRINT BOOK AND YOU
WOULD LIKE MORE INFORMATION
ON HOW TO ORDER A WHEELER
LARGE PRINT BOOK, PLEASE WRITE
TO:

WHEELER PUBLISHING, INC.
P.O. BOX 531
ACCORD, MA 02018-0531